THE NEED FOR DANDELIONS

THE NEED FOR DANDELIONS

ALEX LARKSPUR

The Need for Dandelions

Copyright © 2026 Alex Larkspur

alexlarkspur.weebly.com

Edited by Chris Zable

Illustration by Alex Dingley

Formatting by Talli L. Morgan

ISBN (Paperback): 979-8-9987435-3-5

ISBN (E-Book): 979-8-9987435-2-8

Content Warnings

- Sickness and serious injury
- Death of characters, including the elderly and children
- Self-image issues
- Classism
- Discussions of mass death and plagues
- Discussions of biological warfare
- House fire
- Sewage and bodily fluids
- Childbirth with complications
- Animal endangerment
- Implied sexual content

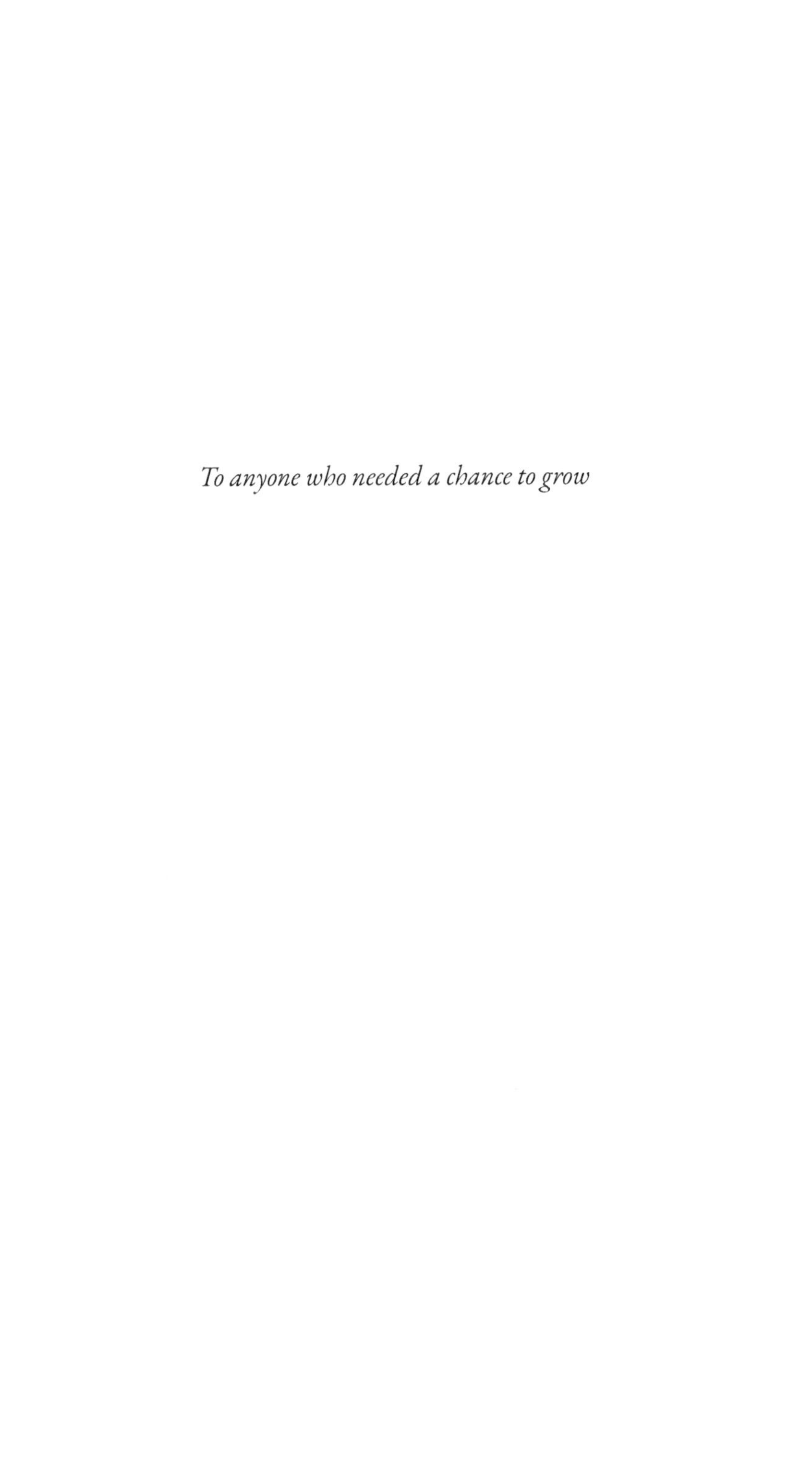

To anyone who needed a chance to grow

Chapter 1

A Meeting

Galen

Galen did not need anyone to protect him in Candiru Quarter. He simply did not. He had been stationed there for almost four years now completely on his own, ever since he took over the assignment from Sister Elowen when she retired. And to be completely honest, living there with Sister Elowen hadn't been very safe when she was still active; she was in her eighties and even a child could have pushed her over and broken her hip. She was still more fearsome than him, but it didn't matter. He did not need someone to protect him. He was safe there.

He had told Bishop Rose this; nevertheless, there was a rather tall, rather muscular, rather bored-looking man in armor standing at his door. The man, wearing the brown and green leathers of the upper city guard, had three different weapons on his belt—which was three weapons too many—and had his arms crossed. His light brown hair was cropped short; his deep brown eyes were sleepy in the early morning light.

He towered over Galen as he stood there with his feet crushing the dandelions poking up between the cobblestones.

Galen did his best to keep his face calm, pleasant, and neutral, though he mourned the flowers. They had just poked their way up out of the cracks now that spring was properly upon Dragonet City. It was fine; dandelions always came back.

"Brother Galen?" the man asked, his voice low gravel.

"Guilty as charged," Galen said, smiling up at him. He couldn't say no to the bishop, or to Governor Maple, who had decreed the safety measures, but he could try and be friendly with this stranger tasked to follow him around for no good reason. However, his small joke may have been a mistake, as the guard's neutral, bored mouth soured into a scowl. Whoops.

Galen cleared his throat and said, "Yes, that's me. The Lady's blessings be upon you. And you are?"

"Sasha Rider," the guard said. He held onto the unpleasant scowl for a moment, but quickly flattened it out to something more neutrally grumpy.

Galen held out his hand in greeting, ignoring the burst of disdain. "Nice to meet you. I take it by your expression that you're about as pleased with this assignment as I am, Mister Rider. Is that the right title? I've never worked with guards outside of an infirmary, and they don't care much what you call them as long as you get the arrow out, you know?"

Galen chuckled to himself, but Sasha did not react at all. He didn't take Galen's hand and Galen retracted it, flexing his fingers nervously. Galen kept his smile, but he knew it must look uneasy. Of course he had been assigned the grumpiest, most humorless guard in the ranks. The Lady of Flowers had a funny way of challenging Galen at every step. The guard didn't seem inclined to speak, just to glower, so Galen took another breath and tried again.

"Have you broken your fast?" Galen asked. "I have water boiling for tea and was about to eat when you knocked. Would you care to join me?"

"What were you going to eat?" Sasha finally stopped glaring and put together a complete sentence. Praise the Lady, it was a miracle.

"I have a couple of eggs, some brown bread and jam, and even some apples, if you like," Galen said, happy for a response, any response. They weren't going to get very far if Sasha was going to restrict himself to terse, scowling questions.

"No meat?" Sasha asked, his voice flat. And they were back to the two-word questions.

"Ah, no, I mean, I am a devotee of the Lady of Flowers. I can't afford to have meat at breakfast," Galen said, struggling to maintain his usual pleasantness.

"Hmm," Sasha said, or grunted, really, and then he waited. Down from two words to none. They were moving backwards. Soon Sasha would be altogether silent and Galen would have no idea what to do.

Galen took a moment, realized Sasha had nothing more to say on the subject, and then stepped aside to let him in. Sasha had to duck into the small abode, and the floorboards creaked under his weight. Galen winced, but as always, the floor still held. Because of the way that Candiru Quarter—really, all of Dragonet City—was constructed, it made him nervous.

The city was built atop an ancient bridge over the mighty Haplin River. It was a precarious spiraling construction with the low districts, like Candiru, at the bottom and the high districts, like Hassar, built above and inward all the way up to Dragonet Palace, where the governor herself lived. It made the city impressive to look at from a distance, but terrifying to live in, like a mountain with no real, solid center. There was a reason that Galen never went higher than Luderick District if he could help it.

Sasha was now standing in Galen's small home with a puzzled look on his face. He glanced around, lip curling up slightly, before he moved towards the kitchen, clearly trying not to bump into things. His dangling weapons made this an exercise in futility. Luckily, none of the things he knocked into, cursing under his breath, were breakable. Or at least they were difficult to break.

Sasha kept running face-first into the dried herbs hanging from the ceiling, and Galen hadn't realized how blessed he was to be so short until he saw Sasha spitting out dried rosemary. He had to suppress a giggle. No need to embarrass the poor man, who clearly had no interest in being here.

"Please, sit down," Galen said, pulling a chair out from his tiny kitchen table for Sasha and then bustling off to gather breakfast.

Galen set the tea to steeping, then piled the table with breakfast items. The brown bread was from Adrian down the street, discounted as a thank-you for setting his son's arm after a nasty fall, and it was delicious. He still had about half of it left, since he always sliced cautiously. Looking at the sheer mountain that was Sasha, he expected that this would mean the end of the loaf.

The four hard-boiled eggs were set on a little blue dish that he had been given years ago in thanks for saving the life of the potter's wife after a kiln accident. Nina would never let him forget how grateful she was. The jam and honey, because he wouldn't be a devotee of the Lady of Flowers if he didn't have honey, were in purple and yellow jars respectively, but these had been left over from the last devotee who lived here. Or maybe even the one before that.

Galen was bending down to grab the apples from under the counter when Sasha cleared his throat. Galen turned back to see that Sasha had not touched the food on the table and was instead staring at Galen with an odd look.

Galen bent, picked up the basket of apples, and then set it on the table as he lifted an eyebrow and smiled with a nod, encouraging Sasha to speak. Perhaps, finally, he'd get to hear more than a single, grunted sentence from the man.

"What did you mean when you said that you could tell that I'm as pleased with this assignment as you are?" Sasha asked, brow furrowed deeply. "Are you not pleased?"

Sasha must have realized that he had revealed his own displeasure—he grimaced, then snatched an egg up and started to peel it. Galen hadn't known it was possible for a man to shell an egg with so much aggression. He almost pitied the egg.

"Well, no," Galen said. "It's nothing against you. I just dislike the implication that I'm not safe here and I need a bodyguard."

Sasha tore his eyes from his egg mutilation with an incredulous look plastered on his face as he glared at Galen. Galen bit the inside of his cheek, certain he knew what was coming next.

"It *is* Candiru Quarter," Sasha said gruffly. "It's not exactly safe."

Of course. There it was. Galen knew to expect it from an upper city guard, but it was disappointing nonetheless. He took a steadying breath before he answered.

"I've been working here as a healer for seven years now, and the last four have been on my own," Galen said. "I've never been accosted in the street. In fact, the one time someone was rude to me, the Kipper Gang beat him up on my behalf. And then I patched him up and he never bothered me again. I'm not worried about my safety."

"The governor feels otherwise," Sasha said firmly, eyes locked on the egg again. Galen had several ideas about where Governor Maple could stick her head full of ideas about the lower districts, but voicing those would be treason, so he kept silent.

"I understand that," Galen said, smiling again, desperate to keep some friendliness between them. "Which is why I'm trying to make the best of it. I'm guessing this isn't the post that you wanted either. Nothing too glamorous about going to the houses of the poor and treating their aches and pains. Tea, Mister Rider?"

"Yes," Sasha said, and Galen poured it into the mugs.

Sasha finally bit into his egg as the mug was slid his way. He chewed on it thoughtfully, glancing around the room with obvious judgement. Galen guessed that Sasha had never been to the lower districts for more than a day or so. Well, he'd need to get used to it.

Sasha swallowed and said, "I would rather have been assigned to the Palace Guard. But it's not my place to complain. Governor Maple wants to make sure that the devotees of the Lady of Flowers are safe, so here I am, bright and early. The Guards of Dragonet City live to serve. Though, I have to admit, you're not what I was expecting."

"What were you expecting?" Galen asked, eyeing him warily.

"A doddering old man," Sasha said, shrugging as though that were the only thing that would have made sense. "Not a young man with a face that…"

Sasha suddenly stopped speaking, his own face scrunched up in mortification that he had even acknowledged what was glaringly, obviously, on Galen's face. Galen smiled sadly and took a drink of his tea. It wasn't surprising; in fact, it was more surprising that Sasha hadn't reacted or brought it up until now.

Galen knew that his face was not a beautiful one. Nearly a quarter of it was covered with burn scars. They covered his left cheek and the area around his eye, and extended all the way down his arm and chest. Not that Sasha was able to see the rest of them. Most people were too polite to say anything; they just gave him a certain look when they were biting their tongue. Sasha drank his tea and didn't meet Galen's eyes.

As he lowered his mug, Sasha said, "Sorry, that was rude."

"Watch out, I'll set the Kipper Gang on you," Galen joked, but Sasha didn't laugh. "It's fine, it's hard to miss. It's just a scar; I don't mind."

Sasha looked as though he didn't believe him.

Galen barreled on. "People stare, and you're a person, so there you go. I joined Aster House when I was eleven, and I started my apprenticeship here, with Sister Elowen, when I was twenty-one. It's been my whole life; I'm a doddering old man in my soul."

Sasha still didn't laugh, just ate his egg in silence. Galen shrugged and sat at the table with him. Galen sliced off a piece of brown bread and offered it to Sasha, who took it with a grunt. Galen vaguely wondered who had taught the guard table manners. He cut his own piece and spread jam on it, then stirred honey into his tea.

They ate in silence, and Galen thought this could work. He could make this work. Maybe Sasha was just not a morning person. The silence was a companionable one, at least from Galen's perspective. It broke after Sasha had finished off Galen's loaf of bread and three of his apples.

"What's the schedule?" Sasha asked.

"Hmm?" Galen said and then smiled again. "Ah, well, half an hour after sunrise, I head out. I have a route that I follow each day of the week, except for my rest day. Of course, I sometimes have to attend to emergencies, and the route changes as people need me."

Sasha winced, perhaps at the early hour, and asked, "And when do you finish?"

"Usually an hour before sunset," Galen said, and laughed. "Well, depending on the time of year. Sometimes I'm out later, if there's a lot of tough cases. But you needn't stay with me past dark."

"I think that that would be when you would need me the most," Sasha said, sighing. "Long days."

"You won't need to come on my rest day," Galen said. "I only go out if there's an emergency."

"And how often are there emergencies when you're what, the only healer in the whole quarter?" Sasha said, grimacing again.

Galen shrugged. "Well, not the only person capable of healing, but yes. I'm the only healer from the Lady of Flowers here. And emergencies happen pretty often if I'm honest. And I am always honest! Don't worry about it, though. As I said, I've been here for seven years and never had any problems."

"Fucking Lion's teeth," Sasha grumbled, and then looked apologetic for swearing in front of a devotee, but Galen brushed it away.

"I hear all kinds of things," Galen said. "Don't worry about censoring yourself. Language gets very colorful when a bone is being set."

"But I do have to be here." Sasha sighed. "You're my charge. I can't let anything happen to you."

"Nothing's going to happen to me!" Galen said brightly. "Even the scum of the scum, the worst criminals—and mind you, that's not Candiru, the people here are just living their lives—but even *they* know that a healer is off limits. Why else do you think I wear such a bright yellow tunic?"

The tunic worn by healers who followed Lady of Flowers was rather garish, but it was meant to be. It was bright, nearly obnoxious, and as pigmented as the dyers in Lavender House could get it. He could always be spotted in a crowd, and if he was running down the street, people saw yellow and knew to move. No one outside of healers wore that bright hue, and very few who were not devotees wore it. It was just logical.

"Maybe you like the color?" Sasha said, but his voice was uncertain.

"I *do* like yellow," Galen admitted. "It's my favorite color; my favorite flowers are yellow. But I probably wouldn't wear it every day like this. You see? It's fine."

Sasha looked unconvinced.

"I can't very well tell my captain that," Sasha grumbled, pulling a hand down his face. "Gods, why'd I have to get this of all the fucking assignments available?"

"Well—" Galen started, but then the bells of Rising Dawn's temple began to ring out through the morning and Galen slapped his face. "Oh, by the Lady, we're late. Behind schedule already. Ah, well, good thing that you ate all the food, less to clean up. Dump the dishes and let's go."

After seeing that Sasha seemed to have no intention of moving, Galen scooped up the plates and bowls himself and dumped them in a basin beside the sink. He pulled on the matching bright yellow cloak, cut short to his waist, and slung his healer's kit over his shoulder. With a few quick checks of the windows and plants, and the ever-important task of making sure that Muffin hadn't sneaked into the house, he walked out the door. Sasha was right on his heels, thankfully.

Galen locked the door and then smiled up at Sasha, saying, "Well, Mister Rider, are you ready?"

Chapter 2

Candiru Quarter

Sasha

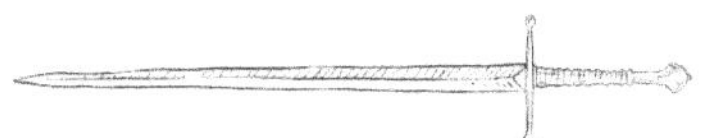

Sasha had not been ready. Not in the slightest. Nothing could have prepared him for the strange little man with the burnt face, bright hazel eyes that seemed to pierce into his soul, and hair that shone like a burnished bronze hilt. He had been pleasant, Sasha supposed, but he was still a devotee of the Lady of Flowers, which meant Sasha disliked him on principle. Even if the tea had been good. And even if Sasha had accidentally eaten all the man's bread. Whoops.

Now Sasha was striding behind the man as he scrambled down the busy morning streets of Candiru Quarter. Lion's teeth, he hated going to Candiru Quarter. For one thing, it reeked to the high heavens. He was sure that even the Evening Star above could smell the stench radiating from its streets. Sewer mixed with animal smells mixed with the sweat and heat from so many bodies in one place.

And that was the other thing; there were far too many people in Candiru Quarter, and far too many of them wanted to pick your pocket or worse. Sasha had tucked his purse against his chest under his leathers to be safe. Well-placed suspicion pricked at his senses as he eyed the solid mass of people they rushed through.

However, he couldn't help but notice that what Brother Galen had said was true. People would spot Brother Galen's horribly yellow clothes and part for him, clearing a path. No one wanted to get in the way of a healer in a hurry, it seemed. Sasha was glad for the long legs that let him keep up with Brother Galen, because the tide of people would crash back together as soon as they passed.

Unfortunately, Sasha's mind kept going back to that pink flower pendant that hung around Brother Galen's neck. He tried not to scowl—he really did—but it was difficult. Lion in Glory, why'd he have to get this assignment of all the ones available? He'd have even taken being a noble's guard. That would have been boring, but it wouldn't have been this. Boredom would be better than bile rising in his throat or a child's world torn away or Anya's sad, tired eyes.

If he could last a year, just one year, he'd be able to request a change in posting. He'd never lasted that long at a posting before in his life, but he'd do it. He'd show Miller, and Tracker, and all of them that he deserved a different assignment. One hopefully far, far away from Candiru Quarter and any follower of the Lady of Flowers.

It didn't take long to arrive at their first stop on what was sure to be a very long day. Brother Galen stopped abruptly, so abruptly that Sasha nearly crashed into him, at a little shack of a house wedged between two shops. Brother Galen knocked and bounced on his toes, humming softly to himself, before turning to look up at Sasha with his odd smile. It was all lip and no teeth, and Sasha didn't trust it.

"Mister Rider, feel free to come in with me, or you can stay out here if you wish," Brother Galen said gently. "It's a bit cramped in there, lots of people in a small space. Fair warning, that's all."

Sasha gritted his teeth. Of course this little devotee was trying to keep him out of his business. He probably thought he was better than a lowly guard just because the Lady of Flowers had blessed him. Condescending lot of self-righteous little scumbags. But naturally he couldn't say that.

Couldn't have this annoying little man go complaining to his superiors about him and ruining his, what was it? Fourth? Yes. His fourth chance with the guard. It was technically a three-strike system, but there was some debate about his second strike. Sasha knew it should have counted, but fortunately for him Captain Tracker thought it should not. He needed the job.

Sasha grunted noncommittally. Brother Galen's smile faltered but then returned as the door opened and he turned back around. Within was a very round, very careworn woman. Her gray hair was piled on top of her head in a slipshod bun, her face was marked with laugh lines and worry wrinkles, and she wore a stained apron over a much-mended dress. Her eyes lit up when she saw the devotee.

"Brother Galen!" she said happily. "Oh, I'm so glad to see you, come in, come in. Little Poppy is doing a bit better today."

"Oh, that's wonderful to hear, ma'am," Brother Galen said, bowing slightly and then walking through the open door. "Oh, and this is Mister Sasha Rider. He's my new, uh, guard. From the governor's initiative."

"Oh, yes," the woman said, rolling her eyes. "We've heard all about that. Well, come in, dear. No use standing outside."

Sasha sighed heavily and moved in. He caught a flash of yellow as Brother Galen disappeared into the next room. He was moving quickly, which Sasha had to admit was probably a good thing for a healer. It gave Sasha a moment to look around the small abode.

It was dark; that was the first thing he noticed. The

windows were open to let in light and air, but this deep into Candiru, the neighboring buildings blocked much of the sun, and the air was as putrid indoors as out. Sasha fought the urge to cover his nose with his hand. If the smell had been bad out in the breeze, it was easily ten times worse in a small space.

"Not from Candiru, are you?" the little woman asked.

Sasha blinked down at her in surprise. Her eyes were bright as she met his gaze with lifted brows.

"No, I was born in Medaka District," Sasha said.

"Not used to the smell yet, eh?" she said, a knowing grin on her face.

"Pardon?"

"I can tell from the wrinkle of your nose and the twitch of your lip," the woman said with a nod. "We're all nose-blind to it, but I'm sure it's quite a shock coming from the upper districts. You'll get used to it, though."

Sasha tried not to grimace. He certainly didn't mind being rude to a devotee of the Lady of Flowers, who deserved it, but he didn't want to be rude to a citizen. Anya would have been disappointed in him, and he certainly had no ill will towards this woman. She didn't seem like the typical Candiru criminal.

"I wasn't meaning to be rude, ma'am," Sasha said, moving to follow Brother Galen and escape this awkward conversation.

"Oh, not at all, Mister Rider," she said. "We know it's bad. That's what happens when you're directly above where all the sewage from up top is dumped, before it gets washed away."

"Ah," Sasha said, trying not to gag at the smell, and worse, the thought of what was making it.

"Oh, I'm Martha Kingley, by the by. Brother Galen didn't introduce me before heading off to see my granddaughter."

"Pleased to meet you, Mistress Kingley," Sasha said, taking another step back.

"Just 'Miss', thank you," Miss Kingley said, then her eyes

sparkled with mischief as her grin widened. "Watch out for the hooligans."

Sasha only had a moment to murmur, "Hooligans?" to himself when a horde of children erupted into the small space. There were at least ten of them; they ranged from small and toddling to awkward and gangly, about the age to take on an apprenticeship, pledge to a temple, or even join the city guard. He was peppered with a hundred questions, which he struggled to answer meaningfully while fending off sticky hands grabbing at his weapons.

"All right, children!" Miss Kingley shouted over the noise, and they all fell instantly silent. "I think that Mister Rider has had enough of you. Let him go do his job."

There was a collective groan, but the children obeyed and disappeared into whatever nooks and crannies they had emerged from. Sasha gave Miss Kingley a grateful nod that she brushed away with a wave of her hand. Then he moved into the room Brother Galen had disappeared into.

The room was small, and the bed took up almost all the space. It was piled high with quilts and Brother Galen was perched on the edge, healer's bag open next to him, talking to an impossibly tiny girl with ruffled dark hair and skin as tanned as Galen's own. The healer was pulling back from where he had been holding a strange funnel-shaped implement to her chest and smiling, no teeth showing of course.

"Your heart is sounding nice and strong, Poppy," Brother Galen said gently. "That's good. Now, I'm going to listen to your lungs too, all right? I'm going to lift your dress in the back and then you're going to take some big breaths."

"Okay," the little girl said.

Brother Galen did just as he said he would, instructing the girl to breathe in and out a few times before nodding, smiling, and putting down the instrument. He didn't seem to notice

Sasha in the doorway, just made notes in a tiny journal and then looked back at Poppy, placing the back of his hand gently against her forehead.

"Your breathing sounds good, Poppy! That's a good sign. That means that you're getting better," Brother Galen said. "You've been fighting so hard. You're very strong. You feel a bit warm right now; how are you feeling today?"

"Better than last week," Poppy said, beaming at the encouragement and revealing a missing front tooth. "I've been drinking the tea that you left with Granny. Even though it tastes yucky."

"Well, how about I bring Miss Kingley some honey she can add to your tea, dear?" Brother Galen asked. "I want you to keep drinking it for a week more, all right?"

"All right," Poppy said with a sigh.

"And keep getting plenty of rest. No running off and slaying dragons just yet," Brother Galen said, smirking as he packed up his bag.

"Okay," Poppy said, giggling.

Brother Galen stood and tucked her back into bed, then turned to leave, smiling at Sasha. It was clear that he was aware that Sasha had been standing in the doorway the whole time but didn't mind. He took a step but stopped when Poppy called out.

"Wait!" the little girl shouted. "Aren't you forgetting something?"

Brother Galen gave Sasha an amused look, then turned around, smacking his head dramatically and saying, "Oh! My dear Poppy! I cannot believe I forgot!"

Poppy giggled again and said, "Good thing I reminded you."

"Good thing indeed," Brother Galen said, reaching into his bag. "Here you go, my dear."

Brother Galen retrieved something small wrapped in wax

paper and handed it to Poppy, who squealed with joy. She unwrapped it, revealing a small, bright hardened piece of sugar that she popped in her mouth with a grin. Then Brother Galen made the sign of the Lady of Flowers, which ruined everything.

Sasha had been enjoying watching how the devotee was with the child until that reminder of why he was there. The Lady of Flowers, here to perform as though everyone owed her something. It twisted Sasha's stomach and he felt the scowl return to his lips.

"See you next week, Poppy," Brother Galen said, then left, patting Sasha on the arm. Sasha fought the urge to brush himself off where the man had touched him.

They made their way out through a throng of children who swarmed Brother Galen asking for candy. He gave it to them, and they scurried away. He gave a pleasant goodbye to Miss Kingley and gave her a jar, explaining that he wanted Poppy to have another week of the special tea. Sasha felt anger bubbling up in his chest, and he gritted his teeth.

As soon as they stepped out of the shack, Brother Galen checked his journal and started walking, but Sasha grabbed his shoulder. The devotee turned around, eyebrows lifted in surprise.

"Why did you do that?" Sasha asked.

"What? Give the kids candy?" Brother Galen asked. He looked stunned at first, but then an easy smile grew on his lips. "My face can look a little scary to children, but I need to treat them when they're sick. It's positive association. I'm just the man with the candy now, not the one with an awful burnt face."

"No," Sasha said. "I mean, why didn't you just wave your hands, say a prayer, and heal her? Wouldn't that be easier for everyone? Isn't that the purpose of your goddess?"

Brother Galen blinked in surprise, and said, "Oh, it

doesn't work like that. I can't just magically heal everyone. That's strictly for emergencies. But I'm trained as a healer to make sure that I can still help people, still follow the Lady's path, you see?"

Sasha didn't see, so he just grunted. Brother Galen smiled at him, then turned and started walking briskly to his next appointment. It made no sense, but Sasha knew that all devotees seemed to believe the same. They were magically gifted by a goddess of healing, so why wouldn't they use that to heal the people they claimed to care for? Sasha swallowed his grumble as he followed Brother Galen.

"So, you met Miss Kingley, then?" Brother Galen asked him as they walked.

"Yes," Sasha said flatly. "She said I was making a face at the smell of Candiru."

"She's a hoot," Brother Galen said with a chuckle. "A very good soul. She cares for all those children while their parents are working, doesn't ask for a penny."

That struck Sasha as odd. He was sure that Miss Kingley had called them her grandchildren, and that Poppy had called her Granny.

"Those aren't her grandchildren?" Sasha asked, brow furrowing.

"Nope, she never had any children," Brother Galen said, then a smile tugged at his lips as he glanced back at the small house. "But she's a perfect grandmother."

Sasha was quiet for a moment, and then asked, "Why aren't they in school?"

"Ah, well," Brother Galen said, shaking his head and looking back at Sasha. "The schoolhouse isn't exactly safe; it got some black mold a few years back and children were getting sick. Then the schoolmaster from one of the upper districts, I think Sillago, refused to come, and the city wouldn't repair the schoolhouse. It's all a mess. But we make do. Like always."

"So the children aren't taught?" Sasha asked again, very confused and a bit disgruntled.

"Oh, they are," Brother Galen said, lifting his hand placatingly. "Just not by the city. There's a devotee from the temple of Rising Dawn who comes here three days a week and teaches them their letters and numbers. She makes them sing songs to the sun's glory at the end, but I suppose that's fair enough."

Sasha ruminated on that, and Brother Galen kept going through his schedule. There were fifteen stops in all that day. Most were fairly quick checkups like Poppy's. There was a pregnant woman named Angelica who had a thousand questions that took up most of their lunch break. This made Sasha rather cross, but Brother Galen didn't seem to mind. At the last stop, though, Sasha saw Brother Galen take a moment to collect himself before he went in.

It was in an apartment stacked precariously atop a shop. Brother Galen waved cheerfully at the man closing up before he climbed up the stairs that were shoved against the building at random intervals. The sun was already close to setting, and the rust-colored sky cast strange shadows between the buildings. Sasha followed carefully behind Brother Galen and watched him show the slightest bit of hesitation before knocking on the door.

"Well, get in here, Galen," a voice called from the other side, clearly old and clearly unhappy.

Brother Galen closed his eyes for a moment, then put on his usual pleasant expression and moved in. Sasha followed him but immediately halted in the doorway. The smell within was putrid. It was more than the sewage that he had started to get used to over the course of the day. The smell was stronger, more concentrated here. There was something almost sickly sweet mixed within it, like rotting flesh. And mildew was the top note of the entire moil of scents. It took all of Sasha's willpower not to gag.

"Who the fuck is that?" an angry voice croaked out.

Sasha saw the source of the smell and the voice. It was a man, lying in a waterlogged and disgusting bed, covered in filth. His clothes were ratty and torn, and his snarl revealed rotten, blackened teeth. Most horrifying of all, his right leg was bulging, splotched with patches of sickly yellow, painful red, and terrifying pitch black. Sasha winced in sympathy, but that apparently made things worse. The man's snarl intensified.

"That's Mister Rider, sir," Brother Galen said, his voice soft. "He's here because of the new initiative from the governor. Every devotee of the Lady of Flowers must be escorted because—"

"And you're stuck with Gap-Tooth Galen?" the man said, sneering as he looked between the two of them. "Oh, they must hate you at the guard station."

"Mister Balsin, we've been over this. Please don't call me that," Brother Galen said, and Sasha could hear a slight tremble in his voice.

"Why not? It's still true, isn't it?" the man spat at him. "Or did you use that fancy temple money to finally fix it? Come on, let's see it. Give Old Harry a smile."

"Mister Balsin," Brother Galen said again, but he was interrupted.

"Smile, boy!" Harry said.

Brother Galen sighed and then smiled, showing his teeth. It was a pained smile, so different from the more cheerful smiles that Sasha had seen throughout the day, but sure enough, there was space between his two front teeth. Harry cackled at him cruelly. Brother Galen sighed and dropped the grin.

Honestly, Sasha was disappointed. Harry was being cruel, yes, but the gap was cute. It was a shame that Brother Galen was embarrassed by it, because it was rather endearing. And then Sasha caught himself. He couldn't believe that he had thought that about a devotee of the Lady of Flowers. It was disgusting that he had found one of her followers cute, even for a moment.

"You see?" Harry said triumphantly. "Now get out, scarface here needs to clean me up."

Sasha crossed his arms and, although there was nothing he would rather do than leave, he said, "No can do, sir. I'm to watch him at all times."

"What, are you a criminal, boy?" Harry asked Brother Galen, who had paled. "Is this guard here to arrest you?"

"Mister Rider, I assure you, it's just myself and Mister Balsin in here," Brother Galen said. "There is no danger. And I...frankly, I don't think that you want to watch this. And Mister Balsin deserves his privacy."

"I'll turn around," Sasha said firmly.

"Is that all right, Mister Balsin?" Brother Galen said, sounding rather defeated.

Harry glowered at Sasha, lips drawn back to show his rotted teeth. And yet he teased Brother Galen about gap teeth in an otherwise cared-for mouth. Unsurprising that this awful old man was an utter hypocrite.

"Fine," Harry growled. "Get turning, dog."

Sasha turned his back on the pair, relieved not to see as well as smell what was happening behind him. Harry snapped at Brother Galen the whole time. Sasha could imagine the devotee lifting him off the bed, sponging him off, switching the sheets, washing the soiled ones, and all the while being overwhelmingly pleasant and patient even though Sasha clearly heard the old man thrashing and even smacking the healer.

It was almost an hour later when Harry screamed, "Come on! I need it! I need it more than anyone else!"

"I know you want me to, but it will only work for a short time, Mister Balsin," Brother Galen said, sounding exhausted, "and then it'll be back. Now, the temple can send a doctor here and they could—"

"I don't want you to cut off the damn thing, I want you to fix it!" Harry spat.

"I can't," Brother Galen said, regret coloring each word. "I can just make it feel a bit better. It's too far gone for me to do anything genuinely helpful at this point."

"Then what good are you, Gap-Tooth Galen?" Harry growled. "What's the point of all this?"

Sasha turned and was shocked at the difference. The man was washed and cleaned, the sheets on the bed were pristine, and the old ones hung drying. The smell was even a bit better, though Harry's leg still looked awful. Sasha could say a lot about Brother Galen, but he would never say that he wasn't a hard worker.

Brother Galen chewed his lip, ran a hand through his hair, and said, "All right. All right, fine."

"Well, the Lady be praised, he actually does his damn job," Harry said, still glaring at the devotee.

Brother Galen arranged Harry's leg and then, with a breath, laid his hands over the discolored skin. The devotee started muttering under his breath and then a pink glow emanated from his hands as well as the pendant around his neck. It was beautiful, it was enchanting, and it was infuriating.

Sasha ground his teeth as he watched the sores heal and the swelling go down. The red disappeared, the black vanished, and the yellow cleared up. Harry sighed in relief. His leg looked shockingly normal.

Brother Galen stood and said, "Be sure to stay off it as

much as possible. And, Mister Balsin, I still really think that the doctor should come."

"Get out of here, scarface," Harry said, rubbing his leg.

Brother Galen sighed. "I'll see you next week, Mister Balsin."

He walked quietly past Sasha into the now-dark night. Brother Galen walked carefully down the steps and, once on the ground, reached into his bag and pulled out a linen pouch. He held the pouch up to his face and pressed his nose against it, breathing in deeply. When Sasha finished walking down the steps, Brother Galen offered it to him.

"It's dried lavender," Brother Galen explained. "It'll help get the scent out of your nose."

Sasha didn't want to admit that he needed help from a devotee of the Lady of Flowers, but he also felt like his nose had been burned. Sasha took it and breathed in the scent deeply. It smelled nice, and it did help to banish the lingering rotting odor. After a moment, he gave it back to Brother Galen.

"Why didn't you just use your magic from the start?" Sasha asked.

Brother Galen was quiet for a moment before he said, "It doesn't last; his leg is too far gone. The magic is just a bandage. We need to remove his leg, so the infection doesn't get worse and spread. I'm...reluctant to use magic on it because he'll just end up relying on that."

"So, you'd let him suffer and stay in pain, just to make a point?" Sasha asked, letting his pent-up anger leak into his voice.

Brother Galen scrunched up his nose, annoyance showing through his carefully crafted healer's persona for a moment before his face became calm again. He squeezed the pouch of lavender in his fingers before he looked back up at Sasha.

"No, that's not the case," Brother Galen said firmly. "I would have given him something for the pain."

"But it wouldn't have been the same," Sasha said, his brow furrowing as he scanned Brother Galen's face.

For a moment, the devotee seemed hesitant to answer. He licked his lips and swallowed. Maybe he realized that Sasha wasn't like most people, that his new guard wouldn't just believe the platitudes that the Lady of Flowers and her followers always gave in place of actual help.

"No," Brother Galen finally said, shaking his head.

"And why not use it on sick folks, like Poppy?" Sasha asked, hot, righteous anger filling his chest. "Wouldn't that be easier than coming back week after week?"

"Her body needs to learn how to heal on its own," Brother Galen said, and he sounded somewhat confused. "That's healthy. The magic might have healed her faster, but..."

"You withheld it to make a point," Sasha said with a huff. "That's just like the Lady of Flowers."

"It wasn't to make a point," Brother Galen said, staring up at Sasha with furrowed brows, shocked and confused. Good. Sasha would knock this oh-so-holy devotee down where he belonged.

Sasha sneered, and then said, "You said you only use magic for emergencies. Is an old man yelling insults at you an emergency, Brother Galen?"

Brother Galen grew quiet, and then ran a hand down his face, and said, "You're right. I only have a small amount that I can use each day. I should have saved it in case there was an actual emergency. I was just...tired. Let's just call it a night, all right?"

As they turned and moved back towards the healer's home, Sasha had to smirk. He had finally gotten one over on the Lady of Flowers. He'd have to start keeping a tally.

CHAPTER 3

THE TROUBLE WITH CITY GUARDS

GALEN

GALEN DECIDED THAT HE DIDN'T PARTICULARLY care for Sasha Rider. It was a grand failing on his part; he tried to like everyone. Seven hells, he even liked Old Harry despite the way the man treated him. At least he had a reason for being mean and grumpy. Sasha, on the other hand, had no excuse that Galen could figure out.

And what was really irritating was that Galen struggled to pinpoint an exact moment where Sasha took it too far. It wasn't a grand moment; it was little comments or looks. Things Galen could write off or say weren't a big deal. Sasha not holding the door for him when his arms were full, Sasha rolling his eyes when he joked with his patients, Sasha needing to spit just when Galen made the sign of the Lady. It all needled at him, slowly but surely.

Week after week, Galen tried to make the best of it. The rest of the first week went by fairly smoothly. Sasha would show up on his doorstep, bright and early and very grumpy. Galen quickly learned to put out three times as much breakfast. Sasha was a big eater, and Galen thought maybe offering food would soften his disposition. No such luck.

Sasha ate his food and grunted; he never said thank you or acted grateful. Galen tried not to let it bother him. He knew that sometimes people were appreciative even if it seemed like they weren't. He'd worked with the sick and injured long enough to know that. Often a patient acted as though Galen were a demon straight out of the seven hells as he set a bone or forced medicine down their throat, only to bring him cookies or newly knit socks a week later. But Sasha was not like that.

However, Galen wasn't going to let that bring him down. The rest of the first week, Sasha tailed behind him and made dismissive grunts. Just as Galen had feared, people trusted him less with a city guard at his shoulder. He understood it completely. In theory, the guards were there to catch criminals and keep Dragonet City safe. In practice, they were often used to make sure that residents of the lower districts stayed there.

Sasha was an upper city guard, so he hadn't been one of the guards with cudgels that beat Candiru residents back when they got too rowdy, but he was still a city guard. And it didn't help that he made faces at bad smells and refused to leave any room that Galen was in. There were a lot of bad smells in Galen's line of work. He was very used to it, and keeping a straight face—making sure that patients who smelled bad didn't feel self-conscious—was an important aspect of healing. One that Sasha was ruining. And while a young person wouldn't mind removing their shirt or pants for the healer, they were much more hesitant when there was a guard standing in the corner. Galen had known it from the beginning: Sasha being there made his job harder.

IT WAS ON THE FIFTH DAY WITH SASHA THAT THEY ran into the Kipper Gang. Galen was leaving the Harrison house—he had been visiting Margaret Harrison, whose bad hip always troubled her in the rainy season—when he turned and nearly ran into Jess.

Jess, who was surrounded by six other members of the gang, all wearing their bright orange bandannas, dodged in time, brushing off Galen's apologies with a good-natured smile and a smack on his back. "No worries, Flower Boy! It's all good. How you been? Anyone giving you trouble?"

"Hello, Jess," Galen said, forcing himself to smile despite his exhaustion. "I'm doing well, thank you. How's the wrist?"

"Good as it ever was!" Jess said, flexing their wrist and showing it off to Galen.

"Wonderful to see," Galen said, all too aware of the guard who was about to emerge from the house. "Now, I hate to chat and run, but I really must get going on my rounds."

"Oh, we'll come with you," Jess said, grinning. "We can watch your skinny little back, my friend."

"Ah, that's kind," Galen said, and then pitched his voice down. "Do you remember that initiative that the governor started? More guards? Well, I now have a guard dog following me around."

"A dog?" Jess asked, a falsely pleased smile playing on their lips. "You know, I always thought you could do with a pet. And not that little rascal that's always running in between your place and the bakery. A proper dog would do you just right."

"Well, not a real dog, I meant I have a—" Galen was interrupted by the shouts of the other Kippers.

"Yuck, a hanging herring!" one young Kipper shouted as Sasha walked out of the house, free from Margaret at last. She had amazingly held him captive for a moment with idle chatter standing in front of the door. Galen had been able to slip out and steal a moment for himself while Sasha had to decide between shoving the old woman out of the way or letting her prattle on.

Sasha scowled, which was his most natural expression. Jess lifted their brows and then nodded, giving Galen an apologetic smile. They whistled and led the Kippers away quickly. Sasha glared at Galen.

"Are those your criminal friends?" Sasha asked.

"They're not criminals," Galen said, although the Kippers took the laws of the city more as suggestions than hard and fast rules. "They just look out for the community."

"Ah, so you're pretending you don't know about their crimes," Sasha said, rolling his eyes. "Of course. That's about what I'd expect."

"The worst thing they do that I know about is break curfew." Galen was lying, but Sasha didn't need to know that.

"Right," Sasha said with a dismissive snort. Galen really did not like him.

～

WORST OF ALL, SASHA HATED MUFFIN. WELL, perhaps that wasn't the worst of all, but it was high up on Galen's list the guard's flaws. Muffin was practically a celebrity on Galen's street. He'd been there for about five years, and Galen still looked back fondly on the chaos that he had caused when he first showed up.

On the third day of the job, Sasha had practically screamed in surprise when Muffin, in a classic Muffin move, zipped between his legs in a flash of blue and white fur, then jumped up onto the kitchen table. Galen had laughed, then tutted at Muffin, scooping the beast up in his arms and putting him back on the floor, scolding him for scaring Sasha and jumping on the table.

"What in the seven hells is that thing?" Sasha asked through gritted teeth.

Galen, who was stroking Muffin's shockingly cold fur, crouched down next to him and said, "It's Muffin!"

"And what is Muffin?" Sasha said, brow furrowing. "A horrible mage's experiment gone wrong?"

Galen hummed in the back of his throat, scratching under Muffin's chin, and said, "Not far off."

"Not far off?" Sasha asked, his face twisted into a mix of annoyance and horror.

Galen looked down at Muffin. In shape, Muffin looked like an especially well-fed, or to be perfectly honest, overfed fox. However, Muffin was, at least partially by everyone's guess, a blink fox. He had sky-blue fur with patches of snow white; his paw pads and tongue were the same shade of white, and his eyes were a deep blue, nearly black. His gigantic fluffy tail was perfect for knocking things to the ground with thunderous crashes. And he was so clumsy that he rarely left everything in the little house intact.

"He's a blink fox," Galen said, smiling. "At least by our best guess."

"He's massive," Sasha said, staring in stunned awe.

"Oh, yeah. His favorite haunting spot is the bakery, and he loves muffins with a fervor to rival a starving dragon. It's why we call him Muffin."

"Where...where did he come from? Aren't blink foxes wild?"

"We're not quite sure," Galen said with a shrug. "He showed up a few years ago. We think that maybe a noble from up top bought him. There are always scammers who are trying to sell wild magic animals as pets. Adrian, that's the bakery owner, thinks that Muffin is the result of someone breeding a blink fox with a cat of some kind, trying to domesticate them, you know?"

"That's illegal," Sasha said, cocking a brow.

"Well, that's not Muffin's fault," Galen said, scratching the sides of Muffin's face as the beast chirruped happily.

"And what, you just let a wild animal run around in here?" Sasha said with a sneer.

"Well, it's hard to stop him, and he's mostly harmless," Galen said. "His victims are usually pots or plates of baked goods. He can't blink that well, which is why Adrian thinks he's a half-breed. But he knows he's not supposed to be in my house, isn't that right, Muffin?" He nuzzled his cheek against Muffin's nose, earning a lick from the creature's cold, blue tongue.

Muffin continued to chirrup as Galen stood, the massive blue and white bundle of fur in his arms. He went over to the door, opened it, and gently plopped Muffin onto his stoop. Muffin looked up at him with a mournful expression and then disappeared in a sharp flash of crackling magic, causing Sasha to cry out in surprise.

Galen turned to see Muffin back in his house, tilting his head to the side and looking up curiously at Sasha. Sasha was pressed up against the wall, glaring down at the plump little animal, his lip curled. He nudged Muffin with his foot, and the blink fox rolled over and showed his stuffed belly.

"I thought you said this thing couldn't blink," Sasha said, glaring at Galen.

"I said he couldn't blink well," Galen said, laughing. "He must have been motivated to make friends with you! Isn't that right, Muffin? Don't worry about Sasha, he's all bark and no bite."

Galen scooped Muffin up again and smiled at Sasha, only for the man to scowl back and say, "Just keep that thing away from me."

"I'll do my best, but Muffin knows no master," Galen said, dropping Muffin gently on the stoop again. This time he scampered away.

"Maybe you should actually try," Sasha grumbled. "That would be refreshing."

And that was the way that things went with Sasha. No matter what Galen did, no matter what he said, Sasha was dismissive if not outright cruel. Galen once tripped on a cobblestone and cut his knee open. He was bleeding, and most people would have helped him up and asked if he was okay, but Sasha just folded his arms and glared at him until Galen had finished wrapping his knee and stood up on his own.

"Graceful, aren't we?" was all Sasha said.

Galen turned that over in his head for days, trying to figure out what he had done that would make the Lady of Flowers want to test him. And Sasha was awful about the way that Galen worshipped her. He came on Galen's first rest day and was annoyed that Galen, a devotee, had the audacity to say prayers to his goddess.

"Must you really do that?" Sasha said, sitting at the kitchen table, using a whetstone on his sword, as he had been for the past hour. The blade must be sharp enough to slice air.

Galen was on his knees with prayer beads in his hands, halfway through his ceremony. He sometimes—well, really, usually—missed his prayers because he was so caught up in his work. He liked to believe that by caring for the people of Candiru Quarter, healing them and making them laugh, he was praying to the Lady in his own way. And it was perhaps even better than the prayers. But he still made sure he kept up with them on his rest days, unless there was an emergency.

"Well, uh, yes," Galen said, turning to look at Sasha with a bemused smile. "I am a devotee. Praying to the god I'm devoted to is well, kind of a large part of it."

Sasha sighed and rolled his eyes. "It's annoying."

"I could try and pray quieter?" Galen offered. "I imagine that the Lady could hear me no matter how softly I speak."

"Then would you mind whispering?" Sasha said, looking at Galen incredulously.

"All right," Galen said, a baffled laugh escaping his lips. This man was ridiculous.

"Good," Sasha grunted.

Eventually, Sasha started coming in late on his rest day, trying to miss the morning prayers even if he also missed breakfast. He still grumbled at the evening prayers though. Galen assumed that he just wasn't religious. And he didn't want to pass judgement, even if Sasha had no problem passing judgment on him. And the awful situation with the guard continued through the weeks they worked together with no sign of improving.

EVERY SINGLE TIME THAT SOMETHING DIDN'T GO perfectly smoothly, Sasha had something to say about it. Whether it was 'well, that could have gone better' or 'you really bungled that one, didn't you?' or even 'wow, well done' said as sarcastically as possible, Sasha couldn't help but comment. And, of course, he never said anything about the majority of the time when Galen helped people successfully and they thanked him.

During their fourth week together, Galen was reaching a breaking point. He had just finished another visit at Miss Kingley's, this time for Andrew, who had broken his arm a month previous. He slipped into Poppy's room, and she was doing so much better that it warmed his heart. Apparently not Sasha's, though, as he stood in the corner with gritted teeth.

Galen walked outside, the sky purpling above him. He was counting his lucky stars that this was his last stop and he would get a reprieve from Sasha shortly. He didn't know if he could handle much more of the grumpy guard. However, that's when a man came running up to them.

Someone running towards a healer was never a good sign. Galen turned to rush and meet him, much to the chagrin of Sasha, who let out an exasperated groan. It was Thomas Sharp, the apprentice at the potter's. He was only eighteen, but he was utterly devoted to his masters. He skidded to a halt in front of Galen, trying to catch his breath.

"Hey, Mister Sharp," Galen said. "Thomas, breathe. What happened? What's wrong?"

"It's...Mistress Mandy...she's..." Thomas gasped out, placing his hands on his knees.

"Mandy?" Galen's eyes widened. "Is she all right? Was it another kiln accident?"

Thomas shook his head, and Galen reached into his bag and pulled out a waterskin, which he gently pushed into Thomas's hands. Thomas drank from it gratefully, draining the whole thing while Galen rubbed his back.

"This seems pressing, do you have time for all this?" Sasha grumped from behind them.

Thomas wiped his mouth and looked guilty while Galen fought with all his strength not to turn around and glare at Sasha. Thomas handed Galen back the empty waterskin with a flush and ran his hand through short, corn-colored hair.

"Not a kiln accident this time," Thomas said, his voice shaking with fear. "Mistress Nina has been very careful since the last time. No, Mistress Mandy is very sick. She has all these black spots on her skin, and she keeps coughing up this...this gross stuff. It's as black as the spots. Black as tar. There's a fever, but she says she's cold. She's so tired, she can barely move or talk, she can't keep anything down."

Galen's mind raced through everything it could be, flipping through his catalogue of sicknesses and diseases, beforc coming up empty. He chewed the inside of his cheek in thought and then took Thomas's arm and started walking towards the potter's.

"When did she get sick?" Galen asked urgently.

"Just hours ago," Thomas said, gripping onto Galen's arm for dear life. "She was right as rain this morning. Oh, Evening Star above, Brother Galen, is it another plague?"

A chill shot down Galen's spine at those words, and he could swear that Sasha made a worried sound, but he just shook his head and said, "Let's not get ahead of ourselves, Thomas. Let me take a look at her. It could even be that she ate something that didn't agree with her. You did well to find me. Can you run again?"

Thomas nodded, and Galen started to pick up speed. Even in the dimming light, people saw the bright yellow of the healer's garb and cleared out of his way. Sasha was close behind him, huffing indignantly at the situation. Well, he could huff all he liked. Galen had a job to do.

CHAPTER 4

IT BEGINS

SASHA

SASHA FOLLOWED BROTHER GALEN AS HE RUSHED into the room. Brother Galen would often look worried or concerned, which made sense, but rarely did he look so panicked. They had made good time, even though Thomas started losing speed as they turned onto the potter's street. Once they had made it inside the premises, the lad had collapsed into a chair and thrown his head back in exhaustion. Sasha couldn't really blame him. Who knew how many streets the boy had raced down trying to find Brother Galen?

Brother Galen didn't slow down, just continued jogging through the workshop to the back. It seemed that he'd been here before. Evidently, he'd been in just about every godsdamn nook and cranny in Candiru. Sasha scarcely believed how friendly nearly every single person was towards Brother Galen. Really, the only exception was Old Harry, but Old Harry seemed to hate everyone. Four visits to the invalid had been more than enough to imprint that firmly in his mind.

But everyone else in Candiru loved Brother Galen. People were constantly waving at him in the streets, smiling at him, pushing gifts of thanks his way, asking for his blessing. It was sickening and made Sasha grind his teeth. Did no one here remember how the devotees to the Lady of the Flowers had behaved during the plague? Sasha's mouth always tasted slightly of bile these days, but this reminder of the past might actually make him vomit.

Sasha followed behind Galen, rounding the corner to see him already unpacking his tools as he spoke softly but urgently to a very tall, muscular woman with tan skin and dark hair tied back into a braid. She was holding the hand of a plump, pale woman who was lying in bed. The patient looked awful. She was probably pale at the best of times; now she looked washed out and pallid, and she was covered in black spots. They varied in size, some as small as a copper coin, others nearly as large as an apple. Her arms and legs had several down their length, but they were crowded together on her torso. There was almost more area covered in the blight than uninfected skin. They continued in small flecks up her neck and marred her face like obscene freckles.

He probably should have averted his eyes to give the poor woman some privacy, but he couldn't stop staring. She was lying there in just her underclothes, and the black spots bloomed all over her skin. They looked so wrong, like circles of rot growing up from under her flesh, each mark outlined in sickly yellow.

Sasha watched in horror as Brother Galen gently pressed on one and his finger sunk into it like it was a tar pool. It took everything within Sasha not to turn and vomit all over the floor. The woman on the bed only whined softly in her throat. Brother Galen seemed unbothered, withdrawing his finger and wiping it on a cloth. Gods above, this was disgusting.

"Thomas said this happened very quickly," Brother Galen said, looking up at the potter for confirmation.

"What?" the potter said, nearly gasping as Brother Galen addressed her. "Yes, she was fine this morning. She was *fine*,

Brother Galen. We did everything as we usually do. I was working in the shop, Mandy was talking to customers, then she just collapsed. The spots started an hour after that. At first, I thought it was just exhaustion, or dehydration like you told us last time she fainted, but not this time."

Brother Galen breathed out, and said, "Okay, okay. She's going to be all right, Nina. I promise."

"I know," Nina said softly. "I know, you're here. You saved her after I nearly killed her the last time, you'll save her now."

"Hey now," Brother Galen said gently, placing a hand over where Nina squeezed her wife's hand. "That was an accident. And Mandy was all right in the end, remember? She's long since forgiven you for that, so you had better forgive yourself, dear."

Nina nodded, wiping tears with her free hand, and then asked, "What is wrong with her, Brother Galen?"

"I don't know," Brother Galen said, shockingly truthfully. "But I am going to try and find out. I'm going to test a few things, and I'm going to ask you some questions. Just answer the best you can, all right?"

Nina nodded again, and Brother Galen started. He asked her mostly about things that Mandy might have come in contact with, or if anyone who looked ill had come into the shop. Brother Galen pulled out a little notebook and flipped through its pages. Sasha peeked over his shoulder and saw one marked for Mandy Poltz-Walker. Brother Galen's eyes scanned it thoroughly.

"Was there anyone that you didn't recognize today?" Brother Galen asked carefully. "Any customers? Anyone who looked like, well, like they weren't from here?"

"I don't really know. Mandy usually was the one talking to all the customers, you know," Nina said. "I think I saw a few folks from the upper districts. Medaka, Sillago, the like."

"Ah, well," Brother Galen said. "I meant more from

outside of Dragonet City entirely. I haven't seen this disease before, so I wonder if it's not local. It's not a reaction to something she ate or touched, that I can tell you with certainty. But with how quickly it came on, and the symptoms, I've never seen anything like this. I'll need to contact the temple."

"It's that serious?" Nina asked, her voice breaking.

"Frankly, yes," Brother Galen said. "I'm sorry, Nina. I'll do my best to make her comfortable for now."

"All right," Nina said, looking dejected. "Thank you, Brother Galen."

Sasha felt his teeth start to grind; Brother Galen had the power to fix this. This was why Sasha hated the Lady of Flowers, this was why he couldn't stand her followers. Why not just fix it? Why all this fuss? He listened to them discuss where the sickness could have come from and scoffed.

He mumbled, perhaps too loudly, "Anything this disgusting must come from Candiru."

Both Brother Galen and Nina turned to him, Nina looking utterly shocked and Brother Galen the angriest Sasha had ever seen him. Brother Galen quickly quelled his reaction, switching to a look of disappointment, but Nina bit her lip and looked back down at her wife. Sasha wished he could take it back; it was too cruel. Anya would have been disappointed in him.

"Careful, Mister Rider," Brother Galen said, his voice a strange mixture of a joke and something far more serious, "or I will set the Kipper Gang on you after all."

"I apologize, Mistress Nina, that was rude," Sasha said, refusing to even acknowledge Brother Galen.

Nina nodded at him, her face pinched in anger before worry and grief overtook it again. Sasha felt Anya judging him, wherever she was. He heard her voice in his head telling him to be careful of the harm he could cause. Guilt stabbed his heart.

But Nina had already forgotten his intrusion and turned back to the person she thought could help.

Nina's voice quaked with fear as she asked, "Is it plague?"

Brother Galen sucked in air through his teeth, then said, "I don't know. Just because it's something that we've never seen before doesn't mean it's plague. It could just as easily be something like measles."

"It came on so quickly," Nina said, her voice quivering.

Sasha may have been an ass, but at least he wasn't doing what Brother Galen was doing. Literally all this pain and worry would go away if he stopped being selfish and used his magic.

"Why not just use your gift?" Sasha demanded.

Once again, Brother Galen and Nina looked up to him as one. Brother Galen had been laying a cool rag on Mandy's forehead, then gently washing the sores, putting an ointment on them before wrapping them. The healer swallowed heavily, probably because he knew he was in the wrong. But there was curiosity in Nina's eyes. She looked over at Brother Galen carefully.

"Could that work?" Nina asked. "I know you used it to help you with...with the kiln accident. And the devotees used it in the plague all those years ago. Would the gift work?"

Brother Galen shook his head and said, "I don't know. There are just too many unknowns right now, and I don't want to risk it. I'll go and talk with the temple elders tomorrow."

"Will you have time? You're always so busy, Brother Galen," Nina asked, her voice shaking. "I don't want you to be even busier, though I am worried..."

She trailed off, her eyes glistening as she looking down at Mandy. Fear and worry were etched into Nina's face as she lifted Mandy's hand to her lips and pressed a kiss to her knuckles, disease or not.

"I'd say this is rather urgent," Brother Galen said, blowing out air. "Maybe I should just go tonight."

"Well, why don't you go now instead of wasting time here if you aren't going to heal her?" Sasha said, fed up with Brother Galen as always.

Brother Galen's shoulders stiffened, and he said, "Mister Rider, I already explained, I'm worried that it might do more harm than good. I don't know what this is yet. I need to talk to the elders at the temple."

"Healing magic? Do more harm than good?" Sasha sneered. "What a wonderful priest you are."

"I'm not a priest," Brother Galen said, throwing his hands in the air and turning towards Sasha. "Only speakers are priests. I'm a devotee, a healer."

"Apologies, I don't know the ins and outs of your little temple." Sasha sighed and crossed his arms.

"Does he have to be here?" Nina asked, gesturing up to Sasha.

"Unfortunately, yes," Sasha and Brother Galen said at the exact same time, then looked at each other in surprise.

Brother Galen sighed and pushed the hair that had fallen from his knot out of his eyes, then dug around in his bag. He continued to treat Mandy as best he could. Well, not the best he could. The magic lingered just below his fingertips, yet he refused to use it. It really was the plague all over again.

It was taking Brother Galen a long time, and Nina eventually excused herself to check on Thomas and send him home. Once she was out of the room, Sasha leaned down so he could speak to Brother Galen while he was working.

"Maybe if she started calling you names like Old Harry does, you'd use your magic," Sasha said, and Brother Galen stiffened.

"Please, Mister Rider," Brother Galen said, sighing heavily.

"I've tried to be courteous to you. I know neither of us like this arrangement, but please stop."

"Why?" Sasha said. "You're just too used to these Candiru rats kissing the ground you walk on. Someone needs to criticize you."

"What did you call the people of Candiru?" Brother Galen spun around and glared at him, that anger from before blazing in his eyes. "*Rats*? That's awfully rude, Mister Rider."

"Oh, don't act so high and mighty, Brother Galen," Sasha said. "I'm sure you think you're reaching down from your heavenly throne to these poor souls in the disgusting Candiru district. What, did you devote yourself to the Lady of Flowers because you couldn't cut it in a fancy university?"

"What?" Brother Galen said, and he sounded very confused. "Aren't you from Medaka?"

"Yes, but I'm just a city guard," Sasha said.

"Meaning?"

"I know rich filth when I see it."

Brother Galen let out a disbelieving laugh and shook his head. "Lady's blessing be upon you, Sasha Rider. You're awfully misguided."

Sasha grabbed Brother Galen and pulled him away from Mandy, gripping his shoulder, and growled out, "Don't you dare say that to me."

Brother Galen stared up at him with wide eyes, fear on his face for the first time since they met, before swallowing and saying, "I'm sorry."

Sasha let him go and crossed his arms, embarrassed to have lost his temper. He rolled his shoulders and watched as Brother Galen warily started tending to Mandy again. Sasha hoped that Nina hadn't heard him. He hated this job, he hated Candiru, but he didn't want to be cruel to someone who was already so worried. Anya wouldn't have approved of that.

"Sorry," Sasha murmured. "I shouldn't have grabbed you like that."

Galen glanced over his shoulder at Sasha and, after a moment of wary contemplation, said, "Thank you. I won't say it again."

Sasha nodded with a grunt.

Silence lingered between them as Brother Galen tried to finish. Sasha noticed that Brother Galen's hands were shaking, which was odd. He had never seen that before, not even when Brother Galen was dealing with Old Harry. Sasha had to say that much for him: he had a steady hand. That was ideal for a man who would be stitching people up and tending their wounds. Sasha watched him carefully, trying to guess why he trembled.

Brother Galen made a frustrated sound in his throat.

"Mister Rider, I know that you are likely looking for something to find wrong about my work so you can properly criticize me," Brother Galen said steadily, "but you hovering over my shoulder like that is not going to make me move any faster."

Sasha snorted and said, "Just wondering why your hands are shaking."

Brother Galen froze for a moment, then said, "Despite rumors to the contrary, I am only human. I've never seen anything like this before. I tried to put on a good face for Nina, but frankly, Mister Rider, I'm a bit scared."

The vulnerability of the statement gave Sasha pause. For a moment, just a moment, Sasha really saw Brother Galen. He was tired. Some people might have been distracted by the burn scars on his face and down his neck, but those people didn't spend all day, every day, staring at Brother Galen like Sasha did.

Brother Galen's hazel eyes were deep pools of exhaustion above deep lines that wouldn't be there if he was ever well-rested. His auburn hair was escaping the knot at the base of his neck, falling to brush across his shoulders. His hideous yellow tunic was stained and worn from the long day and from the fact that he rarely truly rested.

Had it been anyone else, Sasha would have felt sympathy. Hell, if Brother Galen had not been a devotee, Sasha probably would have liked him. Very few people worked as hard. But like all devotees, he held his power out of reach of the people around him like a bully who had seized a beloved toy. However, Sasha did step back with a grunt.

Brother Galen's shoulders relaxed, and he finished up what he was doing. Lion's teeth, it was already so late, and Brother Galen wanted to go to the temple to report this as well. Yet again, Sasha cursed his luck in getting this assignment. It was going to be so late when he finally got back to the bunks. Why him?

But he knew why. This was already his fourth chance. Everyone always ended up complaining about him sooner or later. Ever since he lost Anya, he'd been abrasive. He knew that. Captain Tracker was far too forgiving of him and his mistakes, but now he was paying for them. No one would have volunteered for these long days in the most dangerous and filthy district in Dragonet City. But he doubted that anyone else would have had his particular gripe with the person he was meant to be guarding.

As he had pointed out to Galen, most people kissed the ground where the devotees of the Lady of Flowers walked. This must have been some divine joke from the Lady herself, the bitch.

Galen finally seemed to be finished. He packed up his bag, muttering to himself, then rubbed his eyes harshly. Gods, he did seem tired.

Served him right.

Nina came back into the room and spoke quietly with

Galen, but Sasha tuned it out. He stared at the ceiling and had started to count the cracks in the wood beams when his attention was seized by a great deal of shouting.

"What's happening? Brother Galen, please!" Nina shouted as Mandy started convulsing wildly.

Black ichor spouted from her mouth as she coughed and Nina screamed. Galen had wrapped his arms around Mandy and was trying to turn her onto her side, presumably to keep her from choking. Mandy was bigger than he was—most people were bigger than Galen—and as she thrashed, he was losing the battle. She elbowed him harshly in the nose, and blood started dripping from it.

Galen's head shot up and he shouted at Sasha. "Mister Rider, I would appreciate any help!"

Sasha's instincts bypassed his disgust as the sores on Mandy's body came uncovered. He moved over and gripped her steadily in his strong arms while she vomited up more of the ooze. Galen was trying to figure out what to do. Sasha could practically see his mind working as his eyes darted around.

"Brother Galen, please!" Nina screamed, her voice broken by sobs. "Please do something!"

Galen set his face and placed his hands on Mandy's exposed chest. He started chanting in a language that Sasha didn't know, and then that pink glow returned. It grew brighter and brighter until finally, with a flash, it subsided. The room was silent except for Galen's heavy breathing and Nina's muffled crying.

Sasha set down Mandy's now-still body. She had black ichor around her lips, but the sores had gotten much better. They weren't completely gone, but they weren't open wounds anymore. Mandy was asleep, breathing lightly. Sasha placed the back of his hand on Mandy's forehead. It was cool. The Lady had healed her.

Galen lowered himself to his knees at the side of the bed, still trying to catch his breath, as Nina wrapped her arms around him from behind. It took her a moment to stop crying, and she squeezed Galen tightly in a way that had to hurt.

"Thank you, Brother Galen, thank you," she said softly.

"I'll have to come back to check on her," Galen said, "but I think she'll be all right for now. I'll let you know what the temple says."

"Thank you," Nina said weakly. It seemed to be the only thing she was capable of saying.

Galen gathered his bag, wiped the blood from his nose, and left, wishing the women a good night. He walked out into the cool night air, and of course Sasha was at his heels. And Sasha was furious.

CHAPTER 5

CONFESSIONS

GALEN

A MONTH OF WORKING TOGETHER HAD LED TO THIS. Galen was exhausted. He was so tired, and he was completely drained from using the gift to help Mandy. He had gone to the temple and filed a report with the elders and that had taken another hour, which felt even longer with Sasha's never-ending stream of complaints and criticisms. It was already so late.

They trudged back to his home in the dark. Sasha would drop him there and then be back again in the morning to comment under his breath, to judge his every move, to be entirely too cruel.

They got to his house and Sasha murmured, "Well, that was a mess. Well done, that. Lucky she didn't die, but that would be typical for you, wouldn't it?"

Galen froze. Finally, he turned back towards Sasha, setting his face. He said, as steadily as he could, "Can I just ask, what did I do to make you hate me so much?"

Sasha looked shocked, and he said, "You didn't *do* anything."

"Then what is it?" Galen asked, wishing his voice wasn't shaking. "Is...is it my face?"

"What?" Sasha said, shaking his head. "No. I don't care what you look like."

"But you do hate me," Galen said. He was angry—rightfully so—so why was his face so hot? Why were his eyes starting to water? He couldn't stand that he always did this.

"I don't know if I hate *you*, exactly," Sasha said. "I just hate what you do."

"What I do? Heal people?" Galen said, baffled, hands shaking.

"No, the way you do it. The way *all* of you do it."

An icy tide of realization flooded Galen, and he said, "You hate the Lady of Flowers?"

Sasha was quiet for a moment, as if he were contemplating just whether he dared commit blasphemy. Then he nodded as he said, "Yes. I hate her."

"Why?" Galen asked, shocked.

He knew people hated certain gods. Rival cities hated the Scaled Maiden, plenty of people hated the Crow or Lion in Glory, but he had never heard of someone hating the Lady of Flowers. But Sasha clearly meant it as his eyes bored into Galen.

"I wouldn't expect you to understand," Sasha growled.

Galen clutched his hands into fists at his sides and stared hard at Sasha as he said, "Try me."

Sasha glared back, his fists curled at own sides, and then he finally said, "Fuck it. It's the way you, you devotees, act. Like you know what's best for everyone, like you care just so damn much. But you don't. You have this magical power, and you hoard it while the rest of us suffer. Why are you the arbiters of who gets blessed with the Lady's healing and who doesn't? Why doesn't the Lady just heal everyone in need?"

Galen wanted to snap back 'Why doesn't Governor Maple just use all her money to help the people in need down here?' or perhaps, 'Of course we're the arbiters of the Lady's will! We've devoted our lives to her,' but he knew neither of those would get him far. He didn't want to get into a shouting match that Sasha would win easily. Galen would be calm. Galen would explain.

"I've tried to explain this before," Galen said, trying but failing to maintain an even demeanor. "The Lady only gives us a certain amount of magic each day. We aren't hoarding it up, I promise. We couldn't. The Lady wants us to learn how to use the gifts she's already given, the herbs and the plants, the skills of healing. That's how she leads us."

"Oh, how benevolent," Sasha said, sneering down at Galen.

"I'm...I'm sorry," Galen said, not knowing what else to say. "We're just trying to help people."

"Oh, and you do that *so* well, don't you?"

"Actually," Galen said, trying not to let his voice shake. "Actually, I think we do. I think we help people a lot. And I'm sorry if you think that it makes me condescending, but you've seen me. I'm working here every day, and I *am* helping people."

Sasha scoffed but apparently didn't have a response. The look he was giving Galen was pure malice, and Galen couldn't stand it. He tried to be subtle as he wiped his tears.

"Oh, you're crying to try and make me feel bad?" Sasha asked through gritted teeth.

"No," Galen said as his eyes burned. "No, I just...I don't know why, but I start crying when I'm angry. Trust me, I hate it too."

Sasha rolled his eyes. "I don't know why I bother. It's just excuse after excuse."

"I'm not trying to make excuses," Galen said. "I'm trying

to understand. I've never met someone who hates the Lady of Flowers, or her followers."

"Oh, because you're all just so wonderful?" Sasha asked. "What, are you going to set the Kipper Gang on me?"

Galen shook his head. "That was a joke. I know you hate those. I'm sorry."

"I don't hate jokes," Sasha said, his face twisted into a scowl.

"No, just me," Galen said, exasperated. "Just the temple, and I don't know why! What did they ever do to you?"

"Do you really want to know?"

"Frankly, yes!"

"It's because of you all that my sister is dead!" Sasha shouted loudly enough that Muffin, who had been creeping slowly towards the door, froze and stared at him.

Galen softened as guilt lifted up in his belly. Oh. Oh, of course. It could have been anything, a botched healing, a failed prayer. Galen knew loss like an old friend, and he knew how hard this was. He held out his hands, and looked up at Sasha, imploring him to explain. The man had fixed his gaze on the ground.

"I'm sorry," Galen said, hoping that Sasha heard just how much he meant it. "You don't have to explain if you don't want to, but what happened?"

A muscle twitched in Sasha's jaw. He was clearly fighting back the urge to snap at Galen, but then he asked, surprisingly softly, "Do you remember the plague?"

Galen's brows drew together, and he asked, "The one seventeen years ago?"

"Yeah," Sasha said. "The one that nearly wiped out the city."

"Of course," Galen said. He remembered it intimately.

"Yeah." Sasha gritted his teeth. "My family was mostly lucky. My mother and father didn't get it. Neither did I. But my sister, Anya, did. I was only thirteen, she was eight years older than me, and she...she was the best person I have ever known. She was smart and kind, she was a light in this dark, stupid world. And of course, she got sick."

Sasha stopped speaking. His voice had started to quiver with emotion, and he was taking a moment to gather himself. Galen waited, looking up at him and holding his breath. Sasha ran a hand roughly over his face and sighed.

Finally, Sasha spoke again. "You know that that plague was fucking awful. Very few people got better on their own, and the only reliable way to treat it was the healers from the Lady of Flowers."

Galen knew where this was going. He could see the shape of this story, because he had lived one very similar to it. But he nodded, encouraging Sasha to go on.

"There were so many sick people," Sasha said, closing his eyes, seeming to picture it. "And they had a fucking limit on how many people they could treat a day, you know? They had a waiting list. Of course, my father went and put Anya on the list as soon as she got sick. And we just had to wait as she got weaker and sicker. I went to the temple myself. I begged them to come and save her, and all they said was they would as soon as they could.

"When I got home, I prayed to the Lady of Flowers. I prayed for hours. I begged her to heal Anya, I begged her to save her, but none of my prayers were answered. There was nothing they could do, don't you know?" His tone was barbed and sarcastic.

Galen flinched at his tone but stayed silent.

"They just left Anya to suffer, to die. And I had to watch it happen."

Sasha had opened his eyes and was staring at Galen again. Each word he spoke felt like an accusation, a piece of evidence shoved into Galen's face, saying, *Look, this is what you did.*

"The day after I went to the temple, Anya died. None of us, my mother, my father, me, none of us were ever the same." Sasha's voice broke, but he went on. "She had been my guiding light, she taught me right from wrong, and she was just…just gone. She was going to be a lawyer, defend innocent people, people wrongly accused, and the Lady of Flowers and her followers, people like you, just let her die.

"To make things worse, the day after Anya died, that's when the devotee finally showed up. She told us how sorry she was, but she didn't even bother to stay more than five minutes. She just went on to the next person on the waiting list. It was so fucking mechanical. I had lost my whole world, everything that made me the person I was, and they just checked her name off a list. And I was only thirteen."

Sasha's hands were so tightly clenched that his knuckles were white. Sasha swallowed heavily, eyes flicking down to the pendant around Galen's neck and then back to his face, glaring vitriolically at Galen as though he were trying to banish him to the seven hells.

"So, yes, Brother Galen," Sasha said, his voice a growl. "I hate the Lady of Flowers. I hate her devotees. And yes, I guess I hate you too, because you ruined my life."

Silence hung between them for a moment. Galen had been feeling sympathy for Sasha, he had been feeling horrible about what had happened, but all that had stopped. Instead, he looked up at Sasha and for once, despite unfathomable anger, his voice didn't shake and his eyes were dry.

"I was eleven," Galen said.

Sasha took a breath, and then said, exasperated, "What?"

"When the plague hit," Galen said. "I was eleven years old."

"What does that have to do with anything?" Sasha glared at Galen, his mouth formed into a cruel snarl.

Galen was proud of how steady his voice was as he said,

"You are blaming me for something that happened to you when I was a child. I am very sorry for your loss, the plague was a horrible thing, but you are being very unfair. You hate me for something I was in no way responsible for."

"Yes, but—" Sasha started to say, but Galen cut him off.

"Mister Rider," Galen said. "I let you say your piece without interrupting you. Please let me do the same."

Sasha stared at him and then nodded.

"Do you know why I feel so safe in Candiru? It's not just because it's a perfectly safe district," Galen said, taking a breath. "I'm from here. I grew up three streets away. Old Harry calls me Gap-Tooth Galen because it's a mean nickname from when I was ten years old. These people know me and trust me because I am one of them. And you lived in Medaka, right?"

Sasha nodded.

"I don't want to compare tragedies," Galen said, and he swallowed as the memories washed over him like a tide. "But Medaka is a high district. The plague was bad there. But it was nothing like it was down here in Candiru. There were just...so many dead. You think it smells bad here now? Imagine not only all those who died in Candiru, but all the other dead bodies from the upper districts dumped down here while they waited to be burned. This is where all the sewage goes, so why not the plague corpses too?"

Galen let that sink in for a moment. He stared up at Sasha and watched realization bloom in his eyes, and how the truth struck him. Galen took a breath of the stark night air, thinking back to his time here as a child. The fear, the worry, the never-ending death all around him.

"I'm sorry that your sister caught it, but so glad that no one else in your family did," Galen said, refusing to break eye contact. "In Candiru, it was so easy to get sick, and every single person in my family caught it. Me included. I'm very aware that I'm small. Catching a plague when you're eleven years old tends to stunt your growth. I know you lost your sister to the plague. I am very sorry, I know exactly how you feel. I also lost my sister. And my brothers. And both my mothers. And my grandmother. I was the only one alive, dragging their bodies out to be picked up while I was barely strong enough to move."

Sasha was staring at him, and there was a look in his eyes that Galen had never seen before. His hands had dropped out of their tight fists, and he was flexing his fingers. Finally, something was getting through to him.

Galen swallowed, then continued, "We didn't even know that there was a waiting list to be put on. The devotees were so overwhelmed that it took them two months to even get down to Candiru. I was near death when Sister Elowen found me. She healed me and carried me out of my family's home. I was barely coherent, but I started to panic when they burned the house."

Sasha's eyes widened, and he made a small sound in the back of his throat. He knew what was coming. Galen wet his lips and fought the urge to squeeze his eyes shut.

"It was a plague house. They had to burn it. They tried to hold me back," Galen said. He could still feel the heat on his face even now. "I was convinced that my sister's cat was still in there. It wasn't. It had run away weeks earlier when my sister died, but I wasn't thinking straight. I ran in, and the house collapsed on me. They pulled me out, and I lived, but..."

Galen gestured vaguely to his face. Sasha winced.

Galen paused for a moment, but he had to say it. "My family may not have been destined to become some great lawyers. My family maybe wasn't some gift to the world the way your sister was, but their loss still hurt. It still matters."

"Of course it does," Sasha said, and now his voice was truly shaking. He stopped when Galen held up his hand.

"I joined Aster House as soon as I was healed enough. That's where pledges to the Lady of Flowers live," Galen said. "My face, and my neck, and my chest, are all scarred because they couldn't afford to spare the manpower and the magic to heal my burns when there was a plague going on. I don't mind. I don't care. But I knew that if I was going to do anything with the life that was given to me, I was going to try and help people. That's why I became a devotee. That's why she gifted me. And I do everything in my power to help.

"I saw how hard the devotees worked during the plague, Sasha. If you think that every single loss didn't weigh heavy on them, you're wrong. You're so wrong. Every night, they would break down, sobbing about those they couldn't save. Growers and speakers, devotees who weren't even healers, begged and prayed for the Lady to grant them the power to heal just for a short time so that they could help. I am so sorry that your sister died. She sounds like a wonderful person. But it wasn't their fault, and it is unfair for you to blame us. It's unfair to take it out on me."

Galen finished and let the silence hang heavily between them. He stared at Sasha, challenging him, daring him to disagree. Galen knew that this was probably also unfair, and his mentors would disapprove, but at this point he didn't care. He wasn't a speaker, and he was at his breaking point when it came to Sasha Rider. He hoped that it would hurt.

Sasha swallowed and, with a panicked look in his eyes, said, "Galen, shit, Brother Galen..."

Galen ran his hand over his face, then said, "Please. I know it might be childish. And maybe I shouldn't have told you all that, but I just want you to stop being so mean to me."

Sasha opened his mouth and closed it. He seemed to be struggling with what exactly he could say to try and make this better.

"Good night, Mister Rider," Galen said, barely above a whisper.

Then he opened his door and stepped inside. He felt Muffin slip past his legs. He didn't mind. Having the blink fox sit on his lap would be a good thing tonight. He looked back to see Sasha looking devastated and guilty. Galen shut the door in his face.

CHAPTER 6

AFTERMATH OF CRUELTY

SASHA

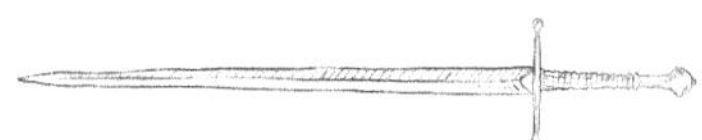

SASHA HAD FUCKED UP. GODS ABOVE, HE HAD fucked up so badly. The moment that Galen shut the door in his face, Sasha nearly knocked on the door and demanded that they continue their conversation. That couldn't be where it ended. That couldn't be it. Sasha had been so convinced that he was going to show Galen just what a total ass he was, but then...

Shit. Shit, shit, shit. Galen was right, he was entirely right, and he had been right all along. And Sasha was the one being a complete ass—to a man who had gone through ten times Sasha's pain. Fucking Lion's teeth. If Anya were here, she would give him a withering look and she would be right to do so.

The strange blue fox had sneaked into the house with Galen, so at least he wouldn't be alone. Sasha ran a hand over his face and groaned. He didn't know what to do, he didn't know how to handle this. It felt so wrong, like missing a step in the dark or having a splinter stuck in his nail bed. Galen baring his soul put Sasha's entire world off-kilter.

Logically, of course, he knew that other places had been

affected by the plague. But he had been so wrapped up in his own life that he simply hadn't cared about how it had affected others. Especially for places like Candiru. And fuck, the things he had said about Candiru to someone who was from there. Galen would have been within his rights to march to the guard station and tell them Sasha was a total and utter ass, and then there would be no more chances. Gods above, he deserved no more chances. He hadn't even deserved all the chances he'd already had.

Finally, Sasha started heading back to the guard bunks. He replayed the conversation and the look on Galen's face. He winced. He never wanted to be the reason that Galen made that face again, that look of hurt and pain. As he walked up the dark streets of Dragonet City, he did what he always did when he knew that he had absolutely ruined something.

He forced himself to relive every stupid mistake that had led him to this point.

After he had lost Anya, his life had fallen apart. He had dashed all his prospects on the ground like a child throwing a tantrum, and he couldn't blame that on the Lady of Flowers even if he wanted to. It had been his choice to drop out of the fancy schools his parents had paid for, his choice to leave home and wander the streets of Dragonet City without purpose, his choice to throw the punch that landed him in jail.

At least that guy had it coming. Sasha couldn't bring himself to regret breaking the nose of a man who wouldn't leave someone alone in a tavern. That had been right, even if the asshole had been rich enough to face no consequences and to get Sasha thrown in jail. Tracker must have thought so too, since she was the one who sprang him and then offered him a chance.

Gods, he didn't know what she saw in him. His parents had been disappointed, and why wouldn't they be? They lost their wildly kind and successful daughter to a vicious plague and were left with their waste of a son, who had more temper than sense. Tracker, though, she sent him to training. She gave him a purpose. And then he had nearly ruined it again.

During his first year, he had ended up in a bloody and brutal fist fight with another guard. Even though the smug bastard had it coming, Sasha wasn't meant to be fighting on duty. That was what had got him in such trouble in the first place. And it had been so stupid. Sasha hoped that they didn't remember what it was about, because Sasha did and it was embarrassing. A strike against him over a stupid game of cards. What was wrong with him?

The second strike was the one that Tracker had gotten expunged, but in truth, he probably still deserved it on his record. It had been a shouting match at the gates of the city with the head chef of an estate, and Sasha let it go too far. The man hadn't filled out the right paperwork for his imports, and that was the only thing that saved Sasha.

He probably shouldn't have called the man a blithering, rabid fool who needed his head checked, though. Gods above, when had he gotten so nasty? No wonder Galen had called him mean. Lion's teeth.

The last strike was by far the most justified. He had broken a merchant's nose, and it wasn't even the right person. He just happened to resemble the man they had been chasing, and when he wouldn't cooperate, Sasha had acted rashly. He had gotten an earful about how the city had to compensate the innocent bystander.

All his strikes lined up in front of him. Beyond that, very few other guards wanted to work with him. The feedback during his yearly reviews said it all. He was sour, grumpy, and not pleasant to be around. And those were only the ones that Tracker had shown him. He was sure that there were worse ones. He was...he was awful. There was no other way to put it. That's why he had been flung to the bottom of the city on a solo job. No one to piss off if he was down there.

No one but the notoriously patient devotee of the Lady of Flowers.

Anya would have hated the way that he had treated Galen. He pictured her walking alongside him in the dark. In his mind's eye, she looked the same as she had before she got sick. Everyone had always told them that they were the spitting image of each other, that it was strikingly clear that they were brother and sister. She had the same creamy skin, lightly tanned from the sun, rich brown eyes, and light brown hair. Hers fell in waves to her shoulders. Sasha had wondered if his hair would have that same wave if he bothered to grow it out.

Gods, he wished she was really there with him. She would speak to him in that soft, reassuring voice that was so similar to...so similar to Galen's. It struck him then how similar they were. The smiles they'd offer people in need, the relentless work to try and make a change, the stupid jokes they'd tell.

Sasha rubbed his eyes harshly, and the vision of his sister seemed to fade away. He was left as alone as he ever was, but now his thoughts raced as he hurried back to the bunks. He couldn't believe how awful he had been, but then again, it made sense. Ever since Anya died, he had been awful. He felt empty and hollow, and he took it out on the world around him.

He couldn't believe that he had told Galen that he wasn't helping people. Sasha had seen how hard Galen worked, how he spent all his days healing people and didn't take any time for himself. Fuck. When Sasha saw that old man, Harry, again, he'd be lucky if Sasha didn't break his good leg. Well, Galen would probably be the one to mend it if he did, so he wouldn't.

By the time he finally got back, it was very late. The Night Guard had already gone out, and it was quiet as Sasha cleaned his armor, washed, and changed into more casual clothes, then headed to the kitchens. He had hoped that there would be no one up, but no such luck. Captain Tracker was there, drinking tea. She smiled and lifted her mug to him as he scoured the cabinets for leftovers.

"Sorry about the long days," she said. "It was the only assignment I could get for you."

"It's fine," Sasha said automatically as he made a plate with cold chicken and rolls. "It's important work."

"Oh? Had a change of heart then?" Tracker asked, her brows lifting.

"You could say that." Sasha gripped the counter and glanced at Tracker out of the corner of his eye.

"Oof, did something happen?" Tracker took another sip.

Sasha swallowed and said, "Just that the devotee I've been working with made me realize tonight that I'm an asshole who carried an unfair grudge for nearly twenty years. And that I've taken out that grudge on someone who was a child when it all happened. And I've been treating him like he's a blemish on society, and he didn't deserve that. And it took me an entire month to realize how fucked up that was."

He turned and met her gaze. She stared at him, clearly considering his barely coherent ramble carefully. Finally, she cleared her throat.

"Do I need to worry that there will be another complaint, and I'll have to kick you out of the guard?" Tracker asked. Her tone seemed light, but it had a very serious undercurrent.

"That's the really fucked up thing," Sasha said, dropping his plate on the table and plopping down in the chair. "He's probably too nice to complain."

"I see," Tracker said. "And this group of people you're talking about? Who do you mean?"

Sasha stared at his food, knowing that he should eat, but feeling like he didn't deserve to. Knowing that Tracker was about to either laugh at him or smack him upside the head, he glanced up and said, "The Lady of Flowers."

Tracker blinked, and then with deep confusion asked, "The goddess? That Lady of Flowers? You were...for what, Rider? That makes no sense."

"Well, yeah," Sasha said, sighing. "I see that now."

"Rider," Tracker said, her voice carefully level, "I've heard you swear. You follow Lion in Glory."

"'Course," Sasha said, shrugging. "All guards do."

"You know that their temples work together, right?" Tracker asked, looking less annoyed and more bemused.

"They...they do?" Sasha asked, lifting a brow.

"Yeah, it's like, fuck, it was explained to me once." Tracker rubbed the back of her neck. "Lion in Glory protects the people while the Lady of Flowers helps them grow. Something like that."

"Oh."

"Maybe that's why you've had such bad luck," Tracker said, taking a drink from her mug. "Lion knows you've been nursing a grudge against his best friend."

"I—" Sasha didn't know what to say to that. It was entirely possible. Once again, he had made his life harder by being a stubborn piece of shit. "Tracker, what should I do?"

Tracker took another sip and eyed him up and down. "What do you think you should do?"

"I need to apologize."

"You didn't apologize tonight?"

"No, he said good night and shut the door in my face."

Tracker hummed and took another sip. Amazingly, there was still liquid in her mug. "What do you plan to do?"

Sasha swallowed heavily. He looked down at his untouched food and mentally reviewed not just the conversation tonight, but the entire month. He didn't deserve forgiveness, that was for damn sure. He didn't deserve yet another chance.

"I really don't know," Sasha said honestly. "I think I may have ruined this beyond repair."

He stared at his hands, but he felt Tracker's assessing eyes on him. She was so thoughtful, so careful, not at all what most people expected from a guard captain.

"Rider, what did you do?" Tracker asked, her voice surprisingly gentle.

Sasha swallowed hard. "He asked me to stop being mean to him."

"He asked you to stop being mean?" Tracker asked, her eyebrows lifting. "Lion's teeth, Rider. That's sad. What the fuck did you say?"

"Many things that I shouldn't have," Sasha said, burying his face in his hands. "I wasn't kidding when I said I was an ass."

He could practically hear Tracker thinking as she breathed carefully in and out. She could take her time. He was sure that the next thing that would happen would be him being thrown out on his ass. And frankly, he deserved it.

"Sasha," Tracker said gently.

Sasha looked up immediately. It wasn't often that she used his given name instead of his surname. She was gazing at him with surprisingly soft eyes as she shook her head.

"I don't think it's a good idea to go right back and talk to him," Tracker said, her voice even.

Sasha didn't agree. He wanted to march back down to Candiru and demand that they continue their conversation so that he could understand just what the hell was going on in Galen's head. Why did he tolerate Sasha's bullshit for so long? It must have shown on his face, because Tracker smirked at him.

"I'm putting you on temporary leave," Tracker said, folding her arms.

"What?" Sasha cried, standing up and towering over her. "No! You can't, I don't have any strikes left and—"

"Did I say anything about a strike?" Tracker asked, lifting a brow.

Sasha hesitated. "No?"

"Right," Tracker said with a firm nod. "This is just a medical leave. You need, let's say, three days to clear your head. I'll send a replacement with the devotee for that time. After your three days are up, come back and see me and then we'll talk. Okay?"

Sasha stared at her, flabbergasted. "Where will I go?"

"Your parents still live in the city, yeah?" Tracker asked, and when Sasha nodded, she looked self-satisfied. "Go spend some time with them."

"I..." Sasha was at a loss, but this was an order. "Okay."

"Good," Tracker said, smiling and standing to pat him on the shoulder. "I think you need a breather, Rider."

"As you say, Captain," Sasha said, slowly sinking down into his seat.

She left him to finish his meal in solitude, which was just fine with him. He made plans for what he would say, turning up at his family's house for the first time in three years. They might be happy to see him, but likely they would be furious. And then he'd have to spend three days in that house where Anya died...

Then he stopped himself. Galen had said he hadn't wanted to compare tragedies, but Sasha found himself doing that. Galen didn't even have parents to disappoint. His entire family had died in the plague, and he didn't blame the one group of people who had been trying to help. No, he had gone and joined them. And Sasha just took out his anger on someone who didn't deserve it.

Gods above, what would Anya think of him? She had told him, repeatedly, that he didn't know anyone else's story. That's why she wanted to be a lawyer and defend innocent people. She always said that everyone deserved a chance, and he hadn't given Galen even a sliver of one. He was a monster. Even worse, he knew Anya wouldn't be proud of him.

When he had finished eating his cold meal, he packed up his meager belongings and started the long trek back up to Medaka. Watching the streets become cleaner, better lit, and emptier the further he got from Candiru reminded him of the large gulf between him and Galen. Gods, he had accused the man of being rich. Why was he like that?

It took about an hour, and it was the middle of the night by the time he arrived at the large, familiar house. It was as dark and cold as he remembered it being, haunted by ghosts of lost time and possibility. Sasha closed his eyes and swallowed heavily. His heart ached like a bruise.

Step by brutal step, he forced himself to go up to the door and knock. He had a key, but using it would feel like breaking and entering into a life where he no longer belonged. It was so long since he had belonged anywhere.

A candle lit up an upstairs room, and Sasha tracked the light's progress as its bearer came downstairs. Sasha held his breath as the door opened, and then he was face to face with his mother. Gods, she looked so much like Anya, a window into an impossible future in which Anya got to grow old.

"Sasha?" his mother asked, eyes wide in surprise.

"Hello, Mama," Sasha said, his voice creaky with unshed, unworthy tears. "Can I please come in?"

CHAPTER 7

SOMEONE NEW

GALEN

GALEN HELD HIS BREATH AT THE KNOCK AT HIS door. Arguing with Sasha on his doorstep, tears running down his face, had been a mistake. The moment he had shut the door in Sasha's face he had regretted it. That was not the way a devotee of the Lady of Flowers was supposed to act.

Dredging up his own past to hurt someone? The Lady must be utterly ashamed of him. But at the same time, he couldn't bring himself to fully regret it. Someone had to set Sasha straight. He couldn't go on acting like that, even if he had been hurt. No, he needed to be set on the right path. And the responsibility had fallen on Galen's shoulders, like so many other responsibilities.

So the light, rhythmic rapping at his door made Galen nervous. He didn't want to spend a day with Sasha so soon after their row. It was odd, though. Sasha had never knocked like that before. He usually gave three strong bangs against the door, followed by another three bangs if Galen didn't answer in twenty seconds or less. This was light, almost musical. Galen couldn't imagine that just one night would have changed Sasha that much. With trepidation, he crept to the door and opened it. Oh.

The woman on the other side was certainly not Sasha Rider. She was clearly a guard: she wore the same brown and green leather armor and had the same weapons strapped to her belt. Well, two of them. She was currently picking her teeth with her dagger. Galen tried not to gape.

She had wavy, golden hair pulled back in a tight ponytail and pinkish, freckled skin. She stared down at Galen with bright green eyes, slowly taking the dagger from between her lips. The look in her eyes was one that Galen was all too familiar with, and he braced himself.

"What happened to your face?" the woman asked, her voice quite loud in the morning air.

Galen tried not to grimace but found that his reservoir of patience was running dry. "I was in a house fire as a child."

The woman folded her arms with an easy smile. "Yeah, but, like, don't you have healing magic or something? Why not just..."

She lifted her hand over her face and gestured in a way that Galen was sure was meant to indicate some kind of magic spell, then grinned at him. Galen took a very deep breath.

"Our gift doesn't work like that," Galen said, trying very hard to keep his voice level. "It can heal things that are currently in distress, but it does nothing for scars."

"Seems like pretty unhelpful magic then," the woman said with a snort. "You'd think that the Lady of Flowers would want things to be beautiful."

Galen felt his face heat rapidly, and then in a rush he said, "I'm sorry, can I help you?"

"Oh, right," she said, as though she had just realized she had an untied bootlace. "You're Brother Galen, right?"

Galen nodded. "Yes, that's me. And you are?"

"Dawn Horner," she said, grinning.

"Well, good morning, Miss Horner," Galen said, and then he tried to paint a friendly smile on his face. "I don't mean to be rude, but what are you doing here?"

"Oh!" Dawn said, laughing. "Right, yeah. I'm the replacement."

Galen felt all the blood drain from his face. Oh, Lady above, he had really messed this up. If Bishop Rose found out about this, or worse, Sister Elowen, he'd never hear the end of his selfishness. He swallowed heavily.

"What happened to Mister Rider?" Galen asked warily.

"Oh, don't worry," Dawn said, lifting her hands. "He just needed to see to his mother for a few days. Some family matter or something. Captain Tracker sent me here to cover for him while he's gone."

Galen couldn't decide if that was a lie or not. It felt cruel to wish that there had been a family emergency, but then at least Galen's greedy little digs at Sasha wouldn't be to blame for his absence. Gods, Galen really was selfish.

"I see," Galen said, and then smiled up at his new guard. "Have you broken your fast?"

DAWN HAD EATEN—HENCE THE TEETH PICKING— but she waited while he ate. They left a bit late because Dawn made a game of chasing Muffin around the kitchen until Galen finally scooped the poor blink fox up and deposited him on the stoop. Muffin stalked away, his tail poofed up in haughty distress.

The events of the night before, both the fight and Mandy's mysterious illness, weighed heavily on his mind, but Galen had no time to wallow. He had to keep on going as he always did. No one else was going to treat the people of

Candiru, and perhaps through his work he could make up for his behavior.

Dawn was very unlike Sasha in a lot of ways. The worst one was that while Sasha stood back and glowered while he worked, Dawn chattered. And the things that she said made Galen's life miserable.

While he was treating a woman named Eliza who had a very upset stomach due to some bad fish, Dawn spoke up and embarrassed the woman nearly to death.

"Lion's teeth, lady," Dawn said, squeezing her nose closed with her fingers. "I don't know what's worse, the stink of the clearly rotten fish or the shit-covered sheets. Are you stupid? Why would you eat something that smelled like that?"

Galen turned to her, red-faced, and said as evenly as he could, "Miss Horner, why don't you wait outside in the fresh air? I'm going to finish up in here and then we'll move on."

Dawn shrugged and left, less of a stickler than Sasha about staying with Galen constantly. When Galen turned back to his patient, she was blushing hard and her eyes glistened.

"Those fish were at a discount," Eliza said weakly. "They were all I could afford for meat this week, Brother Galen."

"I know," Galen said, face softening as he squeezed her hand. "It's not your fault, Eliza. I'll get you feeling right as rain soon enough, okay?"

Eliza nodded, but she asked softly, "Do I really smell that bad?"

Galen wasn't one for violence, but he seriously considered punching Dawn Horner when he finished there. Instead, he smiled and shook his head. "It doesn't bother me in the least. But if you're worried, I could leave some dried lavender with you."

Eliza took it gratefully, and Galen left her with tea to settle her stomach, along with strict instructions to throw out the rest of the fish. So many people in Candiru were taken advantage of by peddlers who would sell their spoiled goods at low prices, telling them that it was a deal.

As he walked out, he looked around and saw no sign of his guard. He huffed in annoyance. At least Sasha Rider never deserted him. He was wasting valuable time looking around for his wayward guard. Finally, he spotted her at an overlook, peering down at the river.

"Miss Horner!" Galen called, then took out his book to double-check his next stop.

Dawn jerked up like a dog hearing its name, spotted Galen, and jogged to meet him. She still had a smile plastered to her face, but Galen had decided that he didn't much like it. It seemed poised to slip in a cruel remark or make a mean-spirited joke.

"The river's awfully close," Dawn said, falling in step behind him. "Never been this far down before, except when leaving the city, you know. You'd think that the river would wash away the smell, but man. It really does not. How can you stand it?"

Galen had fixed his eyes on the path ahead, but he said back, "You do get used to it. It's really not that bad."

"It really is," Dawn insisted, laughing. "I guess it's true what they say about Candiru."

Galen should have left it alone. But, of course, he turned around and asked, "What do they say?"

There was laughter in her eyes when she said, "Rats don't wash themselves," as though it wasn't a vile, nasty thing to say.

Galen bit back a snarl. "It's not very kind to refer to us as rats."

Dawn laughed then, and she said, "I never claimed to be kind. I'm a fucking city guard, Brother Galen. Now, don't get me wrong, you're doing good work here. Everyone respects the Lady of Flowers's charity. But don't expect me not to call a rat's nest a rat's nest."

Galen took a very deep breath. "Please refrain from doing so in my presence."

Dawn rolled her eyes, and said, "Fine. You priests are all so fucking sensitive."

Turning around and stalking down the street, Galen muttered under his breath, "I'm not even a priest. I'm a devotee."

It was like that the entire day. Every stop, Dawn Horner had something to say about the people Galen was treating. Her nasty little jabs rubbed at his skin like stinging nettle. And unlike Sasha, who mostly targeted Galen, Dawn seemed to target everyone else. He hated it. He also wished that she would stop bringing up the smell. It wasn't like anything could be done about it.

When they stopped for lunch, Dawn complained that she couldn't eat any of the food that Galen suggested. When asked why, she gave him a look like it should have been obvious.

"Do you not see what they eat down here, Brother Galen?" Dawn asked. "Rotten leftovers. I could die if I eat that."

Galen stood, staring at her in disbelief. "We eat it all the time. We're fine. You'll be fine if you eat one meal from a food cart, Miss Horner."

She gave him a skeptical look but finally acquiesced. When she bit into the meat pie, her eyes lit up in delighted surprise. She wolfed the entire thing down in minutes, then stood picking her teeth with her dagger as Galen ate. He didn't care for the way she was watching him, as though he was an odd little bug she had caught in a jar.

"You've really become one of the folks down here, huh?" she finally asked him.

Galen arched a brow, pie arrested halfway to his mouth. "What do you mean?"

"Well," Dawn said, waving her dagger dangerously through the air, "you keep saying 'we' do this, and 'we' do that. Like you're right down here with the rats, Brother Galen. But you're a devotee. Not one of them."

Angry chills spread across Galen's skin, but he kept his voice soft and even as he said, "I'm afraid you're mistaken, Miss Horner. I was born in Candiru Quarter. I left for the temple when I was young, but the first decade or so, I lived here with my family. Among the rats, as you say."

Galen couldn't help a feeling of triumph at the stricken look on her face. He was two for two on rebuking city guards for saying cruel things about Candiru Quarter in front of a native. He didn't think the Lady would mind that.

However, it didn't last long. Dawn's eyes widened and she took off at a dead sprint. Galen hardly had time to realize she was leaving and follow her before she had leapt through the air and came crashing down on someone. A pained cry rang out throughout the cluster of food carts where they had stopped.

Dawn stood triumphantly, holding her prey up by the collar of a dingy shirt. The youth, no more than thirteen years old, was clutching a loaf of bread to his chest and looking quite guilty. Galen knew the boy instantly. It was Barty; Galen had treated him and his younger sister a few times. They had lost their mother when his sister was born, and Galen knew that his father had died just a few months ago in a fishing accident. Gods, they must have been starving.

Of course, the guard didn't know any of that, and Galen doubted that she would have cared. Dawn grinned her triumph and marched over to Galen with the thief in tow. Barty stumbled as he was dragged behind the large woman.

"Caught us a criminal, Brother Galen," Dawn said,

beaming with all her teeth. "Now, where's the nearest guard station? I need to turn him in."

The boy looked at Galen with pure panic, and Galen had to act quickly. "Which stall did you take the bread from, Barty?"

Barty pointed at Mister Hatcher's stall, and Galen rushed over to it. Hatcher knew exactly what was happening, and said, "Two copper."

"For a whole loaf?" Galen asked, eyes wide. Like everyone, Hatcher knew Barty's reason for stealing, which was probably why he had pretended not to notice, but Galen didn't want to shortchange the man.

"A discount for devotees of the Lady of Flowers," Hatcher said firmly, looking worriedly over at Barty, held tight by Dawn.

"Fine," Galen said, a bit shortly. He didn't want to risk Dawn losing her patience. He handed over two copper.

"There!" Hatcher called over. "It's been paid for; I'm not complaining. Let the boy go."

Dawn looked at the two of them with disbelief. "I saw him take it!"

"No harm was done," Hatcher said. "Let him go home to his sister. They can have some food in their bellies."

Barty looked near tears, but Dawn didn't release him. Instead, she glared at them and spat, "I saw a crime."

"Not at all," Galen said quickly. "I had agreed yesterday to buy some bread for Barty, and I had forgotten. We're just making good now."

Dawn's sneered, her smile finally gone, but she released Barty. The young man fell to the ground, then scrambled up and ran as quickly as he could away from the angry guard. Galen stared defiantly at her. She crossed her arms, then rolled her eyes.

"And people wonder why Candiru is rife with crime,"

Dawn said, her eyes dark. "Apparently, it's just the done thing here."

"On the contrary," Galen said, closing the distance between them and meeting her eyes, "No crime was committed here at all."

Dawn rolled her eyes but didn't say anything else. As he ushered her away from the crowd of gawkers, he came to a stunning realization. Galen could hardly believe it, but he actually missed Sasha Rider.

CHAPTER 8

CLEANING UP

SASHA

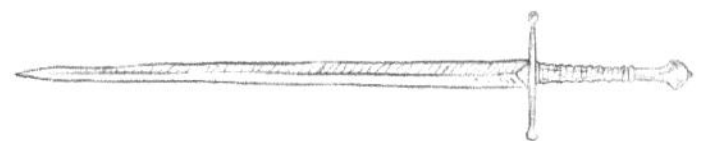

SASHA STRUGGLED TO SLEEP THAT NIGHT. AFTER HIS mother hugged him and led him to his old bedroom (while apologizing that she hadn't aired it out), he tossed and turned in a bed that he hadn't slept in for years. Each tiny barb he had shot Galen's way came back to poke him in revenge.

Every time he closed his eyes, he saw Galen's face. Not the smiling face that he was so used to, but the one he saw as Galen shut the door, full of hurt. What had possessed Sasha to tell the man that he hated him?

In the morning, he got up, got dressed, and then just stood, staring out the window at Medaka's streets. There were people walking about their business, but compared to the streets of Candiru, it seemed desolate. He hadn't realized that he had gotten used to the constant press of the crowd. He hadn't realized that Candiru had become his standard of comparison.

He was still gazing out that window when a soft, tentative knock came at his bedroom door. Releasing his viselike grip on the sill, he turned to see his mother. Her lined face was full of concern, but she still offered him a warm smile.

"Would you like some breakfast?" she asked. "I've got some ham I could heat over the stove, some biscuits from yesterday, oh, and I could always scramble up a few eggs for you."

Sasha smiled at her and then leaned back against the window. "Thank you, Mama. I can help, just set me to it. I've..."

The words got caught in his throat. He couldn't think of any justification to give his mother for his behavior over the past month. Seven hells, she'd be cross at him for grunting instead of saying thank you like a proper gentleman. He cringed to think of what she'd say about the way he had been treating Galen.

"Don't worry, cub," his mother said, her voice still so careful. "We'll have time to talk. But if I know you, you're starving. Come on, can I trust you not to burn the ham?"

"Yes, Mama," Sasha said and followed her to the kitchen.

Being back home with his mother was like being thirteen again. As he took slices of ham from the skillet, placing them onto the ceramic platter, it felt as though Anya might round the corner at any moment. He kept holding his breath, wishing for it to be true. But, of course, she never came.

As they finished eating, and Sasha started to help clean up as he should have been doing at Galen's place, he finally asked, "Where's Pa?"

His mother was wiping the table down with a wet cloth and she sighed dramatically. "Off on some foolhardy venture in Shastian City. Took a riverboat about a week ago, raving about some new mage invention. You know how he is. I'll be lucky if I see him again in a month."

"Oh," Sasha said, dropping the dishes in the washbasin with a loud clatter. Well, at least he wouldn't be horribly disappointing both of his parents at once.

His mother must have mistaken the tone in his voice,

because she came close and squeezed his shoulder, saying, "He'll be sad he missed you, Sasha. We have both missed you so much. I know you've been busy, but I do wish you'd come and visit more often."

Sasha swallowed dryly and stared at the dishes. "I just don't have much to show for my time away. Anya...Anya went to university and made you proud. I haven't done much of anything."

"Oh, come on, cub," his mother said, patting his shoulder. "You know we don't care about that. That was Anya's path, but we're still proud of you."

"I know," Sasha said heavily.

His mother pushed his shoulder, forcing him to turn and look at her. She searched his face, prying him open and looking at his shame and secrets. She made a *humph* sound in the back of her throat, then said, "Clean up the kitchen, Sasha. Then come find me in the sunroom."

She turned on her heel, walking out before Sasha could say a word, leaving him alone with his wretchedness. For a moment, he just stared after her, but then he turned to the dishes.

He scrubbed each plate, each fork and knife, each and every thing that they had dirtied while making breakfast, until it gleamed. He kept having to use the pump, refilling the basin over and over again until his hands were raw and red.

Each time he cleaned something, with each circle of the cloth, he thought of the hurt in Galen's eyes. He thought of his broken voice as he looked up at Sasha and explained just how wrong Sasha had been. With every stroke of his hand, Sasha cursed his life.

It was still the Lady of Flowers's fault, wasn't it? In the end, wasn't it her choice? There had to be someone to blame. There had to be. Right?

Sasha didn't know anymore.

When he couldn't justify scrubbing the dishes any longer, he turned and stared at the table. His mother had wiped it down, but she hadn't scrubbed it. Sasha glared at the table as though it were the cause of all his problems. He dunked a cloth and scrubbed harshly until his arms ached.

When the table was thoroughly clean, he looked down at the floor. Well, his mother had told him to clean the kitchen. At least this was a productive place to put all his pent-up energy. With a determined grunt, he dropped to his hands and knees and started scrubbing the floor.

Again and again, the cloth drew circles in the soapsuds. Again and again, he heard himself say *Yes, I hate you*. He didn't hate Galen. He knew that. There had been so many times when he had thought that if not for the Lady of Flowers, he would have respected him. Galen was not a bad person. He was probably the best living person Sasha knew.

So, he didn't hate him. He had said that to Galen because he knew it would hurt him. Sasha knew that it would stab into Galen's heart, pushing through its protective calluses. It wasn't fair. It wasn't kind. And it made Sasha like one of the monsters roving outside of the cities.

Sasha viciously wiped down the floor, getting even into the low, neglected nooks and crannies under the counter, soaking the knees of his trousers, until he managed to tear the rag he was using in two. He stared at the pieces in disbelief.

The cloth, now dirt-stained and ragged, was a failure. It should have been good at its one job, but after all that pressure, all that pain, it broke. Now it wasn't any use to anyone, and it never would be again. Sasha swallowed heavily. The cloth would never be clean and whole, and he would never be that bright-eyed, hopeful thirteen-year-old again.

Finally, he stood up on shaky legs, looking around for something, anything, else to clean. Unfortunately for him, his mother kept a very neat house. He would just have to go and face her. Holding the rags in his hands like a child about to confess to an accident, he walked to the sunroom.

His mother was sitting in the same worn, comfortable wicker chair that she had used when he was a child. She had her head turned away from him, gazing out the large, clean windows at the well-tended garden. Her hands were folded neatly in her lap, her shoulders relaxed. Sasha hated to disturb her peace, but he entered anyway, as quietly as he could.

"I didn't realize the dishes would take that long," his mother said, her voice heart-achingly gentle.

Sasha wet his lips and made his way to the other chair. "I scrubbed the table and floor too."

As he sat down, his mother turned to him with an arched eyebrow. "Now, what did you do?"

All the blood drained from Sasha's face as he stammered out, "What?"

The knowing look in his mother's eyes was almost too much to bear. She scrutinized him, head to toe, her gaze lingering on the torn cloth in his hands. With a satisfied noise, she turned to face him more fully and smirked.

"I've known you your whole life, Sasha," she said, smiling fondly. "Every single time you've done something bad, you have gone on a penitential cleaning spree. If you were just here for a nice visit with your mama, you would have rinsed the dishes just enough to pass inspection and then been in here in three minutes."

Sasha stared at her, fighting to not let his mouth hang open.

"But today, cub," she said, holding up an accusing finger, "you scrubbed the floors so hard that you tore my favorite dish rag in half. So, what did you do?"

Sasha grimaced and then said, "Mama, I...I don't know what to say."

"Am I right?"

Sasha couldn't speak, so he rested his forearms on his knees, hung his head, and nodded. He had wanted to keep this from her for a bit longer, but that had been a fool's hope. His mother was far too clever to allow him to get away with this for long.

"All right, head up," she said, and he obeyed. "No use hanging there like a dead fish. I know you don't want to tell me, but I promise that you'll feel better if you do, cub. So, tell me. What happened?"

Sasha didn't know where to start. He chewed on it for a moment, holding eye contact with his mother so that she knew he was going to answer. After nearly a full minute, he cleared his throat.

"Is it all right if I give some context?" Sasha asked, and at the look in his mother's eyes, he quickly added, "It's not to make excuses, I promise. I just need to explain. I know...I know that I was wrong."

His mother settled back into her chair and gestured to him. "Fine, give your context, Sasha."

Sasha nodded and then asked a question that caught his mother off guard as much as it did him. "Who was responsible for what happened to Anya?"

His mother's eyes went wide, and her fingers gripped the fabric of her dress as she asked, "What? What do you mean?"

Sasha sighed heavily. "I mean, Anya died because she caught the plague. But...but someone must be to blame, right? She was...she shouldn't have died. We all know that. So, who are we supposed to be angry at? Whose fault is it that she died?"

His mother looked shattered as she said, "Sasha, it was nobody's fault."

Sasha bit down hard on his lip and tasted copper. He had feared that this would be the answer. It was becoming clearer to him at every moment just how much of a fool he had been.

"I know that now," Sasha finally said, looking down at the ground. "For a long time, though, I did blame someone."

"Who?" His mother's voice was full of worry. "It wasn't your father's fault. He would have been the most likely to catch it, but he was careful. I never even left the house." She paused. "Oh, love, you can't blame yourself. You had nothing to do with it. It was just sour luck."

Sasha shook his head, then said, "No, I didn't blame any of us."

"Then who?"

Sasha steeled himself for her reaction, and then said carefully, "The Lady of Flowers."

All sound in the room died away. Sasha licked his lips again and lifted his eyes to his mother's flabbergasted face. The look she was giving him wasn't even anger or disappointment. It was utter disbelief.

"And her devotees," he added to really dig the knife in.

"What?" his mother asked after a few moments of silence.

"I know," Sasha said, burying his face in his hands.

"Sasha," his mother said, "Sasha, how long have you felt this way?"

Sasha didn't answer for a few moments, but eventually he mumbled, "Since I was thirteen."

Silence hung in the air like a sword about to fall. Sasha wet his lips again and looked up. His mother's horrified expression was like a punch in the chest.

"Since Anya died," his mother said once their eyes met again.

And Sasha could only nod.

"Sasha," she sighed. "Gods, we should have made it clearer. We didn't blame the only people who were doing anything to help. The devotees. I suppose you were so young at the time that you didn't realize. The devotees were truly heroes. They worked themselves to the bone. The girl who came running here for Anya could barely stand. She must have been only eighteen."

Sasha didn't remember that. He didn't remember much that day besides staring at Anya's still body and cursing the Lady of Flowers for not saving her.

"She was crying when she realized she was too late, cub," his mother said, and then she lifted a hand to wipe her own cheek. "And she had to keep on going, poor thing. I remember asking if she wanted to have a cup of tea with us, but she told us that she couldn't because there were three other houses she had to try and get to."

Sasha thought of Galen working past dark every night. That exhausted look constantly in his eyes was likely there in the young devotee all those years ago. He bit down hard on his inner cheek.

"I didn't..." Sasha started, but his voice broke. "I didn't remember that. I just remembered her coming and saying that she couldn't help Anya and leaving again. I thought it was just mechanical. Like a checklist."

His mother stared at him, then shook her head. "No, Sasha, not at all. Cub, we were all devastated and angry that Anya was taken from us, but it wasn't their fault. How could it be their fault?"

Sasha nodded, feeling like the vilest scum on the bottom of the bridge. It was even worse than he had imagined. *He* was even worse than he imagined. And now he had to tell his mother why he needed to give that context.

"I know that now," Sasha said, his voice low. "So, I'm sure you've heard about the governor's new initiative to clean up the city, right?"

"Oh, of course," she said. "That auditor, Sir Miller, has been making everyone's life miserable. He kept pestering your father about using magecraft in shipping vessels, saying he had some genius that he had imported from—but that's not what we're talking about."

Sasha nodded. "Part of the initiative is that every healer from the temple of the Lady of Flowers has a guard shadowing them. For safety reasons."

His mother's eyes widened, but she waited for him to continue.

"I was assigned to the devotee who works in Candiru Quarter," Sasha said. "Brother Galen. He is, well, he sounds a lot like the devotee who tried to save Anya. He's compassionate, and kind, and so fucking hard-working…"

"Watch your mouth," she said automatically.

Sasha grimaced and said, "Sorry. But it's true. And I took out a lot of my anger with the Lady of Flowers on him."

"Sasha." His mother had never sounded so disappointed.

"I was so rude, mean…" Sasha swallowed hard. "Cruel."

His mother's mouth was a tight line as she stared at him. Her judgement was worse than any punishment that Captain Tracker could have conceived of. It was as heavy as iron chains.

"We got into an argument," Sasha said, forcing himself to maintain eye contact. "I blamed him for Anya's death. Then, well, he told me what had happened to him during the plague."

As Sasha recounted Galen's story, his mother's pursed lips grew tighter. When he had finished, he ran a hand over his face and sighed heavily.

"I don't know what to do," Sasha said.

His mother scrutinized him for a moment, then she stood up. He followed suit, confusion furrowing his brows at her silence. He had expected her to yell.

"The stairs need to be dusted. Properly dusted, on hands and knees," she said, her voice firm. "Then you could wash the windows, it's been a while, and the maid has too much on her plate. When you're done with that, come find me and I'll have something else."

Sasha stood stunned for a moment before he said, questioningly, "Chores?"

A small, knowing smile grew on his mother's lips. "It sounds like you need to do some penance."

CHAPTER 9

HAUNTED

SASHA

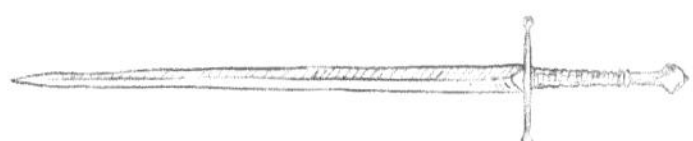

IT WASN'T UNTIL THE THIRD DAY, THE LAST DAY OF his leave, that Sasha finally worked up the nerve to go where he was dreading most. His mother had kept him busy, so very busy, for the entire time he had been there. And anytime there was a break, when he was eating or took a moment to give his hands a rest, she had made him recount the incidents that he had been reliving as he worked.

The disappointment in her eyes, her eyes that looked just like Anya's, was far more punishing than any chore from her never-ending list. He would never complain about any long day with Galen after this. Gods above, he would make this right if it was the last thing he did.

On the final day—he would return to Tracker in the evening, and then to Galen the day after—he finally reached the last chore on his mother's extensive list. He stared at it, and he knew that his mother had put it there for good reason. He needed to do it. He needed to face it.

Clean Anya's Room
Dust
Change Sheets
Sweep

His mother was in the sunroom with a neighbor, and he could hear them chattering away as he worked up the nerve to face the lingering ghosts that would burst forth anew the moment that he stepped into that room.

"It must be nice having Sasha home, Katya," the neighbor twittered. "Been a long time since any of us have seen him."

"Oh, you know how the Rider men are, dear," his mother said with a small laugh. "They get busy, and they forget about everything else in their life."

"Oh, yes," the neighbor said. "Need help getting your boy matchmade? I have a friend who is just wonderful at it. He'd be happy, guaranteed, and it would be a suitable match."

Sasha rolled his eyes, and his mother said, "No, Sasha has other things to worry about right now. I'm more concerned about all this talk about mages lately, you know? Lev has some fascination with mages in other cities, and you know that new auditor..."

"Oh, yes," the neighbor said. "I hate it, you know? We don't need mages in Dragonet. We have enough magic with the temples. And have you heard about that mage from Cyathus City? Their name was Ramil, and they were creating just the vilest..."

Sasha walked away, through with the gossip. He didn't need to eavesdrop on a couple of women talking over tea. He needed to finish this last bit of his punishment and get back to his real work.

He grabbed cleaning supplies, bundled up fresh linens in his arms, and stood outside Anya's door. He stared at it. His hand gripped the broom, his teeth clenched, and his feet refused to move. He didn't want to do this.

He had to do this.

Slowly, painfully, he forced his feet forward. Carefully, he placed his hand on the doorknob and stood stock-still again. This was pathetic. It was just a room. There was nothing on the other side of that door. Nothing but dust and empty space and...and that was the problem. He would open that door and there would be nothing left of his sister.

Sasha finally pushed the door open with a pained grunt. Before he could change his mind, he barreled in and stood staring at the floor. Then he turned and slammed the door shut, blocking out the muffled conversation from down the hall. And then he looked around.

Gods. Gods above, it was just as he remembered it. Her bed was neatly made, the light pink quilt tucked in just how she had always kept it. Her desk bore a tidy pile of books, and her clothes hung neatly in the small closet. There were only two major changes.

Everything was covered in a thin layer of dust, a layer that Sasha was about to remove with a vengeance, and someone had been placing fresh flowers in a vase next to Anya's bed. Sasha had to assume that it was his mother, but he remembered.

He remembered how Anya liked to keep flowers in her room. He remembered the smell of them when he crept in to bother her or ask for advice or seek out a hug. He remembered that when she got sick, she lacked the energy to change them out. He remembered seeing the brown, wilted remnants of the flowers next to her bed as he stared at her body.

But these were fresh and beautiful. His mother must have cut them this morning from the garden. Their light pink blush was perfectly gentle, and the soft scent was comforting. He walked towards them and placed a tentative finger against a petal, smiling even as a sob lifted in his throat.

"You always loved flowers," Sasha said, his voice broken.

He knew that she wasn't really there. Anya had been taken by the Crow nearly two decades before. She was long gone, and at peace. And yet, he still heard her voice. He felt her presence behind him as he stood where she had drawn her last breath.

"I always did," Anya affirmed.

Sasha wanted to turn to her, to see her there. But he knew that the illusion would shatter as soon as he did. Instead, he kept his eyes on the delicate pink flowers. They looked so much like the flower that represented the god he had blamed for so long. The blossoms were just like the one around Galen's neck.

"I really failed you this time," Sasha said heavily.

"Maybe," Anya's voice said. "But you remember what I told you? All those times you got into fights or argued with Mama or Pa?"

Sasha squeezed his eyes closed and swallowed. "It's not too late."

"It's never too late," Anya said, and he could hear her gentle smile. "You can do better. You need to do better."

Sasha nodded and said, "I know."

"So, do it," Anya said. "I know my little brother is a good person."

Sasha laughed brokenly. "I don't know about that."

"Eh, I do," Anya said. "Or are you calling me a liar?"

Sasha spun to face her, crying out, "No! Never!"

Then he was disappointed at the empty space behind him. Of course Anya wasn't there. Anya was dead and had been dead. Nevertheless, her words echoed through his mind. He would do better. He would prove her right.

Sasha started cleaning once more.

HIS MOTHER HAD GIVEN HIM A TEARFUL GOODBYE. She scolded him and told him not to dare to wait so long before visiting again, then kissed him on the cheek. Sasha nodded and took that as well-deserved retribution, then left Medaka to head back down to the guard bunks in Sillago. He had to speak with Tracker again.

It was the first time in a long time that he had gotten to the bunks before the sun set fully. Even when Galen finished early, his long trek normally ended in darkness. It was odd to arrive while people were still milling about.

He made his way through the crowd, ignoring the ever-shouting voice of Dawn Horner as she talked about some disgusting sight she had seen at her post, making exaggerated gagging noises as she described a smell. Finally, he pushed through to Captain Tracker's office.

He knocked tentatively and Tracker shouted, "Come in!"

He opened the door to find Tracker cursing behind a wall of paperwork. She looked up, smiled warmly at him, and gestured for him to sit. He did so, nodding to her and grimacing slightly.

"Feeling better?" she asked, scrutinizing him.

"I don't know if better is the word..." Sasha said, rubbing the back of his neck. "But my mother certainly straightened me out."

Tracker grinned widely. "Good. I knew I could count on her. Now, can I count on *you* to go back down to Candiru and not fumble it this time? I don't think I can stand another night of listening to Dawn Horner complain about it."

Sasha winced. "Dawn Horner was my replacement?"

"Only one I could spare, unfortunately," Tracker said, shrugging. "Now, what do you want to do?"

He pictured the way Galen acted with the people of

Candiru, the way that he smiled and joked, and thought of Anya again. Sasha didn't deserve anything, but Galen deserved an apology at the very least.

"I want to try and make it up to him," Sasha said. "I want to make it right. He asked me to stop being mean to him, and I'm going to. I'm going to try and be nice."

"Good," Tracker said, sighing. "Good. I don't want us to have a reputation of being mean to devotees."

"I know I fucked it up," Sasha said, shaking his head. "I wasn't kidding when I said I was an ass. I'm going to be better. I feel like I should *do* something, though."

"Do something?"

Sasha waved his hands vaguely and said, "I don't know, give him something to try and make up for at least the night we fought. I maybe, sort of, yelled at him and made him cry. And then he told me his life story and, well, I'm an ass. I really should give him something. I just have no idea what to get him."

"He's a devotee of the Lady of Flowers, right?" Tracker asked.

"Yeah."

"Get him some flowers, duh."

"Oh," Sasha said, shaking his head in disbelief at his own stupidity. "Oh gods, I'm an idiot."

"You are, but I love you anyway," Tracker said, smirking at him. "There's a bunch of vendors on your way down to Candiru, just stop at one of them and buy a bouquet."

"Right," Sasha said. "Thanks, captain."

He was thanking her for a lot more than just the advice. Captain Tracker had helped him out of far too many tough situations; she had pulled him out of prison when he was seventeen and straightened out his life. She had given him chance after chance, advocating for him even when he didn't deserve it. He owed her so much, and he didn't know how to say any of it.

"Anytime," Tracker said. "You are a good person, Rider. You just need to start acting like it."

"Yes, ma'am."

Tracker got up with a groan, stretching her arms above her head. "I'm going to bed. Miller was here earlier rooting through my files and that is just plain exhausting. I'll see you around, kid."

"See you around, captain," Sasha said.

He followed her lead, going to bed shortly afterwards. Sleep eluded him for most of the night, but the words of Captain Tracker, his mother, and Anya echoed in his mind. As he thought about Galen, about all he had done to him, he promised himself that he would never make Galen cry again. He promised himself that he would never hurt him.

Chapter 10

Prayers

Galen

Galen stared at the yellow heads of the dandelions that had made themselves a home in front of his door. He was sitting on the small step that led into his house, completely and utterly drained from his third day with Dawn Horner. At least the next day was his rest day, and Dawn seemed to have no qualms about leaving him alone then.

He didn't understand why the Lady of Flowers had seen fit to test him so in the last month. First, Sasha Rider, who was so cruel to him for, well, not *no* reason. Out of very misplaced anger. Then, a strange new sickness that he hadn't even had time to investigate with everything else that had happened. Finally, Dawn Horner, who seemed determined to make everyone in Candiru Quarter hate her—and him.

All Galen wanted to do was bury himself under his covers and scream into his pillow. What he had had before was, well, it wasn't good. It was exhausting, physically and mentally, and he hated how alone he always felt, but at least he hadn't needed to justify his existence to people who weren't even from Candiru.

If he was called a rat one more time, he was going to jump

into the river. He was so tired, but he knew that he couldn't take time to rest or stop, because if he did, the work would continue to pile up. So many people were relying on him that he didn't have time to wallow. With a groan, he pressed his forehead against his knees and squeezed his eyes shut.

Even momentary wallowing wasn't allowed, because not two seconds later he felt an ice-cold nose press against his skin and a pulse of lightning zip through his veins. He sat up with a jolt to see a very curious blink fox staring at him with his head cocked to the side. Just behind him, with an oddly similar expression, was Adrian, the baker. His arms were full of baskets of baked goods.

Galen quickly wiped the exhaustion from his face and replaced it with a smile. "Evening, Adrian."

"Evening, Brother Galen" Adrian said with an uncertain smile. "Are you all right?"

Galen immediately sat up straighter and ran a hand over his hair before saying, "Of course. Just a bit tired, you know. Where are you going with all that? Surely you're not making deliveries. It's so late."

Adrian snorted, then said, "You're one to talk, Brother Galen. You don't get home until near midnight half the time."

Galen shook his head, laughing, and said, "Fair enough, but you didn't answer my question."

Adrian mirrored Galen, shaking his head and laughing, then said, "You caught me. Just a quick delivery of the leftovers to Miss Kingley. I can drop them off no worries since she's on the way to the Sparrow's Roost. I'm meeting up with Rory there once they're finished at the tailor's. I'll have done a good deed, so Rory won't be annoyed about staying out late, see?"

Galen laughed and pulled himself up. "I see. Well then, I'll let you get on your way. Wouldn't want to keep Rory waiting. I'll see you tomorrow."

Galen was about to head inside, but Adrian cleared his throat. "Now, you wouldn't want to come with us, would you, Brother Galen? It's been quite a while since you've been out and, if you'll pardon my boldness, you look like you could use a drink, lad."

Galen tried not to grimace. He didn't want to look as though he needed a drink. He was supposed to be a steadfast healer, a devotee that everyone could count on, not someone who needed looking after. So he smiled and shook his head.

"As tempting as that is," Galen said, spreading his hands out and shrugging, "I'm a bit too tired tonight, I'm afraid. I'd probably fall asleep in the booth, and that wouldn't be any fun."

"You sure?" Adrian asked, his eyebrows knitting together in concern. "There's always room for you at the table, Brother Galen, tired or not. And isn't tomorrow your rest day? You could sleep in."

The offer was incredibly tempting, but Galen couldn't stand to be around people right now. Not when he was so close to a breaking point, hairline fractures spreading across his carefully maintained mask. So, once again, he shook his head. Muffin nudged his shin, demanding attention.

"No, that's all right," Galen said, then bent down to scoop up Muffin. "I'll distract this little rascal while you make a break for it. I'm sure that he's been causing trouble for you."

Luckily, Adrian laughed and said, "He sure has. Just about tripped me three times now. I'm sure he wants me to fall so he can gobble up all the bread that's meant for Miss Kingley."

"There you go!" Galen said triumphantly. "I'll hold back the menace that is Muffin, you go on your merry way. We'll all be happy."

Adrian once again looked slightly sad and disappointed. "If you're sure, Brother Galen. Just know you're always welcome."

"Of course. Thank you, Adrian," Galen said, smiling and moving into his house, blink fox clutched to his chest, before Adrian could look at him with those concerned eyes again.

As soon as the door was closed, Galen rested his head against the wood and sighed heavily. He squeezed his eyes tightly shut, groaned a bit, and let go of the squirming animal. Muffin fell to the ground with a soft thump and then was off to investigate Galen's kitchen.

That was fine. As long as he didn't get into the medicines, Galen didn't care if Muffin rooted through the dried meat and fruits. Galen just stood there, listening to Muffin snuffle around and willing himself to move. He had to eat. He had to clean. He had to take care of himself; he wouldn't be able to keep going otherwise.

With tremendous effort, he pulled himself away from where he stood. He cooked a quick meal and ate it straight from the pan. He cleaned up the kitchen, then washed himself with a cloth and a pot of hot water while Muffin judged him. He pulled on a night shirt and was about to head to bed when he stopped.

Muffin was batting at his small altar. Galen sighed heavily and then moved over to stop the blink fox from breaking anything. As soon as he knelt, Muffin looked up at him, then vanished in a flash of lightning-like magic. Galen turned just in time to see Muffin moseying into his bedroom.

Galen blinked, then rubbed his eyes in pure exhaustion. He was going to pull himself back up, but the sight of the altar, the screen with its painted flowers and the little cup, stopped him. He pursed his lips. Well, he was already on his knees. It had been a while.

Going through the ritual of evening prayers was very soothing. As he poured the nectar from its bottle into its designated cup, a sense of peace washed over him. He had forgotten just how helpful this was for centering himself. It was nice to take the time to say the prayers in Dresian, a language that only devotees of the Lady of Flowers learned in Dragonet City. The words were lyrical, almost musical, and their beauty spoke to him.

After he drained the cup of the nectar, counted through his prayer beads, and completed the ritual, he stayed kneeling. He wasn't sure why, but it felt right. He closed his eyes gently and bent down until his forehead touched the edge of the low altar.

"Lady of Flowers," Galen started, feeling slightly foolish, "I know that this isn't normally how this is supposed to go. But, well, I just..."

He sighed heavily. It was like he was eleven again, back before he knew how to pray properly. He just asked for her help. His face grew red at the thought, but he continued.

"My Lady," Galen said, and his voice broke. "Things have been so bad lately. I know...I know that you have to test your devotees. I respect that, I understand it. But, My Lady, it has been so hard. I am struggling, and there is no one I can tell without causing hurt. And I am sorry if I caused you hurt as well..."

Galen paused to breathe because if he didn't, he'd end up crying again. He was so sick of crying.

"Lady of Flowers," Galen said, and then laughed softly. "Can you please just give me a break? Just for a bit, make it easier somehow. I'd take anything at this point. But please, I'd be so grateful. Just make things a little bit better for me. Please."

When he was done, he stood and bowed and felt like an utter fool. What a terribly selfish prayer, one the Lady would surely dismiss. But at least he had finally said it out loud. A small part of the weight on his shoulders had been lifted. It wasn't much, but it was something.

He went to bed, Muffin jumping up with him and

pushing him to the edge. Galen didn't sleep for a long time. Instead, he gazed up at the ceiling beams and thought about Candiru Quarter and all he had to do.

Then, shockingly, his mind drifted to Sasha Rider. He wished that he hadn't scared the man off. He hoped that their little spat hadn't gotten him fired. Galen was thinking of those deep, brown eyes as he drifted into unconsciousness.

It could have been a dream, or his imagination, but right before he slipped away, he could swear that he heard a voice, warm and rich and melodic, say in his ear, "Well. Since you said please."

CHAPTER 11

FLOWERS

SASHA

SASHA WOKE, BRIGHT AND EARLY, BACK IN THE bunks in Sillago. He had half-expected to still be in his childhood bedroom, another list of well-earned chores awaiting him. However, he was back, and it was time for him to face Galen again. His arms ached from scrubbing floors and his back protested as he got up, still sore from carrying heavy crates around for his mother.

As he splashed water on his face, dressed, and strapped on his armor, he thought about what Tracker had said. Flowers. That was a good idea, surely. If there was one thing that he could be certain of, a devotee of the Lady of Flowers would appreciate a bouquet. The sun was still rising over the city when he left, hopefully with plenty of time to stop, buy his apology gift, and go to Galen's before they had to head out again.

As he walked towards Candiru, he was on the hunt for a flower vendor. He feared that no shop would be open this early, but he could go to one of the little carts that peppered the streets. He was nearly to the district line when he spotted one just opening up shop.

A rainbow of blossoms dangled from the slatted wooden roof, where ribbons and bells were strung to attract attention. The little man, round and short with a shiny bald head and a caterpillar of a salt-and-pepper mustache, parked the cart and was humming to himself as he tied on an apron. Sasha made a fierce beeline towards him.

When the man glanced up and saw Sasha barreling towards him, he paled and took a step back. Sasha doubled his pace, trying to catch the vendor before he turned and ran in the other direction. Luckily, the man was still dancing indecisively on his toes by the time Sasha got within earshot.

"Morning," Sasha said.

"Good morning, sir," the man squeaked. "Is there something I can help you with?"

"Yes, in fact," Sasha said, and the man's eyes widened.

"I haven't seen any crimes lately, sir," the man said, his voice trembling.

Ah, shit. Sasha was in uniform. Of course the vendor was afraid that he was in trouble, or that a guard was about to make his day much, much harder. Sasha groaned internally and tried a smile, which seemed to make the man squirm even more.

"Ah, sorry, that's not what I meant," Sasha said, attempting to be less menacing. "I need to buy flowers."

"Oh," the man said, face and body relaxing. "Oh, of course!"

Sasha sighed with relief and looked at the flowers. Lion's teeth, there were so many kinds. All different shapes and sizes and colors. Sasha had no idea where to even begin. After staring at them helplessly for about a minute while the mustached vendor twiddled his thumbs nervously, Sasha finally gave up.

He cleared his throat and said, "So, what would you

recommend for an apology? For when someone just really, really fu—messed up?"

The man smiled knowingly and said, "Of course. I have the perfect thing."

The man looked through his bouquets until he found what he was looking for. He grinned, then adjusted a few things, removing a few flowers and adding some more. Sasha watched him carefully, seeing pink and red carnations, he thought, along with little white blossoms. The vendor finished by wrapping the blooms in brown paper and tying it all up with a pink ribbon.

"Half a silver crown," the man said, beaming.

Sasha thought it was expensive for a bunch of flowers, but he didn't complain. He paid and took the flowers carefully. He held them as though they were the most precious thing in the world. Despite the instinct to crush them against his chest, or squeeze them with his rough hands, he resisted. He would deliver these in perfect condition.

The entire rest of the walk his heart was pounding. He was in the wrong, and he needed to make it up to Galen. Ever since their argument, guilt had squeezed his heart in a vise, refusing to allow him to even take a full breath. It had only gotten worse after his mother showed him how wrong he had been. As much as the prospect frightened him, he knew that he had to try to make it right.

After battling with himself for a few more streets, he sighed heavily and turned his mind upward for help. He sent a small prayer up to Anya that he was going about this the right way, hoping that at least this would make her proud. Then after a moment, with a mouth as dry as sand, he followed it up with a prayer to the Lady of Flowers.

"Uh, I know that I haven't spoken to you in a long, long time," Sasha said, under his breath, "but, Lady of Flowers, please help me to make this right with your devotee. He didn't deserve how I treated him."

Sooner than Sasha would have liked, he was standing in front of Galen's door, but he couldn't bring himself to knock. He took a breath and hesitated, his hand inches from the wood. Gods above, he just needed to do it. With an oath and a bite of his lip he finally pounded on the door.

For a few terrifying moments, it seemed like Galen wasn't going to answer. But then the curtains twitched, and a moment later the door creaked open. Muffin, the odd little blue and white fox, slipped out between Galen's legs. Galen didn't look good. Bags bruised the soft skin beneath his eyes, and Sasha thought they looked a bit red, as though he had been crying. His auburn hair was loose, frizzy and messy, and touched his shoulders like a kiss. He was wearing not his usual garish yellow, but a plain white tunic. Oh. It was his rest day. Shit.

"Mister Rider," Galen said, looking a bit surprised to see him. His eyes were wide and still full of the hurt that Sasha had put there.

"Brother Galen," Sasha said, cursing himself as Galen flinched slightly at the sound of his voice. Damn.

Galen winced, then said in a low voice, "I just wanted to apologize for the other night. I feel awful for what I said. It wasn't fair to you. I wasn't trying to make our situations a competition, and I feel like—"

"No, Brother Galen," Sasha said firmly. "You have nothing to apologize for. I have been absolutely cruel to you, and it was very, very wrong. I need to apologize for my behavior, and it shouldn't have taken you telling me about the worst moments of your life for me to realize that I've been a total ass."

"You haven't been—"

"Yes, I have," Sasha cut him off. "You were right to call me out. And here, I got you these."

Sasha held out the flowers, and a strange series of emotions flew across Galen's face. Confusion, then shock, then worry that was almost fear. A blush bloomed on his unburned cheek, and he looked up at Sasha with a small, nervous smile.

"I, uh, you don't know anything about the language of flowers, do you?" Galen asked, the tips of his ears as red as the carnations in the bouquet.

Sasha shook his head, and said, "I'm not sure what that is."

"Oh, okay," Galen said, releasing a breath with a small laugh. "So, it's a way of communicating your feelings with what flowers you give someone. Different flowers mean different things."

"Oh, is this one good then?" Sasha asked, trying to smile kindly at Galen. "I asked the flower seller for help. I told him that I needed apology flowers."

"Well, uh," Galen said, another small laugh escaping his lips. "Well, it would be good if I were your, um, romantic partner."

Realization hit him in the chest, hard and sudden as a horse's hoof. Sasha had screamed at the man just a few nights ago, and now he was giving him a romantic gift. No wonder Galen had looked so confused. The Lady of Flowers must be mocking Sasha.

"Oh," Sasha said, eyes widening. "Oh, um...I'm sorry."

"It's fine, really. He must have thought you got into an argument with your partner," Galen said, smiling as he shook his head. "This basically says, 'I'm very sorry, I love you dearly. Please forgive me.'"

Sasha's face was hot with embarrassment. Gods above, he couldn't even apologize correctly. Luckily, Galen seemed to be taking it in stride. He had an awkward half-smile on his face, and his eyes were still a bit wary, but at least it wasn't the previous look of hurt and dismay. Sasha could laugh at himself if it would make Galen feel better.

"Well, if you cut out that middle sentiment, that was what I was going for," Sasha said, trying a small laugh. "I *am* very sorry."

Galen took the flowers from him, smelling them deeply, then said with a coy smile, "Well, it could also be a love confession. Which was why I was a bit confused. Or rather, I thought that perhaps you only felt the extremes of the emotional spectrum."

Sasha's heartbeat fluttered wildly. That was much, much worse. He couldn't imagine what Galen had thought if it looked like Sasha had gone from hating him a few nights ago to saying that he was in love with him this morning.

"Well, I am not in love with you, Brother Galen," Sasha said, trying to stay light. "But I would like to try and make up for how I was treating you. And, uh, I don't hate you. I want to make that clear. I really don't, and I didn't that night either. I was just...I think I was trying to hurt you. And I'm sorry for that."

Galen clutched the flowers a bit tighter, but his slight smile remained. Sasha was sure that he was replaying the conversation as well, perhaps reliving the past month. With all that Sasha had done, Galen would have been well within his rights to slam the door in his face. But instead, he took a breath and let his smile grow.

"Thank you, I appreciate that," Galen said. "And thank you for apologizing. Come on in, I'll put these in some water."

Galen slipped inside, clutching the flowers a little tighter than Sasha had been expecting. Sasha ducked in and tried to reassess the place. He had found it cluttered ever since he got a face full of dried rosemary the first time he walked in. He thought he had just gotten better at avoiding the herbs waiting to be made into medicine, but no, Galen had cleared a path for him. The healer had moved the hanging bundles so that they didn't obstruct his usual path from the door to the kitchen table. Sasha swallowed. The amount of consideration, even in something so small, struck him hard. And he had called Galen selfish.

Galen had already pumped water into a pottery vase, a pale yellow one, so different from the garish yellow of his healer's tunic, and placed the flowers in it. He set them in the window, facing away from Sasha. Sasha moved to the table carefully, pulled out a chair, and sat down. He didn't know if he should break the silence first or let Galen. He drummed his fingers on the table and watched as Galen started to make tea.

Sasha took a breath and started to speak at the exact moment that Galen turned around and started talking.

"Look, I want to let you—"

"I've already—"

They froze and fell silent, staring at each other. Their precarious peace seemed to teeter. Sasha cleared his throat and gestured to Galen.

"You go," he said, nodding at him.

"Ah, no, that's fine," Galen said, shaking his head.

"I insist."

Galen started placing food on the table—Sasha's empty belly was very appreciative of that—and he said, "I have already finished my prayers, so you don't need to worry about that. I understand why you don't like hearing them. I can make sure that I'm done by the time you arrive."

"No," Sasha said, and Galen stilled.

"I, uh, no?" Galen asked, his eyebrows lifting.

"I mean," Sasha pinched the bridge of his nose and said, "don't change your schedule because of me. You made me realize that I was blaming the wrong people for what happened to my sister. I don't know if there is anyone to blame for a plague, but it certainly shouldn't be the people working themselves to the bone to help everyone."

"Oh," Galen said, moving the jars of jam and honey to the center of the table.

"Look, Galen." Sasha winced. "Do you mind if I call you Galen? I can call you Brother Galen if you prefer."

Galen blinked once, then twice, and said, "Galen is fine."

"Feel free to call me Sasha," Sasha said, sitting back. "All the 'Mister Rider' business makes me feel even older than I am."

"Oh, um, I'm sorry," Galen said, eyes widening. "I didn't realize that you didn't like it."

"It's not your fault," Sasha said. "I believe on the first day we met you asked me if Mister Rider was all right. I think I grunted at you."

Galen laughed slightly, and it was good to hear. Laughter normally surrounded Galen like bees around a garden, and Sasha had been trying to kill that. Gods above, what was wrong with him? Anya would have been so disgusted with him, with what he had become. How could he justify the way he had acted?

He couldn't.

"Are you all right?" Galen asked. The tea must have finished, because he was pushing Sasha's usual mug towards him.

"I'm an asshole," Sasha said, "and you're asking if I'm all right."

Galen's wide eyes were scrutinizing him, searching his face. Sasha felt utterly exposed in a way he hadn't been prepared for.

"You looked distressed," Galen said softly.

"Yes, well, I'm just realizing how cruel I was being, again and again, at every moment, and how you didn't deserve it," Sasha said, then gestured up at the ceiling. "You made a path in the herbs for me. Even when I was constantly needling at you. Why?"

Galen shrugged and said, "I assumed that you didn't want a face full of dried herbs every time we had breakfast."

"You're too fucking thoughtful," Sasha said with a groan, then caught Galen's flinch. "That's not a bad thing. Sorry, I'm trying…I'm going to try and be nice. I'm bad at it though."

"I'll settle for not being mean," Galen said, smiling just a bit.

Sasha laughed and said, "You are my last chance, you know."

Galen's smile dropped and he asked, "What?"

"This may be surprising," Sasha said, smirking a bit at himself, "but I'm hard to get along with. The city guard works on a three-strike system, and technically, I already have three strikes. Other guards have said I'm a pain to work with, they didn't like me in the Court of Justice, and when I'm assigned someone to protect, I'm lucky if they don't complain about me. My captain happens to like me, so I have one last chance. And that's you."

"Oh," Galen said, tapping his fingers on his mug. "Well, I wasn't going to complain to your boss. That's why the other night I, well, it sounds rather harsh, but I confronted you. I suppose that's the right word."

"I don't think it's too harsh," Sasha said. "I needed it. Honestly, you could have punched me in the nose, and I would have deserved it."

"Well, yes, but then I'd be the one mending it and I wouldn't want to make extra work for myself," Galen said, and Sasha looked up to see him smiling, the gap between his front teeth just barely showing.

Sasha grinned at him, laughing slightly, and said, "Well, you already work harder than any person I know, so that makes sense. Thank you, though. For giving me another chance."

"Of course," Galen said, and took a sip of his tea.

Sasha really couldn't believe that Galen wasn't going to complain about him. Well, he could believe it, but it was utterly wrong. Galen had more right to complain about him than any other person he had ever worked with, and he was here making Sasha tea and smiling at him.

Galen tapped his fingers against his mug again and said, "I have an idea. Why don't we start over? Clean slate and all that."

He looked at Sasha hopefully, hazel eyes bright. Sasha couldn't believe that either. To be offered not just another chance, but to forget what he had done...Sasha didn't deserve it. He shook his head at Galen.

"I'm afraid I'm bad at that as well," Sasha said. "I won't be able to forget what you told me about your family, or how I was cruel to you when you showed me nothing but kindness."

"Well, I can do the heavy lifting," Galen said, smiling encouragingly. "I'll still remember about your sister, but I'll do my best to forget some of your more...unsavory moments from the past month. How's that?"

Sasha stared at him in disbelief. "I don't deserve that."

Galen's smile was warm, and his eyes were kind. His fingers were wrapped around his mug as he gazed at Sasha like a patient he was figuring out how to treat. After a moment of that silence, Galen took a breath and spoke.

"It's not about what you deserve," Galen said, shrugging. "If that were the measurement, there are some people that I would never treat. It's about giving you a chance to grow, and heal, and sometimes, that requires me to let something go. I know you aren't the biggest fan of her, but second chances are the domain of the Lady of Flowers."

Sasha looked at him, really looked at him, and saw that he was being completely truthful. The small smile, the gentle look in Galen's eyes, despite everything he had gone through, both before and after Sasha interrupted his life, were too much. Sasha didn't realize that he was crying until Galen's face shifted to concern as Sasha's vision blurred.

"Oh, I'm sorry," Galen said quickly, lifting his hands. "I didn't mean to—"

"No, no," Sasha said, wiping his face. "I'm sorry. Fuck, I'm just... Your kindness is a bit overwhelming, Galen. I feel like I've been trampling all over you."

"Well, you've promised to be better," Galen said. "And if you keep that promise, I don't mind. And you even got me flowers, as incorrect as their meaning is, so how could I stay mad?"

Sasha wanted to say *How could you not?* He wanted to take Galen by the shoulders and shake him for how easily he forgave a month of cruelty and bullying, but Galen was smiling at him, so he just shook his head.

"All right," Sasha said, trying to smile again. "As you say."

CHAPTER 12

ORANGES

GALEN

THE NEXT DAY, GALEN HELD HIS BREATH AS HE WENT to answer the door. This would be the real test. It was one thing for Sasha to show up, bouquet in hand, spouting apologies. With those particular flowers, he looked like an awkward teenager who had accidentally offended his first love. For a few terrifying moments, Galen had thought of children expressing romantic feelings through bullying and teasing. But of course, that wasn't the case here. With Galen's face, his bullies were never anything more than bullies.

It would be another thing entirely for Sasha to actually change his behavior. Galen released the breath and, after another moment, opened the door. Muffin pushed past Sasha's legs, chirruping triumphantly as he sped into Galen's kitchen.

"Ah! Sorry, I didn't see him," Sasha said from behind Galen as Muffin tried to burrow his round little body beneath the counter.

"It's all right," Galen said with a laugh as he hurried to the kitchen. "He was probably waiting for the opportune moment. Um, mind helping me?"

"Of course, one moment, uh, let me put these down," Sasha said.

Galen turned around and saw what he had missed, distracted by Muffin. Sasha was holding a giant bouquet, even bigger than the one the day before, and it was wildly and astonishingly yellow. Bright daffodils, yellow tulips, carnations the color of sunshine, and even a few sunflowers exploded from Sasha's arms. As Galen stared at it, Sasha's pale skin flushed.

"So, I went back to the same vendor this morning," Sasha said, crushing the paper as he struggled to maintain eye contract. "I explained what happened. He had a very good laugh about it, but he said he could put together a better bouquet. One about friendship! Because, well, I'd like to try and be friends? And I remember that you said you liked yellow."

Galen couldn't help grinning, and he didn't care if it revealed his teeth. He said, "They're perfect. You really didn't have to, but I'm quite glad you did. These are lovely."

"Oh, good," Sasha said, relief evident on his face. "I was worried that he was having another laugh at me. Okay, let's get that little beast."

Sasha set the flowers down reverently on the kitchen table, and then the two of them wrangled Muffin out from under the counter. Sasha deposited him gently on the stoop and quickly closed the door. Galen surveyed the damage; it wasn't too bad. Muffin had gotten into the dried meat, but nothing else.

"Right, well," Sasha said. "Breakfast? Can I help?"

"Oh, sure," Galen said, picking up the flowers and searching for another vase. "Could you get the tea steeping? The water's on the stove."

Sasha nodded and moved carefully into the kitchen,

getting whacked by a few hanging herbs in the process. Galen winced.

"Sorry, I hadn't moved those yet because—"

"Because for the past month I sat on my ass and let you serve me breakfast every day?"

"Well," Galen said, rearranging the flowers as he set them next to the ones from the day before. "I wasn't going to put it exactly like that. Would you like some oranges? Nina brought them."

"You wouldn't want to keep those for yourself?"

Galen laughed, then said, "She gave me more than three dozen. I couldn't eat all of them before they went bad, not without turning orange, anyway. And my appearance has enough issues as is."

Sasha looked odd as he said, "Your appearance is fine. Is someone making fun of you or something?"

Galen had to take a moment. As long as he could remember, people had made fun of his appearance. That was nothing new. Before he was burned, it was his gap teeth. It was mostly children, but some adults were equally cruel, like Old Harry. After he was burned, spending most of his time in Aster House had been a blessing. Devotees of the Lady of Flowers treated him with dignity, but when he started going out, he was surrounded by whispered comments and pointing children. Rarely did anyone say anything directly cruel about his scars.

"No more than they always did," Galen said, shrugging. "No use in pretending I'm some great beauty."

Sasha grunted and poured the tea, then said, "Old Harry shouldn't talk to you the way he does."

"Ah, well," Galen said, setting the table. "He's a grumpy old man in a lot of pain. Hardly anyone comes to see him, and I only come once a week. If he wants to take out a bit of anger on me, so be it. I don't take it personally."

Sasha shook his head and sat down at the same time Galen did and said, "You're too nice. What if I start being mean *for* you instead of *to* you? Use my power of being a jackass for good?"

Galen laughed and said, "Please don't. I appreciate the sentiment, but please don't."

"Well, since you said please," Sasha said, lifting his brows with a smile.

That caught Galen off guard. Hadn't someone else said that to him recently? But he shook it off. Likely he was misremembering a half-formed dream.

Instead, Galen smiled at Sasha and said, "I think that the reason you being, well, mean to me got under my skin is because I couldn't figure out why. I know why Old Harry is the way he is, but you? You were an enigma. A very grumpy enigma."

"I can't promise I'll be less grumpy in the mornings," Sasha said, sipping his tea.

Galen rested his chin in his hand and said, "You already were less grumpy today, to be fair."

Sasha offered a small smile and sliced off a piece of bread. They ate and then Sasha shocked Galen by telling him to gather his supplies while Sasha cleaned up. Galen just thanked him and nodded, still surprised. It made sense, admittedly, and this was how they should have been doing it from the beginning instead of Galen rushing to beat the morning bells while Sasha sat there. Or worse, Galen having to clean up breakfast before he was able to make his dinner when he finally got back home.

Sasha, evidently, didn't like oranges that much; he had only eaten two at breakfast, which was not very many for him. Galen had eaten one himself, and left a few on the counter, but dumped the rest into a basket. Oranges were quite a useful treat.

They left before the bells of Rising Dawn even started, Sasha scowling at Muffin and using his foot to nudge the animal away from the door. Galen bit back a laugh at that.

He strolled down the street, taking in the early morning sights of Candiru. He loved seeing it as the sun just started to rise. People were waking up and setting up for the day. They called morning greetings to each other, and to him. He always smiled and waved back, and today he watched the eyes of a few citizens drift to the oranges in his basket. It was always nice at this time of day.

Or at least it was until he heard a scuffle behind him. He turned around to see that Jess of the Kipper Gang, along with four other Kippers, had pinned Sasha against the wall. It was obvious to Galen that Sasha was allowing this to happen. If they had tried this less than a week ago, Galen would have been tending to broken noses and limbs.

"Jess..." Galen started, but Jess pulled out a short, wicked-looking knife and held it just under Sasha's throat.

"We've been hearing things, Mister Hanging Herring," Jess spat out in Sasha's face. "We've been hearing that you've been horrible to Flower Boy."

"Flower Boy?" Sasha asked, eyebrows lifting, clearly more amused by the nickname than threatened by Jess.

"Shut it!" Jess shouted, pressing their knife harder against Sasha's throat, and all amusement drained from his face.

"Now, Jess," Galen tried again, but the Kipper wasn't having it.

"We heard you made him cry," Jess said, venom lacing their words.

Galen felt heat rise in his cheeks. How many people had seen his and Sasha's confrontation? He had been crying, hadn't he? He was meant to be unflappable. To be a steady presence in people's lives, someone who could take whatever was thrown at him and offer only kindness back.

"How dare you?" Jess growled at Sasha. "Brother Galen is one of us and the best of us. He never cries! You are a right bastard, you know that?"

And before Galen could say anything, Sasha answered, "I do. I am a right bastard. And an ass. And honestly, not worth Brother Galen's patience or forgiveness."

"That's what I thought you'd say, you...what?" Jess clearly had a takedown rebuttal planned, and Sasha's agreement threw them off.

"I agree with you," Sasha said. "I was fucking awful, and Brother Galen didn't deserve it."

"Right," Jess said. They were now a bit unsure, but still they continued. "Well! Say you're fucking sorry!"

"He already did, Jess," Galen said. "He brought me flowers. Twice."

"He what?" Jess asked, their head whipping so quickly to stare at Galen that their long, dark braid hit Sasha in the face.

Sasha turned his head to Galen and said, "I'm fucking sorry."

One of the Kippers smacked Sasha over the head and said, "Hey, be polite! He's a fucking priest!"

"I'm actually not a priest, I'm a devotee," Galen said, laughing. "And it's fine. I tolerate your swearing with no problem."

"He really did apologize?" Jess asked. After Galen assured them that he had, Jess released Sasha.

"I didn't realize that you would actually set the Kipper Gang on me," Sasha said, smiling.

Galen laughed, but then Jess reached up and shoved Sasha's shoulder so he'd look at them. "Aren't you supposed to be protecting him?"

"Yes," Sasha said, nodding.

"Then why the fuck were you being an ass?" Jess growled.

"I know hanging herrings are awful, but most are nice to priests."

"Uh, not a priest!" Galen called, trying to ease some of the tension. It didn't work.

"I had some... let's call them misconceptions about the Lady of Flowers," Sasha said. "They've been cleared up. I won't be making Brother Galen cry again. I promise."

Jess nodded sternly and said, "See that you don't. Have a good day, Brother Galen. Have the day that you deserve, herring."

Sasha's face fell a bit as Jess turned on their heel, but Galen couldn't leave it like that, so he called, "Wait, Jess!"

They turned around with lifted brows.

"Would you and the Kippers like some oranges?" Galen asked, lifting his basket.

Their face lit up with a grin and they jogged over to nab an orange. The others surged forth and each plucked one from the basket, thanking him and wishing him well. As Galen held the backet steady, he saw Jess behind the gang, a serious look on their face, peeling their orange and speaking intently to Sasha. Sasha nodded firmly, but when Jess walked away, he caught Galen's eye and smirked.

The Kippers went on their way with a blessing from Galen, and soon Sasha was back at his side as they strolled towards their first stop. The basket was a bit lighter, and Galen was sure that at least two of the Kippers had taken more than one orange and they'd get yelled at when Jess found out.

"Sorry about all that," Galen said, looking up at Sasha.

"Oh, it's fine," Sasha said with a chuckle. "I think I deserved that."

Galen laughed as well, and then asked, "What was Jess saying to you?"

"Hm? Oh, well." Sasha's pale face flushed a bit. "They asked if I was courting you, because of the flowers, you know?

I told them I wasn't. I left out the details of my first bouquet. They told me that if I broke your heart, nothing would stop them from stabbing me. They seemed awfully serious when they said it."

Galen laughed and said, "They probably were. At least there's no danger of that."

Sasha nodded, smiling. Soon, they arrived at their first stop of the day. For the first time in a month, Galen could breathe freely while he was working. Sasha wasn't a lingering threat anymore; he was just...there. And now he kept offering to help, too; it was odd. When Galen was treating an infected sore on a young man's stomach, he had to very gently ask Sasha to stop hovering, but in a different way than before.

Sasha was watching him work but not looking for flaws in his techniques or scolding him for not using the gift. He seemed to be trying to truly understand what Galen was doing, and he seemed to appreciate it.

Every visit that day ended with Galen giving the patient, and maybe a few of the patient's loved ones, an orange. The way their eyes lit up at the treat was so gratifying, and it made him want to carry fruit all the time. If only the basket hadn't been so heavy. As they walked out of their last stop into the rust-colored evening, Galen looked down and saw that there were but two oranges left.

"Would you like an orange, Sasha?" he asked, startling the guard out of a reverie.

"What? Oh, sure," Sasha said, and took the orange from Galen's outstretched hand.

They walked together, peeling their oranges as they made their way back to Galen's little house. Galen loved knowing that the scent would linger on his fingers all night. He popped a slice into his mouth and looked up at Sasha, who had a contemplative expression.

"I would offer you an orange for your thoughts, but alas, I gave them all away," Galen said, smiling.

Sasha laughed as he chewed his own orange segment and then said, "I was just thinking about how I made this all harder on myself. Today was…today was nice. I liked watching you work, and I can't believe I was such an idiot that I squandered a month by being bitter."

"Well! You know now, and you'll be able to witness the glories of treating head colds and draining pus-filled sores day in and day out," Galen said, trying not to grin. "But you're right. I thought today was much nicer too. Thank you for keeping your promise."

Sasha stood a bit taller, smiled a bit wider, and said, "Of course. Lion's teeth, who would have known that being nice would make things nicer? Goes to show you."

They both laughed and they were at Galen's house shortly after. Sasha valiantly defended Galen's stoop from Muffin's invasion attempts as Galen slipped inside, wishing the guard a good night. And this time he truly meant it. He set the basket on the kitchen table, then lifted his fingers to his nose and smelled bright citrus. He smiled.

Before he went to bed, he spent some time rearranging the herbs again to accommodate Sasha's new desire to help out in the kitchen. When he finished, he stepped down from the chair and looked up at his work with an unabashed grin. He put his kitchen chair back, and before retiring into his small bedroom for the night, he lifted himself up on his tiptoes and smelled each bouquet deeply. His heart suddenly felt rather full.

Chapter 13

Dandelions

Sasha

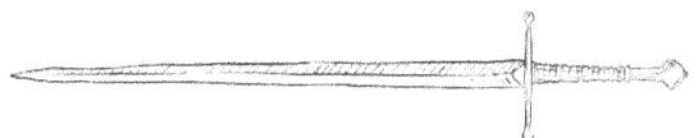

Sasha arrived the next day with another bouquet of yellow flowers in his arms. He didn't know how long he was going to continue to do this, but Galen's surprised smile made him want to keep spending a ridiculous amount of money on flowers every morning. The vendor couldn't believe that he was back a third time and gave him an odd look as he reconstructed the previous day's bouquet.

"I have a lot to make up for," Sasha said in response to the man's cocked eyebrow.

"If you say so," the vendor said, shaking his head with a slight smile and tying the ribbon before relieving Sasha of half a silver crown.

Sasha arrived earlier than usual at Galen's little house, and there was no answer when he knocked. He couldn't imagine Galen was sleeping in; in fact, he struggled to imagine Galen sleeping at all. Whenever he pictured Galen, he was always working. He was tending to patients, cooking breakfast, running through the streets... Sasha was half-convinced that the man simply didn't know how to rest.

After a few minutes, Sasha sat down on the stoop in front

of Galen's house, flowers set down beside him. He tapped his knees and whistled a bit, waiting and looking around the street. In the early morning, before Candiru Quarter really woke up and began its bustling, it was quite peaceful. He could smell the bakery that gave Muffin his name. There were even a few birds twittering above him.

The streets here weren't made of the smooth, flawless stone that he was accustomed to up in Medaka and other high districts. They were patched together, not nearly as perfect. He imagined that a carriage ride through Candiru Quarter would be incredibly painful without the proper cushions. But there was something rather charming about it. The stones were smoothed down, still, by the thousands of feet that made their way over the streets every day. There was something so comfortably human about it.

Sasha was thinking about this, resting his chin on a propped-up hand, when he noticed that weeds were sprouting up between the cobblestones in front of Galen's house. They were yellow flowers, just as bright as Galen's healer's tunic, surrounded by spiky green leaves. Dandelions. If left to fester, they'd soon spread all over.

Sasha sat up straighter. It was a bit surprising that Galen hadn't taken care of these already. A devotee of the Lady of Flowers surely knew the damage that weeds could cause, but then again, Galen likely didn't have time. Lion's teeth, the man barely had time to say his prayers; of course he wouldn't have time to weed. Well, Sasha could help with that.

Sasha didn't know much about gardening, but he figured that even he couldn't mess up pulling weeds too badly. He knelt and started pulling near the base of the stem. The first one he ended up just picking, leaving the roots below. He knew that was wrong. The next one he tugged out more carefully and he was victorious. Sasha smiled. He couldn't help imagining Galen's gratified surprise.

He had been working for a while, perhaps ten minutes, when he heard footsteps approaching. He sat up and was surprised to see Galen, already dressed and ready, holding a basket filled with baked goods. Sasha grinned at him, but Galen's face was horror-struck.

"What—" Galen choked on the word and had to try again. "Mister Rider, what are you doing? What have you done?"

Sasha's brow furrowed; Galen was shaking, and the blood had drained from his face. Sasha stood, carefully, and held up his hands, trying to show that he meant no harm.

"I was weeding?" Sasha said, and it came out as far more of a question than he meant it to be.

Galen swallowed, setting down the basket and folding his arms in front of himself. "I am going to give you the benefit of the doubt. I'm guessing you didn't know that the Lady's followers don't weed wildflowers."

Dumbstruck, Sasha shook his head. Galen rubbed the bridge of his nose and sighed. He muttered something softly to himself before making eye contact with Sasha again.

"I'm sorry," Sasha said, though, truthfully, he didn't feel as though it warranted this reaction. "I didn't know. But, well, they're just dandelions, right? They're weeds."

"Wildflowers," Galen corrected. "Dandelions happen to be my favorite, and I felt blessed that a few had started growing here."

Sasha opened his mouth, then shut it again, before saying, "Dandelions? Really?"

Galen bit his lip and looked up at Sasha. "Really."

"But they're weeds," Sasha said, placing his hands on his hips.

Galen suddenly laughed, shaking his head, before he said, "Are you really going to argue with a devotee of the Lady of Flowers about what is and isn't a flower?"

Sasha felt heat rise in his cheeks, and then he really did feel sorry. He glanced down at the pile of ruined dandelions and bit the inside of his cheek in frustration. Once again, he had made an ass of himself.

"No," he said, looking back at Galen. "No, I'm not. Sorry, I thought I was being helpful."

Galen's eyes softened a bit then, and he stepped closer to Sasha. Sasha held his breath for a moment, but the healer stooped down to pick up the dandelion corpses. He held them almost reverently before he walked to the side of the house and dropped them into a barrel. He picked up his basket and then spotted the bundle of flowers that rested before his door, eyes wide.

"Oh, you didn't need to—" Galen started, his large hazel eyes wide in surprise.

"I know," Sasha said, trying to smile. "I wanted to. I have a lot that I need to make up for. That's what I was trying to do with the weeding."

Galen bent and scooped up the bouquet, which made unlocking his door a bit of a balancing act. Sasha hovered awkwardly, trying to figure out the best way to help, but the door was open before he managed it.

Galen slipped inside and set the basket on the table, then started to search for another vase while Sasha lingered awkwardly in the doorway. It wasn't until he saw a flash of blue and white fur in the corner of his eye that Sasha finally stepped in, slamming the door behind himself. Galen jumped and nearly dropped the vase. He looked at Sasha, eyes wide again.

"I'm sorry if you're angry," Galen said, frowning at him, "but please don't slam my door."

"What?" Sasha shook his head. "No, I'm not angry. Sorry, Muffin was making a run for the open door."

"Oh," Galen said, turning his attention back to the flowers. "All right."

Sasha rubbed the back of his neck and moved towards the kitchen. "Uh, where were you this morning? I knocked, but I assumed you were still asleep. Because it's early, you know."

Galen looked at Sasha with a bit of a smirk, then down at the basket of bread, and then back at Sasha. He finished with the flowers, setting them in the middle of the table instead of the already-full windowsill, then started to unpack his basket. It was nothing fancy, just well-baked bread, but it smelled heavenly.

"I didn't get a chance to visit Adrian on my rest day," Galen said, a small smile playing on his lips. "I usually do, but, well, there were some other things happening. I had to go this morning. Don't worry, Mister Rider, it was just a few doors down. I was perfectly safe."

"Adrian?" Sasha asked, lifting a brow. "Who is that? Is that your swain?"

Sasha didn't really need to ask this. It didn't matter if Galen had a lover or a partner, and it certainly didn't matter if Galen went to see him in the morning. That was none of Sasha's business, truly, but Sasha still wanted to know, though he wasn't sure why he wanted to know.

"My...?" Galen asked, clearly bewildered, before suddenly barking a laugh. "Oh, no. No, no, no. Adrian is the baker. He lives just a few doors down. He sells me bread at a discount because, you know, I'm a healer and a devotee. I don't have time for a swain, Mister Rider."

Sasha didn't understand why that relieved him so much.

"We're back to Mister Rider, then?" Sasha asked, leaning against the table and smirking.

He had meant it as a joke, but Galen suddenly looked stricken and said, "Oh, right. Sasha. I apologize. I just slipped into it again. I was just a bit shocked to see you—"

"Pulling up your flowers?" Sasha finished for him.

Galen nodded, watching his fingers trace the grain of the

beat-up little kitchen table. Sasha sighed and sat down. After a moment, Galen did the same, sitting across from Sasha, the unscarred half of his face hidden by the flowers that acted as a centerpiece. Galen folded his hands and took a deep breath.

"I am sorry," Sasha said, tapping his fingers on the table. "I didn't know. In my mother's garden, she always pulls up dandelions. I thought I was helping."

"I know, and yes, most people do pull them up," Galen said. He rested his cheek in his hand, and suddenly his whole face was gone, hidden behind a wall of yellow. "Dandelions mean a lot to me, you know?"

Sasha huffed out a small burst of laughter. "Is that the 'language of flowers' thing again?"

Galen chuckled and said, "Something like that. Dandelions are very resilient. They grow no matter where they end up; they push through cracks or burst up in gardens. Some people think they're weeds, and do their best to eradicate them, but they always come back."

His face was hidden, but Sasha could picture the determination on it, just like when Galen called him out in front of his house. Eyes bright, face set, and words steady. Sasha could only think of one other person who had ever projected such certainty that they were right and just, and been correct about it.

"Dandelions," Galen continued, "never give up. Even when things are hard, or when it seems impossible to keep growing, they do it anyway. We see those bright yellow petals blooming on the streets year after year. They remind me of Candiru, to be honest."

Sasha smiled a bit, turning Galen's words over and over in his mind like a worry stone. Suddenly, he leaned forward and pushed the vase aside so that he could make eye contact. Galen blinked at him.

"There you are," Sasha said, his voice much softer than he intended.

Galen met his eyes, and Sasha took a moment to take him in. His eyes, though determined, were so tired. There were bags under them and exhaustion weighed on his shoulders like a rock. His hair was mussed, a few strands escaping from the knot and hanging in front of his face, but he was still here. Still ready to keep going.

Sasha smiled and rested his cheek on his hand. "You're rather like a dandelion yourself. Very resilient and determined."

To Sasha's utter surprise, color bloomed in Galen's cheek. He sat up and looked at Sasha with a furrowed brow, trying to work something out. Sasha chuckled then, hoping to break the tension, and stood to start making the tea.

"I mean, you wear their color every day, anyway," Sasha said, glancing over his shoulder and grinning. "Same horrible yellow."

Galen scoffed, then laughed, and said, "Right, just when I thought you were being rather contemplative."

Sasha laughed heartily, then said, "Please, thinking and I rarely go together. That's why I'm always in so much trouble."

Galen shook his head with a smile, then stood as well and started to gather things for breakfast. "Come on, then. We have a long day ahead of us."

Sasha set the water to boil and asked under his breath, "What else is new?"

Chapter 14

Checking Up

Galen

Galen was surprised that they managed to leave the house on time. He looked a bit mournfully down at his dandelion-less steps as they exited, but there was nothing to be done about it now. The flowers would come back eventually. Dandelions always came back.

Sasha walked behind him, seeming lost in thought. Galen kept glancing back at him, mulling the surprising sincerity in Sasha's voice when he compared Galen to a dandelion and the strange way his heart skipped when Sasha said, 'There you are.' A large, strong hand yanked him back, breaking into his reverie.

Galen stumbled, then nearly cried out as a cart hurtled by in front of him, exactly where he had been standing. Galen shook off his shock just in time to hear Sasha shouting after the cart while gripping Galen's arm tightly. Galen looked up. Sasha's face was flushed and he was still spewing obscenities. Why was that so comforting? Sasha stopped as the cart rounded a corner, then looked down and quickly released Galen's arm.

"Sorry," Sasha said, brushing the spot he had been

gripping. "Are you all right? I didn't think I would have time to shout. That ass was going far too fast for a place where people walk. Lion's teeth, he could have killed someone. You are all right, right?"

Galen nodded, and said, "Yes, yes. I'm fine. Thank you. Sorry, I was a bit lost in thought."

"That's fine," Sasha said, shaking his head. "The driver should have watched where he was going. You were nearly run down. What was he thinking?"

Galen sighed and started walking again. "Upper district drivers. They have to come through Candiru sometimes, and they're always in such a hurry. Don't want the stink to rub off on them, you know?"

Galen glanced back with a smile, but Sasha was standing still and scowling. "He could have killed someone."

"Well, he didn't," Galen said, tilting his head down the street. "And we've got a long way to go yet. Come on, Sasha."

Sasha grunted and started following him again. Galen took mercy on him and explained that usually Candiru citizens kept a sharp lookout for those speeding carts. They were taught from toddlerhood to listen for them and move out of the way. Then Galen thanked Sasha once more for saving his life. Sasha seemed satisfied by the time they got to Nina's shop.

"What are we doing here?" Sasha asked, cocking an eyebrow.

"Oh," Galen said, nodding to Thomas, who waved them deeper into the shop, "we're going to check up on Mandy. I want to make sure that she's doing all right after those strange spots. Hopefully it won't take long."

He picked his way carefully through the pots that were scattered all over instead of in Mandy's usual neat rows. He could hear Sasha behind him, following the same path but even more carefully. When he got to the back room, he knocked twice, then waited, bouncing on his toes. He had to keep moving, always moving, because if he stopped for too long, then he'd want to rest, and he didn't have time for that.

Moments later, Nina opened the door. She looked very tired, but her face lit up when she saw Galen. She surged forward and wrapped him in a hug, staggering him back into a piece of pottery that nearly toppled to the ground. He laughed in surprise but patted Nina's back gently.

"Brother Galen!" Nina said, pulling back and beaming. "I'm so glad to see you."

"Good morning, Nina," Galen said, smiling back. He couldn't help it; her warmth was infectious.

"Is that Brother Galen?" Mandy called from further back. "Tell him to tell you that I'm fine! I'm sure the shop is a mess."

Nina rolled her eyes, which made Galen laugh, but she moved out of the way for him. Galen stepped past her to see Mandy, sitting up in bed and looking surprisingly well, not at all like someone who had been on the verge of death just a few nights ago.

"The shop is completely fine," Galen said, smiling at her as he walked in. "Not quite up to your usual standards, dear, but perfectly navigable."

"You see?" Mandy shouted to her wife. "This is what happens when I'm out of commission for a few days. The shop goes to the seven hells!"

"It has not gone to the seven hells!" Nina yelled back, throwing her hands in the air for emphasis. "It's just a little bit messy."

"Oh, a little messy, she says," Mandy said, crossing her arms and leveling a glare at Nina. "I'm sure that's all it is. Just how many pots and jars did you have to clamber over to get back here, Brother Galen?"

Galen laughed, shaking his head as he closed the distance

between them. "Not a one, Mandy. Your wife and your apprentice are doing just fine, and I'm sure you've needed the rest."

"A fine liar you are, Brother Galen," Mandy said, huffing dramatically. "And what would your elders at the temple think? A devotee telling lies!"

"I assure you, Mandy," Galen said, grinning, "I am not lying. May the Lady herself strike me down if I am."

Galen held out his arms and waited, counting to ten slowly in his head. Mandy waited as well, glancing up at the ceiling, over to her wife, and back to Galen. When it became clear that no godly wrath would strike Galen down, Mandy finally huffed her agreement.

"Fine," she said, still obviously quite annoyed.

"Now, Mandy," Galen said, opening his bag and sorting through tools, "I need to do a bit of an examination. I'm sure you remember being quite sick?"

Mandy had always been pale, but she usually had a bit of pink in her cheeks. That drained away as Galen spoke to her. She nodded solemnly and caught Galen's gaze with her light blue eyes. Galen pulled out his little notebook and opened it, ready to write down what he could learn from Mandy's recollections.

"I only remember bits and pieces, to be honest, Brother Galen," Mandy said. "Nina told me afterwards, but I mostly remember feeling very hot and very cold at the same time, though that doesn't make a lick of sense."

"Illness can feel very confusing," Galen said, nodding along and urging her to continue.

"Right, and it felt like my guts were roiling, you know?" Mandy said, holding her hands over her belly. "Almost like a living thing was kicking around inside. It reminded me of when I ate that bad fish a few years back. Oh, my guts weren't happy then."

Galen straightened and asked, "Did you eat anything off that day? If you remember, of course."

"No, that's the thing of it," Mandy said, shaking her head. "We, me and Nina and Thomas, we all ate the exact same thing that day. Except I missed supper on account of being ill."

"And neither of them got sick," Galen said, sighing. "Right, well, I'm going to pick your memory a bit more. You don't happen to remember any odd characters in the shop that day, do you?"

"Odd characters?" Mandy asked, scrunching her face in thought. "Well, Miss Kingley and her gaggle of children came round, they always near give me a heart attack. Running around the crockery like they do."

"No, that's not quite what I meant," Galen said. "More like, strangers. People you haven't seen in the city before."

Mandy thought, and started to say, "Oh! There was—"

Nina interrupted with a shout. "Does he really, truly need to be here?"

Galen turned from his writing and saw Nina, her hand thrust towards Sasha, who was leaning quite innocently against the wall with his arms crossed. Sasha blinked in surprise for a moment before realization dawned. Galen fought off a wince. The things that Sasha had said to Nina when they were here just a few days ago had been quite cruel. Galen had been trained in the art of easy forgiveness, but most had not. Nina certainly hadn't.

To Galen's utter surprise, Sasha just nodded and said, "Shout if you need something."

He stepped through the door, letting Nina close it behind him. She looked just as shocked as Galen felt. It was odd having Sasha trust him. But this was part of it, wasn't it? This was Sasha trying to do better. His gaze met Nina's, and she laughed a bit.

"I'm shocked that worked," Nina said, not lowering her voice in the slightest, ensuring that Sasha would hear her. "Way he was a few nights back, I wouldn't have thought that Lion in Glory himself could have dragged him out of the room. Right bastard, that man."

"We had a heart-to-heart," Galen said, letting a small smile grow on his face. "I think he's working on it."

Nina laughed in a way that clearly indicated that she'd believe it when she saw it, but said, "Good. The world's got enough bastards in it without one personally assigned to make your life hell, Brother Galen."

"I don't think it's quite as bad as all that," Galen said, shrugging. "I do think he's sorry for what he said to you last time. He knows that was out of line."

Nina snorted, and asked, "And what about what he said to you?'

Galen fought the urge to roll his eyes. He was fine. He didn't need everyone worrying about him when they had their own problems. He was there to make their lives easier, not cause any anxiety. He'd handle it himself, seven hells, he *had* handled it himself. If there was one thing that working in Candiru Quarter on his own for all these years had taught him, it was that he had to be resilient. Like a dandelion.

"Really, Nina, I'm fine," Galen said, then tapped his notebook. "Mind if I finish this examination? As much as I'd love to linger here today, I do have other patients."

"Right, of course," Nina said, her face softening a bit. "You'd tell us if you needed help though, right? Brother Galen?"

"Of course," Galen said, smiling at her. "And you've helped plenty. I use the jars and vases you've given me all the time. I appreciate them."

Nina smiled at him, but she didn't say anything else. There

was a bit of sadness in her eyes that Galen couldn't quite make sense of, but this was the second time that Nina had nearly lost her wife. It was understandable that she was feeling uneasy.

"Right, so, who did you see?" Galen asked, turning back to Mandy.

Mandy explained that she hadn't seen anyone from outside the city, but there were definitely a few customers from the upper districts. Occasionally, that did happen, but more often than not, those in the upper districts would send servants or runners to pick up orders, not come themselves.

It was odd, yes, but Galen failed to see any connection with the strange disease. Surely, if something like that was happening up top, he would have heard about it and been given a treatment plan that he'd have to modify to work for Candiru. Resources were plentiful in the upper districts, but down here, he'd have to make do.

He completed a physical examination, but besides a sore throat and a few bruised areas where the worst of the spots had been, Mandy seemed perfectly healthy. At least Galen knew how to treat it if it popped up again. It seemed rather fast moving, and it was unfortunate that using the gift was apparently the most reliable way to treat it. He could only rely on that magic so much.

"Well, Mandy," Galen said, standing and packing his things. "I'm clearing you as healthy and ready to get back to work as soon as you'd like. Just keep on drinking tea with honey to help that throat, all right?"

"Finally!" Mandy said, standing up as well. "I'm going to get dressed and see how big of a mess my shop is. Brother Galen, do come by and pick out something to take with you, won't you?"

Galen smiled, and said, "As soon as I get some free time, you'll see me at your door."

"So, we'll never see you?" Nina asked as she pulled her wife close to press a kiss to her temple.

"Now, that's not what I said—" Galen said, laughing at the identical incredulous looks on their faces.

"Might as well be," Nina said, sighing. "How many stops have you got today?"

Galen flipped through his book, winced, and said, "Twenty-four after this one."

"Galen!" Mandy said, eyes wide. "Rising Dawn, that can't be right. You're just one man."

"Just one man, doing his best," Galen said, smiling and holding up his hands to ward off their concern. "Don't worry about me, I'm fine. I'm used to it by now. You just focus on feeling better. Have a good day, both of you."

And before they could say anything more, Galen turned and rushed out the door to the next person in need.

CHAPTER 15

THE KIPPER AND THE HERRING

SASHA

GALEN LOOKED A BIT OVERWHELMED WHEN HE LEFT the back room of the pottery shop, but he didn't slow down. "Galen!" Sasha called as the devotee stepped out into the street, his eyes fixed on the little journal he always had with him.

Sasha had been standing awkwardly, trying not to disturb any of the precariously placed vessels, and had to scramble to follow Galen. He nearly knocked down a large pot in the process, but between Sasha and Thomas, it was saved.

When he finally reached the door, Galen was vanishing into the swell of people now out and about in Candiru Quarter. Sasha grunted in frustration and attempted to push his way through the crowd, trying to keep the flash of yellow tunic in his sight. Normally, the buffer around Galen made walking through the streets a bit easier. It was still speeding the little healer on his way, but without that deference, Sasha had to fight through the never-ending stream of people on their way to work, to shop, to visit friends, none of whom cared for a single guard trying to push through.

The uneven streets made things even harder; he tripped over the cobbles a few times. The abrupt shifts of incline from steep to gentle and back to steep made his footing unsteady. He was stumbling as he searched desperately for that bright dandelion in a crowd of tans and browns. By now, he should know Candiru Quarter better, but he didn't. He had been too focused on the wrong thing, and it was coming back to bite him. The Lady of Flowers and Lion in Glory must be having a fine laugh at his expense.

Sasha was continuing his fruitless chase when someone grabbed his wrist. He spun around violently, ready to attack, but stopped himself upon seeing Jess. They were wearing all dark colors except for the bright orange bandanna around their neck. Their long braid swung as they backed up, holding their hands up with a cheeky grin.

"Well, hey there, herring. You lost?" Jess asked, eyes dancing with unvoiced laughter.

Irritation rose like bile in Sasha's throat, but he bit it back. This was Galen's friend. They had threatened him with a knife the day before, but he could find it in his heart to be civil. He clenched his teeth to avoid saying something he'd regret and gave them one firm nod.

Jess's grin grew positively feline, and they said, "Thought so. You're missing Flower Boy. Can't very well do your job of hovering over him like a gargoyle when you've got yourself stuck on the busiest street in Candiru."

Sasha's self-control slipped and he rolled his eyes. "I don't hover over him like a gargoyle."

Jess snorted. "You most certainly do."

"No, I don't." Sasha's voice cracked with frustration.

Jess's eyes practically glittered as they latched onto a game. "Yes, you do."

"I don't have time for this," Sasha said, turning away from

the Kipper and starting to pick his way through the crowd again.

Moments later, Jess was back, looping their arm through Sasha's and saying, "Ah, come on, don't be like that, herring."

Sasha grunted at them, which only made them laugh. However, with Jess leading him, walking was much easier. Sasha was able to make his way through the crowd without pushing up against people. He glanced down at Jess in surprise, and they rewarded him with another catlike grin.

"Do you know where you're going?" Jess asked.

Sasha shook his head. "I normally just follow Brother Galen, but he was in a bit of a rush, and we got separated."

"Mmm," Jess hummed, nodding solemnly. "Yeah, I know he's got a lot on his plate. Don't hold it against him, yeah?"

"I wasn't planning to," Sasha grumbled, looking back down the street and searching for yellow. But for all he knew, Galen was already with his next patient, and then he'd never find him. Sasha was going to get in so much trouble for this.

"Don't worry, herring," Jess said, patting his arm condescendingly. "We'll find him. Just give me a moment."

Jess whistled sharply. Surprised by the sound, Sasha flinched. A few moments later, another young person dressed in black and sporting an orange bandanna appeared. He grinned at Jess and Sasha, revealing a few missing teeth.

"Danny, go find out where Brother Galen's at, will you?" Jess said, voice suddenly far less playful. "Then come back and tell me."

"Gotcha," Danny said, wiping his nose on his sleeve. He was perhaps younger than Sasha had first thought. "Is someone hurt?"

"Nah," Jess said, giving the boy a smile. "I just need to get this lost hanging herring back where he belongs."

Danny snorted a laugh, gave Jess a mock salute, and disappeared back into the throng. Jess laughed to themself and continued leading Sasha down the street. Sasha let himself be led but huffed out through his nose.

"What?" Jess asked. "You have a problem?"

"Wouldn't it make more sense for us to stand still so he can find us again?" Sasha asked, glancing down at Jess.

"Don't worry, he'll be able to find us," Jess said, laughing. "He'd have a harder time finding me if I stood still, to be honest. We're always on the move down here."

"Fine, whatever," Sasha said, looking forward again at the waves of people. "You'd know better than me."

"So very grumpy," Jess said, their voice mocking but jovial. "Just what *is* your problem?"

"Nothing," Sasha said.

"Sure," Jess said, snorting again. "And I've got a job in the governor's palace."

"I don't need to explain myself to you, you stupid little—" Sasha grumbled, and then Jess stopped abruptly.

Sasha turned to look at them, and their glare was sharp and deadly. Sasha nearly staggered back from it. Jess crossed their arms in front of their chest and looked up at Sasha with enough fire in their eyes to set the city ablaze.

"Let's get one thing straight, Sasha Rider. I don't have to help you. In fact, I'd rather not help you," Jess said, words flung like daggers. "Galen seems to believe that you're trying to do better and be better. But the way you've been acting towards him for the past month? One fucking apology isn't going to fix that."

"Look—"

"I wasn't done," Jess said, holding up a finger. "Galen may have an abnormal tolerance for rudeness, but I don't. I'm happy to leave you here wandering the city until you lose your stupid job. I was doing Galen a favor, not you. But if you're going to be rude to me? Farewell, and bad luck to you."

Jess gave Sasha a sarcastic little bow and started to turn

away, but Sasha grabbed their shoulder. Jess whipped around, the annoyance on their face palpable and what little patience they had left for him clearly at its end. They lifted a brow, looking at Sasha suspiciously. Sasha took a deep breath and steadied himself.

"I apologize for being rude," Sasha said. "Being polite doesn't really come naturally to me, even when someone is being nice to me. Please don't leave me in the streets. I'll never find Galen on my own."

Jess placed their hands on their hips, looked Sasha up and down, tossed their head, shrugged, and finally said, "All right. Apology accepted."

Sasha sighed in relief as Jess took his arm again and started walking. Jess let Sasha bump into a few things, but Sasha kept his mouth closed about that. He deserved a few stubbed toes.

"Can I ask a question?" Sasha asked after a few minutes.

"You certainly can," Jess said, smirking. "Whether or not I'll answer it is another story."

Sasha managed not to roll his eyes and asked, "Why is it that Brother Galen is so busy? He makes at least a hundred visits a week, and sometimes even more. It doesn't make sense to me. I don't remember a devotee visiting when I was sick as a child."

Jess thought for a moment. "Where did you grow up? And don't lie, I know it wasn't Candiru."

"Medaka," Sasha said.

Jess let out a low, sardonic whistle, lifting their brows. Sasha rolled his eyes. Medaka wasn't even one of the rich districts. His family was just comfortable.

"Guessing you had a family doctor," Jess said, turning a corner and pulling Sasha with them.

Sasha considered this and said, "Yeah, we did. Dr. Hammerstone. They'd visit when we were sick."

"Right," Jess said. "Doctors cost money, right? That

probably wasn't a problem for your parents. I mean, if you lived up in Medaka…"

"No, it wasn't," Sasha said. "The only time we ever had a healer from the Lady of Flowers was during the plague."

"When it was the only option," Jess said, shaking their head. "Yeah, well, most people down here? We can't afford a doctor. It's too expensive when there's rent, and food, and taxes…if things are bad enough, sure, we might be able to scrounge up enough for a doctor, but even then, a lot of doctors want us to go up to the high districts to visit them, rather than coming down here."

"Oh," Sasha said, brow furrowing. "That seems…"

"Fucked? Yeah, I think so too," Jess said, abruptly turning another corner, nearly letting Sasha smash his face against a wall. "But the Lady of Flowers? They help for free. You just have to sign up, or have someone sign you up. And it may not be the fastest, but Brother Galen always gets around to treating everyone on the list."

"But still, there have to be some people who don't sign up," Sasha said, sighing. "It seems like a lot."

"There's a lot of people in Candiru." Jess shrugged. "More than you'd think. And Flower Boy, bless his soul, refuses to turn down anyone. His life would certainly be easier if he did. But he doesn't."

"Why?" Sasha asked, baffled.

"I really don't know," Jess said, sounding frustrated. "Maybe he believes he owes it to us for surviving when other people didn't. But that's not how that works, yeah?"

"Yeah," Sasha agreed. He kept thinking about how heartless he had been. If Galen really was so worried about helping people, how must he have taken Sasha telling him that he was doing everything wrong?

"Anyway," Jess said, stopping in front of a little door, "we're here. Galen's just through there."

"What?" Sasha said, blinking. "How?"

"Danny showed up a bit ago and I started following him," Jess said, grinning at Sasha again. "Learn to pay attention, herring. Anyway, nice chat. Good luck. Stop being an ass."

And with that, the Kipper dropped Sasha's arm and vanished into the crowd.

CHAPTER 16

ANOTHER LONG DAY

SASHA

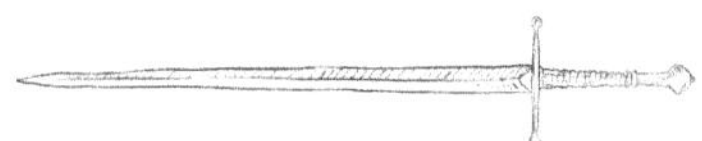

SASHA STARED AT THE PLACE WHERE JESS HAD disappeared for a moment before he shook his head and stared at the door. Just as he was about to knock on it, the door flew open and Galen rushed out—right into Sasha's fist.

With no real power behind it, it couldn't be called a punch, but Galen staggered back with a cry. Galen was holding his nose and looking wide-eyed up at Sasha.

"Oh, fuck, oh, Lion's teeth." Sasha pulled Galen out of the house, but was unsure what to do next. "Galen, I'm so sorry, I didn't mean to hit you. I was about to knock and then—"

"It's fine!" Galen said, waving him off and digging around in his bag. As soon as his hand left his face, Sasha saw that he had given Galen a bloody nose. He winced.

"I am very sorry, Galen," Sasha said again. "Lion's teeth, I hope your nose isn't broken."

Galen wiped his nose with a rag, then pinched the bridge and ran his fingers down the sides. "It's not. Don't worry. I think you'd need to actually punch me for that, not just knock on my face like it's a door."

Sasha barked a surprised laugh, then immediately felt awful about it. "Sorry. I won't punch you."

Galen grinned at him as a bit more blood dripped from his nose. "Good to know. How did you find me? I just realized I had abandoned you at Nina and Mandy's. That's why I was rushing out."

Sasha laughed again, rubbing the back of his neck. "I don't think you'd believe me if I told you."

"Oh?" Galen said, raising his eyebrows. "Try me. Come on, let's walk and talk. I've still got twenty-three more stops today."

Sasha blanched at that as Galen started walking, tucking his little book back into his bag. Sasha jogged a few steps to catch up with his charge and glanced down at him. His nose was still bleeding, and every so often, he'd lift the rag and wipe the blood off again. Galen hadn't seemed angry, but as Jess had said, Galen had an abnormal threshold for rudeness.

"I know I keep saying it, but sorry about your nose," Sasha said.

Galen laughed a bit, then said, "You've already apologized. Beating yourself up about it won't make it heal any faster. And it most definitely was an accident. You know what, make it up to me by telling me how on earth you found me. I want to see whether I'll believe it."

Sasha bit back another pointless apology. "Jess found me wandering around. They sent some kid to find you, and then they led me here."

Galen turned to look at him with his brow furrowed. "Is that all?"

"Yeah," Sasha said, smiling uneasily.

Galen shook his head with a smile and said, "That is extremely believable. Despite the front they put on, Jess is an absolute sweetheart. Of course they'd take pity on you. I would have been more surprised if you had found your way to me yourself. No offense."

"They didn't take pity on me," Sasha said, suddenly appalled at the notion. "They may have just wanted an opportunity to lecture me."

"And yet, they led you straight to me," Galen said, smiling broadly enough to show the little gap between his teeth.

Something about that smile made warmth bloom in Sasha's chest, and all he could do was nod. "I suppose they did. I know, I should appreciate gifts, no matter the package they come in."

Galen laughed again, then patted his arm. "That's the spirit. Now come on, it's going to be a bit of a long day, unfortunately."

That ended up being quite an understatement. Galen went to house after house, room after room, patient after patient. It was relentless. Sometimes it was something simple and easy. Someone had a sore throat that wouldn't go away, and Galen gave them packets of tea and honey. Someone had sprained their ankle a week ago, and Galen checked their wrapped foot and watched their progress in walking. Someone had a splinter that they just couldn't get out on their own, and Galen had to dig for it with a needle.

It didn't matter how small the problem was. Galen would still come into the home with a smile and a reassuring voice. Everything would be okay, he'd do his best to help them, and the Lady would bless them. The face he put on was incredible, and only Sasha saw the hairline fractures in the mask as the day went on.

It was only Sasha, who stayed by Galen's side, who saw the bone-deep exhaustion underneath the friendliness and the good-natured jokes. Galen would leave the house, calling goodbye to a patient and their family after handing out sugary treats to the children. For a moment just before he stepped out into the street again, on to his next assignment, it showed.

Galen was haggard. His eyes grew unfocused for a moment, his shoulders slumped, and his hands hung by his side. For a moment, his eyelids would start to droop as though he were asleep on his feet, but then it was gone. Galen would take a breath and then his normal, cheerful self was back. Sasha had never seen anything like it. And it worried him deeply.

After the tenth visit, the monotony had started to drive Sasha mad. He would just stand in the room, leaning against a wall if he could, and let the visit fade into the background as he longed for a break. He truly didn't understand how Galen did it.

He watched him, the gentle smile on his face, appreciating how he made every single person feel as though they mattered, even if their ailment was just a splinter. Galen's obvious happiness when someone thanked him or hugged him was very endearing. The appreciation always seemed to take Galen by surprise. It shouldn't have.

After the thirteenth patient, Galen rolled his shoulders as they left the house and said, "We're about halfway done, Sasha. I'm sorry, today's a long day."

"Not your fault," Sasha said, shrugging.

"Want to take a quick lunch break?" Galen asked. "Mistress Gladden gave me a silver crown even though I tried to refuse her. I'm buying."

Sasha smiled weakly and nodded. He hadn't realized just how hungry he was until Galen mentioned food. A rather embarrassing rumble emerged from Sasha's midsection, which made his face heat and made Galen laugh.

"Well!" Galen said triumphantly. "It seems like you agree."

Galen led him to a little stall where a cloth awning kept the sun off customers who bent over bowls of hot soup. He sat them down on wobbly, worn-down stools at the end of the counter and waved to the attendant.

When the woman saw Galen, she broke into a grin and rushed over to him. She was wearing a dress of a shockingly pristine white and a matching flower in her dark hair, which was tied into a similar knot to Galen's.

"Brother Galen, so good to see you," the woman said in a very pleasant voice. "How are you today?"

"I'm very busy as usual, Gwen," Galen said, smiling. "How's the leg treating you?"

Gwen laughed and said, "Very well, thank you! I don't know what I would have done if not for you, Brother. I'm usually not so foolish as to get in the way of a cart, but..."

"Accidents happen. I was almost run down this morning myself. I'm just glad that you're all right," Galen said, setting the silver crown on the counter. "Now, if you would, two bowls."

Gwen smiled slyly. "Oh, Galen, you know that your money is no good here. They're on the house."

Sasha watched the conflict on Galen's face, until the devotee finally said, "Gwen, no, I...You need the money more than I do. I don't have rent to worry about."

"Galen, I'm not going to lose my house because I gave away two bowls of soup," Gwen said, leaning closer to him. "Let me do this."

After a moment of an apparently heated internal debate, Galen sighed and said, "All right. Just this once."

Gwen grinned triumphantly and left to get their soup. Galen buried his face in his hands and muffled a disbelieving laugh. Sasha patted him softly on the shoulder.

"Think of it this way, she's giving back to the temple," Sasha said. "Giving you the energy to continue on today."

Galen rubbed at his eyes and said, "Right. Sure."

"You all right?" Sasha asked, pitching his voice down. "You seem really tired."

"You think?" Galen said, turning to him and giving Sasha the kind of look that Sasha's teachers would give him when he was being particularly frustrating.

"I do," Sasha said, nodding.

"Strange that," Galen mumbled before rubbing his eyes again. "Sorry, I'm just frustrated that I'm only halfway done. I'm going to sleep among the worms tonight."

"Mmm," Sasha said in response. "Maybe the back half will go quickly."

To Sasha's utter surprise, Galen leaned his head back and groaned dramatically before slumping against the counter again, folding his arms and burying his face in them. He made another agitated sound.

"Uh, what's the matter?" Sasha asked, baffled.

Galen sat up, just in time for the soup to come, and said, "You never say that. It just curses us to have a hard afternoon."

Gwen slid the bowls across to them, waving away their thanks as she offered them spoons. Galen stared at his soup as she left, sighing heavily much to Sasha's amusement.

"Oh, come on," Sasha said, grinning at him. "You don't really believe that, do you?"

Galen took a dramatic spoonful of soup, swallowed it, and said, "Just watch."

Unfortunately for both of them, Galen was right. The afternoon was awful. Each visit seemed to drag on forever. Either the patient had a thousand questions, or they were causing problems in their own unique way.

One man had injured his back the week before, and Galen

had told him that he needed to rest for it to heal. But he had continued to work, and it had made the injury so much worse. Previously, the man could get up and walk, but now it was so bad that he couldn't even sit up without excruciating pain.

Even worse, his partner was yelling at him for not listening to Galen, for going forth and trying to work with his back in such a bad state. Then the man yelled back at them, saying that they would have lost the house had he not worked, and back and forth and back and forth. Sasha had never felt so uncomfortable in his life.

Galen tried to mediate the conflict while massaging the injured man's back and rubbing ointment along his spine, attempting to persuade the man's partner to watch so that they could do the same throughout the week. Eventually, Galen gave them the silver crown he had been given earlier that day. Hopefully, the man would take off work to heal with the extra bit of money on hand. Before he left, Galen promised that he would send a speaker down their way to help.

Next came a young person who was so embarrassed that they wouldn't even tell Galen the problem for a good twenty minutes. Eventually, Galen was able to pry out that it was a venereal disease, which made the patient cry and flush so deeply that Sasha was worried for their health. Of course, Galen was composed and kind the entire time, even when he kicked Sasha out for the patient's privacy. Sasha left without comment.

The sun had long since set when they arrived at the home of the last patient, a woman with chest pains. Galen arrived and started the examination, listening to her heart and lungs with his strange little funnel. He asked her questions and listened along, nodding and writing things down in his journal. In the end, he had no real answers.

"I'm sorry, ma'am," Galen said, packing away his tools. "I'm not quite sure what it was. It could have been anything from something you ate to spending too much time out in the sun. And your chest doesn't hurt right now?"

"No," the woman said, her face stuck in a scowl. "No, it's fine now. But you're telling me that I waited all day for you to see me, and you can't even tell me what the problem is?"

Galen nodded. "I'm sorry. I am not a doctor, just a healer. If you are still worried about it, I can ask the temple to send a doctor. However, there is quite a long waiting list. We only have a few doctors working for us right now."

The woman scoffed and said, "More waiting! Really! That's the best you can do?"

Galen looked sympathetic, but also very, very tired. He tried to smile at the woman, but it was clear that he was worn down from the long day. He nodded and started to speak, but she cut him off.

"This is ridiculous," she said. "You know, I donate to the temple all the time. I make sure that you people have the money to work. But the one time that I need you, I'm let down. This is all so infuriating."

"I am very sorry, ma'am," Galen said. "I don't know what else I can offer you. I'll ask the temple to move you as high as they can on the list, but that's the best I can do."

"Of course," the woman said with an agitated huff. "Fine, if that's the most you are willing to do. I thought that you devotees were about helping people."

Sasha had had enough. "Hey, lady? Why don't you back off?"

Galen turned and looked at him in horror as the woman, whose name Sasha hadn't bothered to catch, gaped at him. "Excuse me?"

Galen raised his hands. "Sasha—"

But Sasha was undeterred. "He's been going since the sun rose. You're his twenty-fifth patient today, and tomorrow he's going to do it all again. He's exhausted and he doesn't need you screaming at him to cap off his day from the seven hells. Sorry that you had some indigestion, but that doesn't make you priority number one."

The woman glared at him, and said, "And what is your name? I ought to report you—"

True fear shot down Sasha's spine, but luckily Galen was there to save him, holding up his hands and saying, "Please, forgive him. He's not used to the long days yet. I'll put you on the waiting list for the doctor, all right?"

The woman looked back and forth between Sasha and Galen for a moment, then said, "Fine. Now, get out of my house."

"Have a good night, ma'am," Galen said, then pulled Sasha out into the street.

The night air hit them hard, but Sasha was still indignant. He fumed, crossing his arms and gritting his teeth as Galen sighed without speaking. Galen started walking up the empty street and, despite the late hour, it was clear that he wasn't heading home.

Sasha followed behind him and said, "You're really going to put her on that waiting list? After the way she spoke to you? What's the matter with you?"

Galen didn't answer at first, just continued walking, but then he turned and glared at Sasha. The steep incline put their eyes on the same level. He was clearly extremely annoyed.

"Sasha," Galen said, clearly choosing his words carefully. "I am very tired, so I apologize if I'm short with you, but this is what I do. I did not need you to step in and yell at a patient for me. I am not going to be flustered by some woman who was angry that I took a long time to get to her and is annoyed about a waiting list. I seem to remember that you were rather cross about a waiting list once as well."

Sasha felt the words like a dagger to the heart, and Galen clearly regretted them the moment that he said them.

"No, sorry," Galen said, sighing. "No, I didn't mean that. I am just very tired."

"I know," Sasha said, shaking his head. "It's all right."

"It's not," Galen said, folding his arms. "I'm meant to be better than that. I shouldn't have...Well, anyway. It's not just for her that I need to go to the temple, but I might as well take care of her issue while I'm there, right?"

"Right," Sasha said.

"I'm sorry," Galen said, again. "I just need a good night's sleep. I'll be all right."

Sasha nodded. After the temple, he walked Galen back home. As he left, exhaustion weighing his own steps down, he wondered how in the world Galen kept doing this without breaking.

CHAPTER 17

IT RETURNS

GALEN

GALEN HAD GOTTEN SO USED TO SASHA'S ILL treatment of him that this reversal took some getting used to. But it was, well, it was nice. It was nice not to have to worry about whether his day was going to be ruined by glares or awful remarks. No, Sasha had been true to his word. And he hadn't only stopped being mean; he had started being nice.

Sasha had made a habit of bringing him flowers, though after he ran out of vases, he asked Sasha not to bring them every day. And Sasha actually listened! He limited himself to only bringing flowers on rest days—wonderful bouquets, which Galen had to admit were nice to receive. On one such day, Sasha had sheepishly asked Galen about the language of flowers.

"Oh, well, it's more of an important thing with the growers," Galen said as he placed another sunshine-colored bouquet into a vase. "But all the devotees are taught it. It's fun, you know. When we were young, we could be a little snippy with each other without getting into too much trouble. Nothing sends a clearer message than someone leaving a bundle of thistles on your seat in chapel."

Sasha laughed and after a moment said, "Thistles mean back off? They are all prickly."

"They can," Galen said, leaning against the table and smiling. "It depends on the context. But if someone was, say, pestering you to sneak out into the gardens with them and begging for kisses, a bouquet of thistles would definitely send that message."

Sasha chuckled, sipping his tea, and said, "I can't imagine you were on the receiving end of any thistles, you're too nice. Did you have to resort to that at any point? It sounds like you're speaking from experience."

"Ah, no," Galen said, feeling heat rise in his cheeks. "You're right, no one ever gave me thistles, but um, no one was really ever inviting me out to the gardens or for an evening stroll. I helped a few friends steal them when they had to resort to that, though."

"That's hard to imagine," Sasha said with a snort.

"What? You don't believe I can be devious and break rules?" Galen said, mock offense on his face as he held a hand to his chest. "I'm hurt! You're the one who accused me of having criminal friends."

"No, not that," Sasha said, shaking his head and grinning. "I meant that no one invited you for a tryst, or whatever the euphemism was. Going out to the gardens."

"Oh," Galen said, feeling flushed. He turned his scarred cheek, the one that wouldn't show the blood gathering there, towards Sasha. "No, that wasn't really a worry for me. No one was interested in me like that."

"I don't understand why not," Sasha said. "But I'm sorry. Didn't mean to be rude."

Galen shrugged and said, "You weren't. Uh, anyway, the language of flowers. Great for love confessions. I can't tell you how many times I helped my friends steal carnations from the gardens. The growers have a well-founded hatred of teenage pledges."

Sasha laughed, and then asked, "So, you've mentioned this before, but growers? Speakers? And healers? What does that mean?"

Glad to be on more solid ground, Galen turned back to him with relief, saying, "Well, there's three paths you can choose among when you pledge your devotion to the Lady of Flowers. I know it's similar in other temples too. Lion in Glory has four paths, I believe. But, for the Lady, you can choose to be a grower, someone who tends to the gardens, a healer, someone who tends to the bodies, or a speaker, someone who tends to the hearts and minds. The Lady is really into tending."

Sasha laughed. Galen felt a smile tugging at his lips.

"You don't officially choose your path until you're eighteen, so you learn a bit from each. They all kind of build into each other. Like, I know about herbs and medicinal plants from my time learning from the growers, and I know how to keep my composure, usually, even when people are shouting or upset, from my time with the speakers. And that's why, even though I'm primarily a healer, I do know the language of flowers."

"And only speakers are priests?" Sasha asked.

"Right," Galen said. "They specialize in reaching hearts, taking confessions, praying, that kind of thing. I'm not the most, uh, diligent with my prayers. My specialty lies elsewhere."

Sasha nodded, then asked, "So, do the speakers and growers have gifts too?"

"Yes," Galen said, smiling. "Growers can help make plants, well, grow. And very quickly. Once, I saw a grower propose to her lover by making their favorite flower spring up from the plot they were working in. It was very romantic, and then she was yelled at for ill use of her gift. Speakers can do a couple of things, speak directly to the Lady, for one, and they can take confessions. Uh, by actually looking into your memory. It's a bit daunting, but it is helpful."

"I can imagine," Sasha said, sighing. Then his voice took on a strange tone. "Devotees can take lovers. You aren't all celibate?"

Galen snorted, and said, "No. That's only the Evening Star, and gods know why he requires that of them. No, I would have been in trouble long ago if that were the case."

Galen couldn't help but notice how Sasha's cheeks pinked, and his eyes widened a bit, and then he seemed to have to clear his throat. Galen bit back a laugh, and sat down across from the guard, fighting a full-faced grin.

"What, does that surprise you?" Galen asked, resting his elbows on the table and propping up his chin.

"I'm more wondering where you find the time," Sasha said, recovering and smirking at him.

"Well," Galen said, losing the battle against his grin, "before you came along, I didn't always have a babysitter, and I could find a bit of time here or there."

Sasha barked out a laugh, and then shook his head before saying, "Anyway, the language of flowers."

"The language of flowers," Galen repeated.

"Can you teach me?" Sasha asked, rather earnestly. "Unless it's something private, only meant for devotees."

"If it were only for devotees," Galen said, smiling and tilting his head slightly, "your flower vendor wouldn't know about it. But, sure. Maybe you'll find a creative way to insult me with it."

"That wasn't my intention," Sasha said, but luckily he was laughing again.

Good. Galen liked it when Sasha laughed. His laugh was low and rich, like his voice. It made the walls of Galen's little house rumble, and it was nice to hear someone else's laugh in his home.

It took a couple of those rest days to teach Sasha the basics, but then Sasha would arrive with bouquets that bore different messages. *You're too kind* or *You're a good friend* or *I appreciate you*—it was nice. Galen liked having someone who stayed with him, who didn't leave after treatment.

He found himself wishing that the governor had implemented something like this before. Not guards, not that Sasha wasn't doing his best, but another healer. There weren't many other resources in Candiru. There was an old hedge witch who would take on small illnesses, there was the midwife, and then there was an alchemist with questionable methods. That left most things for Galen, and it was too much for one person. It was no wonder that he hadn't had time for sex in nearly three years.

AT THE START OF THE FOURTH WEEK AFTER THEIR confrontation, when Sasha had been kind as long as he had previously been cruel, Galen saw just how much Sasha had changed. They were chatting as Galen steered them through the crowded streets of Candiru. Two months into his tenure, Sasha had gotten much better at navigating the masses of people but still wasn't perfect. It was good to have the little bubble that people left open for Galen as a cushion for Sasha.

The sun broke across the sky and beat down on everyone. Summer was coming, and the smell of Candiru would get worse when the baking heat brought it out of the river just beneath the district. Already, he saw folks with face masks and pouches beneath their noses to help block out the scent. Galen had left his cloak behind today, opting for just the bright yellow tunic. Poor Sasha still had on all his leathers and

Galen could see him sweating, constantly having to wipe his brow.

Galen was about to suggest stopping to pick up some chilled fruit when a panicked young woman wearing the orange bandanna of the Kipper Gang rushed up to Galen with wide eyes. Galen froze and turned his full attention to her, luckily remembering her name as she skidded to a halt in front of him.

"What's the matter, Fynn?" Galen asked.

"Brother Galen, I don't know if you can actually do much," Fynn said, grabbing his wrist and running, leaving Sasha to jog behind them, "but it's awful. The guards are here and they're clearing out Figlove Lane! They're kicking people out, arresting people, smashing up tents..."

Galen's heart leapt into his throat. Figlove Lane was near the bottom of the city and housed many, many people who had lost their homes for one reason or another. Losing jobs such that they couldn't afford rent, house fires, mold, any number of reasons, really. Galen went to Figlove Lane once a week to see if anyone needed anything, and the people there needed more help than most.

Sasha had, in the past, made his disgusted face when they were there. He had since softened and helped where he could. Just last week, he helped a group from Rising Dawn's temple move enormous crates of food to distribute there. They were just people, people in need, and if guards were there, that meant only bad things in store.

"Right, okay, I'll do what I can," Galen said firmly.

They raced down, down, down further through streets of Candiru until they skidded to a halt in front of the wretched street. Galen was appalled at what he saw. High guards, the top rank outside of the palace guards, wearing blue uniforms similar to Sasha's green one, were using axes to break apart tents and smash belongings. Their closed wagons were full of people crying, shouting, begging for mercy. Galen didn't stop as Fynn babbled about when it started. That didn't matter; it mattered that it stopped.

Galen rushed forward and put himself between a guard and a tent, and it was only because Sasha grabbed the man's arm mid-swing that he didn't strike Galen. Oh. Galen was unendingly grateful for that; it would have been difficult to explain why the guards needed to stop if he were bleeding out on the ground.

"Who's in charge here?" Galen asked, narrowing his eyes at the young man.

"Ah, you're a devotee, right?" the young guard said. "Uh, hold on, I'll get him. Sir Miller!"

Galen breathed in carefully as a tall, thin man with stark silver hair and a closely cropped beard turned at the name. He was wearing a crisp, clean navy surcoat, spotless trousers, and polished boots that gleamed in the sunlight. He could not have been more out of place amidst the chaos.

The young guard motioned him over and the man stalked through the wreckage of the camp, crushing people's belongings beneath his careless feet. Galen felt Sasha standing behind him, strong and steady. By the Lady, he was so glad that this was happening now and not back when Sasha hated him.

"What seems to be the problem?" Sir Miller asked and then looked behind Galen with a bemused smile. "Ah, hello, Rider. I heard that you got stuck down in the gutter. Got used to the smell yet?"

Galen spoke before Sasha had a chance to say anything, asking, "What's the meaning of this? Why are you arresting these people? Why are you smashing up their camp?"

Sir Miller's face took on an expression often seen on outsiders addressing Candiru folk. "Governor's orders,

Brother. They were blocking the street; that's against the law. It's disruption of the peace."

"Disruption of the peace?" Galen repeated in disbelief. "They were just living their lives. Many of them have jobs, families that they need to care for. I know these people. None of them are criminals."

Sir Miller smirked at him and said, "Well, they were breaking the law, which makes them criminals, Brother. Look, I know you devotees, especially your kind, have a soft heart. I get it. But if we don't crack down on this crime, nothing will ever change, and the city will just get worse."

"The people living on Figlove Lane weren't making things worse," Galen said, aghast. "You can't just arrest them like this!"

"We can and we did," Sir Miller said. "Sorry, Brother. It's part of the initiative to make the city safer. The same reason you have your guard shadowing you."

Galen glanced back at Sasha, then faced Sir Miller again and said, "They aren't violent. They haven't hurt anyone."

"Tell it to the governor," Sir Miller said, shrugging. "Look, think of it this way. What if a wagon needed to get through and all these people and tents were here, blocking the way? What if the wagon contained, for example, life-saving medicine that needed to be delivered posthaste? Would it really be worth trying to find a new route when there was a perfectly acceptable one here, just clogged up?"

Galen didn't like the insinuation that the people who lived on Figlove Lane were clogging up the city, as though they were the sewage beneath the bridge. Galen clenched his fists and gritted his teeth, standing his ground but knowing that there was very little he could do here and now.

"I will be talking to my temple about this," Galen said, glaring up at the man.

"Please do," Sir Miller said, spreading his arms open in a way that said *Do your worst. I know that you really can't do anything.*

Galen swallowed and asked, "Where are you taking them?"

"To Minuca Prison," Sir Miller said. "It's not a long sentence."

"But once they're out, they'll be arrested again soon after," Galen said flatly.

"Who's to say?" Sir Miller smirked.

Galen was about to say more, but he felt Sasha's hand on his shoulder, and the guard said, "Thank you, Sir Miller."

"Not a worry, Rider," Sir Miller said, then glanced down at Galen. "Hopefully you're able to transfer to a better assignment soon. Candiru is a dangerous place."

Galen fumed as Miller stalked away to continue tearing down the camp. He spun around, easily freeing his shoulder from Sasha's grip. Sasha stood there with a neutral expression, hands held up in surrender.

"Why'd you thank him?" Galen asked, outraged.

"He was going to try and find an excuse to have you arrested next if you kept going on like that," Sasha said. "Miller's a real dick that way."

"You should have let him," Galen expostulated. "Then the Lady's Temple would have had to get involved and fix this."

"If I had, who would take care of Candiru?" Sasha said, folding his arms.

Galen opened his mouth to reply, sighed, and said, "You have a point. This is wrong, though. Who is he, anyway? He's not a guard."

"He's a pain in my ass, is what he is," Sasha grumbled, then sighed. "He's an auditor. You know, trying to fix the city, find the problems, bury everyone in paperwork. He's been working with the governor for a while now, and he has all these grand plans to improve the city. It's weird seeing him out of the palace, actually."

"He's been the one coming up with all of the initiatives?" Galen asked, placing his hands on his hips as he winced at the destruction around him.

"Yeah, so, you have him to thank for me!" Sasha smiled weakly at his own joke before his face fell and he rubbed the back of his neck. "Look, you talk to your temple, I'll talk to my captain. She's more reasonable than Miller is. Maybe between the two of us we can do something to help."

Galen nodded, looking over at the broken remains of what had been a fine section of temporary homes in the street. The guards were piling the trashed remnants into wagons, likely to be dumped. Galen breathed in sharply through his teeth, and then quickly dropped down and started searching through the wreckage.

"What are you doing?" Sasha asked.

"Grabbing personal effects, things that can't be replaced," Galen said, picking up a sketch of a family that had been folded and refolded so many times that the charcoal had vanished from the creases. "I'll give them back once this has been sorted out."

"Oh," Sasha said, taking a moment to take in what Galen said. "Mind if I help?"

"Please," Galen said, smiling up at him, and Sasha joined him.

Fynn must have seen what they were doing and called for help, because minutes later there was a group of Kippers doing the same thing. Galen had to stop himself from laughing as Jess appeared and narrowed their eyes suspiciously at Sasha. But it was nice, and the Kippers brought sacks to help. Sir Miller and the high guards may have rolled their eyes, but Galen didn't care.

He was interrupted by someone from the locked wagons calling, "Please! Get Brother Galen! He's right there, he can help!"

Galen stood immediately, dumped the things he had gathered into the nearest Kipper's sack, and jogged over, saying, "Hey! I'm here. What's wrong?"

"William is sick!" a woman called, sticking her face out of the bars as far as it would go. "Something's wrong with him and it's going to get all of us in here ill! Please, mister guard, let Brother Galen take a look!"

Galen turned to the guard, pleading, "Please, sir, I need to look inside. I'm a healer. I can help. Please."

The guard seemed nervous, as though he had orders not to open the wagon for anything but also didn't want to say no to a devotee. After much hemming and hawing, he finally agreed. While he was debating, Galen washed his hands with water from his skin and readied himself to take a look. When the guard opened the back of the wagon, Galen stilled.

William, a healthy young man the last time that Galen had seen him, was on his side and coughing up large amounts of black ichor. What Galen could see of his skin was covered in familiar black spots. He was shaking, but Galen could feel the heat radiating from him. By the Lady, it was the same as Mandy. Galen swallowed heavily. He hadn't seen this in a month; he had hoped Mandy's sickness was a fluke.

The rest of the occupants had crowded against the back of the wagon, as far as they could get from William. Galen shook off his wariness and sent a quick prayer up to the Lady that there would be no need for the gift later today. He stepped close, laid his hands carefully on William's chest, and started chanting.

After a flash of pink light and the familiar warmth in Galen's hands and chest, William was back. He wiped his mouth, apparently not as far along as Mandy had been, and blinked slowly at the space around him. Galen called for water and Sir Miller. While they were being fetched, Galen took William by the shoulders.

"Hey, William, feel better now?" Galen asked, struggling to keep his voice calm and even.

William nodded weakly and whispered, "Thank you, Brother Galen."

"Don't worry about it," Galen said. "I need to ask you a couple very important questions, okay? Do your best to answer them, all right? I need to know this so that no one else gets sick."

William nodded and spoke barely above a whisper. "I'll do my best."

"Thank you, William," Galen said, smiling and gently squeezing the young man's shoulder. "Okay, when did you get sick?"

"Just a couple hours ago," William said. "Right before the guards got here."

"Right," Galen said, chewing on his lip. It was fast, whatever it was. "Did you talk to anyone you didn't know this morning? Before the guards came?"

William shook his head. "I didn't talk to no one. I was sleeping, I have a night job, you know. And then these guards came, and I couldn't stop coughing..."

One of the Kippers arrived with a fresh waterskin, and Galen handed it to William, who drank greedily. Galen sighed, putting a hand on his hip and racking his brain. He had asked the temple, and they hadn't found anything either. It had gone away, and he had written it off as a fluke or a freak occurrence, but now it was back. Whatever it was.

"Wait," William said. "Okay, this was weird, but it wasn't anybody talking to me, you know?"

Galen turned to him and said, "Yes? Anything you can think of."

"Well, there was this guy who like, bumped right into me when I was coming home from work. But it wasn't an accident, couldn't have been. Nearly knocked me right on my ass. And I shouted at them 'cause they didn't even say 'scuse me or nothing. But they didn't even turn around. But I remember them 'cause their cloak was real fancy, you know? Had to be from the upper districts. Probably nothing, though. Upper district folks are always rude."

Galen nodded, and said, "Thank you, William. Take it easy, well, as easy as you can, all right? I'm going to try and get you and everyone out of jail soon."

William nodded, a sad look in his eyes, and of course that was when Miller arrived. Galen turned around to face him, furious even though he had to look up quite a distance to meet the man's gaze.

"You need to take everyone out of this wagon and get a new one before you move these folks," Galen said. "There was an unknown sickness in here, and this wagon will need to be burned."

Sir Miller scoffed and said, "No can do, Brother. We've got to get a move on. So, why don't you take yourself back to do your job and—"

"If you don't listen to me, you will be in violation of the law," Galen said, keeping his voice firm despite the mix of anger and fear churning in his belly. "In times of sickness, or in the event of an unknown illness, if a healer is present, their commands must be followed for the good of Dragonet City. It's the law"

Sir Miller stared at him for a moment, scowled, and then said, "Fine. Fine, listen to him."

He turned on his heel and stalked away. Sasha snickered from behind him. Galen stayed and watched to make sure that the guards did everything by the book, which of course took hours. When that was finally done, he still had the rest of his route to complete, which took more time since everyone wanted to hear about what had happened on Figlove Lane, and then he had to go and file another two reports at the temple, and only then could he finally go home, well after dark. Sasha must be exhausted.

"Hey, well done with Miller," Sasha said as they got to the door. "He's a real asshole, but you dealt with him well."

"Thank you," Galen said. "Sorry about another late night."

"It's fine, not your fault," Sasha said, shrugging and clearly fighting a yawn. "That weird black spot sickness is back?"

Galen sighed, and said, "It was definitely another case today, but I don't know. It didn't seem that Nina or Thomas ever caught it, despite being right by Mandy. I don't know how it spreads. I told the temple, and hopefully they'll know what to do. And hopefully they can help Figlove Lane. Ah, it's just so much."

Sasha reached forward and patted him on the shoulder, and he said, "You're doing the most you can. No one could ask more from you, you know that, right?"

"Right," Galen said, looking at Sasha's hand in wonderment. Sasha kept it in place.

"Everyone here appreciates you, Galen," Sasha said. "Rest well, all right?"

"Thanks. Um, good night."

"Good night," Sasha said, letting go of Galen and smiling.

When Galen went in, he breathed in the scents of dried herbs and slumped against the door, closing his eyes. His fingers drifted up to where Sasha had set his hand earlier that day when he was talking to Sir Miller and again just now. Sasha's hands were so large, calloused from sword work, and comfortingly warm. Galen liked it when one of those hands was on him. And then, horrified at himself, he shook his head and pushed that thought away, locking it in a chest and shoving it to the back of his mind. He couldn't deal with that on top of everything else. And he knew better than most that nothing good came from thoughts like that.

FEELINGS

SASHA

SASHA WAS UNHAPPY WITH HOW HIS REPORT WITH Tracker went. He wasn't able to make it for another three days because they kept missing each other. It made sense; Sasha was out working with Galen past when most day guards had had their post-work drinks and were heading to bed. Finally, though, he managed to corner her early one morning.

All she could say was "we'll see what we can do" and "well, you know how it is in Candiru" and his least favorite, "it was the governor's orders."

Sasha, who had once regarded Governor Maple's orders as akin to divine proclamations, was about a second away from shouting "Hang the governor!" and losing all possibility of using his station as a guard to fix this.

Unfortunately, while Tracker lent a sympathetic ear, the other guards in the room did not. The fact that there even were other guards in the room was his fault; Tracker had offered to go into her office, but no, Sasha just had to have it out in the middle of the hall.

"Why are you bothering with this anyway?" Dawn

Horner, annoying as always, said with crossed arms. "Sounds like the high guard were just doing their job."

"Well, Dawn," Sasha said with a sigh, "it's because the people on Figlove Lane didn't do anything wrong, so, you know, it's not right."

"Camping on the street is against the law, you know," Andre said as he leaned casually against the wall. He had a cushy posting in a noble house. "And I wouldn't put it past the Candiru rats to be up to something in those tents."

Sasha didn't realize what he was doing until he had already done it and Andre was pushed up against the wall with Sasha's arm pressed up against his windpipe. He had been sure that he had gotten better at keeping his temper under control, but Tracker had to pull him off and give him laundry duty on top of his already excruciatingly long days guarding Galen. Andre accused him, jokingly, of having a "rat lover" and it was lucky that Tracker was there in between them; otherwise, that would have been Sasha's last day as a city guard. Even Tracker wouldn't have been able to keep him from being fired.

When they were alone in her office, Tracker sat Sasha down and said, "Lion's teeth, boy. What's gotten into you?"

Tracker was nearly sixty, so she had a right to call thirty-year-old Sasha a boy, especially when he was acting so childishly. Sasha slumped and ran a hand over his face. He hadn't been able to shave properly for days with how busy they'd been and his stubble was uncomfortably bristly.

"Sorry, captain," Sasha said. "I'm just a bit tired, and I didn't have a lot of patience for someone who's always done before sunset talking poorly about the people I'm supposed to be protecting."

"Well, actually," Tracker said, folding her arms as she sat, "you are only supposed to be protecting your charge. The devotee. Is that going better?"

"Loads," Sasha said, feeling himself perk up. "Brother

Galen is such a kind soul. He works harder than probably any other person I know. I still can't believe I was such an ass to him, but it's better now. We're getting along. I buy him flowers every rest day."

"You buy him flowers?" Tracker asked, a smirk on her lips and her eyebrow arching up. "That's interesting. You mentioned that Brother Galen was from Candiru originally? And that he cares deeply for the place?"

"Yes," Sasha said, a smile growing on his face as he thought about Galen. "And you know, he insisted that Candiru was not dangerous, and I didn't believe him at first, but he's right. The worst thing I've seen there was a teenager stealing from a market booth, but that'll happen all the way up in Lenok. I really shouldn't doubt him."

"Right," Tracker said, and then she smiled. "You know, I can probably find you a different assignment if you don't think you can keep things strictly professional."

"What?" Sasha said, brow furrowing. He had no idea what she was talking about.

Tracker laughed disbelievingly and said, "Oh, come on. Flowers? The way you lit up when you were talking about him? The way that you slammed Andre against the wall when you heard him talking bad about where Brother Galen is from?"

Pieces started to fall into place. Sasha could guess what she was getting at, but he was as stubborn as they come, so he crossed his arms and said, "Speak plainly, captain."

"There's no shame in falling for a kind man," Tracker said, grinning at him, "and I know that the devotees of the Lady of Flowers aren't celibate. I've courted one myself in the past."

Sasha's face heated, and he was sure he was bright red. His mouth fell open, then snapped tight shut. Tracker's silent laughter only made him more embarrassed as he gathered his thoughts.

"It's not like that!" Sasha said quickly. "Besides, you're the one who told me to get flowers!"

"Once!" Tracker said through a laugh. "Not every godsdamn week!"

"Well, I was doing it daily until Galen said he was out of vases," Sasha grumbled.

Tracker's smile consumed her face as she held out her hands, as though presenting evidence as plain as the sky above.

"Rider, come on!" Tracker said, her eyes gleaming. "Really?"

"I had a lot to make up for!"

"How expensive was that?"

"Not that...it doesn't matter," Sasha said, shaking his head. "The point is that I don't have, er, feelings for Brother Galen. He's a friend. They have all been friendship flowers and I had him teach me the language of flowers so I wouldn't accidentally give him a love confession bouquet again."

"Again?" Tracker asked, delight on her face as she leaned forward across her desk.

"Yes, well, the first bouquet apparently had an... unfortunate meaning," Sasha said, reddening. "But that's not important."

"I beg to differ," Tracker said. "That's very important to my own personal amusement."

"Captain, please." Sasha buried his face in his hands. "Stop. I swear, I am not in love with my charge! He's just been right about a lot of things, you know?"

"Who said anything about love?" Tracker said, her smile threatening to break her face in two. "I thought it was lust, maybe with a bit of infatuation, but it could be resolved if you took him to bed..."

"Captain!"

"All right, all right," Tracker said, chuckling and lifting her hands in surrender. "I'll let you alone. I think that was punishment enough."

Sasha sat up. "You're not going to put me on laundry duty?"

"Frankly, I don't know when you'd have the time," Tracker said, shaking her head. "You're out the longest of any day guard I know. And then we'd have no clean clothes. Speaking of, aren't you late?"

"Shit!" Sasha said, jumping up so fast he knocked over his chair then picking it up quickly. "Ah, fuck, sorry! Thank you, captain. I've got to run."

AND SASHA DID RUN ALL THE WAY TO CANDIRU. THE bells of Rising Dawn were already clanging before he even made it to the district. When he got there, Galen was already standing in front of his house, yellow tunic on and his medical bag slung across his chest. He was writing something in his little journal, swaying back and forth, fingers drumming. He didn't see Sasha pushing towards his door.

"Galen!" Sasha called. "Sorry I'm late!"

Galen's head shot up and a look of relief washed over his face, followed by his closed-mouth smile. He put away his journal and tucked a loose strand of hair behind his ear.

"Sasha! Good morning," Galen said, relief evident. "I'm sorry, we don't really have time for breakfast. I was about to set out, and I was going to leave you a note with directions. Is everything all right?"

"Yes," Sasha said, nodding firmly. "My captain just had to talk with me. Don't worry about breakfast, I'll be fine."

Galen had started walking, Sasha following behind him, and the healer turned his head back and said, "Oh? You'll be fine? Should I give this sweet bun to someone else?"

Galen pulled out a pastry wrapped in a patterned tea cloth and waved it temptingly in the air. He smiled at Sasha, and Sasha grabbed the bread from him with an answering grin. Warmth bloomed in his chest at how Galen had thought of Sasha even when he was the one making them late. But that wasn't as important as the slight buzz he felt in his fingertips when his hand brushed briefly against Galen's when he grabbed his breakfast.

"Thank you," Sasha said before taking a bite of the delicious bread.

"No worry," Galen said, brushing his hand through the air. "I've got a couple apples too, if you like."

Sasha grinned at him, and said through a mouthful, "You're too nice."

"On the contrary, I think I'm the exact right amount of nice," Galen said. "And did your parents never tell you that it's rude to talk with a full mouth?"

Sasha swallowed the bread down and said, "Oh, yes. If my mother found out about my manners, I'd be scrubbing the floor for a week."

"Should I contact her then?" Galen asked, laughter dancing in his eyes. Sasha felt his heart skip.

"Please don't," Sasha said, and he couldn't help imaging how much his mother would love Galen.

"Well," Galen said, smiling again, "since you said please."

They went along the route, and Sasha was a bit taken aback by how much it had changed since he first got here. They didn't need to visit Poppy anymore, though they'd still see her when they walked past Miss Kingley's place and were swarmed by children demanding candy, which Galen happily gave them. There were always new illnesses, new injuries, new aches and pains, and Galen was always there to care for them.

The one stop that never changed was Old Harry. As they moved down towards where the old man lived, Sasha could see

Galen growing more tense, the dread obviously building up in him. When they arrived at the bottom of the steps, the shop below the apartment long since closed, Galen paused. Sasha couldn't help it; he reached forward and squeezed Galen's shoulder. Galen's face broke into a small smile, he took a breath, and he started walking up.

It was the same as always, Harry being incredibly cruel and Galen just taking it. Even at the start, two months ago, Sasha thought this was disrespectful, but now? Sasha was barely able to contain his rage when Harry spit in Galen's face and laughed. After Galen was finally done, and was bullied again into using the gift, Sasha stayed behind for a moment while Galen stepped outside to catch his breath.

Although Galen had told him not to, Sasha didn't care. It was one thing for a one-time visit, but this persistent abuse was intolerable. Sasha was done with it, and he was going to put an end to it tonight.

"You really ought not to talk to him like that," Sasha said, which was the nicest way that he could say it.

"I'll talk to him however I choose," Harry hissed through his rotten teeth. "He works for me."

"Actually, he works for the Lady of Flowers," Sasha said, stepping closer and marveling at how acclimated he had gotten to the smell. "And being an ass to a devotee of a goddess is going to have consequences."

"What, is that why you started acting like he was some precious gift to the world?" Harry said, glaring at Sasha. "I know you wouldn't be bedding him, not with a face like his."

Once again, Sasha didn't really know how he got there. He had his hand fisted in Harry's shirt front, lifting the man half off the bed, and his face was inches from Harry's. The old man was glowering at him with all the vitriol in his body, which was quite a lot.

"Don't you dare talk about him like that, you absolute

waste," Sasha said. "He has been nothing, absolutely nothing, but kind to you and you repay him with this? I was a fool, but I learned. I want you to know that the only reason that I haven't broken your nose is because it would create extra work for Galen, and he doesn't deserve that."

"Well, aren't you a knight in shining armor?" Harry said, baring his teeth.

"It'd be better for you if I was," Sasha spat. "Then I would have more reservations about threatening a sick old man. But unfortunately for you, I'm an asshole. And I'm an asshole who happens to really like Brother Galen. So, be fucking nice to him, you cretin."

Harry curled up his lip, but said, "Fine, fucking asshole."

"Now you're getting it," Sasha said, dropping Harry back on the bed and leaving without another word.

Galen was sitting on the bottom step, the pouch of lavender held up to his face and his eyes closed when Sasha stepped down beside him. Galen stood, then offered the pouch to Sasha, who took it gratefully.

"What took so long?" Galen asked, sounding very tired.

"Ah, well," Sasha said, shrugging. "Guard business."

"Oh," Galen said, voice a bit distant. "Okay. Ready to head back?"

"Of course," Sasha said. "You okay?"

"Mister Balsin always leaves me a bit tired, but yes," Galen said, a weak smile on his face. "Thanks for asking."

They walked back through the streets of Candiru, the few streetlights now lit around them, casting a warm glow anytime they passed under one. They walked in companionable silence, and occasionally Sasha would glance over and catch the glow illuminating Galen's face. The gentle light was very good to him, and he looked warm and soft. A piece of auburn hair was dangling in his face, and Sasha fought the urge to tuck it behind his ear.

If only Galen would smile fully, as he so rarely did. Sasha wanted to see that gap tooth again, remind himself of just how cute it was and...Sasha cut off that train of thought. He licked his lips as they climbed the steps to the street that Galen lived on. It was perfectly normal and reasonable to admit that a coworker was attractive. Hell, Sasha knew that Tracker was very attractive, and he could admit that Andre had his charms when he wasn't talking. It didn't mean anything.

"Good night," Galen said, smiling, as they reached the door.

"Night," Sasha said. "Sorry about being late."

Galen opened the door and looked back at him with a shrug. "Sounds like it wasn't your fault."

"I suppose," Sasha said. "Thank you."

Galen smirked, and said, "For what?"

"I...I can't remember now," Sasha said, fighting a smile.

"Okay," Galen said, laughing. "That's all right."

Just then, a streak of blue and white zipped past their legs and into Galen's house. Galen yelped and Sasha swore, and soon they were on a Muffin hunt. For such a round animal, he was astonishingly good at hiding. They found him curled up under Galen's bed, and Sasha had to lift the frame up while Galen pried Muffin from the floorboards. Galen was clutching the creature to his chest as Sasha set the bed down.

"Uh, sorry about the mess," Galen said with a little laugh.

Oh. Sasha realized that this was the first time that he'd been in Galen's bedroom. It was surprisingly untidy. There were books scattered on a little table, dirty clothes strewn across the floor, mostly a cacophony of yellow, and trinkets and baubles everywhere. Though, after a moment of thought, it seemed entirely and incredibly Galen. Sasha smiled at him and took Muffin from him.

"No worry," Sasha said, holding tight to the squirming fox. "I'll see you tomorrow."

"See you tomorrow," Galen said, smiling back at him.

That smile struck him like an arrow to his heart. It buried itself deep in him and woke something he had thought long dead. He felt cold. He felt hot. He felt as though the world were spinning. Oh. *Oh.*

"Good night." Sasha was surprised that he was able to get out those two words as everything tilted around him.

"Good night." Galen's smile could melt the deepest snow; Sasha was sure of it.

Once Sasha had left the house and set Muffin down, once he made sure that the door was firmly shut, he looked down at the fox. Muffin was looking up at him curiously, tilting his head to the side with a small chirrup. Sasha buried his face in his hands and groaned. Flowers every week...the way he was looking at him...how he defended him... Sasha lifted his head and stared at the fox, who still had not scampered off. He probably thought Sasha had food and was just being rude about it and not sharing.

"Muffin," Sasha said, and the animal perked up, listening to him. "People think about their friends like that, right?"

Muffin tilted his head to the side, as if to say *Like what?*

"Like..." Sasha waved his hands through the air. "Like they're funny. Like they're attractive. Like they're...they're...."

Sasha glanced back towards Galen's house. The lights were out in the kitchen; he was probably already in bed, thinking that Sasha was on his way back to the bunks.

"Like they're wonderful," Sasha finished softly, looking down at Muffin.

Muffin was still there, ears perked, but he had started washing his face like a cat would, licking his paw and wiping it across his nose and cheeks. Noticing that Sasha was staring at him, the fox looked up and blinked in a way that said *So?*

"So...so..." Sasha said, then grunted with frustration and sat down on the ground amongst the dandelions that had started to return. "So, I don't know. We're just friends, aren't we? I can't go from hating a man two months ago to being…"

Sasha cut himself off before he could say it, but Muffin was staring at him with anticipation, as though the creature was saying *Well? Get on with it.*

"To developing, *ugh*, feelings for him," Sasha said, folding his arms grumpily. "What was I supposed to do? He saved oranges for me. He gave me a bun this morning, even though I made him late. He's so fucking thoughtful. And, Lion's teeth, have you heard his laugh?"

Muffin blinked at him, and Sasha read a lot into that blink. Mostly *Well, oranges and bread are much more normal things to give to friends than flowers every godsdamned week. And yes, I have heard his laugh. I've known him a lot longer than you have, you know.*

Sasha sat, his forearms resting on his knees, thinking. Whenever he did this, he usually regretted it, but he needed to do it right now. He needed to take out his heart, bitter, broken, and shriveled as it was, and examine it. And when he did, he found it warm and healing. He found that it had been tended to, whether he had liked it or not. And there was one reason for that.

"Muffin," Sasha said, partially to the blink fox and partially to himself, "I think I've gone and fallen in love. Fuck!"

CHAPTER 19

A New Blossom

Sasha

The next day, Sasha showed up bright and early and brought muffins with him. Muffins were safe. Muffins didn't mean anything. You could give muffins to a friend, and no one would question it at all. There was no language of muffins. Was there?

"Muffins!" Galen said with delight as he opened the door. "How thoughtful. Come in, we don't want an extra *Muffin* sneaking his way in here again."

It took Sasha a moment, because Galen had smiled fully for just a second when he had opened the door and his gap tooth showed, sparking fresh warmth in Sasha's chest. But then the joke registered as Galen's smile faltered a bit and Sasha burst out laughing, perhaps a bit too much and a bit too loud, but Galen looked happier. Sasha stepped in and Galen shut the door quickly behind him.

"Sorry, took me a second," Sasha said. "Must still be waking up, you know."

"Very fair," Galen said as he moved towards the kitchen. "I'm glad you weren't delayed today. I like our breakfasts together."

Sasha stumbled a bit as he tried not to read too much into that. Damn Tracker. Damn Muffin. And most of all, damn his stupid heart for realizing that what he felt for Galen wasn't just warmth. He quickly recovered as Galen turned to place the mugs on the table. Sasha set the muffins down and then looked for a way to help. Standing there, head moving back and forth between different items, he must have looked like a right fool. Luckily, Galen took pity on him.

"Could you put out the jam and the honey?" Galen asked, then smiled brightly. "I'm going to get the butter. It's a rare treat to have muffins at breakfast."

Sasha would have bought muffins every day for the rest of his life if he could see that smile again. Oh, *fuck*. Galen had apparently been extremely right when he said that Sasha could only feel two extremes of the emotional spectrum.

Galen disappeared around a corner and, after slamming the jam and honey down on the table, Sasha tried to get a hold of himself. He couldn't be acting like this. He had absolutely no right to think of Galen this way. Lion's teeth, why was he like this?

He had promised Tracker that he could be professional, that she had nothing to worry about. Ah, what a stunning end to his career that would make, though. So many strikes and disciplinary issues because he had a bad temper and a sour disposition, was difficult to work with and was rude to people, only to finally be dismissed because he made someone uncomfortable by falling in love. The Lady of Flowers must be taking her revenge.

Galen returned a minute later, triumphantly holding a dish of butter above his head, and it was downright adorable. Then he set it down on the table and motioned for Sasha to sit. Fuck, it was probably odd that he wasn't sitting already. Was it odd that he hadn't started eating yet? It was definitely odd that he hadn't touched his tea.

Galen set a dish with six hard-boiled eggs on the table and sat, saying, "Are you feeling all right? You look a little flushed."

"Oh," Sasha said. "Um, I..."

"Oh, not an insult! I'm just, well, I'm a healer," Galen said, shrugging. "I tend to notice things like that."

"I'm fine," Sasha said. As Galen gave him a skeptical look, he held up his hands. "Really, I'm fine. It must be the heat; it's getting warmer out."

Galen made a humming noise and nodded, apparently satisfied. It *was* getting warmer, but that wasn't the reason for the heat in Sasha's cheeks. They ate, and Galen complimented Sasha's taste, since Sasha had bought muffins from the bakery that had given Muffin his name. It was...it was nice.

And Sasha was definitely not staring at Galen as he chewed muffins or sipped tea. He definitely was not thinking about how Galen's hair, not tied back for the day yet, brushed his shoulders like a ghost of a kiss. And he definitely wasn't thinking about how that hair would feel between his fingers.

"Do I have something on my face?" Galen asked and then gave him a half-smile. "I mean, besides the obvious."

Sasha blinked, and then with a silent curse said, "No, why?"

"You were staring at me," Galen said.

"Was I?" He very well knew he had been. Fuck.

"You were." Galen laughed.

"Sorry," Sasha said, shaking his head. "I was spacing out a bit. Didn't mean to be looking right at you."

Galen shrugged with a smile. "No worry. Well, in good news, it should be a shorter day today."

"Oh?" Sasha asked and was slightly horrified that he felt disappointment.

A shorter day meant less time with Galen, which was the last thing he wanted. He would wander the streets of Candiru all day and all night if it meant being with Galen. The floodgates had opened, and Sasha was getting washed away in the tide.

"Yes, just four stops," Galen said, laughing and shaking his head. "I'll hardly know what to do with myself. We should be done before lunch."

"Wow, it's been so busy lately," Sasha said. "But that's good, you deserve a bit of a break. Well, honestly, a very large break."

Galen laughed again and said, "Kind of you to say. Maybe I'll get to go to the temple this afternoon. That'd be nice."

Galen looked a bit pensive, a touch of sadness on his face, and Sasha would have done anything to wipe it away. But, as quickly as it had appeared, it vanished, and Galen was back to smiling at Sasha.

They finished, and Sasha cleaned up while Galen tied back his hair and put together his bag. Sasha really was so upset with himself for how he had acted that first month, how childish and boorish and ignorant. It was a miracle that Galen was still friendly with him, and Sasha realized as he scrubbed the mugs that Galen would never feel the same way towards him as he felt towards Galen. And that was nothing but fair. He rinsed out their mugs and put everything away and was done by the time Galen was ready to go.

The morning went surprisingly quickly. All four stops were brief checkups with no problems. It seemed almost unreal after the many long days that Galen had worked, but they were done by lunch. Galen took Sasha to a little stand that served the oddest sandwiches, each one a single puffy piece of flatbread topped with meat and vegetables, then wrapped into a cone that allowed the filling to peek out. Galen told him with a smile that during festivals, they had a dessert version with cinnamon and cream.

"I've only had it a few times," Galen said, after swallowing a bite of his cone, "but I still think about it embarrassingly often."

"We'll have to try it at the next festival, then," Sasha said, promising himself that he'd buy Galen a dozen if he wanted.

"If I'm not working, sure," Galen said.

"You're always working," Sasha said, shaking his head disappointedly.

"That's not true," Galen said, laughing. "I'm not working right now."

"And how rare is that?" Sasha asked. "I swear, you work far more than any single person I know. It's not fair. Why doesn't the bishop station another healer down here? It's too much for one person."

Galen rolled his eyes and took a huge bite of his cone, then couldn't answer because he was chewing. Sasha sighed and ate his as he watched Galen chew on Sasha's questions as well as his food. When he had swallowed, he pursed his lips and exhaled sharply.

"Bishop Rose doesn't have a say in how many healers are stationed here," Galen said, staring at his hands as if he was worried about how Sasha would react. "I'm sure that she would have stationed a fair number of people here because you're right. It is too much for one person."

"Hey, I can be right every once and a while. It's not all that shocking," Sasha said, bumping against Galen's shoulder.

Galen chuckled and shook his head. "It's the governor who decides. She said that Candiru only needed one healer, but there are three stationed in Medaka alone. They each only work three days a week, and only one day solo. The rest of the time they can spend in contemplation or working in a garden or..."

Galen trailed off, looking far more tired than Sasha had ever seen him. It was as though Galen was holding a pile of stones on his back, slouching under the weight of responsibility for not just an entire district, but *his* district. His home, his people. Galen looked as though he could fall asleep standing up.

Sasha said, "Medaka is smaller than Candiru. I mean, not size-wise, but there's fewer people."

"I'm not trying to sound, I don't know, bitter or something," Galen said, finally looking up at Sasha, "but it doesn't make sense, does it?"

"No, it doesn't," Sasha said. "Why would she not keep more healers stationed here? And why doesn't the temple argue?"

Gale scoffed a bit before regaining his composure.

"The temple is funded partially by the governor," Galen said, shaking his head. "The government makes substantial donations to all the temples, and that's a big reason why we can do what we do. Especially for the Lady of Flowers. Those who rely on her the most tend not to have a lot of disposable income to donate. We have to listen to the governor's orders, or rather, we have to pick our battles."

Sasha remembered Figlove Lane, only a few days ago, and bit his tongue.

Galen was quiet for a bit longer, and then he said, "I sometimes think...no, it's a bit of a conspiracy theory, never mind."

"Oh, come on," Sasha said, grinning. "Now I have to hear it."

Galen reddened and took another bite of his lunch to buy himself time, but Sasha didn't mind waiting. For Galen, he had all the time in the world. Finally, Galen sighed.

"It's just that...Governor Maple is always talking about cleaning up the city," Galen said. "And you've seen what she means by that firsthand. Seven hells, she hired an auditor to help her do it. It's not just getting murderers and cutpurses and other criminals out of the city; it's clearing a street of homeless people or assigning a guard to follow me around and make my job seem dangerous and make it harder."

"I make your job harder?" Sasha asked, suddenly deeply concerned.

"Well, not anymore," Galen said. "Now that you aren't constantly glowering. But think about what most people here associate guards with."

"Oh," Sasha said, brow furrowing. "Oh, right."

Galen waved his hand. "They trust you now. Especially since the Kipper Gang went and told everyone that you like to give me flowers, and you helped with Figlove Lane. But I don't know, sometimes it seems like Governor Maple wants Candiru Quarter to just disappear."

Sasha was trying to fight a blush at the mention of the flowers, but he still shook his head and said, "I'm sure it's not that. I mean, she's not making the best decisions, but the governor wouldn't just write off that many people. She's the governor. She probably just doesn't know how bad it is. She's got a lot on her plate, running all of Dragonet City."

Galen was quiet for a second, then he shook his head and said, "Yeah. Yeah, you're right. That's probably it. Sorry, just tired, you know."

"Very fair," Sasha said. "You should take it easy today."

Galen nodded, and they both finished eating. He wiped his hands on a worn tea cloth and passed it to Sasha. As Sasha finished, a young woman ran up to Galen in an utter panic. Galen was, of course, immediately on alert.

"Brother Galen," the young woman said, grabbing his arm and tugging him along. "Please, come quickly, Angelica is in labor!"

"What?" Galen said, following behind. "But she isn't due

for another month! Where's Midwife Ariel? We can get a runner to find her…"

"That's the problem!" the woman was frantic. "Pansey Choplin's in labor too. Ariel is over there. Can you deliver the baby? Please!"

Galen blinked, but he nodded and said, "Yes, yes, of course! Come on, who's with Angelica now?"

"Charlie, her husband, you know," she said. "But Mother is out of town, it's just me and Charlie, and we didn't know what to do, and I ran all the way to find Ariel, and she wasn't available because you know, delivering another baby, but then I thought of you, and I came running and…"

"Relax, Susan," Galen said, calmly and steadily. "I'm here now. Your sister will be okay."

Sasha had been running behind the two of them, trying to piece together what exactly was happening, and that last bit of information finally slid everything into place. It obviously wasn't anyone's fault, but Galen's time off was vanishing. Sasha cursed under his breath on Galen's behalf. Had there been another healer here, Galen could have continued to relax a bit. Hell, had there been another healer, Galen could have had more than just one weekly rest day that was often interrupted by emergencies.

They jogged a couple of streets down into a more residential area. There were people hanging clothes on lines between the buildings, children chasing each other in the streets, and loud screams coming from one of the houses. Sasha nearly stopped in his tracks, but both Susan and Galen charged forward to that house.

"Oh, Rising Dawn alight, sounds like she's gotten worse," Susan said, wringing her hands.

"Don't worry," Galen said, and he rushed in.

Sasha followed closely behind but was struck by the scene before him. The home was half very neat and tidy and half in total disarray. Shouts and curses emanated from a back room, and of course that's where Galen disappeared to. Moments later, a very harried-looking man with tired eyes and a mess of red hair emerged with a sigh of relief. He spotted Sasha and gave him a puzzled look before realization washed over him.

"Enter at your own risk there, friend," the man, presumably Charlie, said. "I've been cursed to all seven of the hells twice over for being the one who got her pregnant."

Sasha wasn't sure if he was supposed to laugh at that, but he was saved by another shout. He nodded to the expectant father and went into the room. Galen was already set up, crouching to look between the woman's legs and talking soothingly to her. Susan was holding her sister's hand and doing the same.

"You're doing so well, Angelica," Galen said. "Keep pushing."

"It hurts! Brother Galen, Ariel didn't say it would hurt this much!" Angelica said, and then screamed again, squeezing her sister's hand like a vise.

Galen nodded and then made the smallest sound in the back of his throat. It almost sounded like he was worried. He stood and glanced meaningfully at Susan before nodding to Angelica.

"I think I know why it's hurting, Angelica," Galen said, and then with a breath, he continued. "The baby is coming out the wrong way."

"What?" Angelica bellowed at him, but Galen didn't even flinch.

"The baby will be fine," Galen said. "But it's coming out feet first instead of headfirst. It'll be okay, I know what to do, but I'll need a bit of help, okay? Mister Rider?"

Sasha hadn't even realized that Galen knew that he was in the room, but he stood straighter and said, "Yes?"

"I hate to ask you to do more than your duty, but would

you please get Charlie and bring a basket and as many clean blankets and towels as you can find?" Galen asked, his voice steady and commanding.

Galen looked back over his shoulder at Sasha, his gaze full of purpose. The exhaustion from earlier had faded away for now as the devotee blazed with urgency. The gaze sent a pleasant tingle down Sasha's spine.

"Of course," Sasha said, hoping that he sounded as steady as Galen did.

As he turned out of the room, he heard Galen telling Susan to boil water and bring it back as soon as possible. Sasha hurried and caught Charlie's arm, relaying the message as calmly as he could. Charlie gathered up the blankets and pushed them into Sasha's arms, then ran next door to borrow a basket.

Sasha returned with the blankets and saw that Galen had Angelica sitting up on the bed, breathing in quick rapid breaths that he was demonstrating to her. Sweat was running down her face and there were tears in her eyes as she screamed again. Sasha stood awkwardly until Galen spotted him.

"Where's Charlie?" Galen asked.

"Gone to get a basket, he'll be back," Sasha said.

"He had better!" Angelica growled out as she gripped Galen's arm tightly.

As if on cue, Charlie ran in with three baskets in his hands, "I didn't know what size to grab, so I got a variety."

"Good," Galen said. "The one with the handles will work. Now, you two come here, you're going to hold her up and help her stand."

"What?" Charlie and Sasha asked at the same time.

Galen seemed to be trying very, very hard not to roll his eyes, but he quickly explained, "It is a bit easier to give birth squatting rather than lying on your back, so it might help it go quicker and ease her pain. But because the baby is coming out the wrong way, I need to help guide it. That's why you two are going to be holding her up, okay?"

As he was speaking, he started laying blankets out on the ground. He finished by lining the bottom of the basket with another blanket and setting it in the center of the others. He dropped to his knees and rolled up his sleeves, placing his medical bag beside him. Then he looked back at the two stunned men.

"Well?" Galen asked, lifting a brow. "The sooner the baby comes, the sooner she'll feel better. Get to it."

Sasha and Charlie both scrambled over to the frantic Angelica. With Galen's directions, they maneuvered her to stand with legs apart, over the basket. Her skirts fell, covering her bottom half completely, and Galen sighed heavily.

"Mister Rider, I expect that you will respect Angelica's privacy, yes?" Galen asked.

"Yes?" Sasha replied, confused at what exactly he meant, until Galen reached up and tucked Angelica's skirts up into her waistband. Sasha blushed and fixed his eyes on a distant point in the room.

Galen continued to work, adjusting Angelica's stance and speaking softly to her, until Charlie asked, "Is the baby going to drop into the basket?"

"It's just there as a precaution," Galen said, his hands reaching up into a place that Sasha didn't want to think about, his voice still calm. "In all likelihood, it won't be necessary."

"But what if it is necessary?" Charlie asked again.

Galen started to answer, but Angelica snapped at Charlie, "Unless you are Brother Galen, I don't want to hear you speaking, do you understand?"

"Yes, love," Charlie said, and he fell silent.

In minutes, Susan returned with a pot of hot water and Galen gave her a few more instructions. She nodded and ran off again. Scurrying back and forth, she brought a strange collection of items: a dishrag which Galen soaked in the water, then laid across Angelica's large belly, another rag that Susan rolled up for Angelica to bite down on, and more pots of water as the first one cooled.

Sasha felt as though Angelica was going to break his hand and blow out his eardrum, but as he caught the rolled-up rag and held it out for her to bite down on again, he at least felt he was being useful. Her moans of pain went on and on, and Galen watched steadily, his hands moving. Sasha kept his eye fixed across the room, but he couldn't help but see the movement in his periphery.

There was another sudden shout, and a squeeze, and Galen sprang into action.

"Baby's coming, Angie," Galen said. "Okay, okay, you're doing so well, keep pushing, the feet are out! They didn't get tangled and caught, that's good! Keep going, dear."

And it went on like that. Charlie yelped once at his wife's grip. Sasha understood that but also was endlessly glad that it wasn't him who had made a sound. Angelica's glare could have melted a man. Galen's steady presence was probably the only reason things were as civil as they were. Her struggles went on for what felt like at least an hour, and it was exhausting for all of them. Finally, they were almost done.

"One last push! Come on, Angie, you've got this!" Galen cheered, and there was one last scream from the woman between them. "You did it! One moment."

Angelica collapsed on her husband on shaky legs, tears running down both of their faces. Sasha did his best to continue to hold them upright, feeling like he was invading what should have been a very private moment. But he supposed that it was better that than the two of them sprawled on the floor.

It took a moment of silence before Angelica lifted her head

from Charlie's shoulder in panic. "Why isn't it crying? Galen, what's wrong? Is the baby all right? Is it okay?"

"Everything's fine!" Galen called from the floor.

Suddenly, crying punctuated the air, and both parents sighed with relief. Galen stayed on his knees for a while longer, probably cleaning up the baby, before he rose, plucked another clean blanket up, and wrapped the child. He handed the baby to Angelica, who had tears pouring down her face.

"She had a caul," Galen said, smiling. "You'll want to take her to the temple of the Evening Star when she's old enough; she might have visions."

"A girl," Angelica said, her eyes glued to the new babe's face. "She's so beautiful."

"A new blossom in our world," Galen said. "The Lady of Flowers offers her blessings. Take a moment if you need, and I'll finish up with you once you give her to Charlie, all right?"

"All right," Angelica said, but she seemed utterly enchanted by the infant.

Just then, Susan rushed in, followed by another woman. She was round with gray hair that puffed up like a cloud and when she spotted Galen, she rushed to him. Galen looked at her, tired but smiling.

"So sorry, Brother Galen," the woman said. "How'd it go?"

"It was a footling breech," Galen said. "She had a veil. But she seems healthy now. How'd the other birth go, Ariel?"

"Smooth as butter," Midwife Ariel said. "Go on, then. You look exhausted, boy. I'll finish up here. Thank you greatly."

Sasha thought Galen would normally have protested, but he just nodded. He was covered in blood: all over his yellow tunic, his arms, and his face. His hair was a mess, and his eyes were utterly worn out and drained. Lion's teeth, it must have been worse than he was letting on.

Galen said goodbye to the new parents and aunt, scrubbed his hands clean in their kitchen, then stumbled out of the house with Sasha close behind him. They walked a few streets in silence until Galen suddenly turned down an alley. Sasha followed, confused, until Galen stopped and slumped with his back against the wall.

"Sasha, is there anyone around?" he asked.

Sasha looked around, and then said, "No."

"Thank the Lady," Galen said, then he slid down into a squat, pulled out a cloth, bundled it into a clump, and screamed into it.

Sasha jumped back in shock. Galen pressed his face against his knees, and the sound was muffled by the fabric. It was only when Galen had lifted his head and started muttering to himself that Sasha dared to move closer. What he heard nearly killed him.

"Fuck, fuck, fuck, fuck, shit, fuck, holy fucking shit..." Galen's profanities continued in a constant stream.

"I, uh, are you okay?" Sasha asked, eyes wide.

Galen stared up at him with unhinged eyes. "No! No, I am not fucking okay. I've never been so scared in my life! Holy fucking shit."

"I've never heard you swear like this," Sasha said, and he couldn't help the laugh that escaped his lips.

"Yeah, well, I've never delivered a baby before today," Galen said, raking his hands through his hair. "And fucking feet first and with a fucking caul! The Lady continues to test me."

"What?" Sasha was flabbergasted. "There's no way, you were so calm!"

"That's why all of this is exploding out of me now," Galen said, resting his head in his hands. "Couldn't have very well done it in there and scared the shit out of Angelica and Charlie. Fuck!"

"Come on, you must have delivered a baby before," Sasha said, grinning. "You knew exactly what to do."

Galen glared up at him and said, "I've *assisted* before. I've never done it by myself. Gods above, I thought I might have a heart attack."

"Glad you didn't," Sasha said, sitting down next to him. "You really were great in there, you know. I would have never known you were so scared. You kept everyone so calm, I was amazed. You were like this steady rock that everyone was holding onto, even when there was this river of panic that was going to wash us away."

Galen was silent for a bit. Sasha looked at him carefully. Even coated in blood and gods knew what else, even exhausted and frazzled, Galen looked incredible. What Sasha dearly wanted to do, which he would never do, was tilt Galen's head up and kiss him. At that thought, Sasha decided that he needed to go to a temple to do penance, or maybe his mother's house again, because how was he thinking about that when Galen was overwhelmed and distraught?

"Thank you," Galen said, a smile tugging at his lips. "That was elegantly put."

"Oh, don't act so surprised," Sasha teased. "I can string together a sentence well when I want to."

"I didn't mean it as a bad thing," Galen said, shaking his head. "Just, thank you. That was very stressful, and I'm just glad that the baby was okay. And that no one knew just how panicked I was. All right, I think I'm better now. I got it all out."

Sasha stood and offered Galen a hand, which he took. Sasha pulled him up and rested a comforting hand on his shoulder. Galen sighed and ran a hand over his face.

"I didn't even know that you knew how to swear," Sasha said, laughing.

Galen tried to blow the hair out of his eyes, but it was

stuck firmly there by all manner of dried liquids. He said, "As you may recall, I did say that I hear people swear a lot. It happens when they're in pain. Also, I am twenty-fucking-eight years old."

Sasha burst out laughing, and Galen joined him after one more moment of trying to be stern. He laughed until tears rolled down his face. Sasha stopped first, and ended up just watching Galen as he was lost in mirth. Galen's laughter turned into a snort, which just made him laugh harder. Warmth bloomed in Sasha's chest, and his smile must be vague and dreamy, but seeing Galen as this absolute embodiment of joy, he couldn't help it.

When Galen had subsided into giggles, Sasha asked, "Is there a bathhouse nearby?"

Galen snorted again, trying and failing to keep his unhinged laughter at bay. "Sure, why?"

"You're going to get cleaned up," Sasha said. "And then I'm taking you out."

CHAPTER 20

APPRECIATION

GALEN

GALEN DIDN'T KNOW WHAT HE HAD DONE TO deserve Sasha, but whatever it was, he was grateful. Sasha had insisted on the bathhouse, which he paid for, and Galen had to admit that he desperately needed it. He had felt gross and sticky, and worn out from the birth, and—after a thorough dousing by an attendant horrified at his appearance—he had sunk into the warm water with a sigh of utter relief. Luckily, he had another set of clothes to change into; it was wise to be prepared in his line of work. You never knew what you'd get covered in.

When he walked back out to the front of the bathhouse, his hair still damp, Sasha was waiting for him. He was leaning up against the counter, arms crossed in front of his chest and an easy smile on his face. It wasn't surprising that he hadn't noticed Galen yet. He was talking to the pretty attendant at the front desk, distracting them from their work, but they didn't seem to mind. They both laughed, and Galen's heart skipped a beat.

He had been getting along so well with Sasha, and he had been enjoying their time together. And maybe that's why when he saw Sasha happy, a smile on his face as if it had always belonged there, his breath caught. He thought of Sasha's hand resting comfortably on his shoulder and the way that Sasha would give him a smile or laugh at his jokes, and he knew it was all leading somewhere dangerous.

Objectively, Galen knew Sasha was handsome. It was no wonder that the bathhouse attendant was flirting with him; Galen certainly couldn't hold it against them. Sasha had a striking face, warm eyes, and a strong jaw, and gods knew that he was muscular and solid. But Galen had seen him without his armor, and he knew that he wasn't sharp like some people got. There was softness there that Galen would love to run his hand across and...and Galen needed to stop thinking about this.

Just as he knew that Sasha was objectively handsome, Galen knew that he himself was objectively ugly. He would have just been plain if it wasn't for the scars, but he had the scars. People sometimes recoiled from him, and if they didn't, they looked at him with pity. Pity and attraction didn't mix well. Just because Sasha was being nice to him now didn't mean that he'd want to be anything more than friends. In fact, Galen couldn't even imagine why he was thinking about this.

Galen didn't have time for romance; he didn't have time for anything. Not when Candiru was still suffering so much and no one seemed to care. It was his job, his responsibility to try and take care of that. He lived when so many others had died; he couldn't take the time to indulge in a pretty face, pleasant though the fantasy was. There was work to do.

Sasha's eyes drifted away from the attendant, and when he spotted Galen, he called, "Oh, you're done!"

Galen couldn't help but notice how Sasha's face lit up when he saw him. He couldn't help but notice how he pushed up from the counter and moved towards him, abandoning the pretty young worker mid-sentence. Sasha's hands flexed at his sides, as though he wanted to reach for Galen. But that was simply untrue. There was no way that Sasha felt any kind of way towards Galen.

Well, he knew that was a lie, because Sasha had felt an overwhelming animosity towards Galen, and then he had tried to make friends...maybe it was just respect. Sure. That made sense. And besides, Sasha was only giving him flowers because Galen was a devotee of the Lady of Flowers. Of course Sasha would assume that's what he'd like. And he wasn't wrong, but it made things a bit more difficult for Galen's stupid, confused heart.

"Thank you for this," Galen said when he realized that he hadn't said anything. "I didn't know how much I needed it."

Sasha beamed at him and said, "And deserved it. Oh, uh, hold on."

Sasha suddenly reached around Galen's waist, and Galen felt himself flush as Sasha's face moved right in front of his own, mere inches away. Galen stilled until he felt Sasha tug his tunic down in the back, straightening it. The guard's hands lingered there for a moment, brushing the small of Galen's back. Chills like the sparking cool of Muffin's touch zipped through Galen's veins, and he was mortified. As Sasha stood back to his full height with a smile, Galen released a breath. Of course, that was all it was, that he had been looking like a fool.

"Thank you," Galen said softly.

"No worry," Sasha said, grinning. "Come on now, what's the best local tavern?"

"You're not really taking me out," Galen said, laughing in disbelief.

"Oh, I definitely am," Sasha said, wrapping an arm around Galen's shoulder and squeezing, and Galen tried not to savor the warmth too much. "You deserve a godsdamn drink after what you went through today. Unless the Lady of Flowers prohibits drinking? That'd be odd, right? Sex? Absolutely fine, no problems there. Drinking? Hard line, not allowed."

Galen's laugh grew larger, and he rolled his eyes. "Yes, we're allowed to drink. You've seen me with a glass of wine before."

"I don't know if I have," Sasha said, walking him out of the bathhouse and into the street. "It's mostly tea."

Galen huffed in annoyance. Though, perhaps he had always waited until Sasha had left to pour a glass. And it had been more often in the early days that Galen needed a glass to deal with the feelings that Sasha had been giving him. Now maybe he'd need a glass to deal with very different feelings.

"Okay, well, I do drink," Galen said, shaking his head and smiling. "I suppose we could go to the Sparrow's Roost. It's a bit calmer than the bigger taverns."

"Perfect, lead the way," Sasha said, looping his arm through Galen's. Galen was glad for the layers of fabric between their skin. Without them, that lightning he had felt earlier would be too much to handle.

When they made their way there, it was less Galen leading the way and more Galen giving directions to Sasha as he practically dragged Galen behind him, hurrying through the streets. Galen knew it was easy to do; he was a lot smaller than big, strong Sasha, but there was a bit of indignity in it. When they got to the tavern, Galen was relieved to see that it wasn't busy.

Sasha nearly pushed him in, and Galen had to just roll his eyes and accept it. Moments after he entered the space, however, Galen realized his mistake. He was wearing the bright yellow healer's tunic and, upon seeing him, the patrons of the tavern froze. He recognized most of them and guessed that they all recognized him. The yellow meant something very specific to the people of Dragonet City: that someone was hurt, and he was there to help.

"Uh," Galen said, trying to think of a way to explain his arrival and failing.

"Do you need something, Brother Galen?" the barkeep asked, her voice steady but concerned. "Need some strong alcohol or anything? I've got plenty of clean rags."

"Oh, well—" Galen said but was saved by Sasha slinging his arm around Galen and grinning at the barkeep.

"He needs some strong alcohol, but for enjoyment! I'm making him take a break," Sasha said, flashing a charming smile at the patrons. "You all know even better than I do, Brother Galen doesn't take enough breaks."

Galen's face blazed, and he was about to duck out from under Sasha's arm and run off to find some malady to treat when a round-faced man burst out laughing and shouted, "He needs one! I'll buy you a drink, Brother Galen. If you hadn't set my shoulder, I'd be out of a job. To Brother Galen!"

"I'll buy you a drink too!" A woman with dusty brown hair lifted her drink. "You helped my Johnny get over that fever."

Suddenly a chorus of voices joined in, saying that they'd buy him a drink and giving reasons why, listing all the ways that Galen had helped them. Galen was overwhelmed. A tidal wave of emotion was forming in his chest, and saltwater started rising in his throat, threatening to spill from his eyes.

"Thank you, everyone," Galen said, and he was surprised at how the room fell quiet as he spoke. "I don't know if I'll be able to drink all of that. I am just one man."

A chuckle rippled through the room, and Galen smiled, then said, "Sorry it's been a while. I've just been a bit, well, busy."

"For the past decade, it seems!" a server yelled as she set a mug down on a table. "You're only ever in here to tend to bar fight wounds, you know. Or to buy yourself a bottle of wine."

"I was a bit too young for taverns before I became a

devotee," Galen said, and he could feel heat rising in his cheeks again.

"Oh, that's right," a man came up beside Galen and placed a hand on his shoulder. "You got working even younger than most. Come on, take a load off, Galen. Oh, uh, Brother Galen."

Galen laughed lightly and said, "If I'm in the tavern for fun"—he shot Sasha a meaningful look—"I suppose I can just be Galen tonight."

A cheer rose up through the Sparrow's Roost and before he knew it, Galen was being swept around the room. People kept pushing things into his hands, and Galen couldn't possibly hold them all. Sasha started taking them from him as his arms became full, carting them to a corner table, and then returning for more. There was a mountain of trinkets by the time Galen was finally able to sit down, not to mention six drinks.

"Oh dear," Galen said.

Sasha's laugh shook the table, and he said, "See? This is why I assumed that you didn't know how to swear."

Galen glanced over at him with an undignified snort, and said, "And what's wrong with saying 'Oh dear'? What would you rather have me say?"

"What's clearly just behind your lips."

"Which is?"

"Holy fuck," Sasha said, grinning broadly as he took one of the mugs.

Galen squawked indignantly, certainly not on purpose, and that set Sasha off laughing again. It was the same deep rumble that shook the walls of Galen's house and rattled his ribcage. Tonight, looking at the joy in Sasha's eyes, hearing that rich laugh, the warmth in Galen's chest spread through his whole body.

Galen tried to take it slow and easy, but every time he

finished a drink, two new ones had arrived. This would not end well; Galen had hardly had more than a single glass of wine in a night in years. He must have looked exasperated because Sasha couldn't stop grinning at him like a cat.

"What?" Galen asked, wiping away foam from the ale he had just downed. It was nearly impossible to slur just one word, but somehow Galen managed it.

"Nothing," Sasha said, his smile threatening to break his face. By the Lady, Galen loved that smile. It was full of mirth, without a lick of cruelty behind it. He wished he could smile like that.

Instead, Galen laughed and said, "Oh, I know what this is. You've just been pretending to be nicer this whole time. So you could lull me into a false sense of security and then get me drunk and make me make a fool of myself. I see you, I know what you're doing."

Sasha's smile plummeted as he stammered out, "No, no, that's not it at all. I really just...I thought that you needed a break, and after today and how stressed you were, I just thought that this could help you unwind, you know? I wasn't meaning to—"

Galen cut him off with a quick laugh, lifting his hands, and said, "I was joking! It was a joke. I know."

"Oh," Sasha said, immediately relaxing, the smile returning and his shoulders dropping. "Right. You do that."

"I do that," Galen said, shaking his head with a huff of laughter.

"But, hey, look at it this way," Sasha said, gesturing to the mugs of ale. "They're showing their appreciation."

"Sure," Galen said, rolling his eyes, but he couldn't help but smile.

He wasn't sure how to make sense of it; it was a lot. Apparently, word had spread that he was in the Sparrow's Roost, and even more people showed up until the small tavern was packed to the walls. A new patron would enter, spot him, and push their way through the crowd to clap a hand on his shoulder or cheerfully sing his praises, or even tearfully hug him. And always, *always*, buy him another drink. He was grateful that Sasha was taking some of them, but he felt guilty about the still-full mugs sitting on the table.

"Whoa! I'd never thought I'd see the day!"

Galen looked up and saw Jess, a wide grin on their face and their dark hair pulled up into a topknot instead of their usual braid. They had their hands on their hips, but soon they were tugging Galen up out of his seat and towards the back area of the tavern, which was reserved for dancing.

"Jess, Jess, no," Galen said, stumbling after far too many ales. He looked back to Sasha for help, but the man was laughing and watching with sparkling eyes. Traitor.

"Oh, come on, Flower Boy," Jess said, kicking people out of their way. "You never come out. You've got to dance!"

"Sasha, err, I mean, Mister Rider forced me to," Galen said as people cleared a path for him as they did in the streets.

"Sasha, eh?" Jess said, calling to the bard holding a lute on the upturned crate that functioned as a stage. "Hey! Play something we can dance to!"

"What does that mean?" Galen asked with a sigh as the music started.

Jess and Galen started jigging. Several others had joined them. Galen barely remembered the steps, and the fact that the world was tilting slightly wasn't helping any. He kept bumping into people and apologizing, and stepping on Jess's feet, but they just laughed him off.

"Sorry, it's been a while since I've danced," Galen said after the third time he stepped on Jess's toes.

"It's all right," Jess said, grinning as they spun him around, which tossed Galen's stomach in horrifying ways. "So, first-name basis?"

"What?" Galen asked when the world stilled enough for him to think. "Oh, with Mister Rider. Yes, we're friends now. He really has stopped being such a...such a..."

"Flaming, stinking asshole?" Jess offered helpfully.

Galen barked a laugh, then said, "Well, yes. He's been very nice the last month or so."

As Jess spun around him, they scrunched their face in disbelief. Which, Galen had to admit, was probably fair. He copied their footwork as best as he could and tried to amend his statement.

"Well, maybe not nice, sometimes he's still rude as the seven hells, but never to me." Galen winced as he bumped into Jess, who luckily just looked amused. "He keeps looking out for me and trying to make me happy. I mean, he's been...he's been..."

"Kind?" Jess said, clapping their hands in time with everyone else, Galen scrambling to copy them a beat later.

"Yes, words are escaping me tonight," Galen said, laughing. "Thank you."

Jess grabbed his arms, and they started spinning. The world tilted again, only Jess's strong hands keeping Galen upright, and then they stopped. The music ended, and everyone was clapping. Galen joined in, then the next song started.

"This is so surprising, you know," Galen said suddenly.

"What is?" Jess asked, hooking their arm through Galen's and pulling him to join a line of similarly linked partners.

"That all these people came," Galen said, glancing at Jess. "I mean, isn't everyone busy?"

"Not everyone works like you do, Galen," Jess said, smirking. "In fact, I'd say that most people don't work like you do."

Galen shrugged as they followed the line of couples through a tunnel of lifted arms formed by their fellow dancers.

At the end, they took their place, forming an irregular slump as Galen's height caused a bit of a problem. He would have had more qualms about it if he wasn't so relieved to be standing still for a bit.

"You do know that you're very beloved in Candiru, right?" Jess asked as another linked pair of dancers ran through the tunnel, ducking under Galen's arms. "Everyone knows you, and everyone loves you."

"Well, not everyone," Galen said, his mind drifting to Old Harry.

"The people who don't are assholes," Jess said as though it were a simple matter of fact. "Adrian, the guy who owns the bakery on your street, he had to talk the Kippers, me included, down from beating up your guard after the first week. Nobody liked that ass when he was being a dick to you."

Galen blinked in surprise. He hadn't even been sure that people had noticed the way that Sasha spoke to him back then. Sure, Sasha had been rude to a few citizens, and he wasn't surprised that people had heard their fight after the first month, but after the first week? Galen hadn't realized anyone was paying attention.

"It wasn't because he's a guard?" Galen asked as they moved to circle each other, the tunnel portion of the dance sadly over.

"Sure, that was part of it," Jess said, "but most people were mad that he was being so fucking rude to you. Miss Kingley had a fit about it."

"Oh," Galen said, glancing back over to Sasha, who was talking cheerfully with a few other patrons, though his eyes kept drifting back to the dance floor.

"But he's better now, yeah?" Jess asked. "He's been bringing you flowers and baked goods, I hear. He's not trying anything untoward, is he?"

Galen barked another laugh and then shook his head. "No! No, not at all. You don't need to worry about that, Jess."

Jess stared at him for a moment, and then said, "You like him like that?"

"No," Galen breathed, smiling softly.

Jess gave him an incredulous look, lifting their brows. "You sure?"

All the blood rushed to Galen's face, which wouldn't help his already weak argument. "No, I mean, yes, I'm sure. I don't like him, uh, romantically."

Jess didn't respond, just grinned as they continued to dance.

"I'm just glad that we're friends now," Galen said in a rush.

"Okay," Jess said, laughing. "Friends."

Galen, to his dismay, continued, "Honestly, I don't think he has a lot of friends, so he's not sure how to act."

"Uh-huh," Jess said, spinning around again.

"That's why he keeps bringing me flowers." Galen flushed and grabbed Jess's hand to stop them. "Please don't tell him I said that."

Jess's eyes sparkled, their smile threatening to split their face in two, but they said, "Sure. Lips are sealed. Well, you tell me if his hands start wandering, and I'll cut them off."

"Jess!" Galen said, burning red as they spun him and cackled.

"What?" Jess said when they were facing each other again. "I've got to look out for you. We all do. Certainly seems like your temple and the fucking queen herring don't give a damn."

Galen shook his head, and said, "I appreciate it, I do, but you don't need to worry. With a face like mine, I don't have to worry about men's hands wandering. They usually don't get too close."

He had been trying to make Jess laugh, but instead, their mouth bent into a frown as they pulled him from the dance floor and whispered sharply, "Did your city guard say anything about that? I'll break his fucking nose."

"No!" Galen said, shaking his head vehemently. "No, no, Sasha has been very nice about it from the start. Even when he was still being, as you said, a flaming stinking asshole, he never said anything about my face. He never even stared like others do."

Galen glanced over at Sasha, who actually was staring at him now. He was staring, but it wasn't the way Galen was used to. It was as though Sasha was watching his every movement, measuring them, and making sure that he was safe. Galen didn't think that he minded that staring at all.

Jess looked him over carefully, then nodded, and said, "Good. Rising Dawn, Galen. You let me know if anyone says fucking anything about your face. Me and the Kippers will set them straight."

Galen nodded, but thought, *Well, you just guaranteed that I'll never tell you, because I don't want to have to deal with extra broken noses and stab wounds.* Eventually, Jess relented and returned Galen to his table. They glared a warning at Sasha before disappearing back into the crowd.

"Welcome back," Sasha said, lifting yet another mug of ale. "Have fun?"

Galen smiled and said, "I'm going to have to treat Jess for broken toes tomorrow, I'm sure of it. It's been a while since I've danced."

"No offense, but I could tell," Sasha said with a laugh and a shake of his head. "You are a *terrible* dancer."

"I know," Galen said, laughing, and then burying his face in his hands. "Oh, Lady of Flowers, I know. It doesn't help that I'm tipsy too."

"When was the last time you went dancing?" Sasha asked.

Galen thought, and then said, "I think when I was nineteen. We went out to celebrate someone's wedding."

Sasha's mouth hung open for a moment, then he said, "Lion's teeth, man. I'm going to make you go out more often. That's unbelievable. Nearly ten years?"

Galen shrugged and said, "I got busy?"

"No one should be that busy," Sasha said. "It's unfair to you."

Galen shrugged again. He didn't really want to talk about this yet again. He knew it was unfair, but that was Candiru Quarter. Things were always unfair here, and he didn't want to think about it right now. Not when people were buying him drinks and making him dance. Luckily, another throng of people came up to greet him then, and the conversation slid away.

It was after dark when Galen finally told Sasha that he was tired and needed to get home. Sasha agreed and carefully extracted Galen from his crowd of admirers and pulled him out into the street. The night had cooled the warm spring air, and it felt nice after the stifling warmth in the Sparrow's Roost.

Sasha had to help him walk after the first street; he was stumbling far too much. He leaned against Sasha's arm, his cheek pressed against the leather armor, while Sasha held him up with his other hand. Galen appreciated the steady, solid mountain of Sasha in that moment. He smelled like leather oil and campfire, with a bit of sweat. But Galen didn't mind that at all. It was nice to have someone to lean on, someone to rely on. Just as a friend, of course.

By the time they got back to Galen's little house, Sasha was half carrying him. Galen opened the door and stumbled in, and Sasha lingered just long enough to accidentally admit Muffin. Sasha cursed, which set Galen off laughing so hard that he fell on his ass on the ground. Sasha hurried over and helped him up.

"Sorry, I really didn't know that all of Candiru Quarter was going to conspire to get you absolutely sloshed," Sasha said, sitting Galen in a kitchen chair. "Any magical or medical hangover cure you can use?"

Galen snorted, then said, "Hand me the leftover muffins and that pitcher of water."

Sasha did as he was told and then started hunting for the blink fox. Galen tore through the remaining five muffins with the same voracity with which Sasha ate all food and then started drinking directly from the pitcher.

"Huh," Sasha said.

Galen looked up and saw that Sasha had captured Muffin and the blink fox was scrambling to break free of his arms. He was staring at Galen with what looked like wonder and awe, and Galen snorted. Sasha put out the invading ball of fluff, then quickly shut the door. He leaned against it with crossed arms and continued to stare as Galen drank the rest of the pitcher.

"What?" Galen asked when he was done, standing to refill the pitcher.

"Nothing, I just thought..." Sasha said, waving his hand vaguely. "I thought there'd be some trick."

"There are tricks," Galen said, pumping water into the pitcher. "But I've always found what works best for me is a belly full of food and a lot of water. I'll have to use the chamber pot a few times tonight, but it's better than a pounding headache tomorrow. The muffins came in handy, so thank you again. I did finish them off, sorry."

Sasha shook his head and said, "They were for you, that's fine. I'm glad you know what works. Did you have fun at least?"

Galen took a drink from the refilled pitcher, then nodded.

"I did. It was nice knowing that what I'm doing here doesn't go unnoticed, you know?"

"I know," Sasha said, and then he smiled warmly. "I wanted to show that to you, you know. I wanted you to know that the people of Candiru appreciate you, Galen. You're a hero."

Galen laughed and said, "Oh, I wouldn't go that far, Sasha."

"I would."

Galen frowned. That wasn't right. He was just doing his job, following the Lady's path for him. He wanted to help people, and he supposed that being a healer was what most would consider a noble pursuit, but he was not a hero.

The silence must have lingered for a bit too long, because Sasha cleared his throat and said, "Right, well, I'll see you tomorrow. Have a good night. Rest well."

"Thank you," Galen said. "You as well."

Sasha smiled warmly once more and then slipped out. Galen stood in the kitchen, clutching the water pitcher to his chest, and considered that warm smile for quite some time.

CHAPTER 21

IT SPREADS

GALEN

IT HAD BEEN SO NICE TO BE WITH PEOPLE, NOT JUST as their healer, but as a member of their community. Galen had forgotten what it was like, if he had ever known what it was like in the first place. After his family had died, he had joined the devotees so quickly that he hadn't really had time to experience normal life. And he didn't mind, truly he did not mind. How could he when so very many people were counting on him? That would be selfish.

Life went on, and Sasha kept threatening to take him out to a tavern again. Others did too when he saw them on his rounds. A week passed, and then another, but nothing ever came of it. Galen just got too busy again. Miss Kingley and her brood of children all got head colds, Fynn of the Kippers twisted her ankle, and, of course, he had to do follow-ups with Angelica and Charlie and their new baby girl. That, at least, was enjoyable.

For all the trouble that bringing the little baby into the world had been, she seemed the picture of health now that she was here. Galen wondered privately if the Lady of Flowers

217

really had blessed her. Her bright brown eyes followed his finger easily, and she burbled happily.

"She's the easiest baby, you know," Angelica said, smiling dreamily. "Hardly cries a spot and isn't fussy at all. Sometimes she stares off in the corner, but I remember what you said about the Evening Star, Brother Galen."

Galen smiled as he handed the baby back to her mother and said, "It'll be a blessing, I assure you. Have you decided on a name?"

"Oh, yes!" Charlie said excitedly, then he looked to Angelica for confirmation.

"We're naming her Marigold," Angelica said after rolling her eyes at her husband with a fond smile. "We thought we ought to honor the Lady for sending you to us, Brother Galen. Our little flower wouldn't be here without you."

Galen had to fight back tears as he held a hand to his chest and said, "I think that's perfect, very fitting. Do you know what marigolds mean?"

Angelica and Charlie shook their heads, and Galen continued, "Inner strength and power, and the light that burns inside each person. She had such a difficult start to life, so I think the name suits her very well."

"Well! And here I just picked them because I thought they were pretty," Angelica said, lifting Marigold up to look at her. "My little Marigold, so strong and beautiful. You will be a light to this world, my love. Thank you, Brother Galen."

"Of course," Galen said, smiling and gathering his things. "Please let me know if there's anything else I can help with."

After their goodbyes, he and his shadow stepped out into the street. Sasha had been oddly quiet during the whole exchange, and Galen glanced back to check if, perhaps, he had somehow made Sasha angry again but was shocked. The man was wiping tears from his face.

"Oh, goodness," Galen said, holding up his hands, unsure what to do. "Sasha, are you all right?"

Sasha nodded and took a breath, then said, "Sorry, yes. I'm fine. It just made me emotional. The name was so perfect, and they didn't even know. Marigold, a light in the world, you know?"

Galen couldn't help smiling, but he nodded and said, "I know."

LIFE WENT ON. THERE WERE HARDER CASES AND easier ones. Sasha was constantly there. Galen had thought of him as a mountain before, and he really did seem like one. Galen had, of course, never actually seen a mountain. He'd never left Dragonet City, and rarely left Candiru, and there were no mountains around them. There were just the plains and the large expansive river, but he imagined what mountains must be like. Huge, steady, unmoving, and reliable. Sasha was all those things. If Galen could count on one thing, Sasha would be at his door every morning.

The most surprising thing he found, however, was that the next time that he visited Old Harry to clean him up, he wasn't nearly as awful. He was still grumpy, but he didn't call Galen names or spit at him, and he wasn't making him miserable on purpose. Galen almost wanted to check if Harry was feeling well, but then he caught how Harry stared at Sasha in the corner and how Sasha glared back at him when they both thought he wasn't paying attention. Oh.

At the end, when Galen made his usual tenuous suggestion that a doctor from the temple could come and look at Harry's leg, he almost keeled over when Harry finally agreed. Galen breathed sharply in and nodded. Instead of bullying Galen into using the gift, Harry acccptcd the pain medication and the assurance that the doctor would be there as soon as possible.

After they had descended and breathed in dried lavender, Galen looked up at Sasha and said, "You did that, didn't you?"

"I don't know what you're talking about," Sasha said, but he was an awful liar. He was beaming at Galen.

"Thank you," Galen said, softly, and smiled back up at Sasha. "I guess I did need your 'powers of being an ass' after all."

Sasha laughed at that, quite loudly, and Galen had to shush him. It was after dark, and children were probably sleeping.

He quieted himself and said, "I know you said you could handle a grumpy patient, but I couldn't take it anymore. Sorry for taking it into my own hands."

Galen smirked and shook his head. "I'm not above admitting that I can be wrong as well."

Sasha's beaming face seemed to light their path home.

As time went on, those captured on Figlove Lane returned, and Galen checked them over for any signs of the strange sickness. The temple still hadn't discovered anything about it, at least nothing that they had shared with Galen. The temple was normally quite good about that, so Galen assumed that there was nothing to share.

The way it cropped up on William after a month with no sign of it worried him. So did the mention of someone in a fine cloak bumping into William before he got sick, but Galen didn't know what to do with that. He knew it hadn't been a poison; that was the first thing he checked after he checked for one of those reactions to food or plants that some people were born with. He had no idea what it was. He just desperately hoped that it wasn't another plague.

Galen found himself almost wishing that it would make itself known again. He had sent messages to all the other healers stationed in various districts in the city, but no one else had seen anything like it. It was just twice, and just in Candiru. Every rest day, when there wasn't an emergency, he was at his table, writing in another little journal, tapping his chin with his charcoal and thinking about it.

"What are you working on?" Sasha finally asked him three weeks after the Figlove Lane incident.

"Remember the black spots?" Galen said, looking up at him.

"Like the ones on your chin?" Sasha said, smirking and tapping his own chin.

Galen sighed, used his sleeve to wipe his face, then said, "No, I mean, like what happened to Mandy and William."

"Yeah," Sasha said, sitting beside him. "Yeah, I do. What about it? You think it's coming back?"

Galen shrugged and said, "I'm not sure. I almost wish it would, and that I could catch it earlier. I want to understand it. The first step to stopping something is understanding it, you know?"

"I suppose," Sasha said, giving him an odd look. "It seemed painful though."

"I know," Galen said, burying his face in his hands. "I know. I don't really want anyone to get sick, but it feels like it's looming over me waiting to drop. I would almost feel better if it finally did."

Sasha nodded in understanding, and said, "I get it. Well, maybe your temple will dig something up soon."

Galen looked up at him again, and said, "One can hope."

～

Unfortunately, Galen's wish came true two days later. It had been a normal day, neither exceedingly harsh nor very easy, but still tiring, as always. The sun was just starting its descent below the horizon, turning the sky rust colored, when there were sudden calls for help from just down the street. Of course, Galen went running towards the sound with Sasha close at his heels.

This time, there were two people, and that terrified Galen. He knew them, the blacksmith's children. They were twins, Mackley and Marlyn, and they were only seventeen. They had been miracle babies during the plague that had swept through Dragonet, and their mother had lost her life to that same sickness not two months after their birth. Now Galen stood over them, looking down at their bodies, covered with black spots as tar-like ichor dripped from their mouths.

Their father had carried them to the bed they still shared; the blankets and pillows scattered across the floor as he stood wringing his hands and chewing on his bottom lip. Galen leaned down and started examining them. They didn't seem as far along as either Mandy or William had been. He inhaled sharply. There was a rotten egg smell about them that he hadn't noticed with the others.

"When did it start?" Galen asked, his eyes flicking up to Mister Priestly, the blacksmith.

"Just an hour ago," he said, running a hand over his bald head. "Brother Galen, what is this? You know the twins have had everything this side of the seven hells. Fevers, measles, flu, but I ain't never seen anything like this."

"I've seen this before," Galen said, trying to sound reassuring. "There were two other patients. I had to use the gift to cure them, and I will use it for Mackley and Marlyn."

"Oh, thank you, Brother Galen," Mister Priestly said, sighing. His worried face melted into relief.

"But," Galen said, wincing at what he was about to ask, "could I ask you a favor?"

Mister Priestly looked uncertain but nodded.

"They are nowhere near as far along in the sickness as either of the other two were," Galen said. "I want to know if you would mind if I observed them for a bit, since I'm trying to gain a better understanding of it. The moment either of them takes a turn for the worse, I will use the gift. I swear it on the Lady. But this could help a lot."

Mister Priestly was silent for a moment, then he said, "I'm not sure."

"If the answer is no, I understand," Galen said, lifting his hands immediately. "I'll use the gift right now. They'll be fine."

Mister Priestly looked at Galen, searching his face, and then looked back down at his two unconscious children. They were both breathing heavily, but steadily. Every once in a while, a finger would twitch, or their eyelids would flutter. The black spots on their skin looked deep and terrifying. Galen tried not to be disappointed to lose this opportunity. He knew that Mister Priestly would care for his children's safety first.

"Well," Mister Priestly said, drawing out the word and drumming his fingers against his arms in thought.

Sasha suddenly cleared his throat, stepped forward, and said, "I'm sure you already know this, Mister Priestly, but Brother Galen always has everyone's best interests at heart. If he thinks that he'll be able to keep them safe and learn more about the disease, I trust him. He always has a good reason for what he does."

Sasha glanced over at Galen and offered him a little half-smile. Galen gave him one back in thanks. Mister Priestly sighed heavily and nodded. Galen breathed out a sigh of relief then pulled out his notebook. He kept observations for a couple hours, watching how the sores spread and deepened, listening to how their coughs worsened and noting how more ichor was produced. It was terrifying, but he started to understand the timeline of the disease better.

He still didn't know the exact time of contraction, but it seemed like it progressed over the course of about five hours from when the spots first started showing up. It was quick, terrifyingly so. Eventually, he breathed in, then placed a hand on each twin's shoulder and started praying. Pink light filled the room, and soon two annoyed teenagers were sitting up and wiping ichor from their mouths.

Galen had already questioned their father very thoroughly, but he wanted to ask the victims themselves just one thing. "Was there someone who was wearing a nice cloak who bumped into you or talked to you?"

The twins looked at each other, and then Marlyn said, "Didn't bump into us, but they stopped us on the street and told us that they had something to show us."

"Marlyn!" Mister Priestly shouted, making his daughter wince. "We've talked about this!"

"Yeah, Pa, that's why we told them to stick it where Rising Dawn can't reach it," Mackley mumbled. "But they got all huffy and tried to grab our wrists to pull us. Marlyn kicked them a good one in the shin."

"Did their skin touch your skin?" Galen said, perking up and listening carefully to every word.

Once again, the twins glanced at each other, and then Marlyn said, "Maybe? I'm not too sure. It's kind of a blur."

"When did you start feeling sick?" Galen asked, his mouth dry.

"Maybe an hour after the weird guy stopped us," Mackley said. "Least for me. Marlyn?"

"Yeah, that's about right," Marlyn said with a nod.

Sasha must have been able to tell that Galen was reeling,

because he came up behind him and placed a steady hand on his shoulder. Galen thanked him with a small smile. Then he nodded to the family, telling the kids to get some rest.

"Ain't you forgetting something, Brother Galen?" Mackley said with a grin on their face.

"Oh! Right!" Marlyn said, lifting her eyebrows.

"What?" Galen asked, looking between the two of them. He truly had no idea what they meant.

"Candy," Mackley stage-whispered to him.

"Oh!" Galen said and then laughed. He produced two pieces of candy and gave them to the twins. Their father lightly smacked the backs of their heads, and they chimed out their gratitude.

"Thank you too, Brother Galen," Mister Priestly said. "I don't know what I would have done if I lost them."

Galen moved closer to Mister Priestly and took his hands, squeezing them gently.

"I'm glad it didn't come to that," Galen said, smiling at him. "And thank you for your patience. I know that this wasn't easy and that you put a lot of faith in the Lady and in me. I promise that I would never have done anything that would have actually put your children in danger."

Mister Priestly's voice cracked as he spoke. "I know, Brother Galen, it's just hard because their mother... I couldn't have lost them too, you understand?"

"I understand." Galen nodded, squeezing his hands. "I do. Thank you for trusting me. Hopefully, this will help shed some light on what's happening. You and Marlyn and Mackley will have helped a lot of people."

Mister Priestly smiled, tears threatening to spill as he gazed at his two children. They were laughing, making a game out of trying to get Sasha to break his stoic expression as they told jokes or pulled ridiculous faces. Mister Priestly laughed, a few tears escaping down his rough cheeks. He squeezed Galen's hands in turn.

"You're welcome, Brother Galen," he said hoarsely.

After saying their good-byes to the Priestlys, Galen and Sasha walked out of the blacksmith's shop into the night air. Oh, gods, it was late again. Galen looked up at Sasha apologetically.

"I'm sorry," Galen said.

"Huh? What for?" Sasha asked, looking at him with genuine surprise.

Galen rubbed the back of his neck. Sasha was taking this all too well. He couldn't believe that he was forcing the man to linger, stealing all his time and energy away from whatever life he had outside of his job. Galen didn't have anything, but Sasha must have something.

"It's another late night after a hundred late nights," Galen said, sighing. "If it were just me it was affecting, it wouldn't matter, but I'm dragging you along too. I don't know what else to do. I have to figure this out, but you're stuck with me, and..."

"Galen," Sasha said firmly, and Galen stopped.

Sasha took a deep breath, examined Galen for a moment, and then said, "Your work is important. It isn't your fault that you're the only person here; in fact, it's not fair to you. But you don't ever need to feel guilty about keeping me out late."

Sasha hesitated, but with a breath he continued, "I like spending time with you. It's better than with literally anyone else I know. And I feel like I'm actually helping with something important when I'm with you, not just twiddling my thumbs at some pointless guard post or, gods forbid, harming people. I like being with you."

Galen felt a pleasant chill roll over him despite everything that had happened over the night. He stared up at Sasha in disbelief, but Sasha seemed completely sincere. He liked spending time with him. Every touch that they had shared, every smile, came rushing over him like the current of a river. Suddenly, Galen craved Sasha's warm touch. He wanted Sasha's hand on his shoulder, his comforting presence. And maybe...

"Well, thank you," Galen said, feeling as though his breath was being stolen from him. "That does...that does help."

Sasha smiled and placed his large, warm hand on Galen's shoulder. Galen's heart skipped a beat as he stared up into Sasha's deep, warm brown eyes. He was possessed by a vision, a desire for Sasha to move his hand up and cup his cheek. Galen imagined Sasha's strong, calloused fingers stroking the damaged skin of his scar. Heat spread through his body.

His reverie was interrupted when Sasha said in his deep, steady voice, "Come on, then. Let's get you home. I'm sure tomorrow will be full of important work as well."

"Right," Galen said, nodding.

"And I'm sure you're exhausted as usual," Sasha said, his tone playful, but his eyes wide and full of concern.

Galen shrugged, fighting back a yawn. Luckily, that made Sasha laugh. Galen let that laugh fill him up from the ends of his toes to the tips of his ears. And then they walked back together through Candiru, back to Galen's home, and the warmth in his chest was real and palpable.

CHAPTER 22

A MUCH-NEEDED CONVERSATION

SASHA

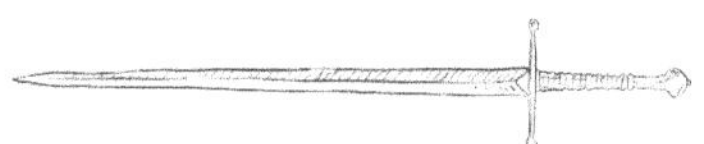

SASHA WAS CERTAIN THAT GALEN KNEW HOW HE felt. Galen was smart; he would definitely pick up on the fact that Sasha was following behind him, panting like a puppy and ogling him like a schoolboy with his first crush. Gods above, he had it bad. Had he ever been this obsessed with someone? If so, he didn't remember it.

When he was about ten, he had a crush on a boy in his class and couldn't talk about anyone or anything else. Every day when he'd come home from school, he'd regale the family about Wallace: how smart he was, how he came up with the best games, how his eyes were the exact color of the river... Anya teased him relentlessly for the few months it lasted, and he could only imagine what she'd say now. This was truly pathetic, because he was a full-grown adult and full-grown adults didn't have *crushes*. And there was no one he could gush to about Galen because he spent almost all his time with Galen, which just compounded how he felt about Galen and then even when he wasn't with Galen, Galen was all he could think about and...

This was unhealthy.

He had almost given the game away the night after Galen had treated the twins with the strange black spot sickness. Galen had looked up at him with those hazel eyes full of shame and regret and apologized to him. Sasha had been about to confess that he was in love with Galen, but luckily, he caught himself at the last second.

His friendship with Galen already felt tenuous enough; he had been so awful to him. It was hard to believe that Galen tolerated him at all, since Galen was far too good for someone like him. As much as Sasha wanted to have Galen for his own, to hold him, to kiss him, to peel off that garish yellow tunic and see what lay beneath, he knew that he had no right to. Hell, he had already hurt Galen enough. How dare he try to derive pleasure from him? Sasha was determined to keep his inappropriate desires to himself.

ANOTHER WEEK PASSED WITH NO FURTHER SIGN OF the black spot sickness, but Galen was clearly still uneasy. At every visit, Galen asked whether anyone had seen a stranger in an expensive cloak. Eventually, word must have gotten around to the Kippers, because one morning they walked out of Galen's house and nearly tripped over Jess, who was sitting on the ground cross-legged and scratching Muffin between the ears. Ah, two over-energized annoyances at once.

"Looking for someone?" Jess asked, leaping to their feet with surprising agility.

If Galen was surprised, he didn't show it. Sasha, on the other hand, had been taken off guard and immediately reached for his sword, only to sheepishly slide the half-drawn weapon back into place as Jess laughed.

Galen gave Sasha a reproachful look, then asked, "What do you mean?"

Jess had been giving Sasha a rather triumphant (and annoying) grin, but they turned to Galen and said, "Heard you were asking folks if they'd seen a guy in a fancy cloak down here. So I got curious. Looking for someone?"

Galen smiled and shook his head, then said, "Just looking into something, don't worry about it."

Jess leaned their weight on one leg and tilted their head, letting their long braid dangle in the air. Their assessing look eventually made Galen shift uncomfortably, and then they said, "When you say not to worry about something, Flower Boy, it definitely makes me worry about it. It makes me think someone's giving you trouble again."

"They're not. No one is," Galen said, and Sasha watched as color rose from beneath Galen's tunic all the way up to the tips of his ears. "I promise, nobody is bothering me. I would tell you if someone was."

Jess exchanged a concerned look with Sasha, but then they looked back at the healer and said, "Okay. But you'll tell me, yeah? You know I've got your back, right? We all do."

"I know," Galen said, "and I have yours."

Jess grinned and strode up to him, hugged him, and then ruffled his hair as Galen squeaked, saying, "You be careful out there, Flower Boy. Watch out for him, Sa-sha." They emphasized Sasha's name with an impudent drawl.

"That should be Mister Rider or Sir to you," Sasha said, folding his arms.

Jess released Galen, sent Sasha a rude gesture and a smirk, and ran down the street, cackling. Sasha sighed heavily, but Galen just laughed as he tidied his hair. Sasha's eyes were immediately drawn to the action.

Galen so rarely let his hair down, and Sasha loved seeing it. The auburn locks brushed his shoulders just slightly as he used his fingers to comb out the snarls Jess had put there, and then he tied it back into its knot. Sasha started to imagine just what it would be like to run his hands through that hair, to feel the softness that he was sure was there, to twine the locks through his fingers...Lion's teeth, he needed to stop.

"Why do they call you Flower Boy? Is it because you're a devotee of the Lady of Flowers?" Sasha asked in an effort to stop picturing how that hair might look splayed out around Galen's head. If, say, he lay back on a soft surface. Like a bed.

"Hmm?" Galen said, turning to him. "Oh, uh, it's an old nickname. Actually, it's older than Gap-Tooth Galen, believe it or not. Jess and I grew up on the same street. Our lives took different directions though."

Galen smiled as though he were reminiscing, and Sasha snorted, then said, "Well, you became a decent sort."

"Jess is a decent sort too," Galen said defensively. "Not everyone can just go and join a temple."

They were walking towards the day's first stop, but Sasha saw the tension in Galen's shoulders, the way he suddenly crossed his arms. Fuck. He'd fucked up again.

"Sorry," Sasha said. "I didn't mean...Well, I mean, they are in a gang, aren't they?"

Galen snorted quietly, and then said, "No, no, that's fair enough. It used to be worse down here, you know. There were bad gangs and crime, or so I'm told. The Kippers helped clean things up a lot in Candiru. They were regular heroes during the plague. That's why Jess joined them, the way that I joined the temple."

Sasha nodded. It suddenly made a lot of sense. The city had left Candiru to rot during the plague, so the people of Candiru stepped up to take care of each other. Jess did seem rather concerned about the district, much the way Galen was. He couldn't imagine them working in a temple though. No temple walls would have been able to contain them.

"And why did they call you Flower Boy?" Sasha persisted.

Galen laughed and said, "My mothers were flower sellers. I

was their oldest, so I was going to be apprenticed to them. I was already learning about it, and apparently I wouldn't shut up about flowers. Jess started calling me Flower Boy whenever I got too passionate."

Sasha snorted, and then said, "Really? There is no way."

"Oh, there is," Galen said. "Trust me, I was thoroughly teased when I became a devotee of the Lady of Flowers. Jess told me that they had the right to call me Flower Boy for the rest of my life. I don't mind it. It fits well. Better than Gap-Tooth Galen, or scarface, even if those fit just as well."

Sasha felt anger bubbling up in his chest, anger that those names seemed to stick to Galen and dig into him like burrs. If there was anyone in the world who didn't deserve that, it was Galen. Sasha tightened his hands into fists at his sides.

Finally he growled, "No. They don't fit."

Galen looked back at him, wide-eyed and bemused, and said, "I do have a scarred face. I do have gap teeth."

"Yes, but that's nothing to be ashamed of," Sasha said. They had stopped walking and were facing each other, the crowd moving around them like a river around two stones.

Galen was still looking up at him, his eyes suddenly glistening, so Sasha continued, "Those names are just trying to hurt you. No one should be using them."

"I know," Galen said, touching the scarred skin of his left cheek, then dropping his eyes. "I know. It's just…"

Sasha wanted to grab Galen's hand and hold it, bend to kiss Galen's cheek, the place where his fingers had brushed damaged skin. He wanted Galen to know that his face was beautiful, that the scar didn't matter to Sasha, that it shouldn't matter to anyone. But that was an impossible fantasy.

"Sorry," Galen said, shaking his head. "Never mind. Come on, we're already late."

Galen turned on his heel and wove through the streets. Sasha matched his breakneck pace, trying not to sigh. It wasn't a bad day, but Sasha kept thinking about the look in Galen's eyes when he touched his scar, and he kept imagining what it would be like to kiss it away. Gods. He needed to go dunk his head in the river, things were so bad.

∾

After they finished for the day, Sasha wandered slowly back to the guard station, stopping at a small shrine to the Lady of Flowers and dropping half his week's pay into the donation plate. The priest, who Sasha assumed was *actually* a priest because she had been speaking to people, looked up at him in shock and disbelief. Sasha smiled weakly and turned to go.

"Wait!" she called, and Sasha turned around. "That was quite the donation. Did you need to talk about something?"

Sasha stood for a moment, hands clenching and unclenching, and then he finally nodded. She gestured for him to join her on the stone bench she sat on, but he glanced around at the few visitors to the shrine. She smiled gently and dismissed each person quickly but politely until it was just the two of them. He sat heavily on the bench, dwarfing her.

"So, my child, what can I do for you?" she asked, smiling at him.

She was older, perhaps seventy, and her dark gray hair was tied in much the same fashion as Galen's. Instead of the garish yellow tunic of a healer, she had on a deep blue robe. However, the same pink flower hung around her neck, marking her as a devotee. Her head was adorned with a crown of light pink flowers, and her face was heavily marked with laugh lines. Sasha wondered if this was what Galen would look like when he was older. He breathed in deeply.

"Well, Sister, uh, is that correct?" Sasha asked, glancing at her.

"That's fine," she said warmly. "Sister Amber, if you like. I'm a speaker."

"I'm Sasha. I thought you might be a speaker," Sasha said, nodding. "I have a...friend who's a devotee. He explained it to me."

"Oh, really? Who is it? I may know him," Sister Amber asked, smiling broadly.

"Brother Galen," Sasha said, turning to stare at a patch of well-tended blue flowers.

"Oh, ah," Sister Amber said, and he could almost hear her smile drop. "Yes."

"Is something wrong?" Sasha asked, swallowing heavily. His gaze remained fixed on the flowers.

"No, well," Sister Amber said, and then sighed. "We all know Brother Galen. He is a very sweet man, but, well..."

"He's overextended," Sasha said flatly.

"Yes," Sister Amber said. "It seems you do know him."

"It's not fair," Sasha said, his voice breaking unexpectedly. "He shouldn't be alone down there. It's too much."

"That's true," Sister Amber said, her voice calm and low. "His predecessor was much like him, and she worked herself until she was nearly dead waiting for what she deemed an appropriate replacement. That was Galen."

"He's going to do the same, isn't he?" Sasha said, wincing as he pictured Galen completely burnt out. "Unless something changes, he's going to kill himself trying to serve the entire Candiru Quarter on his own."

"I hope that something changes," Sister Amber said. "He is too good a man to be broken."

"I agree with that more than you know," Sasha said, breathing out. "You know the initiative from Governor Maple?"

"Guards with each of the devotees working as healers?" Sister Amber asked. "Are you Galen's guard?"

Sasha nodded and said, "I am. I've...I've seen everything that he does. I know him so well, and it's not..."

He drifted off, and after a moment, Sister Amber asked, "There's something with Brother Galen that you want to talk about, isn't there?"

"Yes," Sasha said, intently examining the scuffs on the toes of his boots.

"I see," Sister Amber said, folding her hands. "I will do my best to help, if you like."

"I don't know how you can help," Sasha said, his voice breaking again.

"Sometimes just talking about something can help," Sister Amber said, resting a careful hand on his shoulder.

Sasha swallowed and squeezed his eyes shut for a moment. He focused on the gentle pressure of Sister Amber's hand. If he didn't say it, he could still deny it. But he didn't want to deny it. Gods above, he couldn't deny it any longer. It would kill him if he did. He took a shuddering breath, opened his eyes, and spoke.

"I'm in love with him," Sasha said, looking over at Sister Amber. Saying it to someone who was not a blink fox was daunting.

Sister Amber blinked once, smiled gently, and said, "That's what's weighing on you?"

"Yes," Sasha said, biting down hard on his inner cheek. "I'm not worthy of him."

Sister Amber gave him an assessing look, and then asked, "What makes you believe that?"

"Well, just look at me," Sasha said with a derisive laugh. "And then think of him."

Her eyes scanned him up and down, then she tilted her head to the side in a gesture that reminded Sasha hysterically of Muffin. He bit down on his inner cheek again to avoid bursting out in unhinged laughter. He tasted copper.

"I don't see anything wrong with you," she said finally. Her smile was full of truth.

"You ought to," Sasha said, a broken smile on his lips as he looked at her.

"Why's that?" The priest's eyes were unbearably kind and soft.

"I'm an utter dick," Sasha said, looking down at his hands. "I'm cruel and stubborn and mean. I've only just now pulled my head out of my own ass long enough to realize that I'm the problem and the world's not out to get me. And I acted that way to Galen. I was so cruel, and then he fucking forgave me. He acts like none of it happened, and it doesn't make sense. He's too good for me, and it's pathetic that I could even start to imagine that I could be worthy of him. I don't deserve someone like him. Lion's teeth, I don't deserve anyone."

Sasha realized halfway through the speech that he was crying, and he hated that. How did he deserve tears when it was his own damn fault? He wiped his face. Sister Amber was silent for a moment, waiting to see if he really was done. She hadn't interrupted him once, just sat and listened. Only after he swallowed and nodded at her did she answer.

"Would you like advice, or were you just looking to get it all out?" Sister Amber asked, her voice soft as a well-loved blanket.

"Advice," Sasha said, his own voice gruff and broken.

"Brother Galen is a devotee of the Lady of Flowers," Sister Amber said, and then motioned with her head for him to sit up and look at her, which he did. "That means that he is very forgiving. You understand this?"

"Yes, but..." Sasha said, but Sister Amber held up a hand.

"I'm not going to let you wallow," she said, her voice firm but kind. "We are trained to be forgiving. Not to the point where someone could seriously harm us, of course, but we understand the need for second chances. Yes?"

"What if I did seriously harm him?" Sasha asked, forcing himself to look into the speaker's eyes.

"Did you?" she asked, brows lifting.

"I don't know," Sasha said. "I made him cry."

"Well, you cried just now," Sister Amber said, pointing at him as he opened his mouth. "Were you seriously harmed?"

Sasha swallowed. "No."

"Hmm," Sister Amber said, and then held out a hand. "Did Galen explain what the gift speakers have is?"

"He did, and you shouldn't waste it on me," Sasha said, and started to get up, but she stopped him with a look.

"Now, if you don't want me to see your past because you want it to remain private, that is fine," Sister Amber said. "But if you don't think you're worth my gift, that's another matter entirely. I am choosing to use it to help you. That is what devotees of the Lady of Flowers do, my friend."

Sasha paused, and then after a moment, he nodded and took her hand. "How does it work?"

"Just relax," Sister Amber said, smiling gently at him, "and breathe."

Sasha did as he was told. He breathed in deeply. All he could smell was the flowers around him, and they smelled lovely. Sister Amber's hand was warm and calloused, in the way he imagined Galen's hands were calloused, from hard work and care for others. It made him very, very comfortable. He breathed out. Then it started.

Sasha felt Sister Amber in his mind, examining his memories like Galen examining an injury. Sasha's chest felt very tight. Oh, gods, this incredibly kind woman was going to see how he acted. She was going to see how he had treated Galen. Oh, fuck. Fuck, fuck, fuck.

She must have felt his panic, because she said gently, "I am not here to judge you, I'm here to help you sort out your feelings. Don't worry, Sasha."

Sasha nodded, but a pained noise escaped the back of his throat. Galen had been right, of course. This was terrifying. Sasha tried to relax, to just breathe, but every time Sister Amber plucked at a new memory, he'd get a flash of something he had said or done, and a new wave of revulsion would sweep over him. She had said she wasn't here to judge, and he believed that that was her intention, but he knew that she would have to judge him in the end. How could she not, with all he had done?

Then, Lion's teeth, she plucked at the memory he had feared the most. It was the night that he and Galen fought in front of Galen's house. He saw Galen's battle against tears in a whole new light. Jess had been right. Galen never cried, and yet Sasha had made him cry. And that look of hurt when Galen had shut the door, fuck. How could Sasha claim to love someone he had done that to? Sasha wanted to yank his hand away from Sister Amber, to shout "See! I told you!" but her grip was shockingly firm.

Then he saw the past two months. And gods, he fell in love with Galen all over again. The way Galen smiled, his kindness. Fuck, it was too much. Sasha sighed wistfully. His cheeks, and, well, other places, heated at the memory of Galen coming out of the baths, his tunic still hitched up in the back, his damp hair touching his shoulders. He decided that once he was done here, he'd take a long, ice-cold bath.

He rewatched Galen dancing with Jess in the tavern. He really was a terrible dancer. But gods above, that made Sasha love him even more. Every time Galen laughed in his memory and Sasha saw that flash of a smile, Sasha's heart sank into his belly. The impossible gap between who Sasha was and who he wanted to be made him want to scream.

By the time it ended, Sasha felt like more of a monster than ever. How could a man like him presume to love Galen? As Sister Amber released his hand, he couldn't meet her eyes.

He just held his hand to his chest as though it were wounded.

"You see?" Sasha said, his voice sounding odd in his ears. "I don't deserve him."

To his utter surprise, Sister Amber laughed. His head snapped over to her, and she was shaking her head with a bemused look. His mouth gaped open like a fish's. She smiled gently and placed both hands on his shoulders.

"No, Sasha," she said. "Listen. Yes, you were, what was it you said, an utter dick?"

Sasha nodded silently.

"Yes, an utter dick," she said again, with more confidence. "But listen to me. You have been doing what you are supposed to do."

"What?" Sasha asked, blinking in disbelief.

"You have been working to make it up to him," Sister Amber said, smiling at him, eyes warm. "And many people wouldn't. I promise you, Galen is as good as his word. He's long since forgiven you. You've been working towards being kind to him longer than you were an utter dick."

"It's very strange to hear a devotee say 'utter dick' so many times in quick succession," Sasha said, bewildered.

"Well, get over it," Sister Amber said, waving her hand to brush off his concern. "What's important now, I think, is that you understand that it is all right to forgive yourself."

"But I don't deserve forgiveness," Sasha said, staring at her. "I don't deserve to want him like that."

Sister Amber let him finish, then said, "Have you kept your promise to be better to him?"

"For the most part," Sasha said, "I'm still sometimes an ass."

"But you apologize then try to do better," Sister Amber said, smiling. "Does that not show that you have a willingness to change?"

"I guess." Sasha shrugged.

"So, you don't really have anything that you need to be forgiven for anymore," Sister Amber said.

"I wouldn't say that," Sasha said, wincing.

"I would," Sister Amber said, looking smug.

"But what about my feelings towards him?" Sasha asked, running a hand through his hair. "Aren't those...isn't that...it's awful, isn't it?"

"Why?"

"Because I was, and here I am saying it again, an utter dick!" Sasha said, throwing his hands up in exasperation. "So what right do I have to pine after Galen when there are so many other people who would be better for him?"

"Oh, does Galen have suitors lining the streets?" Sister Amber asked, holding a hand to her chest in mock surprise.

"No, but he should," Sasha said glumly.

"Here's a thought," Sister Amber said, lifting an eyebrow. "How does Galen feel about you?"

Sasha paused and carefully said, "I suppose he sees me as a friend now. But imagine if he found out, he'd be horrified, wouldn't he?"

"Why?" Sister Amber asked, and Sasha started to despise that word.

"Because he's so much better than I am," Sasha said, almost desperately. "I've gone over this."

"Maybe he doesn't care," Sister Amber said, "or, more likely, he doesn't think himself better than you, or anyone. We devotees do tend to be rather humble."

Sasha ignored the quirk of her lips and said, "He should care. He deserves the best man in the world, someone who will be kind to him and make him smile. Someone who will listen to him and help him, and someone who will treasure him."

"Like you do," Sister Amber said, a triumphant grin on her face.

"I do not!" Sasha said, appalled that she could think so.

"I literally dug around in your memories," Sister Amber said, tilting her head towards him. "You do. You buy him flowers every week, for the Lady's sake."

"I suppose." Sasha felt as though he was at the top of Dragonet City, standing on a precipice, about to fall to his doom.

"Sasha," Sister Amber said, placing a hand gently over his. "Listen to me. If you let this simmer, it will eat you alive from the inside. If you tell him, and he rejects you, at least you will have a clean break. But, my dear, I don't think he will."

"How can you be so sure?" Sasha asked, voice dropping low.

"Because Galen deserves to have someone like you in his life," Sister Amber said. "He'd be a fool not to realize that, and Galen is no fool."

"He's not," Sasha said, throat dry.

Sister Amber suddenly wrapped him in a tight hug. After a moment of shocked silence, Sasha reciprocated, squeezing her tightly to him and trying desperately not to cry again. He buried his head in her hair, the gentle scent of flowers washing over him. She pulled back, then plucked a now-crumpled pink flower from her crown and tucked it behind Sasha's ear.

"You'll do what's right," she said, smiling.

As Sasha left the shrine, he couldn't help but notice the dandelions growing tall and proud at the entrance, not confined to any garden. Their bright yellow in the setting sun reminded him again of Galen, of the way that he kept going and kept growing no matter what. He turned Sister Amber's words over as he walked back to the barracks and wished he had her confidence.

CHAPTER 23

LOSS

SASHA

IT WAS A REST DAY. OVER THE PAST FEW DAYS, SASHA had turned Sister Amber's advice over and over in his mind like a worry stone. She was probably right, in the same way that Galen was always right. He needed to tell Galen, but he didn't know how. Or when. Galen was so overwhelmed that adding anything to his plate would be monstrous.

Maybe. He didn't really know.

Confessing with flowers could be sweet now that Sasha firmly knew their meanings. Just show up with his weekly bouquet, but this time it would speak truly. That would be romantic, right? However, when he arrived at the vendor, he immediately chickened out and bought another bouquet of yellow sunflowers. Coward.

Galen greeted him cheerfully and happily took the flowers, holding them up to his face and inhaling as he always did. Sasha hadn't thought they had much of a smell, but that certainly didn't seem to stop Galen. In the moment that Galen held the blossoms up to his nose, eyes closed, he looked completely free of worries. That, more than anything, was why Sasha loved to bring him flowers. He could tell that they brought him happiness, real happiness, and that's all Sasha wanted to do. If he could just bring some relief, some carefree moments to Galen for the rest of his life, that would be all Sasha would need.

Except it wasn't. Sasha wanted more, and he knew that he wanted more, and he hated himself for wanting more. Galen moved into the kitchen, now completely cleared of hanging dried herbs, and started to fill a vase with water for the flowers. Sasha watched him carefully, moving to the table and drumming his fingers against the well-worn wood.

"What do you do with all the flowers?" Sasha asked suddenly, if only to get his mind out of the rut it was in.

"Hmm?" Galen said as he turned. "Oh, well, I put them in water for a few days until they get droopy, and then I compost them. They're helpful for gardens, and it's improved our compost quite a bit. And I think people appreciate that there's more eggshells now thanks to you, too."

"Like, a community compost?" Sasha asked, eyebrows lifting.

"Yes," Galen said, grinning uncontrollably. "It was Sister Elowen and Miss Kingley's idea years ago. We all bring what we can, and people take compost as they need for their gardens. The original idea was a community garden, but the governor wouldn't sanction it. Oh, um, the compost bin isn't actually sanctioned. You won't report it, will you?"

"What?" Sasha said, and at Galen's wince, he clarified. "No, of course not, but why wouldn't she sanction a community garden?"

Galen shrugged as he placed the flowers in the vase. "Is it really all that surprising?"

"Yes," Sasha said. "We had a community garden in Medaka, and I know that other districts have them. I thought they were a staple in districts."

"Well, that's lovely for them," Galen said, sighing. "But we weren't allowed to have one in Candiru."

"But that's foolish," Sasha said, his forehead wrinkling. "It doesn't make sense."

"Yes," Galen said, hands tightening around the vase and his voice growing heavy as his mouth started to twist into a frown. "Yes, I know. I've been to other districts and seen the community gardens there. I've seen all the nice things that they have there that the governor endorses."

"But why would Candiru be different?" Sasha asked.

"Why do you think?" Galen said, nearly slamming the vase down on the table, his teeth gritted. He glared at Sasha with wet eyes. "What possible reason do you think that Governor Maple, the same person who cleared out Figlove Lane and left us to rot during a plague, wouldn't let us have a community garden to help the people here? What could it possibly be?"

Sasha was surprised, and he stood up straighter. Galen rarely got angry, but he sure was now, and it had happened so suddenly. There was a heavy lump in Sasha's throat, and he swallowed, thinking back to their conversation the day Galen had helped with the birth. When Sasha dismissed what Galen said about the governor.

"I didn't mean to imply that..." Sasha said. The times others had called the people of Candiru rats, the times he had done the same, echoed in his mind. "I'm sorry, Galen, that was..."

Galen's fingers were shaking as he let go of the vase, and then he ran his hands over his face, scrubbing their heels into his eyes. He took a deep breath and then visibly calmed down. When he opened his eyes again, he smiled apologetically.

"Sorry, I didn't mean to get angry," Galen said. "That wasn't fair to you."

"No, it was," Sasha said, and as Galen shook his head, he pushed on. "It was, Galen. You're right."

Galen crossed his arms, looked away, and then muttered, "You're not the one putting laws into place."

"Governor Maple seems like she's been preoccupied, huh?" Sasha prompted, hoping that this would be the right direction.

"Yeah, sure," Galen said with a shrug, and then sighed. "Anyway. Breakfast, morning prayers, I've got to work on a few salves and ointments, so the kitchen is going to be a right mess. Maybe we can get something from a cart for lunch."

Galen clearly wanted to move on from the governor and her treatment of Candiru, and Sasha had to oblige. Breakfast went the same as always, and Sasha watched carefully from the table as Galen set up his small shrine and said his prayers to the Lady of Flowers. The shrine was simple: a small painted screen, a wooden cup filled with light pink liquid, a flower that Galen had plucked from the bouquet, and a misshapen beeswax candle. Galen placed them all out with reverence before he knelt.

Sasha couldn't believe that there had been a time when he had been annoyed at the mere sounds of prayer. It truly sounded beautiful. Galen used a string of prayer beads, counting on each bead as he said the prayers in a near whisper. Sasha knew the whisper was his fault, and he winced. When he first started working with Galen, Galen's prayers had been loud and confident, but he had told Galen that they annoyed him. Like an ass.

Once Galen had finished, drinking down the contents of the cup and putting away each of the holy items, Sasha spoke up. "You don't have to whisper your prayers."

"What?" Galen asked, turning and staring at him with bright hazel eyes.

"I mean, the reason you're saying them so quietly. That's because of me, isn't it?" Sasha said, eyes dipping. "You don't have to. You can shout them if you want."

Galen smiled, running his fingers over the beads in his hands, and then said, "Thanks, but honestly my neighbors probably appreciate me being a bit quieter."

"Right," Sasha said, smirking, "though I could go over and tell them to fuck off if they're being rude, if you like."

"No, thank you," Galen said with a laugh. "No, I'd like to think I'm on mostly good terms with my neighbors."

"As you wish," Sasha said, and then glanced at the beads in Galen's hands. "Can I look at your prayer beads?"

"You want to?" Galen asked, joining him at the table. "I mean, sure."

Galen held out the beads and Sasha took them, his fingers brushing across Galen's ever so slightly. At the touch, sparks ran down Sasha's spine and he struggled to calm down. The beads were still warm from Galen's grasp, and Sasha savored that feeling. It was almost as though he was holding Galen's hand.

He held up the beads to look at the string more carefully. Each orb would have been clear glass, it seemed, if not for the perfectly preserved petal at the center. There was a rainbow of colors, each apparently from a different flower. It was beautiful, and Sasha held the string with reverence.

"Part of what takes us from pledges to full-fledged devotees is making our prayer beads," Galen said, breaking Sasha from his trance. "Well, it's not as though the moment the beads are made we're suddenly devotees, but the gift normally isn't given to us until they're done. I don't know if that's the Lady's doing, or if that's just skillfully timed that way. I suppose I'd know better if I were the bishop or something."

"You made these?" Sasha asked, brows lifting.

"Yes," Galen said, and he grinned wide enough to show his gap teeth. "We had help, of course, but I'm rather proud of how mine turned out."

"They're beautiful," Sasha said, handing the string back to Galen and savoring the small touch of their fingers again. On one hand, he did mean the beads, but he was also mesmerized by Galen's smile.

"Thank you," Galen said, and then with a laugh, "Be careful, I might end up getting a big head if you keep complimenting me. I mean, I already walk around Candiru as though I own the place."

Sasha laughed, shook his head, and said, "Well, we can't have that."

THE REST OF THE MORNING WAS EATEN UP AS GALEN started on his salves and ointments, grinding plants into pastes and mixing them. Boiling things in the kitchen, gathering bits of dried herbs, stuffing the completed mixtures into jars. Sasha felt very in the way.

At first, he had tried to help, but Galen had to keep stopping to correct the way he was doing things, and he eventually gave up. Instead, he sat and watched, chair pulled out of the kitchen and into the small entryway, waiting until there was a task he could do, like getting something down from a high shelf.

They were at it for a few hours, Galen chattering away as he laid out dried yarrow and watched a bubbling pot over the fire, when there was a frantic pounding at his door. Since Galen was elbow-deep in his work, Sasha got up and turned to answer it. He hoped that it was something easy, a child with a bloody nose or someone with a sore throat, but instead he opened the door to a frantic Jess.

They barely even looked at him before they shoved past shouting, "Galen! Galen, come quick! There's been an accident and he's dying!"

The moment Jess had burst into the house, Galen had dropped what he was doing and rushed over. He grabbed his short yellow cloak despite the heat of the day and pulled it on as Jess babbled at him. Sasha watched as Galen's head whipped around, and Sasha realized he was looking for his bag. Sasha had seen it on the small, beaten-up sofa in the back. He rushed past and grabbed it, tossing it to Galen at the door.

"Here!" Sasha called, and Galen snatched it out of the air with a nod of thanks, then ran after Jess.

Jess darted down the street with Galen close on their heels, and Sasha understood exactly why Galen had donned the cloak despite the heat. People cleared the way as soon as they saw the bright yellow. Sasha felt sweat running down his face and back as he struggled to keep up with the pair.

It wasn't long until they skidded to halt in front of Nina and Mandy's pottery shop. Sasha would have been worried that the black spot sickness had returned if it were not for the devastating scene in front of him.

A wagon, clearly from one of the upper districts, had crashed right in front of the pottery shop. The wagon's driver kept tearfully explaining that he didn't know what had spooked the horses and that he lost control and that he was sorry. The two women who owned the shop, and whom Sasha had been rude to, were clutching someone who was covered in blood, whose limbs weren't bending the right way, who didn't seem to be breathing. Galen, of course, didn't stop. So Sasha followed him.

It was even worse up close. The wagon's wheels had run over the person, and the horses had trampled him. His stomach had been torn open and glistening entrails peeked through the open wound, his skull had collapsed in at places, his eyes were swollen shut. Horrifyingly, there was a raspy breathing sound, even as blood poured out of his mouth at every exhalation.

"Galen, Galen, please," Mandy begged. "He's so young, he was putting out pots for me and he had a big one, and the wagon came and I think he didn't want to drop it, and then..."

Sasha realized with horror that he knew this man. This was Thomas. This was the young man who had come running to get Galen to help Mandy. He was just an apprentice, and yes, he was too young. Galen threw his bag open and started digging around before making a panicked sound in the back of his throat and moving to use the gift. He placed his hands on Thomas's stomach wound first, then shook his head and moved to place them on his head, then grunted and moved back to the stomach.

Oh, gods. Oh, Lion's teeth, this was so much. Galen started chanting and the pink glow appeared, starting to stitch together wounds, and then without warning, it faded and stopped. Galen made that panicked sound again and then moved his hands up to Thomas's head and started chanting again, but this time, no pink glow flickered. Galen was breathing heavily.

"No, come on, please!" Galen cried, keeping his hands in place and chanting again, but nothing happened. "Please!"

Galen lifted his hand and wiped his face, smearing it with blood. Thomas wasn't breathing anymore. He was gone. But Galen kept chanting, kept pressing his hands, desperation in his voice. Thomas wasn't moving, though, and everyone could see it. He was gone.

"Galen," Nina said, gently touching his shoulder as he continued to chant.

Galen turned his head to face her, breathing hard, his eyes wide and red rimmed. He looked terrifying with the blood and gore smeared over his face. Nina shook her head and squeezed his shoulder.

"Galen, he's gone," she said. "It's not your fault, you got here as soon as you could, but he's gone."

"No, no, he can't be," Galen said, voice shaking as he turned and started to chant again. "Come on, Lady of Flowers, please!"

"He's with the Crow now, Galen," Mandy said softly. "You did your best. It was just a horrible accident."

Galen was already on his knees, but he sank further into a crumpled mound. Jess squeezed his shoulder gently as well. Galen seemed far away, looking at Thomas's mangled body, but also looking past it. Sasha finally stepped forward and pulled Galen to his feet.

"Come on," Sasha said softly. "You've done all you can."

He walked the blood-soaked healer back through the streets of Candiru to his house. Galen didn't speak the entire walk home. His eyes were devoid of light, and he kept stumbling as he walked. Sasha supported him, one hand around his waist, the other at his elbow in a twisted parody of their trip home from the tavern just a few weeks previous.

Sasha didn't know the streets of Candiru as well as Galen did, but at this point he could always find Galen's house. When he spotted the little door with a few of the dandelions that had returned peeking up between the cobbles, he sighed with relief. Sasha opened the door and brought Galen inside. The kitchen was exactly as it had been, except that the pot was boiling over. Sasha swore and quickly sat Galen in a chair, then pulled the pot from the heat, burning himself in the process.

He hissed in pain, and Galen said quietly, "There's burn cream in the cupboard over the pump."

Sasha turned to him, and said, as gently as he could, "I'll take care of you first."

Galen stared at him, his eyes flat and far away, and then said, "You don't need to. I'm not hurt."

Sasha ignored him and went to the pump, picking up a bowl and filling it with water. He grabbed a washcloth and pulled a chair up to Galen. He dipped the cloth into the bowl and then, as gently as he could, he started washing the blood from Galen's face. Galen went incredibly still as Sasha cleaned him. It lasted for a few minutes, Sasha wiping away the remnants of the loss while Galen stared at him in disbelief. Finally, Sasha took a deep breath.

"I think you are hurt, Galen," Sasha said, keeping his voice low and soft. "It's okay, though. It's okay."

Galen's face suddenly twisted, and then he let out a sob. Tears poured down his face. Galen lifted a hand and scrubbed at his eyes as Sasha put down the cloth. Sasha's hands clenched and unclenched; he wasn't sure what to do, so he just watched Galen cry.

"It was my fault," Galen said in between gasping sobs. "It was *my* fault. If I had been faster, if I had been..."

Sasha grabbed Galen's shoulders and said, "How, in the name of all the gods, is a wagon losing control and hitting someone when you were five streets away *your* fault?"

"I should have been faster," Galen said. "Maybe I should have been out in the streets."

"You have one day off a week," Sasha said, squeezing his shoulders. "And you were using it to make more supplies for healing. Galen, what else could you have done? This was not your fault."

"It's my responsibility," Galen said, choking down another sob. "Thomas is dead because I couldn't save him. If I had been there, if I had made a decision sooner, maybe I could have called on the Lady in time and then..."

"Galen!" Sasha shouted, making Galen jump. "You are one person! You can't be everywhere. I'm sure this isn't the first time you lost somebody."

Galen stared at him, eyes wide and glistening, breathing

hard. He clenched his teeth, his mouth twisting into a deep frown, until he finally found the words.

"No," Galen said. "Of course not. I've lost plenty of people, but still…"

"Galen, what?" Sasha said, searching Galen's face for the right thing to say. "This wasn't your fault. Why are you blaming yourself?"

"Because I'm all they have!" Galen cried, his face growing red as tears poured freely again. "I am all that they have. No one else seems to fucking care, so I have to. I have to, Sasha. Governor Maple doesn't care; she'd let us rot or exterminate us like rats. The temple is sympathetic, but all I hear about is how their hands are tied. The guards certainly aren't going to do anything. I suppose I have the Kippers, but who knows how long it'll be until the governor decides that they need to be arrested too. I am all that they have, and I keep letting them down."

"You are not letting them down, Galen!" Sasha said. Shouted. "Lion's teeth, how could you think that? You give more than any other person that I have ever met, and you still want to give more. I cannot believe the situation that you are in, Galen. If anything, you are the one being let down, by everyone and everything in this godsforsaken city!"

Galen stared at him, wide-eyed. His face was still wet with tears, his eyes were still red, but his lips were pursed in thought, and his brow was wrinkled. He blinked and then opened his mouth to speak, only to close it again. Then his shoulders slumped.

"I'm just so sorry that you're alone," Sasha said. "It's not fair."

Galen closed his eyes for a moment, then opened them and said, "But I'm not alone."

"What?" Sasha asked, baffled.

"I...I have you," Galen said, a sob interrupting his sentence.

Sasha wished that he could be bold enough to kiss Galen then, as his heart really wanted, but that would be wildly unfair to Galen, who had just been sobbing and breaking down in the face of the injustice of the world. So instead, Sasha leaned forward and wrapped Galen in a strong hug. Galen was stiff for a moment, but then his shoulders relaxed, and he wrapped his arms around Sasha. He collapsed his head against Sasha's shoulder, giving in to everything.

The sobs started up again, but Sasha was able to rub small circles into Galen's back, to let him know that yes. He had him. And for as long as Galen would have him, Sasha would be there. No matter what.

Chapter 24

It Consumes

Galen

When Galen woke in the morning, he didn't want to get out of bed. Every time he lost someone, this happened. He asked himself if he was worthy of this post, he asked himself if he deserved the trust people put in him, he asked himself if he could even face the day. But he knew that he had to, so he did. He pushed himself up and forced himself to wash and get ready for the day. He dressed in the yellow tunic that he didn't deserve. Swallowing down the last of his self-pity, Galen moved into the kitchen to start on breakfast. Sasha would be there soon.

Sasha had stayed late last night, and it had been so kind of him to do so. He had held Galen while he cried, he had cleaned up the kitchen and then redid it when Galen clumsily knocked over an entire jar of pickled ginger, sending shattered glass, liquid, and yellow slices all over the kitchen floor. Sasha hadn't even scowled, just sat Galen back down and told him not to apologize. He spent the next half hour watching Sasha scrub his floor, a sight that both baffled and warmed him.

Sasha had bought them a late lunch and dinner with what Galen assumed were his own funds, though he grumbled about the cart workers' rudeness. He had stayed well after dark just to make sure that Galen was okay, and Galen felt like his heart was going to break.

He knew people appreciated him, but everyone was so busy. They'd give him bread, or buy him an ale, or greet him on the street, but this was different. It was so obvious that Sasha cared for him. He had cleaned the blood off his face, he had talked him down, and he had held him while he cried. No expectations, just the comfort of someone holding him. He hadn't known how much he had needed that. He hadn't known just how much he needed someone. He hadn't known how much he needed *this* someone.

Galen wrapped his arms around himself, closing his eyes and squeezing his sides. He could pretend, just for a moment, that it was Sasha's arms around him. When Galen's face had been pressed against Sasha's warm, solid chest, he had thought to himself that he wouldn't mind staying there. When Sasha had rubbed circles against Galen's back, Galen had wanted him to never stop.

Sasha's touch was so firm and so steady, and Galen craved it. His hand drifted up to his shoulder, the place where Sasha had rested his large, rough hand so many times. The ghost of it was there again, and Galen sighed. He knew that it'd never be more than a hand or a steady hug, but Galen would take it. He would take any touch between them.

Still mulling over Sasha's comforting touch, Galen went to start the tea. As he stood in the kitchen, his unfocused eyes not really seeing the bubbling water in the pot, he heard a commotion outside. Two loud voices were shouting angrily. He couldn't make out the words, but he swore he recognized one of them. Setting the mugs down, he moved over to the door and listened. He winced. Sasha was arguing with someone.

"There is absolutely no reason that you need to bother

him," Sasha was saying in his stern voice, the one that told people to kindly fuck off.

"Actually, Rider, there was a death, and he was involved, so I do need to ask him some questions," the other voice replied. This second voice was also familiar, but Galen couldn't place it, not in the same way that he instantly knew Sasha's.

"I didn't realize that you were a guard, *sir*. Isn't this below your paygrade?" Sasha asked, and Galen could practically hear him cross his arms.

"I'm not," the other voice said, "but the wagon was from Lenok District and the fact that it caused a death puts the incident within my purview."

"An accidental wagon death seems like a strange thing for an auditor to take an interest in," Sasha growled.

"I really don't know why you're being so touchy about a Candiru rat," the voice said huffily.

Oh dear. It was time to intervene before Sasha broke someone's nose. Galen quickly opened the door, allowing a very perturbed and poofed-up Muffin to slip inside the house and hide under the table. Galen looked back at the frightened blink fox and sighed but then stared in disbelief at the man Sasha had been shouting at.

The auditor from Figlove Lane, Miller, was standing there, fists clenched as he glared at Sasha. He turned and looked down at Galen with a contemptuous smirk before putting on a polite veneer. He nodded to Galen, and a vile, insincere smile spread across his lips.

"Good morning, Brother," Miller said. "I do apologize if our discussion disturbed you."

"Good morning," Galen said, eyes flicking over to the very cross-looking Sasha. "It's all right. I was already up and making tea. I just wanted to see what all the hubbub was."

"Yes, well, I understand that you witnessed the death of a

young man yesterday, a Mister Thomas Sharp?" Miller asked, lifting a brow but not dropping his nasty smile.

"Yes, sir," Galen said, trying to hold his voice steady. "I was called to the scene by a citizen. They ran to get me, and Mister Rider and I went to the scene as quickly as possible. Unfortunately, Mister Sharp was too far gone by the time I got there. I tried to use the gift, but it was too late."

Galen was proud of the fact that his voice didn't break, but the sympathetic look he got from Sasha over Miller's shoulder almost did him in. Miller hummed thoughtfully and then nodded.

"So you did not see the accident itself?" Miller asked.

"No, sir," Galen said. "Only the aftermath. For what it's worth, I think it was truly an accident. The driver seemed very repentant."

"Oh, no doubt," Miller said. "I just needed to get your statement. Things are a bit more, let's say, organized in other districts. They're a bit stricter and I needed to make sure everything was in order. We aren't all so cavalier as you are down here in Candiru."

He had to be trying to get a rise out of Galen, but Galen just smiled and said, "Well, we do our best. Was that all, sir?"

"Not quite," Miller said. "I was wondering if I could talk with you in private. Without your assigned guard listening in."

Galen blinked in surprise, then asked, "Right now?"

"If it's not too much trouble," Miller said in a voice that clearly indicated that he did not actually care how much trouble it would be.

Galen glanced over at Sasha, who had his arms crossed and appeared to be trying to make Miller's head explode just by glowering at him. Sadly, the effort seemed to be failing. Galen eventually sighed and nodded.

"Apologies, Mister Rider," Galen said to Sasha. "Hopefully this won't take long."

"*You* don't have anything to apologize for," Sasha said, clearly imagining Miller in a much more dire state than he was currently in.

Miller gave Sasha a dismissive glance, then walked into Galen's house. Galen gave a grumbling Sasha one last apologetic smile and then followed Miller inside. Miller was giving the room a once-over, looking at the jars of ointments that Galen had refilled, assessing the worn wood of the shelves and tables, and then staring at the vase of yellow flowers. Galen felt his face heat, though he couldn't have said exactly why.

"Honestly, this is precisely what I imagined this house would look like," Miller said, with a laugh and a shake of his head. "You're just a devotee of the Lady of Flowers to your core."

Galen couldn't decide if it was an insult or just an observation—with Miller it certainly wasn't praise—so he just took a deep breath and said, "Sir Miller, I don't wish to be rude, but I do have a very full schedule ahead of me today and I would like to get started as soon as I can."

"Of course," Miller said, pulling a chair out from the table. "Your time, like mine, is very valuable. This will be quick, if you'll have a—good gods, what is that?"

As Miller had moved the chair, Muffin had emerged and stared at him. As he shouted, though, Muffin suddenly vanished, then reappeared behind Galen's legs. Miller was staring at the blink fox in disgust and disbelief but then shook his head.

"Your...pet?" Miller asked.

"Of sorts," Galen said, scooping Muffin up into his arms. "He belongs to the street if he belongs to anyone. This is Muffin."

"Ah," Miller said, regaining his composure. "A pest, then. I can send an exterminator, if you like."

"No!" Galen said, and he could hear the defiance in his own voice. "He's not doing any harm. Just likes to sneak into my house, that's all."

"All right, then," Miller said, chuckling dismissively. "I know how you devotees like to care for strays. I understand. Speaking of, that's what I wanted to talk to you about. Strays."

"Strays?" Galen asked, holding Muffin tighter to his chest.

"Yes, your guard. Mister Sasha Rider. How has he been treating you?" Miller asked.

"Sasha? Oh, he's been...well, he's been great." Galen felt a smile grow on his face. "We got off to a bit of a rocky start, but he's been very helpful as of late."

"Really?" Miller asked with a huff of surprise. "That's quite something. Sasha Rider has a bit of a, well, let's be kind and call it a reputation. There've been a considerable number of complaints about him and his demeanor. Especially towards devotees."

"Right, ah, he may have mentioned that," Galen said, shrugging.

"And I just wanted to make sure that you weren't covering for him," Miller said, placing his hands on the table. "I know that devotees, especially those from the Lady of Flowers, have a high tolerance for bullshit, pardon my frankness, Brother, but if Rider is acting inappropriately, I will step in. I could do a bit of auditing."

Galen went cold at the thought of losing Sasha, but he cleared his throat and said, "No worry. Well, as I said, we did get off to a bit of a rough start. Off on the wrong foot, I suppose, but we have since reconciled. Sasha has been very thoughtful and kind, and endlessly diligent in his duty. I've never felt safer than when I'm with him."

"I find that rather hard to believe," Miller said coldly, staring daggers at Galen.

"I am not lying," Galen said, making a shield of his own stare. "If you do not believe me, I'd be happy to accompany you to the temple of Rising Dawn and you can have a truth-seeker interview me."

Miller hadn't seemed the type to be surprised, but his eyelid twitched slightly in annoyance, and he said, "I don't think that will be necessary."

"Glad to hear it."

"You really have no complaints?"

"Not one."

Miller sighed deeply and said, "Well, then, I suppose I will stop wasting your time. Have a good day, Brother."

"You as well, sir," Galen said.

Miller left, nearly walking directly into Sasha, who was lingering at the door. The moment the door was open, Muffin scrambled out of Galen's arms, scratching his cheek in the chaos, and bolted out into the street. Galen sighed, lifting his fingers to his cheek to wipe the blood away only for Sasha to bombard him with concern.

"Are you all right?" Sasha said, grabbing Galen's hand and taking his chin to turn his face and look at the scratch.

"I'm fine, Sasha," Galen said, heat coursing through him at Sasha's touch. "It's only a scratch. Muffin was just eager to leave."

"That asshole," Sasha grumbled.

"Muffin?" Galen asked, smirking.

"No, Miller, of course," Sasha said, releasing Galen and then adding with a blush. "Oh, you were joking."

"Yes, and I do agree with your assessment," Galen said, sighing.

"Did he say something to you?" Sasha asked, his face changing from the red of embarrassment to the nearly indistinguishable red of anger. "What was it? I'll break his fucking nose."

Galen shook his head. "No, you will not. He didn't say anything about me, personally."

"What did he say, then?"

"Well, he was asking about you."

Sasha suddenly paled and asked carefully, "What did he want to know?"

Galen looked at the floor and sighed, then said, "He asked repeatedly if you were being respectful. He said that you had trouble before, and he wanted to make sure that I wasn't being too forgiving."

Sasha was silent for a moment before he asked, "And what did you tell him?"

"The truth," Galen said, and at Sasha's terrified look, he clarified, "I told him that we got off to a bit of a rocky start but now we're on good terms. I told him that you had been very courteous and kind, and a good protector, and that I had no complaints."

Sasha suddenly sat down and said in a low voice, "That can't be the truth."

Galen sighed, offering Sasha a small smile. "It most certainly is. What you did for me yesterday made it obvious that you're a good and kind person. If you think I don't see that, well, then you're a fool, Sasha Rider."

Sasha looked at him with a very odd gleam in his eye and then chuckled to himself, shaking his head. That was where they left it, and Sasha hurried to help with breakfast to make up for the late start. Galen noticed that any time Sasha's hand brushed against his skin, it lingered there for a moment longer than it needed to. It must be because of the odd interaction in the morning. There could be no other reason. Nevertheless, he savored the touches.

~

THEY LEFT AS THE BELLS OF RISING DAWN RANG AND went through their day. Nothing too horrible, nothing too difficult, just helping people who needed to be helped. Galen enjoyed it: he relished having Sasha right behind him, ready to help the moment he asked. He tried not to think about the worry in Sasha's eyes when he thought that the auditor might remove him.

It wasn't until nearly another week had passed that things started to go wrong again. Galen had another rare short day and was taking a lunch break, leaning against the wall that separated pedestrians from the long drop to the river. It was a gut-wrenching height, but Galen liked it. It reminded him of how small he was in the face of everything. Sasha did not like it as much and had told Galen quite a few times that he was strange for enjoying it.

Sasha was trying to convince him that it was a perfect day to go to a tavern again when a small child ran up to him brightly flushed, sweat pouring down his little face. Galen raced to meet him; it was Andrew, Miss Kingley's little one who had broken his arm not long ago. He was panicking.

"Brother Galen!" Andrew cried. "Brother Galen, it's so bad, there's a bad sickness. I think that Beth is about to die. There's all these black spots and she's coughing up black stuff!"

Galen's lunch fell from his hand and was still travelling down to the river below when he started running towards Miss Kingley's house, leaving both Andrew and Sasha shouting after him. He would not lose anyone to this disease; he had sworn to himself that he would stop it.

As he rounded a corner, he glanced back and saw Sasha running a few steps behind him with Andrew in his arms, clutching the guard's broad shoulders. Fine, that was good.

He'd have to thank Sasha later. It still took far too long to get to Miss Kingley's house. Candiru was too big.

He didn't even knock, which was rude, but the urgent situation trumped politeness. He heard violent coughing as he ran past the horde of scared children in the front room. He pushed into the back, where Miss Kingley was trying to help an older girl who was writhing on the bed, coughing up a tide of the black ichor, the sores on her body spreading more of the viscous liquid across the sheets.

"Move!" Galen shouted, already lifting his hands, but he was too late.

Beth arched off the bed, released one final rattle of breath, and then collapsed back down, dead. Galen stood in shock for a moment, horror, guilt, and anger overcoming him.

Then all that was struck from him.

Around Beth's body, the puddle of ichor started to move. Miss Kingley froze in abject horror, but Galen's eyes fixed on the trembling mass. The black tar-like substance under and around the dead body quivered, then tendrils of sludge burst out of the muck, flailing in the air as though searching for something. Galen's fingers twitched, his instincts screaming at him to rush back away from the bed, but he couldn't tear his eyes away from what was emerging from Beth. The tendrils gripped the quilt, leaving sticky black stains where they touched, pulling the blob forward.

More of the ichor flowed out of Beth's sores, leaving her body to shrivel. The black goo gathered into one gelatinous body, about the size of Muffin, and continued to reach with searching tendrils. A sound emerged from the newly formed monster, a high screech that made the hair on the back of Galen's neck stand on end. He was about to cover his ears, but Galen's intuition told him moving could be a mistake. So he gritted his teeth as it rose in pitch and the monster took shape.

Miss Kingley made the mistake of moving.

She took a step back, away from the monster, and its tentacles sprang forward and wrapped around her arms, neck, and face. Her scream was choked off as the creature propelled itself forward, burrowing past her teeth and down her throat. Lady of Flowers, it wasn't a sickness at all. It was a parasite.

Miss Kingley was choking and screaming, tears streaking down her wrinkled face, and that finally broke Galen out of his stupor. He rushed forward and placed his hands on either side of her face, chanting intensely. The pink glow appeared around them and soon the parasite within her was dead. It leaked from her mouth as a black sludge, dripping onto the ground, completely immobile. The inky blackness of the terror was not the same abyss of darkness it had been. The light of the Lady had dulled it, leaving it washed out. Once it was done, they stared at each other, disbelief filling the space between them.

"What was that?" Sasha asked from the doorway.

Galen dropped his hands, turned around, and said, "I'm not quite certain, but be damn sure I am going to figure it out. Miss Kingley, I am very sorry for your loss. I am going to the temple of the Lady of Flowers right now. If you would like, I can request that they send a speaker to you."

Miss Kingley was silent for a moment, then nodded and said, "Yes, if you would, Brother Galen. That would be appreciated."

"Of course," Galen said. "I am so sorry."

Miss Kingley just nodded, wiping her eyes and letting her hand slip down to her throat. Galen looked at Beth's body one last time, his heart aching that he couldn't save her. Instead, he would just have to end this. No one else would die from this. He turned to walk out, but his way was blocked by Sasha, still lingering in the doorway and staring. Galen had to gently push Sasha to get him to move. Sasha did, and the two of them walked silently past the group of children huddling in the front room. They didn't even ask Galen for candy.

Once they were out on the street, Sasha grabbed Galen's shoulder and said, "I've never seen anything like that."

"Neither have I," Galen said, biting his lip. "It's not a sickness."

"What is it?" Sasha asked. "It looked like...like a monster, but cities aren't supposed to have monsters. That's the whole point of cities."

"I think it's a parasite," Galen said. "And yes, a monster. That would explain why it's not spreading like a sickness. It would have to kill its host first and then move to the next living thing. Gods, I'm just lucky that the Lady of Flowers has been killing it when I heal people."

"But if you were killing it, how has it been spreading? You've healed at least five people with it, right?" Sasha asked.

"It just confirms my suspicion. Someone is infecting people on purpose," Galen said. He looked up at Sasha. "We need help."

CHAPTER 25

THE GOVERNOR

GALEN

"Interesting," Bishop Rose said. "Very interesting."

Galen was kneeling in front of her in one of the temple's central gardens. He hadn't changed before leaving Candiru to go three districts up to the main temple of the Lady of Flowers. Black splotches of ichor marred his bright yellow tunic. It hadn't taken that long to explain the story to the bishop, and although she would have believed him without corroboration, Sasha had been standing behind him confirming everything.

The bishop motioned for him to stand, and he did so immediately. Bishop Rose was an older woman with sun-tanned skin and a careworn face. Her hair was a deep salt and pepper, tied up in a knot at the base of her neck, just like Galen and half of the devotees of the Lady of Flowers wore their hair. The bishop's robes were pale pink elegantly embroidered with the colors of all three branches of devotees: the bright yellow of the healers, the deep blue of the speakers, and the dark green of the growers. She was staring at him and tapping her chin.

"I apologize, your grace, I just don't know what to do," Galen said, wincing.

"Oh, no apology needed," Bishop Rose said, brushing her hand through the air. "I wouldn't know what to do in your position either."

"I see," Galen said. "Well, glad to know that I'm not the only one at a loss."

Bishop Rose laughed, then continued, "Sometimes, that is the most helpful thing, isn't it? Just knowing that you're not alone."

Galen nodded at that, because it was true, but then said, "Yes, but I would still appreciate a way to stop this."

"Oh, of course," Bishop Rose said, closing the small distance between them and taking his hands. "Don't worry. Well, maybe worry a bit. We're going to have to ask for the governor's help."

"Oh," Galen said, biting back the more intense things that he wished to say, since he was in the presence of the bishop. "I can do my best, but I don't know how well it's going to go."

The bishop smiled gently, and said, "My dear Galen, I am not sending you up there on your own. You'll have a speaker with you to do the, well, speaking. You'll be there for clarifying questions and eyewitness reports."

Galen felt himself relax slightly. "All right, that'll be good. When will we seek audience?"

"In about an hour, maybe two, I would think," Bishop Rose said.

"An hour?" Galen squeaked, and the bishop smiled again.

"This is very pressing, isn't it?"

"Yes." Galen's heart raced sickeningly at the memory of that creature crawling into Miss Kingley's mouth.

"We'll brief the next available speaker, you'll change into something cleaner, and then you'll head on up," Bishop Rose said. "Mister Rider?"

"Yes, ma'am?" Sasha said, straightening up immediately.

"You'll go with, of course," Bishop Rose said. "Corroborating stories and all that."

"Yes, ma'am," Sasha said. "I wouldn't leave Brother Galen alone."

Something fluttered in Galen's chest at those words said in Sasha's deep and steady voice. He hoped that it didn't show too much on his face, but he still turned to the guard and offered him a thankful smile. Sasha smiled back at him in turn.

"Wonderful," Bishop Rose said, releasing Galen's hands to clasp hers together. "Wait here. I'll find a speaker."

She swept back into the towering temple that surrounded the garden courtyard where they had had their meeting. Once she was gone, Galen breathed in deeply, closing his eyes and taking in the medley of garden scents. The earthy fragrance of soil, the sweet aroma of honeysuckle and roses, the sharp smell of mint and rosemary; they all wrapped him in a comfortable, familiar embrace. He really missed this sometimes, his time in the temple. He loved helping the people of Candiru, and he knew it was necessary, but there was so little time to do just...this. One of the directives of the Lady of Flowers was to stop and smell the flowers, and that was a directive that he often had to ignore.

"Galen?" Sasha's voice broke the peace.

Galen opened his eyes and looked up at the guard. "Yes?"

"Sorry, I didn't mean to disturb you," Sasha said, wincing. "But, well, are you all right? This is a lot."

Galen shrugged. "What else can I do?"

Sasha opened his mouth, but thought better of it, closing it and then just crossing his arms. He chose a peony that apparently offended him and glowered at it with vigor. In an effort not to laugh, Galen closed his eyes again to breathe in the garden. He was able to do so for a few minutes before he was interrupted once more.

"Brother Galen?" a voice asked.

He opened his eyes and saw a young devotee, probably newly graduated from pledge, standing in front of him in the dark green tunic and brown pants of a grower. Their mousy brown hair was tied into a knot and their feet, like many growers', were bare.

"Come with me," they said. "We have new clothes and robes for your visit with the governor. Also, you may want to, uh, wash up."

Galen smiled at them and nodded, then turned to Sasha, "I won't be long, but don't worry. I'm safe in the temple."

"I know," Sasha said. "I'll just, uh, appreciate the flowers?"

"I planted those daffodils over there," the young devotee said with a smile, pointing to the patch of yellow. "In case you want to appreciate them."

Galen laughed lightly at the bafflement on Sasha's face, then let himself be led away to the baths. They weren't particularly busy at this time of day, and Galen got a pool all to himself. He had told Sasha he wouldn't be long, but that ended up being a lie. The luxury of hot water that he could soak in, not just a wet, soapy cloth to wipe himself with, made him linger.

When he finally got out and dried his body and hair with a fluffy towel, he was given a brand-new healer's tunic, as well as new trousers and a healer's robe. That was the real surprise. It was white with the edges bordered with yellow silk, instead of the simple wool that he thought he deserved. These were only given out on special occasions to deeply important healers. Galen felt unworthy of it as he pulled it on. His chipped and dull flower pendant seemed wrong set against the new luxury.

The devotee, named Lark, helped him tie his hair again

and then placed a flower crown on his head. It was made from lemon-colored yarrow, to represent the healers, and, of course, pink primroses to represent the Lady. Galen looked at himself in the small mirror and breathed in.

He was almost the picture of a perfect healer. Almost. As always, the vision was ruined by his scar. Devotees of the Lady of Flowers were meant to be friendly and approachable, but the giant marred section of his face tended to scare away children and repel adults. Instead of the smooth tan skin of the rest of his face, his scar was white and puckered, twisted in unnatural patterns from when it struggled to heal. The mark clawed its way just under his eye, and he remembered one of the healers telling him how lucky he had been that the fire hadn't stolen that as well.

Unbidden, his hand lifted and his fingers brushed against the rough skin there. It was as rough as a dried lemon, no softness to be found. His throat closed up and his eyes grew hot as he imagined what could have been. What *he* could have been. He wished he could just smooth away the imperfection, but it was his to bear. It was his reminder that he had lived while his family had died; it was his reminder of his duty to Candiru.

He released the breath in a sigh, lowered his hand, and turned to move back into the garden. Blinking away the unshed tears, he shook his head and reminded himself that there were far more important things than his vanity at stake. When he walked into the open air, he was surprised to see Sasha talking animatedly with a speaker. He recognized her instantly as Sister Amber. She was well-known in the temple and wore a speaker's white robes with blue silk edges. Her crown of primrose and forget-me-nots was beautiful, and she wore it far better than he did his.

When she spotted him, her eyes twinkled, and she called, "Brother Galen! We were just talking about you."

To Galen's utter surprise, Sasha's face flushed brilliant scarlet. He held up his hands in denial as Sister Amber laughed. Galen moved beside them, the shortest of the trio, and smiled gently at Sasha.

"It wasn't anything bad, despite this one's reaction," Sister Amber said, grinning. "Well, I've been briefed. Are you ready?"

"As I'll ever be." He tried to smile, but he suspected the result was wavery at best.

"Fantastic, the carriage should be here shortly," Sister Amber said.

Sister Amber strode out of the garden with the confidence of someone who knew that she would be followed. She was right, of course. Galen and Sasha both trailed behind her. Galen fought the urge to lift the robe as he walked, knowing he didn't need to. It was remarkably well-fitted and wasn't too large for him, which he would have expected.

"You, uh, you look nice," Sasha said as they walked through a hall full of vases of flowers with devotees bustling around. "Really nice. It suits you."

"Oh, thank you," Galen said, fighting a growing blush. He really shouldn't be blushing. "I don't really feel as though I've earned the right to wear something this important, truthfully."

"If anyone has earned the right," Sasha said, staring at the stained-glass symbol of the Lady of Flowers above the entryway as they continued to follow Sister Amber, "it's you. I'll admit, I don't know much about the Lady's teachings, but you seem to embody them, based on what I've learned."

Galen pressed a hand up to his chest, trying to hold in the emotions gathering there, and said, in a surprisingly broken voice, "Thank you. That means a lot."

He and Sasha exchanged a glance, and Sasha offered him one of those warm, kind smiles and placed his large hand on

Galen's shoulder, squeezing it comfortingly. With Sasha standing beside him, he could do this. He was certain of it. Sasha would support him and he would be kind, and with that in mind, Galen could face Governor Maple.

The carriage was one usually set aside for Bishop Rose, so it was quite nice. It was made of light wood with the Lady's symbol painted in pink on the side. The driver was not a devotee, but Galen recognized him as a temple employee. He helped Sister Amber in, then did the same for Galen. Sasha declined the hand and just pulled himself up.

The interior had cushioned seats but no proper windows, just slats to let in air. There was a magelight within, though, and that luxury deeply surprised Galen. Magelights were expensive to buy and to maintain, especially in Dragonet City, where mages were few and far between. The river city didn't have the types of universities or libraries that would attract mages. Galen would bet good money that fewer than two dozen mages could be found within the city's boundaries.

"I know," Sister Amber said, watching Galen stare at the magelight. "It's amazing, isn't it? Apparently, they're very common elsewhere, and nowhere near as pricey."

"I visited Shastian City once when I was younger," Sasha said. "Every home had at least one, and most businesses had several. But they are the 'Shadow City,' so it makes sense."

"Oh, yes," Sister Amber said. "Even Dresia has them more commonly. The Grand Temple there is richly adorned with them. It can be very striking. Have you ever made the trip, Brother Galen?"

Galen looked between the two of them, then shook his head, saying, "I've never left Dragonet City."

"Really?" Sasha said, his brows lifting. "Not even to the riverbanks?"

"No," Galen said. "Just to other districts. And not even all of those."

"Huh," Sasha said, gazing at him. "I could take you out to the countryside, at least. If you want. My family has a small cottage out there, if you need a vacation or something."

Sister Amber suddenly snorted and gave Sasha a look. In response, Sasha mumbled something unintelligible and then scowled. Galen ran a hand over his face. He had really hoped that Sasha could be civil with such an important member of the temple, but that was apparently wishful thinking.

"I don't really take vacations, but the offer is appreciated," Galen said apologetically.

Sasha just smiled sadly in return. "You should. You deserve one."

Sister Amber and Galen shared one bench and Sasha took up the other. Theoretically, they could have fit a fourth person in the carriage, but it would have been a tight fit with Sasha's width. Galen was rather small, though, and he could probably fit on the bench with Sasha if he didn't mind Sasha's side pressing up against him, his warmth pushing against Galen, comforting and strong... If Galen could have done so without the others noticing, he would have pinched himself. It was embarrassing how smitten he was.

Sasha was being nice, he was being kind, but that didn't mean anything. People didn't like Galen like that. Galen was meant to embody the Lady of Flowers. He was meant to help people, not do whatever it was that his mind was conjuring. And how could he selfishly think about that while someone was in Candiru infecting people with a parasite? What was wrong with him?

"You're rather quiet, Brother Galen," Sister Amber said, smiling at him.

Galen startled and then mirrored her smile, saying "Yes, sorry. Just lost in thought."

Sister Amber patted his knee. "Understandable. Don't worry, I'll handle Governor Maple. I've dealt with her before."

"You have?" Sasha asked, his brows lifting spectacularly.

Sister Amber grinned at him. "I have indeed, Mister Rider. I'm rather high ranking in the temple, in fact. I do enjoy going to the small shrines, though. Helping those who need to talk about something. Telling people what they need to hear."

Sasha looked away from her, folding his arms and grunting. Galen wanted to kick Sasha's shin and tell him to stop being rude, but Sister Amber was laughing. She took her hand from Galen's knee and patted Sasha's thigh good-naturedly, making the guard sigh heavily. This was...this was odd.

"Not right now," Sasha said, his voice low.

"Then when?" Sister Amber asked, smiling away.

Sasha was quiet for a moment, chewing on his lip, and then said, "Soon."

"Good," Sister Amber said, clasping her hands together. "Remember what I told you."

"I know," Sasha said, sighing.

Galen looked between the two of them, and then asked unsteadily, "Do I want to know?"

"It's a private matter for now," Sister Amber said. "I'm sure you'll know soon enough."

"Right," Galen said, shifting uneasily on the cushioned bench.

His mind ran through a thousand different scenarios. Perhaps Sasha had asked for help with telling Galen that he was leaving. He was tired of the excruciatingly long days and persistent loneliness that came with Galen's station. It would be disappointing, but Galen wouldn't be able to fault Sasha. But maybe...

Maybe the opposite was true, that Sasha had something far sweeter to tell him. Maybe the lingering touches, the soft looks, the kind words just for Galen all meant something more. Galen allowed himself a small indulgence, following that train of thought. If Sasha cared for him as more than just a friend, Galen didn't know what he'd do.

He stared down at the floor of the carriage, willing himself not to blush. This was neither the time nor place for such thoughts, but they still raced around his mind like a pack of wild blink foxes. It was making him giddy, even if he knew they were mere fancies. No one could ever want him, least of all Sasha Rider.

It took far too long, and not nearly long enough, to reach Dragonet Palace. The carriage door opened and the wind slammed into Galen. They were high up, far above the river, and it was dizzying, even if he couldn't bring himself look down at the steep, winding streets that had led up to their destination. He could *feel* the height.

The palace itself sparkled, made of a hard, white stone that caught the sun and reflected it back. Galen tried to imagine what it took to cart that amount of stone up to the top of Dragonet City and was horrified at the prospect. Sister Amber squeezed his shoulder and Sasha patted his back. Taking a bracing breath of the sharp air, Galen followed them into the palace.

As they made their way through wide, sparkling halls, Sister Amber cleared a path through clerks and guards with her quick speech all the way to the governor's audience room. Galen followed silently behind, barely taking in the tapestries and portraits, the polished floors, and the guards in glittering plate armor, so much nicer than Sasha's leather armor. Suddenly, something surfaced in his memory.

"Didn't you say you wanted to be a palace guard?" Galen whispered to Sasha while Sister Amber cajoled the governor's secretary.

"Hmm?" Sasha said, and then his brow furrowed. "You remember that?"

Galen nodded and said, "You mentioned it the first day we met."

"That's right," Sasha said with a sigh. "I don't want to anymore. I like working with you."

"Oh, really?" Galen said, chuckling. "You would rather be down in the bloody trenches with me in Candiru than here in a glittering palace wearing shining armor?"

"Yes," Sasha said with finality.

Galen laughed, shaking his head. "I'm not sure I can believe that."

Sasha huffed, then said, "You should. I've told you before, I like spending time with you."

Galen was still formulating a response when Sister Amber called back, "Come on, boys! We're in."

The governor's office was exactly what Galen had been expecting. He had never met the governor, but apparently his assessment of her from afar had been correct. Rich was the only word for it. There was a grand window that would have let in a lovely amount of sunlight if it weren't covered by heavy velvet curtains of such a deep crimson that they were nearly black. Instead, an abundance of magelights lit the room, which was larger than Galen's entire house.

The carpet beneath his feet was plush and his shoes sank into it. That felt very odd. The wooden desk and chairs were dark and polished to an impossible shine, and plush cushions on the chairs matched the drapes. They looked almost brand new, without a single wrinkle or spot of wear blemishing their surface. Behind the desk was a larger-than-life-size portrait of the governor herself standing on the banks of the Haplin River with Dragonet City behind her. He knew it was just perspective, but she looked like a giant.

Governor Maple herself was a pale woman with golden

hair that sat in a heavy braid on her shoulder. She stood just to the side of her desk, resting her carefully manicured nails on the wood without doing anything as revealing as tapping them. A coral silk dress trimmed with pink lace brought out the color in her otherwise pale skin. It was lovely; in fact, it probably cost more than most citizens in Candiru made in a year. She held her face neutral, not letting any emotion through the mask.

Sister Amber gave a small bow, just a dip of the shoulders, and Galen copied her. Sasha gave a quick salute. Governor Maple remained rigidly upright, staring at the three of them, making only the slightest nod of acknowledgment.

"Sister Amber, and another devotee, always a joy to meet with the representatives of the Lady of Flowers," Governor Maple said, her voice as neutral as her face.

"Governor Maple, I am so thankful that you made time in your busy schedule for us," Sister Amber said, smiling.

"As I understand it, you didn't give me much of a choice," the governor said. "I heard you berating my secretary."

"I wouldn't call it berating," Sister Amber said, her smile resting easily on her face, "more like speaking with intention."

"Of course you would," Governor Maple said, a small sigh breaking through her carefully cultivated neutrality. "Well, what is it this time?"

"May we sit?" Sister Amber asked, gesturing to the chairs.

The governor narrowed her eyes slightly, then waved her hand in a way that Sister Amber must have interpreted as permission, because she sat. Governor Maple moved behind her desk and sat as well, steepling her fingers. Galen sat beside Sister Amber, but Sasha remained standing protectively behind Galen.

"Well, Governor Maple, you know me," Sister Amber said, her voice light and pleasant, "but I'd like to introduce Brother

Galen. He's a healer working in Candiru Quarter. And this is Mister Rider, Brother Galen's assigned guard."

For the briefest moment, Galen thought he saw something flicker in the governor's eyes when Sister Amber mentioned Candiru. It seemed deeper than the disgust that so many from higher districts felt, so far as he could tell from that glimpse.

"Hello," Galen said, lifting a hand. Sasha just grunted.

"Hello," Governor Maple said. "I assume that you're here for a purpose, not just to see about my sniffles?"

"Yes, but I'd be happy to look into your sniffles if the palace doctor can't help you," Galen said, keeping his voice light.

Thankfully, the governor smirked and said to Sister Amber, "Well, get on with it."

Sister Amber proceeded to explain the black spot sickness that was not a sickness much more succinctly than Galen ever could have. She presented Galen's suspicions that someone had been infecting the people of Candiru with a parasite as the actual truth, not merely a theory. She made it clear that it was a deeply important matter that needed to be solved soon. It was incredible to see a master at work.

When she had finished, the governor sighed deeply and said, "And I assume you want me to spend resources to look into this problem in Candiru?"

"Of course," Sister Amber said with a smile that could cut through stone. "It is your job, after all."

Governor Maple scowled, and then looked at Galen carefully, as though evaluating him. He tried not to shift under her gaze, tried to look as confident and sure as Sister Amber, tried to look as steady and firm as Sasha.

"And why did you not bring this up sooner, Brother Galen?" the governor asked.

"I brought it up after the first case, and I reported every

case after that," Galen said, willing his voice not to shake. "What I saw today, though, was different."

"And you did not push for action sooner?" Governor Maple asked, lifting a plucked brow.

Sister Amber cleared her throat and answered for him, "Brother Galen has been very busy. He is the lone healer in Candiru, a district that contains nearly a tenth of the city's population. Honestly, it's a miracle that he was able to spare the time to be here now."

"Well, the gods do bless us, it seems," Governor Maple said with a sigh. "Is there any worry that it will spread to the rest of the city?"

"No, that's the problem," Galen said. "It's not like a plague, it's a living being that's consuming those who are sick, but I've killed it every time I've found it. If I wasn't, it would presumably spread, but there is someone infecting people with it. This needs to be acted on immediately."

"And who might this someone be?" Governor Maple asked, her voice sharp.

"Well," Galen said, fighting to keep meeting her eyes, "every one of my patients who suffered from this reported encountering someone in a fine cloak who bumped into them or touched them."

"A fine cloak? That isn't much to go off." She seemed deeply unimpressed, just as Galen had feared she would be.

"It's odd for Candiru Quarter," Galen said. "All of the people who were infected were natives of Candiru. We know when someone isn't from Candiru."

"We?" Governor Maple asked, her head tilting to the side ever so slightly.

Galen felt the blood drain from his face, then braced himself and said, "I am from Candiru originally."

"I see," the governor said. "I hope that you are not insinuating that someone from the upper districts is purposefully going down to Candiru to infect people with a, what was it? A parasite? You don't think that they would have better things to do with their time?"

Galen was a bit stunned by her callous question. It seemed as though Sister Amber was as well; she somehow sat up even straighter to look searchingly at the governor. But it was Sasha who shifted and placed a hand on Galen's chair, clenching his teeth and nearly growling.

"You know, governor," Sasha grunted, "you seem to be rather cavalier with the lives of your people. You don't appear concerned about this at all."

"Sasha," Galen said quietly, and he felt the man relax infinitesimally.

"I didn't realize that your guard was so protective," Governor Maple said, resting her chin in her hand.

"That is my job," Sasha said, his voice low and angry.

"Sasha," Galen said, and then took a breath before looking at the governor. "He has a point, ma'am."

"Oh, does he?" the governor asked.

Galen gathered himself and said, "The people of Candiru are also citizens of Dragonet City. You are the governor of Dragonet City, which means that you are responsible for their lives, not just the lives of those in wealthier districts. I know that they may not fit your ideal picture of a citizen, but the city runs on their labor, you understand? If someone is out there trying to kill them, and trying to make it look like another plague, something is wrong in your city. You are the governor. It is your job to fix that, is it not? I'm sorry that it isn't happening in a place that is more convenient for you, but it is happening. So, what will you do about it?"

At some point during his speech, Galen had stood up and moved closer to the desk. He didn't realize he had done so until he felt Sister Amber's hand on his wrist. He blinked and muttered an apology before stepping back and dropping into the chair again.

"No, Brother Galen," Sister Amber said, the easy smile gone, replaced by a look of fierce determination. "Don't apologize. Well, Governor Maple, would you care to answer his question?"

Maple sneered at her and then directed her gaze back to Galen before saying, "I will investigate it, Brother Galen. The Lady of Flowers does not need to threaten me in order to make me *care* about my citizens. Trust me, I do care deeply about every district in Dragonet City and about every person, too."

"Thank you," Galen muttered, but he didn't truly mean it.

The promise was empty, hollow words from an empty, hollow person. If the governor truly cared about Candiru, Galen would jump into the Haplin River from the top of the city.

"Was that all?" the governor asked Sister Amber. "Or is there some other crucial matter you need to bring to my attention? A loose dog that you wish to badger me about, perhaps?"

Galen flinched at that. He couldn't help it, and he felt Sasha step forward at the movement. Luckily, Sister Amber was there and grabbed the guard's wrist, halting his progress. It wasn't the time or place.

"That is all, Governor Maple," Sister Amber said, keeping the peace as only a true speaker could. "Thank you for your time."

The governor nodded in dismissal. Sister Amber stood first, giving that same short bow again, followed by Galen moments later. She started to walk out with dignity and grace, whereas Galen was trying to stop his heart from beating out of his chest in panic. He could feel Sasha right behind him and wished that Sasha would place a warm hand on his shoulder. He desperately wanted that bit of comfort after such a terrifying confrontation.

They were almost to the door when Governor Maple suddenly called, "Oh, Brother Galen?"

All three of them turned around, and Galen asked, "Yes?"

"Please let me know if I can send a court face painter down to teach you how to cover that scar," Governor Maple said, a falsely considerate smile etched into her face. "I'd be happy to do it. It's rather intimidating, don't you think? Are children afraid of you? How do you manage to examine them?"

The world spun and saltwater lifted in Galen's throat. He only managed to stutter out, "I—" before Sister Amber reached suddenly around him and grabbed Sasha's arm as he took a quick step towards the governor, his face a mask of fury.

"Obviously, governor, he has been managing just fine," Sister Amber said, her voice smooth and steady. "He has handled all of Candiru on his own for years and they love him down there."

"Well, no accounting for taste," Governor Maple said, picking up a letter to read as if their mission was of no consequence whatsoever.

Sister Amber had to tug both men out. Sasha seemed determined to rush the governor, and Galen was frozen in shock. Once they had somehow made it back to the carriage, Sister Amber pulled Galen into a tight hug. He squeezed her back for a moment, and then the driver helped them in.

Sasha sat with his arms crossed, rage barely contained, and the moment they started moving, he said, "What a bitch."

Galen choked out a surprised laugh, and Sister Amber just chuckled and shook her head. "Couldn't have put it better myself. She loves to dig a knife into a wound, you know? I am sorry about that, Galen. You did not deserve it. You were brilliant, though."

"You were," Sasha was quick to affirm. "You were incredible, called her right out on her bullshit."

"Oh," Galen said, feeling heat rise in his cheeks at the praise. "I suppose I did, didn't I?"

"Not that it makes it right, of course, but that's probably why she made her little jab about your scar," Sister Amber said. "You backed her into a corner by forcing her to answer for what's happening in Candiru, no beating about the bush. It was rather direct and effective; have you ever considered a career as a speaker?"

"Oh, no, I'm not cut out for that sort of thing." Galen said, marveling at the compliment. It was high praise coming from such a well-regarded speaker.

"You're probably the bravest person I know," Sasha said, smiling warmly at him. "Most guards would piss their pants facing down the governor like that."

"You have such a way with words," Sister Amber said, laughing. "Have *you* ever considered a career as a speaker?"

Sasha rolled his eyes with huff and grumbled something unintelligible.

Galen smiled, though, and said, "Thank you. Gods, I just hope that I didn't make it all worse."

"Ah, she's all bark, no bite," Sister Amber said, brushing a hand through the air. "A nasty woman, but she'll be forced to do what's right in the end."

"I hope so," Galen said.

The carriage stopped at the temple, and Sister Amber started to make her way inside. Galen knew that he and Sasha would be making the long walk to Candiru in the setting sun. He shrugged off the white robe and tried to give it back to the temple, but Sister Amber took him by the shoulders and shook her head.

"Brother Galen, you have earned it. Keep it," she said.

"That can't be right," Galen said, smiling and still trying to give it back.

"Oh, it most certainly is right." Sister Amber smiled, pride on her face. "I'll be in touch, dear. I need to look into a few things."

"All right, thank you." Galen laughed, still not quite believing it. "And thank you for coming with us today. I couldn't have done that alone."

"I think you're selling yourself short," Sister Amber said. "However, I understand. You healers are always so humble. Oh, and Sasha?"

Sasha stood up straighter and looked at her with a bit of fear in his eyes. "Yes, ma'am?"

"Do remember what I said, will you?" Sister Amber said, grinning. "No time like the present."

"Right," Sasha said, and Galen could have sworn he blushed.

Soon, they were walking together down towards Candiru. It was a peaceful walk, neither of them saying much of anything, though sometimes Galen would glance over, and he could swear that Sasha was trying to work up the nerve to speak, the gods only knew what about.

When they got back to Galen's house, he opened the door to step inside and Sasha stopped him for a moment, placing a hand on his shoulder. Galen looked back up at him in puzzlement.

"Is something wrong?" Galen asked, hoping to the Lady of Flowers and any other god that might be listening that there wasn't.

"No, I...I just..." Sasha started, and then he cleared his throat. "Looks like some of the dandelions have returned."

Galen looked down at his feet and sure enough, about a dozen bright yellow flowers had pushed their way up between the stones. He looked back up at Sasha and nodded.

"They have; I told you. They come back. They're very resilient." Galen fought the urge to cross his arms as he looked up at Sasha.

"Just like you," Sasha said, his gaze soft as he looked at Galen. "They're tough. Just like you with the governor."

Galen shook his head, and said, "I don't know. Everyone keeps telling me that I'm something special, but..."

"You are something special, Galen."

Galen felt his lips tug up into a smile, and he said, "Thank you. I couldn't have done it without you, you know."

"Really?" Sasha clearly didn't believe him. There was a look in his eye that Galen couldn't quite parse.

"Yes, well." Galen took a moment to breathe. "With you standing behind me, I feel as though I can take on the world, even the governor. As though I'm not so alone."

That was the perfect opening, wasn't it? Galen had suspicions of what Sasha had discussed with Sister Amber, and that would be the perfect space for him to say it. Galen stood and waited, trying not to let hopes rise when there was no solid reason for it.

"Oh," Sasha said, his eyes wide. "Well, I'm glad that I could be there for you."

Galen tried not to let his disappointment show on his face. Sasha was a friend. He was only a friend, and that was good. A friend could keep away loneliness just as well as... The governor had spelled it out plainly, hadn't she? Galen's face would only scare people away. If he expected more from anyone, he would just be setting himself up for disappointment. He took that feeling and tucked it away, locking it deep within himself.

"Me too," Galen said. "Good night, Sasha."

And he shut the door.

CHAPTER 26

CONFESSIONS, AGAIN

SASHA

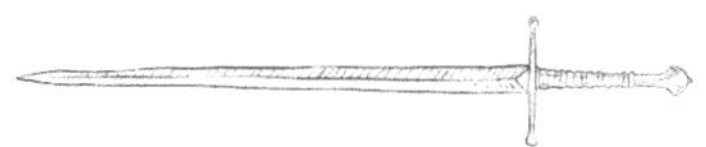

SASHA HAD LEFT GALEN AT HIS HOUSE, BUT HE couldn't stand it anymore. Sister Amber's words were ringing in his ears, and she was right. He needed to tell Galen, and he needed to tell him now. It really would eat Sasha alive, and seeing Galen's courage today had only made Sasha more sure. He knew how he felt for Galen, and it was unfair to keep it from him any longer.

Although the sky was rust colored and rapidly turning purple, he rushed to the next district up. He was practically sprinting, but he didn't care. The effect of a running guard in leathers was similar to that of a running healer in yellow; people got out of his way.

By the time he saw what he was looking for, he had sent up prayers to every god he knew and several that he may have made up asking, no, begging that he'd find it in time. And as he was babbling at the Lady of Flowers for probably the fourth time, he spotted it. The flower stall he had gone to that first day. The man looked like he was about to close, but seeing Sasha charging towards him, he smiled and waited.

"Ah! If it isn't my best customer," the vendor said, grinning. "How can I help you?"

"Hello, sir, sorry, I ran all the way here from Candiru," Sasha said, breathing heavily.

The vendor was kind enough to give him a moment to let him catch his breath, and he asked, "Emergency flowers?"

"Yes," Sasha said with a look of pitiful desperation. "Do you remember the first bouquet I bought from you?"

The vendor suddenly broke into a grin, and he said, "I think I have enough of everything to make another."

Sasha smiled and thanked him. He watched carefully as the man gathered the same collection of flowers again, almost reverently this time. As the baby's breath was placed next to the pink carnations, Sasha's nerves started to catch up with him. His heart raced along with his mind, which played a million scenarios of Galen slamming the door in his face or laughing at him or telling him off, but he remained steadfast.

"Now, this is a bit unprofessional," the vendor said as he handed Sasha the finished bouquet. "But I simply must know. Is this for the same person you bought the first bouquet for?"

Sasha swallowed. "Yes. A lot has changed."

"It seems so," the man said, and then as Sasha reached for his coin purse, the man held up his hand. "This one time, it's free. Good luck."

Sasha thanked him again and then took off back to Candiru. He wasn't as fast as he had been before, a jog instead of a sprint. As he made his way down, clutching the flowers to his chest, he practiced what he would say over and over. He constructed the perfect way to say it. He'd be romantic, he'd be suave, he'd sweep Galen off his feet.

And then he froze in front of Galen's door. He held the flowers close to his chest and lifted a hand to knock, but it just stayed there, like a parody of what had happened just a few months ago. With one last deep breath, he knocked gently. It was moments before Galen opened the door.

"Hello, Sasha, did you forget—" And Galen stopped speaking. He stared at the flowers in Sasha's arms, his hazel eyes wide. Color gathered in his right cheek.

Every perfect line, every practiced phrase, everything that Sasha had planned to say to Galen fled his mind at once. He gazed at Galen, perfect, kind, wonderful Galen, and he could only say the simplest thing that was in his heart.

"I think I love you," Sasha breathed out.

"What?" Galen asked, his voice shockingly soft.

Sasha swallowed and repeated himself. "I think I love you."

Galen's eyes darted to the flowers in Sasha's arms and then back up to his eyes. Sasha licked his lips nervously and was shocked to see that Galen's eyes were glistening, tears pricking at their corners.

"Galen," Sasha said. "Galen, please say something."

"I don't..." Galen started, and Sasha was terrified at how that sentence was going to end, but then he continued as his head dipped down, "I don't appreciate being made fun of."

"I'm not making fun," Sasha said. "Galen, I really..."

Galen's head shot up and the tears at the corners of his eyes fell freely as he said, "Why? I'm...look at me! Why would...would someone like you want someone like me?"

"Why?" Sasha asked, and he blinked back his own surprising tears. "Galen, you're the most amazing person I've ever met. You're so brave, and selfless, and, gods, hard-working."

Galen stared at him as though he still didn't believe him. He let out a small huff of breath and shook his head.

"I'm...I'm hard-working?" Galen asked, his voice quiet.

"Not just that, of course," Sasha said, quickly. "Of course, not just that. It's just one thing that I love about you."

"How romantic," Galen muttered, and he lifted a hand to wipe away the tears, his face burning with embarrassment.

Galen turned and walked inside, but he didn't close the door. Sasha followed him, gods, he'd follow him anywhere, and shut the door carefully behind himself. He scrambled with his words.

"No, Galen, listen. You're laughter and sunshine, and, I don't fucking know, just joy itself," Sasha said, clutching tightly at the flowers. He needed Galen to understand.

"Sasha," Galen said, sighing.

"And gods, Galen, you're beautiful," Sasha said, reaching for him.

Galen suddenly spun around, shaking his head, and said, "Don't lie. Please, stop. I know... I know..."

"I don't know who made you believe that you are ugly," Sasha said. "But if I find out who they are, they better leave the city because I will destroy them. Galen, you are fucking beautiful. I wouldn't lie to you."

Galen suddenly buried his face in his hands and let out a startled sob. Sasha set the flowers aside and stepped carefully towards Galen. As gently as he could, he took Galen's wrists and pulled them down. Galen looked up at him, tears streaming down his face. Sasha ran a thumb across Galen's scarred cheek, pushing the wet from it.

"There you are," Sasha said, gazing at Galen and staring into his warm, tear-filled hazel eyes.

Galen blinked quickly, forcing more tears loose, sending them cascading down his cheeks. His breath kept hitching, and guilt prickled in Sasha's heart again.

"I promised I'd never make you cry again," Sasha said, softly. "I'm sorry."

Galen laughed brokenly, jostling free a few more tears, and he shook his head. Sasha smiled as gently as he could and held

Galen's cheek as he looked into his eyes. Galen swallowed and placed a hand over Sasha's.

"I really do love you, Galen," Sasha said. "I'm not making fun. I would never."

Galen was quiet for a moment, and then asked, "You really do?"

"I really do," Sasha said immediately. "I want...how do you feel, Galen?"

Galen took a shuddering breath, and then said, "I don't know. I never let myself think that this was even possible."

Sasha breathed in, and then said very carefully, "I would understand if the answer was no. I was vile to you when we first met. It would make sense."

"No, Sasha," Galen said, and Sasha's heart skipped a beat when he heard how Galen said his name barely above a whisper. "That has long since been forgiven and forgotten. You've made up for it, more than made up for it... I just find it hard to believe that I could...that you could..."

"I can, I already did," Sasha said, placing his free hand on Galen's shoulder. "You are incredible, Galen. It was so easy to fall in love with you."

"I'm sorry," Galen whispered, looking away. "I don't mean to, I don't know, ruin this for you... I'm just not sure how I..."

Sasha nodded, feeling his heart start to shatter, and he pulled back. Before he could, Galen squeezed his hand and took another slow breath.

"This...this may be foolish, and I'm not trying to lead you on," Galen said, unable to meet Sasha's eyes. "But maybe you could kiss me? That might help me sort out my feelings."

Sasha's heart stopped shattering. Instead, it started hammering in his chest, echoing in his ears and rattling him. He placed a finger under Galen's chin and gently lifted it so he could meet those hazel eyes. Galen's breath seemed to catch as Sasha smiled.

"All right," Sasha said.

He leaned in and pressed his lips against Galen's. Galen was, at first, very still. Galen seemed unsure what to expect, what to do. He had become rigid as Sasha kissed him, but then something shifted almost imperceptibly. Galen reached up and hooked his hand behind Sasha's neck and pressed closer. Sasha tried not to break the kiss by smiling, but he wanted to dearly. Instead, he started to move against Galen's lips, and, to Sasha's delight, Galen matched him.

Sasha moved his hands to either side of Galen's face to push his fingers into his auburn hair. He deepened the kiss, easing his tongue into Galen's mouth, which made Galen flinch and gasp, and that shook Sasha out of the trance he was in. He pulled back quickly and looked down at Galen. Galen looked dazed; his lips were wet and very red. He lifted his hand and touched those lips before flicking his eyes up to Sasha again.

"Uh, so..." Sasha started, but then left the space hanging open for whatever Galen wanted to say.

Galen blinked once, then twice, and how had Sasha not noticed until now how long his eyelashes were? Galen lowered his hand and took a breath. Sasha held his own breath as he watched him carefully. A small smile grew on Galen's face.

"Well," Galen said, and then seemed oddly at a loss for words.

"Well?" Sasha asked, trying not to sound desperate and failing miserably.

"I think I know what I'm feeling," Galen said, then, with a bit of laughter in his eyes, he looked up, "but I don't know if I'm sure. I think you might need to kiss me again."

Sasha laughed then, big and full, and he couldn't stop grinning as Galen broke into a smile that showed off the cute little gap between his teeth, until he did stop because he had pulled Galen into another kiss, holding the back of that beloved head and wrapping an arm around that tempting waist and pulling him closer.

Galen was much more receptive the second time, and he wrapped his hands around Sasha's shoulders. It was the best kiss that Sasha had ever had, and he felt quite silly for not doing this sooner. Then it was the easiest thing in the world for him to scoop Galen up from the ground.

Unfortunately, that resulted in Galen breaking the kiss to squeak out, "Sasha!"

Sasha beamed at him and spun around, only to collapse on the sofa with Galen straddling him. Galen's face was bright red everywhere aside from the damaged skin on his left cheek, but he was laughing and not hiding his smile at all.

"Lion in Glory, Galen, I love your smile so much," Sasha said, leaning in and kissing Galen's neck.

"Oh, stop! I thought you said you weren't going to lie to me," Galen said, shoving Sasha's shoulder gently.

"I'm not lying," Sasha said, smiling at him. "Your smile is cute."

"It's not!" Galen said, looking truly baffled. "I'm... I'm Gap-Tooth Galen, remember?"

"Uh-huh," Sasha said, grinning stupidly. "That's exactly why it's so cute. I thought that the first day I met you. At the time, I was mad at myself for it."

Galen stared at him, mouth hanging slightly open, and then he shook himself out of it and blushed, saying, "You did not. You're mistaken."

"I did so!" Sasha cried, trying to sound offended, but only sounding hopelessly lovestruck. "I most definitely did! I distinctly remember thinking that it was cute. I would not forget that."

Galen laughed and moved to cover his mouth, but Sasha snatched his hand and kissed it. "Please don't hide that. I'm not lying, it's adorable."

"People don't call me adorable," Galen said, snorting. "Especially not strikingly handsome men like you."

"Well, I'm going to have to remedy that," Sasha said, becoming preoccupied with kissing Galen's hand again before smiling slyly at him. "You think I'm handsome?"

"Well, I do have two functional eyes," Galen said, blowing a loose strand of hair from his face. "So, yes. Come on, Sasha. You must know that you're handsome. I'm sure you've had no trouble picking anyone up at a tavern or anything like that."

Sasha considered it for a moment as he busied himself kissing Galen's neck again. He hadn't ever really thought about his own looks, but Galen wasn't wrong. He knew that if he was pleasant and smiled, he usually could go home with whomever he wanted. Galen's hands were gripping his shoulders and Sasha realized that this was the only person he'd ever want to go home with again.

"Well, I'm glad I at least have that to offer you, if nothing else," Sasha said against Galen's neck.

Galen suddenly pushed him back and looked at him with a deadly serious expression. "Don't say that."

"What?" Sasha asked, confused, because he had meant to make Galen laugh.

"The fact that you're handsome is...is a bonus, I suppose," Galen said, red blooming on his cheek. "But that's not why I like you. I don't swoon over every handsome man I meet."

"And where are all these handsome men you're meeting? Because I've been with you every godsdamn day for three months and I've never met any handsome men," Sasha said, grinning. "Well, besides you, but you don't seem the type to swoon over your own looks."

That might have been the wrong joke, because Galen's laughter sounded just a bit pained, but he said, "No, silly."

Sasha shouldn't have liked being called silly as much as he did, but a smile spread across his face and he said, "Okay, go on. What hidden depths do I have? What do you like about me?"

"You're kind," Galen said, humming and tracing the curve of Sasha's ear with his finger.

Sasha shivered pleasantly, but then laughed and said, "No, I'm not! Did you forget how much of an ass I was to you? To everyone?"

Galen let his fingers linger on Sasha's neck and tilted his head slightly to the side. "I didn't say you were nice. Being nice is a challenge for you, but you've been kind to me since that night."

"What's the difference?" Sasha asked, leaning into Galen's touch.

"Nice is being polite, and being nice isn't always kind," Galen said, moving his hand up to Sasha's cheek. "But being kind means that you help people. You do it through actions. Like, it may not be nice to force a child to take medicine, but it is kind."

"Oh, and I'm kind?" Sasha said, grinning.

"You are," Galen said, and as he pushed his fingers through Sasha's short hair to the back of his head. "You really are. Like when you made Old Harry stop being mean to me."

"He needed to be stopped," Sasha said, fighting the anger bubbling up in his chest to focus on the movement of Galen's fingers. "That was just right."

"And it was kind," Galen said, his eyes drifting across Sasha's face, "when you...when you comforted me after Thomas and the wagon..."

Sasha leaned forward and pressed a kiss to Galen's forehead. "I would have done that even if we were just friends."

Galen laughed lightly, and said, "You see? Kind."

"Is it greedy to ask what else?" Sasha asked.

"No, I don't think so. Okay, well, you're willing to change

your mind when you're wrong," Galen said, his voice quiet. "I like that. Not everyone is like that."

"It took a lot for me to change my mind, though," Sasha said, staring into Galen's eyes.

"Not really," Galen sighed, smiling gently. "A few days after...after I confronted you, you had changed. You were trying to do better."

"You had told me that the Lady of Flowers was just trying to do good and I ignored that," Sasha said.

"After I found out why, I understood," Galen said, tilting his head. "There, I like that we can both be understanding. How's that?"

"I like that too," Sasha said. "What else?"

"Now you're being greedy," Galen said, laughing.

"I'll show you greedy later," Sasha said, grinning at Galen's sudden blush.

Galen paused for a moment, and his fingers stopped their tracing, which was a great disappointment to Sasha. Galen tapped his fingers a few times against his skin and hummed a bit. Then he took a short breath.

"I like that you make yourself known, you know?" Galen said. "Like, you always let me know your opinion, good or bad. I suppose you talked with Sister Amber today, then realized that you had fallen in love with me this evening, and then you ran and bought a bouquet to confess."

Sasha laughed so hard that it bounced Galen in his lap, and he had to hold onto him. Galen looked at him with puzzlement, which only made Sasha laugh harder.

"Sorry, I'm not laughing at you, Galen," Sasha said, once he had calmed down a bit. "It's just that, no, I've been in love with you for a while now. I just couldn't keep it to myself any longer."

"What?" Galen asked, his eyes wide.

"Oh, please, Galen," Sasha groaned. "I was not that subtle."

"I just… I don't…" Galen seemed at a loss for words, until he finally spat out, "Since when?"

"Remember when I told off Old Harry and then he was nicer to you?" Sasha asked.

"Yes," Galen said, slowly.

"That night," Sasha said. "At least, that's when I admitted it to myself, and Muffin. He was there too."

Galen stared at him for a moment, and then cried, "That was over a month ago!"

"Yeah," Sasha said, grinning. "I was bringing you flowers and hanging on your every word. Gods, Galen. I know you're busy, but I thought I was being obvious."

"I thought you were just being friendly," Galen squeaked. "At least, that's what I told myself. Because why would you be interested in me?"

Sasha moved his hands to Galen's hips, and then leveled his eyes at him before saying, "Galen, do we really need to go over that again?"

"No," Galen said. "No, I know. Now I'm the one being silly."

Sasha smiled wickedly. "It's been over a month since I realized that I desperately wanted to know what you look like under all that hideous yellow."

"Oh," Galen said, and suddenly his face was a deep shade of maroon.

Whoops. Sasha may have gone too far with that one. He cleared his throat and tried to find a way to take it back that wouldn't ruin the moment, but he was too enraptured by Galen to think of anything. He started to stumble through an apology, but Galen covered his mouth with a firm hand.

"Don't take it back," Galen said, his voice a little

breathless. "It just took me off guard. But that doesn't mean that I didn't like it."

"Okay," Sasha said indistinctly through Galen's hand.

"It'll be nice to admit that I am curious about just exactly what is under all of that armor of yours," Galen whispered in Sasha's ear, making him buzz with excitement. "Though, if you want, we could just find out tonight?"

Galen lowered his hand just in time for Sasha to shout, "Really?" like an excited schoolboy getting his first kiss.

Galen grinned at him and said, "Really."

"Could we, I mean, if you want to of course," Sasha said, his heart nearly beating out of his chest. "Could we find out right now? Please?"

Galen's eyes sparkled, and he said, "Well, since you said please."

Galen laughed beautifully at Sasha's expression, and Sasha caught that laugh with another kiss. Then he stood, lifting Galen up with him, and carried him into the bedroom.

CHAPTER 27

MORNING

GALEN

GALEN WOKE TO POUNDING AT HIS DOOR. HE WAS confused, because Sasha didn't pound on his door anymore and, anyway, it was his rest day. But as he blinked back into the waking world, he realized something else was wrong, because there was a heavy arm draped over him and Sasha's soft snoring in his ear. The previous night came rushing back to him like a bucket of cool water being poured over his head. Oh, by the Lady. Had he really...? That had been real?

Galen rolled over and saw Sasha, shirtless and snuggled against Galen's pillow, with a blissful look on his sleeping face. Galen's reaction was pure and unbridled panic. No one had ever stayed the night. There was one man who kissed his forehead before he left, but that had been at least three years ago. Galen's heart pounded furiously as he waited for Sasha to wake up, see his face in the daylight, and regret everything.

There was more pounding at his door, then Sasha stirred, sleepily opened his eyes, and saw Galen. There was a moment of confusion, then clear recollection, and then, amazingly, a slow, warm smile spread across Sasha's face. He closed the small distance between them and kissed Galen gently.

"Morning," he drawled sleepily. "Are you all right? You looked worried."

"You stayed," Galen said breathlessly.

"Yeah," Sasha said, tightening his arm around Galen and pulling him closer before pausing. "Sorry, was that okay? I didn't really ask. I think we both just kind of fell asleep."

"Of course it was okay," Galen said, his voice soft and disbelieving. "It's just that no one ever stays."

Sasha brushed his lips against Galen's again, and then said, "I'm not planning on going anywhere."

Galen had meant to say something romantic or meaningful in response to that, but then there was more banging on the door. Galen's eyes widened and he sat up. Sasha moved his arms in time; otherwise, he would have easily held Galen down. Galen wouldn't have minded that, if not for the knocking.

"The door!" Galen said, jumping out of bed and moving to dress quickly. "That's what woke me, someone is at the door. Oh dear, what if someone's injured?" Galen swallowed hard. "Or what if it's the parasite?"

He glanced back to see Sasha resting on his elbows, watching Galen tug on pants with appreciation and maybe a little disappointment. "If it was a desperate emergency and you didn't answer, they probably would have moved on, yeah?"

"Maybe," Galen said, pulling a white tunic on. "Hold on, hopefully I'll be right back."

Sasha gave him a little salute with a grin, which Galen found unspeakably cute, and then that made Galen blush furiously because he was allowed to find Sasha cute now. He nearly giggled to himself but held it in. He needed to sober up in case it was a medical emergency. It wouldn't be appropriate to answer the door laughing and blushing if someone was in dire need of help.

The pounding continued and Galen rushed to the door, running a hand over his face. He took a deep breath and then opened the door. Oh. Oh, that had not been what he was expecting. Standing there was a severe woman with short-cropped chestnut hair streaked with gray dressed in the uniform of the guard captains. She had to be in her late fifties, and she looked incredibly cross.

"Hello?" Galen said, smiling weakly. "Can I help you?"

"Is Sasha Rider here?" the captain said, and there was a surprising tinge of worry in her voice.

Oh, if this was Sasha's captain, he couldn't afford to spill the beans on, well, them, could he? What was the policy? Would Sasha be reassigned? He didn't want that, gods, he couldn't let that happen. But lying to this captain seemed like a bad idea as well.

"He is," Galen said. "He, uh, it was late when we got back. Very late. He spent the night."

Without warning, the captain pushed past him, charging into the home and calling, "Rider!"

Galen heard a thump and a curse, and then Sasha appeared in the bedroom door, a blanket wrapped around his waist. He was blushing furiously, and Galen quietly closed the door. Well, so much for subtlety. Hopefully Sasha wouldn't be reassigned.

"Hello, captain," Sasha said, smiling weakly.

The captain sighed heavily, then, startlingly, a grin broke out on her face, and she punched Sasha's shoulder. "I fucking knew it! When?"

"Last night?" Sasha said, and the captain gave him a skeptical look. "No, really! Just ask Galen. Brother Galen, shit!"

The captain looked back at Galen, and Galen was sure that he was just as red as Sasha. She laughed and shook her head. Then she wrapped her arm around Sasha's shoulder and shook him bodily, jostling the blanket from his grip. Oh dear.

"Go put some pants on!" she snapped at him. "Making the good brother answer the door when I'm sure that—"

"Tracker!" Sasha cut her off. "Gods, just give me a moment."

Sasha disappeared into the bedroom, probably hunting for his lost pants. Galen tried not to move, to stay invisible, but no such luck. Tracker, the captain, looked at him and grinned broadly.

"Was my boy a gentleman?" she asked.

Galen somehow blushed even harder and looked at the ceiling with interest before saying, "He was very, um, respectful."

"Good," Tracker said, sighing. "Been training him since he was seventeen and I know what he can be like."

"Mmhmm," Galen said, still not making eye contact. Gods, this was something else.

Sasha reemerged, sans armor but with clothes, and smiled apologetically at Galen. Tracker took him by the shoulders and shoved him into the kitchen with a laugh. Then, to his utter surprise, she took Galen gently by the elbow and sat him down at the table.

"Make us breakfast," Tracker said. "That's what you do for someone after you've bedded them, and for me because you scared the living shit out of me!"

"How?" Sasha demanded, ignoring the first part of the sentence despite the way Galen buried his face in his hands.

"I thought you had been arrested and were rotting in prison," Tracker said pointedly. "Half the guard is talking about how you threatened the blessed governor, Rider! What were you thinking?"

"I was thinking that the governor was being cruel to the

man I love," Sasha said, crossing his arms. "I would gladly be thrown in prison for that."

"I would prefer that you stay out of prison," Galen said softly. "I like you being here with me."

Sasha darted across the distance between them and pressed a kiss to the crown of Galen's head. Galen looked up at him in wonder, feeling the blush lifting under his skin again as Sasha smiled warmly at him. For that moment, it felt like they were the only two people in the world, and it didn't matter what was happening outside. Galen had told Sasha that he made him feel less alone, and that was never as true as right now.

"Well, this is definitely the more positive possibility," Tracker said, drawing Galen out of the moment. "You're still going to be able to guard him?"

Tracker was staring at Sasha with her lips set in a firm line. Sasha nodded. "I would rather die than let something happen to him."

"I don't know about that," Galen said. "I don't want you dead."

"Good," Tracker said. "Right, well, I won't get in your way."

"You're not staying for breakfast, then?" Sasha asked, his hand resting on Galen's shoulder and his finger tracing circles on his tunic.

Tracker stood, looked between the two of them, and said, "I'm not quite so cruel that I'm going to tease you when you so clearly want to spend the day together. Wish you well."

She smiled and lifted her eyebrows twice at Sasha and then left. Sasha seemed to be holding his breath until they heard the door open, then close, and then he knelt in front of Galen and kissed him fully on the mouth. Galen had marveled the night before at how gentle Sasha was with him, and he marveled at it again now. His lips were insistent, yes, but so careful, as though he was afraid to make a wrong move.

When he broke the kiss, he smiled and said, "Sorry about that."

"It's all right," Galen said. "She clearly cares about you. I was just worried that you were going to be reassigned."

"Oh, Tracker won't do that," Sasha said with a laugh. "She will be rubbing this in my face for the rest of my life. She called me out before I knew it myself."

Galen laughed, shaking his head. "So, want to spend the day together?"

"I would have rather lingered in bed with you this morning."

Galen smiled back and said, "Well, there's no rule written that we can't just get back into bed. Why not?"

Sasha grinned immensely and scooped Galen up in his arms. Galen squeaked in surprise. He should know by now that Sasha could pick him up easily, but it still took him off guard. Sasha's rumble of a laugh shook Galen, and he wrapped his arms around Sasha's neck.

"You like this, right?" Sasha asked, his voice tinged with nerves.

"What, being thrown around like a sack of potatoes?" Galen grinned at him. "Yes, actually."

"I thought I was being more careful than treating you like a sack of potatoes," Sasha grumbled, so Galen pulled himself up and kissed his cheek.

"I'm teasing," Galen said. "You're being a perfect gentleman."

"Well," Sasha said, a wicked grin spreading on his face. "I don't know about all that."

Galen barked a laugh, and then said, "True enough. I don't know if you're being *perfect*. But I'm enjoying myself."

"That's all I care about," Sasha said, his voice dropping soft and low.

Sasha carried him into the bedroom and carefully placed

him on the bed. Instantly, he was looming over Galen and kissing him again. Then he gripped Galen's tunic and pulled it over his head, throwing it to the side. Galen's heart started beating hard against his ribs again. There hadn't been a decent amount of light last night. Sasha probably hadn't been able to see how his scar continued down his neck and covered his shoulder, arm, and part of his chest.

"What's wrong?" Sasha asked, pulling back. "You okay?"

"Yes, it's just…" Galen swallowed, and looked away.

"Hey," Sasha said, angling his head down to gaze into his eyes and tucking a piece of hair behind Galen's ear. "Do you need to slow down? It's all right if you do. I don't mind. I'm happy just being in the same room as you."

Galen smiled at that and then shook his head. "No, I just… you didn't get a good look at my scar last night, the whole thing. Sorry, I'm just a little nervous about you seeing it."

Sasha's brow furrowed, a small frown formed, and then he very gently started trailing his fingers across the scar. He began just below Galen's eye and drew his fingers along his neck, across his shoulder, and then down his chest. Galen was holding his breath, watching Sasha's face carefully as he traced along Galen's skin, waiting for disgust to twist his features. It never happened.

"Every inch of you is beautiful," Sasha whispered. "Believe me."

"Okay," Galen said, his voice just as quiet as Sasha's had been. "I believe you."

He wasn't sure if he really believed that it was true in general, but he was sure that Sasha believed it. Sasha moved his hands to lace his fingers in Galen's hair as he held the back of his head and then leaned in to press a kiss against his lips. It was lovely to kiss Sasha; Galen had never felt so loved and treasured in his life. When Sasha pulled away, he was grinning.

"I've been wanting to do this for so long," Sasha said.

"What? Kiss me? Well, go on, keep at it." Galen said, laughing.

"No, well, yes, but not what I meant just now," Sasha said, running his fingers through Galen's hair. "I've been imagining what it would feel like to touch your hair for so long. I love your hair so much."

Galen stared at him in utter disbelief, not because he had any strong convictions about his hair, but precisely because he didn't. He didn't think much about his hair at all, except to tie it back when it got in the way. Sasha was still working his fingers through the tresses, his nails scraping pleasantly against Galen's scalp.

"Mmm, oh, um," Galen said, blushing. "That feels nice. I never really thought of my hair as anything special."

"You're so fucking special," Sasha said slowly. "And gods above, your eyes. Your eyes are so pretty, Galen. I could just get lost looking in them for hours."

Galen was silent again for a moment, and then said, "Your eyes are nice too, you know."

Sasha snorted. "Sure. My eyes are brown."

"They're warm and rich," Galen said, lifting a finger to trace just below Sasha's eye. "Like freshly tilled earth, and they're beautiful."

"My eyes look like dirt?" Sasha asked, smirking. "And they're beautiful? Really?"

"If you're asking if a devotee of the Lady of Flowers thinks that soil is beautiful, then yes. Where else do things grow?" Galen said, smiling up at him.

Sasha looked at him with pure shock for a moment, then a smile spread across his face. With slow reverence, he moved in once more to kiss Galen, and the two of them sank slowly against the bed in the early morning light.

Galen forgot to say his morning prayers.

CHAPTER 28

IT ROTS

GALEN

SASHA DIDN'T STAY EVERY NIGHT, BUT HE STAYED often enough that Galen's neighbors must have suspected. Galen didn't care. He finally had something for himself that no one could take away.

Whenever Sasha spent the night, Galen nearly suffocated in the morning. His bed was far too small for two people, especially when one of them was Sasha's size. Sasha's habit of lying on his stomach would have been okay, except that he chose to do it on top of Galen. Galen would have to heave Sasha up, or try to wake him quickly, to get him to move off. Sasha was far less apologetic when he was half-asleep and would sometimes wrap his arms around Galen to prevent him from leaving.

"Sasha, if it were a rest day, I would agree, but I have patients to see," Galen said, trying to extract himself from the guard's strong arms.

"You should have more rest days," Sasha murmured against Galen's skin, but he let him go.

The people of Candiru must know. Sasha, as he had said, was not subtle. Especially now that he felt no reason to hold back, his comments and touches must show people how lovesick he was. Only someone maddeningly in love would gaze so starry-eyed at a man in a garish yellow tunic drenched in vomit and pus.

It was endearing but annoying, in the way that Muffin could be annoying. Both were a bit too clingy, a bit too in Galen's space, but ultimately, they were cute and cuddly, and Galen didn't mind.

FRUSTRATINGLY, THE PARASITE HADN'T SHOWN UP again since the meeting with the governor. The problem was real, but for the two weeks that investigators from the upper city were nosing around Candiru, nothing happened. Galen didn't want anyone to be infected, but godsdamn if someone wasn't infected soon, the governor's agents would write it off as a non-problem.

Galen was examining Margaret Harrison's bad hip again when something finally happened. She was thoroughly ignoring Galen as he massaged out the aches and pains and was looking up at Sasha and batting her eyelashes, even though she was easily old enough to be his grandmother. Sasha was rolling his eyes and sending exasperated looks Galen's way. All Galen did was smirk back at him.

The door to the small house flew open, revealing Fynn, the young Kipper, ashen-faced and wide-eyed. Galen, Sasha, and Margaret all stared at her until she took an unsteady step forward and collapsed onto her hands and knees.

Galen abandoned Margaret's hip and rushed to the young woman, who was breathing hard, and asked her desperately, "Fynn? Fynn, what's wrong? What happened?"

"Brother Galen, you have to come quick," Fynn said, her voice shaking. "You must come now. Please."

"Right. I'm sorry, Mistress Harrison," Galen said, helping Fynn up. "Tell me on the way, Fynn. Is someone hurt?"

They stepped out into the hot day, the smell of sunbaked sewage nearly overwhelming, but sheer panic kept Galen moving. He had to work to push away the memory of the awful wagon accident, which he had also learned of from a Kipper at his door.

Fynn kept starting and stopping, unable to get the words quite right. "I've never seen anything like it, Brother Galen. We were just doing rounds, you know, checking in on things, and picking up, er, payments for services."

Sasha grumbled at that, but Galen ignored it and kept asking Fynn questions. When he realized what the problem was, his heart leapt into his throat and he blamed himself. He had been hoping for this.

She led him and Sasha down just a few streets to a large house. It was owned by the Perkinses, one of the wealthier families in Candiru. Despite their success, they were very poor by the standards of the rest of Dragonet City. Galen couldn't remember the last time he had been to the house; the Perkinses could afford a doctor and rarely needed a mere devotee.

As they got to the door, which was swinging slightly open, Galen's heart threatened to explode out of his chest. Sasha grabbed his shoulder and pulled him back before he could walk in. Galen stared up at him in confusion.

"Let me look inside first, make sure it's safe," Sasha said, his voice a whisper.

"I don't think there's nothing living in there," Fynn said.

Galen's stomach dropped, and Sasha said, "Humor me."

She nodded, and Sasha disappeared through the door. The few minutes it took for Sasha to scope out the building felt far longer. Galen stood on the stoop wringing his hands and picturing one of the parasitic creatures burrowing into Sasha's throat.

"Oh, you two are a couple now, ain't you?" Fynn suddenly asked.

"What?" Galen asked, turning to look at her, and was a little shocked by her smug expression. "Is this really the time?"

"Oh! So, you are!" Fynn said, grinning. "I cannot wait to tell Jess."

"Oh, please don't," Galen groaned. "They said they were going to cut Sasha's hands off and I quite like his hands."

Fynn laughed. Galen wondered at her timing, but then he noticed how carefully she was avoiding looking at the door. Oh. Laughing and teasing Galen meant she didn't have to think about what lay within.

When Sasha reappeared, Galen grabbed his wrists and tugged him forward, scanning for any signs of the parasite under his skin or around his mouth. Sasha submitted to his careful examination.

"It's clear," Sasha said, but he had the same ashen look that Fynn had earlier. "Galen, though... It's a lot."

"I've seen plenty of horrors," Galen said, eyes still roving over Sasha. "Nothing tried to crawl into your mouth?"

"No, I'm fine," Sasha said, and then he took Galen's hands in his, stilling their search of his skin. "Galen, it's really bad."

"Let me see," Galen said, pushing past his lover.

The first thing he saw was the hollowed-out body of a middle-aged woman. A novice might not have seen the hollowing, but he had been examining human bodies for years. The way her stomach fell in, the lack of mass, was disturbing.

Her skin was covered in the telltale tar-like spots. Black ichor dipped from her mouth, her nose, her ears, even from her eyes in a parody of tears. She had been trying to get to the door, perhaps trying to get help. Or she may have just been trying to escape. Galen swallowed and moved on.

There were seven bodies, all of them as bad or worse. Most

horrifying were the three children in the nursery, the youngest barely a year, lying in puddles of ichor in their beds. They must have been dead for days, but no rats had nibbled at them and no flies had gathered. It was as though the bodies were no longer even flesh.

Galen staggered out of the room and collapsed against a wall. He took deep breaths, but the air in the house was so stale that it barely helped. He squeezed his eyes tight shut and tried not to blame himself. There was no way that he could have known that this was happening. There was nothing he could have done to stop this.

Still, it tore him apart.

Then he felt Sasha's hands on his shoulders. "Hey, Galen. I know. I know."

Galen stood up from the wall and collapsed against Sasha, who squeezed him to his chest, holding him tight. Galen tried to burrow his face under Sasha's armor. He didn't cry, he couldn't cry, but he needed to soak in Sasha's warmth.

Sasha pressed a kiss to the crown of his head and said, "The Kipper ran off. She said she had to tell Jess something."

"Ah, fuck," Galen whispered.

"Oh, it must be bad if you're swearing," Sasha said, struggling for lightness.

"No," Galen said. "Just, when they show up later tonight to threaten you, let me do the talking."

Sasha released a breath of a laugh and kissed Galen's head again. "Are you all right?"

"No," Galen said, pulling back. "But there's nothing you can do. And I'm worried. Where are the monsters that were inside these folks?"

"They probably went to find new victims," Sasha said. "Right?"

"And I'm not there to stop them," Galen said, running a hand over his face. "I've got to look for them, but there's the

Henderson girl who I need to check on, and Malcom Carter broke his arm last week, I need to make sure it's healing all right, and then there's..."

Sasha took Galen's face in his hands and said, "Galen. You need to ask for help."

"You saw how well that went last time." Galen sighed heavily.

"Maybe this time it will be better. You have a whole house full of evidence."

"Evidence... These are people," Galen said, eyes drifting back to the nursery door.

"That's not what I meant. I'm sorry," Sasha said quickly.

Galen pulled back from Sasha, shaking his head, and said, "No, I'm sorry. That isn't fair to you. You're right. Come on, let's make sure there's nothing we missed."

Sasha made sure that he was the one to open each door, that Galen was safely behind him. There couldn't be anyone left to jump out, since Sasha had already checked the whole house, but Galen allowed it. It would make Sasha feel better.

They were almost back out again when Galen saw ink-black tendrils unfurling from beneath a narrow closet door, reaching towards Sasha's boots. Galen wanted to shout a warning, but he couldn't get the words out in time. As Sasha opened the door, a maid's dead body dropped out. Worse still, the parasite emerging from within her sprang through the air towards Galen.

Steel flashed and black ichor sprayed around him. Two distinct halves of the creature landed with two resounding plops, their tentacle-like appendages still flailing. Galen stared in shock at the severed creature, and then in awe at Sasha. Galen realized in a moment of absurdity that he had never seen Sasha use his blade outside of the drills Sasha went through on their rest day.

"You okay?" Sasha asked, noticing Galen staring at him.

Galen nodded in disbelief.

"Good, and hey, we found out something important," Sasha said, a hint of a grin on his face.

"What's that?" Galen asked.

"Looks like you can kill it with good old-fashioned violence," Sasha said, pointing his sword at the mess on the floor.

It had stopped moving, and its tendrils lay uselessly in the black ichor. Sasha nudged one of the halves with the tip of his blade and it didn't react. Cautiously, and with a groan of despair from Sasha, Galen did the same with his toe. It didn't move.

"It can be killed," Galen said. They both looked like they had been drenched in black ink, but he grabbed Sasha and kissed him.

CHAPTER 29

WHISPERS IN THE DARK

SASHA

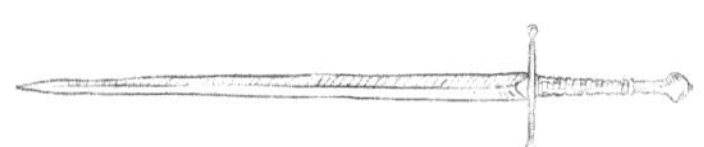

SASHA WAS DESPERATELY IN LOVE, AND HE WOULD do anything for Galen, even drag him to the Candiru guard station—despite his protest that he had patients to see—and demand that someone go look at the Perkins house.

Of course, there was a lot of hesitation. The guards of Candiru were busy with criminals and were very annoyed that a bodyguard was bothering them with such nonsense. The captain was a tired old man who eventually sent a runner to the guardhouse in Lenok District because this was 'above his pay grade.'

"Can you at least set someone outside the house to make sure no one goes in until the investigator gets there?" Sasha asked.

"If I had someone to spare, but we're spread thin down here," the captain said. "Watching an empty house isn't the best use of manpower."

"It's not empty. There are bodies in it."

"Sure, but they're not going to get up and go anywhere, are they?" the captain said. "Just go back in an hour or two. There should be someone who can help you then."

Sasha accepted this only because Galen was so antsy to get back to work. While Sasha had been talking with the captain, Galen was luckily able to change into his spare healer tunic. He looked incredible in anything, but he did seem more comfortable without the muck.

They continued through Galen's stops in a haze, and Galen was nowhere near as personable with his patients as usual. Instead of staying and talking, Galen did what was necessary as quickly as possible and moved on. When they could finally race back to the house, Sasha's heart dropped at the sight of Sir Miller waiting for them.

"Ah, hello again, Rider. Brother. It seems the gods will that our paths cross once more," Miller said, smiling falsely.

"Hello, Miller," Sasha said in a barely contained growl.

"So, what's this problem you claim we have?" Miller asked, ignoring Sasha's disrespect.

Sasha was about to answer, a sharp and rude reply ready on his lips, but Galen stepped in. "Someone is infecting people down here with a parasite. This family was infected and killed by it. There had been some government inspectors looking into it recently, but they've left Candiru."

"If it's a disease, isn't that more your area?" Miller asked, smiling sardonically. "I believe you told me as much once when I was cleaning up some riffraff."

Sasha saw Galen's jaw twitch as he bit back a remark about the insult to the people of Figlove Lane, instead saying, "Normally, yes. But if someone is deliberately infecting people with a deadly parasite, that is murder, is it not? I assumed that a guard captain would be sent here, but maybe you can be of more help. You're even better than a captain because, perhaps, you could convince the governor to take this seriously."

The polite warfare between Miller and Galen was a wonder to watch, but Sasha didn't really want to waste time, so he said, "Sir, will you just look inside? It's all there."

"Very well," Miller said.

The bodies still lay where they had left them. Miller crouched down and looked carefully at the woman near the doorway, his face twisted in disgust. There was still an air of unshakable wrongness in the house, which was made worse when Galen suddenly froze.

Sasha leaned over to Galen and whispered, "What's wrong?"

Galen whispered back in halting tones, "It's gone."

"What's gone?"

Galen pointed to a spot near the maid's body. There was a puddle of the black tar in front of her, but the creature that Sasha had sliced in half was gone. Oh, Lion's teeth. Panic welled up in Sasha as tried to think what could possibly have happened. He was sure that it was dead. What could survive being cut literally in half?

"What are you two blathering about?" Miller asked, turning around as he straightened up.

"There was a dead parasite here," Galen said. "Sasha killed it. But it's gone now."

Miller smirked. "Rider didn't finish the job? Why does that not surprise me?"

Sasha stepped forward, teeth bared, but Galen laid a hand on his arm and said, "I don't understand what you find so funny about this, Sir Miller. People are dead. I am not sure what happened to that creature, but when I checked it, it was dead. We asked the captain here to station a guard at the house, but he told us that there wasn't one to spare. I am as concerned if someone took it, for whatever reason, as I would be if it were still alive."

Miller sighed, and said, "Oh, all right. You win. This is not amusing, I apologize. It's just a bit of gallows humor, as it were."

"I thought gallows humor was for one's own imminent

execution," Galen said, staring up at the man. "Not about other people's deaths."

"Ah, well, perhaps working to fix Dragonet City has skewed my sense of humor," Miller said, shrugging. "I'm sure Rider has made an off-color joke now and again."

"Not really," Galen said.

"Well, Rider isn't that good of a guard, so I suppose that makes sense," Miller said, eyes flicking to Sasha's face for a moment. "I fear we must apologize for that."

"On the contrary, there's no apology necessary. Sasha is a fantastic guard," Galen said, his gaze and voice steady and firm. "He saved my life today. And he's been a wonderful help. We've had this discussion before, Sir Miller."

Sasha reached down for Galen's hand as if by instinct, squeezing it to comfort them both. He realized it was a mistake as soon as he saw Miller's eyes flick down to their joined hands. The auditor's lips curled up in disgust.

"Oh, I see," Miller said, eyes glued to their hands. "Right, well, I'll have investigators come around again. Don't worry, Brother Galen. This is in good hands. Why don't you and Rider clear out? Retire for tonight. I'm sure you two will enjoy each other's *company*."

Sasha squeezed Galen's hand tighter, and said, "I'm sure. Thank you, sir."

Galen looked like he was going to say something more, but Sasha pulled him outside. The sky was just starting to turn rust-colored as the sun dipped behind the city's crest. Galen took over, marching up towards his house, but kept hold of Sasha's hand.

"I can't stand that man," Galen said.

"That makes two of us," Sasha said, running his thumb against the back of Galen's hand. "Maybe we can talk to the temple instead."

Galen nodded. "Yes, tomorrow. I'm just so tired. I haven't felt this worn out in a long time."

Galen leaned his head against Sasha's arm, making Sasha rejoice internally. Galen hesitated to make any public show of affection, but Sasha would have shouted his love from the rooftops if Galen was all right with it. Even such a small gesture of closeness was a reason for celebration. His joy was ruined, sadly, when Jess jumped out in front of them with a giant grin on their face.

"Galen," they said, eyes full of delight. "When were you going to tell me?"

"Eventually," Galen said, his face extremely red.

"Oh, *eventually* he says," Jess said, then grabbed Galen's free hand and pulled him from Sasha. "I had to wait until Fynn told me! Fynn, of all people! Come on, Galen. I thought we were friends."

They wrapped their arm around Galen's shoulder and shook him gently. Galen looked like he would rather be anywhere else. Sasha let one small chuckle out and Jess's head snapped towards him. They released Galen, pointed a finger at Sasha, and stalked towards him.

"You!" Jess shouted.

"Me?" Sasha asked, lifting his hands in surrender.

"Yes, you!" Jess said, shoving a hand against Sasha's chest. "You said you weren't going to court him."

"Ah, yes, well, I didn't plan to," Sasha said. "It just happened. You must admit, Galen is rather extraordinary."

Galen laughed at that and looked away. Luckily, Jess softened and, after a moment's thought, said, "Fair enough. I guess I won't stab you just now. But if you break his heart..."

"I'll submit to stabbing," Sasha said with a smile. "I'd deserve it."

"Glad you know it," Jess said, and then playfully punched

his arm. Sasha rubbed where they had hit, smarting at the sting.

They moved back over to Galen and said something low that Sasha couldn't make out. Galen shoved their shoulder, but he laughed. That unworried, unabashed laugh after a day of horrors was a balm to Sasha's soul. He smiled.

Jess ruffled Galen's hair, much to the healer's consternation, then ran off to attend to some sort of Kipper business. Galen sighed and took down his hair to retie the knot. Sasha was back at his side in moments and reached for his hand again. He thanked every god he knew when Galen took it back. They walked through the sunset-painted city streets in comfortable silence.

"I hope you don't get in trouble," Galen said once they were almost back to his house.

"Why would I?" Sasha asked. "For standing up to Miller? I don't report to him."

"No," Galen said. "For me."

"For you?" Sasha was confused for a moment before he realized what Galen meant. "Oh, no. Of course not. Tracker knows already, obviously. It'll be fine."

They got to Galen's door, and Galen turned and said, "I hope so. Can I ask you a favor?"

"Of course, anything."

"That's a lot of power." Galen chuckled. "What if I told you to go jump off the bridge into the river?"

"I'd ask if I could take off my armor first," Sasha said, reaching for Galen's waist, "but I'd do it."

Galen laughed again before his face became serious. "But really. Do you... Do you think you could talk to Captain Tracker about what happened? Tonight, if you don't mind."

"Oh," Sasha said, and he hoped that his disappointment didn't show. "Yes, of course."

"I promise I'm not trying to get rid of you," Galen said,

lifting a hand to Sasha's cheek. "I just want someone other than Miller to look at it. You seem to trust Captain Tracker, and I don't want to waste time."

"Oh, no," Sasha said. "I understand. I get it. I'll go right now. Though, can I ask you for a favor too?"

"All right," Galen said, lifting a brow.

"Just a good night kiss," Sasha said with a sheepish shrug.

Galen smiled and grabbed the place where Sasha's shirt peeked out of his armor and pulled him down into a kiss. It was a good kiss, one that promised more at another time, and Sasha knew that promise would be kept. When Sasha pulled back, he was grinning at Galen. Galen shook his head and went inside.

SASHA PRACTICALLY FLOATED BACK UP TO THE guard bunks, his fingers continually drifting up to his lips. He tried to fight the smile plastered to his face, since people tend not to trust a grinning guard, but the effort was futile. He was just too godsdamn happy.

When he arrived at the building, he asked after Tracker, but apparently she was still out. He huffed out his annoyance at having to sit around the bunks waiting when he could have been with Galen. He supposed that he could take care of trivial tasks like washing himself or eating dinner.

It took an hour to finish off the mundane chores of food and hygiene, mostly because other guards kept asking what he was smiling about. He did his best to brush them off. They might guess that he was infatuated with someone, but they didn't need to know that it was Galen. That he'd keep to himself for now.

He moved down the hall towards Tracker's office and was relieved that candlelight flickered from beneath the closed door. Sasha was just about to knock when he heard a conversation through the wood, and one voice gave him pause. It was Miller. Sasha swallowed heavily and lowered his hand. He glanced down the empty hallway and turned his ear to listen.

"We are still working on it," Miller said, and he sounded exhausted and annoyed.

"I just don't understand why that little healer is still guarded," said a voice that Sasha didn't recognize. "He should have dismissed Rider months ago; this whole thing should have long since kicked off. What is taking so long? You said Rider's record is abysmal. According to you, the devotee should be rotting on the streets."

Sasha had to bite his lip to stay quiet. The speaker was right, of course, but it still hurt.

"Well," Miller said, nearly growling, "I didn't really expect Rider to start fucking the devotee, now did I?"

Sasha took a sharp breath and hoped that it wasn't as loud as it felt. Fuck, fuck, fuck.

"And that is the case?" the unknown voice asked. "It's not just rumors?"

"I confirmed it for myself tonight," Miller said. "Why anyone would want that scar-faced little busybody, I'll never know, but Rider sure does. By the Maiden's fin, it would be comical if it weren't so inconvenient."

"It does complicate things," the other voice said. There was a long pause. "Could we get Rider suspended for courting his charge?"

There. Sasha heard it. The accent of the other voice was decidedly upper city, likely the top two or three districts, but it wasn't quite the upper city accent that Sasha knew. There was a nearly imperceptible twang. Sasha knew he had heard it before, but he couldn't place it.

"No, unfortunately. His captain is sticking out her neck

for him," Miller said with a heavy sigh. "I don't know what Tracker sees in that man, but she's been protecting him for years."

Sasha felt his shoulders ease. Tracker wasn't working with Miller on whatever this was. She didn't know. She was still his protector, still his friend. Gods above, bless her.

"Yes, unfortunate." The other voice sounded just as annoyed as Miller now.

Sasha had almost placed the accent. He had heard it when one of his father's trading partners from another city had dined with them, back when Sasha still lived at home. What city was this person from?

"I say we still go forward with the plan," Miller said. "Rider will fail, of course, but we can just say that it was one bad apple. And with his record? The city will believe he's rotten to the core."

"I just can't believe that the devotee hasn't given up yet," the other voice said. "With the death seekers on top of his usual work, he ought to be dead from exhaustion already. Twenty-three percent of the population of Dragonet City is under his care, did you know?"

"Scaled Maiden, really?" Miller asked. "Almost makes me feel bad for him."

"Oh, I do feel bad for him," the other voice said. "And most of them rely on him because they can't afford doctors, you know? The plan will work. They've got to be tired, so he'll be vulnerable."

Sasha remembered the source of the accent. Cyathus City. His father had been trading with a mage guild there, selling some useless magical trinkets. That was where that twang was from, he just knew it.

"Right, well, the top will be pleased, won't she?" Miller said.

"Oh, yes," the other voice said. "Reconstruction can't start until Candiru is wiped out, and that won't happen until Brother Galen is dead. Pesky little devotee, isn't he? Are you ready, my friend?"

Sasha heard a guttural noise as he backed away from the door, but he didn't wait to find out anything else. He turned and started running towards Candiru and Galen. He had to warn him.

CHAPTER 30

IT DESTROYS

GALEN

"SASHA, ARE YOU SURE IT WASN'T A DREAM?" GALEN asked again, but he shook his head adamantly.

"I'm not creative enough to dream up something like that," Sasha said, pacing in Galen's kitchen and stepping carefully over Muffin, who was weaving between his legs. "It was Miller and some bastard from Cyathus City talking about killing you!"

Galen ran a hand over his face, fighting exhaustion once more. He had been in bed, completely asleep, when he was awoken by frantic banging on his door. His ears were finely tuned to that sound in case there was a dire emergency in the middle of the night, which happened often enough. He was surprised when it was Sasha, breathing hard, sweat pouring down his face and panic in his eyes. Of course, Galen had pulled him inside. The fact that Muffin had also raced in was a minor annoyance.

The story sounded fantastical, and Galen had immediately assumed that Sasha had fallen asleep while waiting for Tracker. He didn't mind comforting his lover after a nightmare, but he would have preferred doing it while lying in bed together, not sitting groggily in his kitchen while Sasha ranted at him and a blink fox nipped at his heels.

"Okay, so what do we do?" Galen asked, fighting a yawn.

"That's the thing. I don't know," Sasha said, raking his hands through his short hair. "I think we can trust Tracker, but I don't know where she is, and Miller might figure out that I know something, and I don't think we can trust the governor. Maybe we can go to your temple for help, but they already have tried to help, and what I really want to do is just keep you in here, locked up and safe, but I know that you won't let me do that and—"

"Hey," Galen said, standing and grabbing Sasha's hands, bringing his relentless march to an end. "Breathe, sweetheart."

Sasha stopped, took a deep breath, and then, furrowing his brow, asked, "Did you just call me 'sweetheart'? Really?"

Galen laughed and then lifted Sasha's hand to his lips before saying, "Yes, because you are sweet. Maybe a bit sour as well, but you are sweet."

Sasha blinked at him. "If you say so."

"I do," Galen said. "And I broke you out of your spiral. Now, what is our plan? Because you're right, I'm not going to let you lock me up when people need my help."

Muffin pushed between their legs, the cool buzz of his fur making the hair on Galen's bare skin stand on end. A shiver ran through him, and Sasha took the opportunity to pull Galen to his chest and squeeze him tightly.

"I just don't want you to get hurt," Sasha said, his voice breaking slightly.

"I know," Galen said, sighing. "I know, but I can't let others get hurt in my stead."

"I'm never going to leave your side," Sasha said, holding Galen even tighter. "I'm not going to take my eyes off of you for a moment."

Galen laughed, and said, "All right, then. I feel safer already."

Eventually, Galen calmed Sasha down enough that they were able to go to bed. Silently, he regretted the loss of sleep over something that he doubted Sasha had heard correctly. Surely Miller wasn't planning on killing him. Galen was a devotee of the Lady of Flowers; people just didn't murder devotees of the goddess of healing.

THE NEXT DAY, SASHA WAS UP AND DRESSED BEFORE Galen. He was already in his leathers and had a hand on the largest weapon on his belt, a sword. He seemed even more on edge than he had been the night before.

They set out on their rounds, and Galen realized that he did in fact think of them as *their* rounds now, not just *his*. Despite the start of summer having arrived, it was gray and cloudy. The heat was still there, of course, but it felt trapped and suffocating, especially in Candiru. Somehow, it made the smell even worse. He donned a face mask that had been treated with rose oil and offered one to Sasha, who put it on gratefully. Nearly everyone in Candiru had such a mask, and nearly everyone who didn't have a mask had dried herbs which they sniffed from periodically.

Sasha had been in Candiru long enough now to recognize many faces, but with half of every face covered, it wasn't enough anymore. More than once Galen had to greet someone loudly by name when he noticed Sasha reaching for his blade. The guard always seemed a bit embarrassed afterwards, as he should have been, but it certainly didn't stop him.

Other than the general unpleasantness of the weather and the threat to Galen's life, the day was ordinary. It ended with their weekly visit to Old Harry, which was nowhere near as daunting as it had once been. The doctor from the temple hadn't amputated Harry's leg yet, but there was a date set now. Harry himself seemed resigned to it since he knew that eliminating the pain from the rot would make it worthwhile.

Galen climbed the crooked staircase with his shadow close behind him and knocked on the door as usual. He waited for Harry to tell him to hurry up already, but no sound came from within. Galen hummed slightly to himself. The silence was unusual, but perhaps Harry was asleep. He knocked again, more loudly.

Still, nothing happened.

"That's odd," Galen said, and then a new fear formed in his chest.

The infection could have taken him. Galen was the only one who came to see Harry; no one would know. Ah, Lady of Flowers, how could he have let this happen? And just when Harry had finally agreed to the operation that would have saved his life. Galen was a fool. A selfish, selfish fool.

"Mister Balsin, I'm coming in!" Galen called, and he opened the door.

As he opened the door, Sasha said, "Wait, Galen, it may be a trap—"

The room was dark, but there was enough light from the open door that Galen could see the scene before him. Old Harry was dead. Worse still, his body was eviscerated and devoured. The only part of him that wasn't flayed open and scored with the black ichor was his bad leg, which seemed completely untouched. In the center of the crater that was all that was left of Old Harry lay a very still mass of black.

It was horrifying, worse than Galen had ever seen, but it made a sick kind of sense. It appeared that because there hadn't been another host, the parasite had just consumed all of Harry that it could, though it wasn't interested in his infected leg. Galen was infinitely grateful for the mask, because he was sure that the smell was putrid. Despite Sasha placing a hand on his shoulder to stop him, Galen walked in.

His boots squelched through the tarry puddles, and he winced at each noisy step. He prayed to the Lady of Flowers that the parasite had starved, that it was dead, because it was bigger than any that he had seen before. But he had to look. He had to make sure.

The mass, nearly the size of a child on the cusp of their teenage years, was curled up on its side, or what Galen thought of as its side. These creatures didn't adhere to the rules that Galen was used to, and it threw him off. As he closed the distance to the bed, he heard Sasha scream his name.

"Galen!" Sasha roared, and he heard the accompanying charging footsteps. "Look out!"

That was the warning he needed to dodge out of the way as a tentacle the size of Sasha's arm shot out towards him. The thing had been playing dead, waiting for him to get close. Oh, dear. That meant these things were at least somewhat intelligent.

Sasha's sword plunged into the mass, which screeched like a colony of bats that had been set on fire. Both men winced at the sound, stumbling back. Did these things have vocal cords? Galen shook his head at himself. He couldn't believe that he was focused on the monster's anatomy when it was actively trying to consume him.

The tentacle shot out at him again, plunging towards his mouth, stopped only by the facial mask. Sasha was hacking at the monster from the other side and made eye contact as another tentacle tried to do the same to Sasha and failed because of that piece of fabric. Ah, brilliant! To Sasha's horror, Galen grasped onto the failing tentacle in front of him.

"Trust me!" Galen called and then started chanting.

Pink magic blossomed around him and flowed into the tentacle. Everywhere the Lady's touch met the parasite, it dissolved. More horrid screeching filled the room, but Galen didn't care. He simply shouted over it, expending all the magic he had for the day as he destroyed the creature in front of him.

When it was nothing but ash, Galen felt his legs start to give out, but then Sasha was there, holding him up and leading him from the room. Galen let himself be led to safety, and only then did he let himself start to mourn Old Harry. The man had been a bastard, but he had changed. He had gotten better. And even if he hadn't, he didn't deserve the death that came for him.

Once they were outside and down the stairs, Galen leaned against the wall and tore down his mask, taking in giant gulps of fresh air. Even as rank as it smelled, it was better than that horror. Sasha pulled down his mask too, only to pull it back up immediately afterwards as he patted Galen on the shoulder.

"Sasha, we have to tell someone about Old Harry," Galen said. "That was the biggest one I've seen yet, but I'm spent. I don't think I can make it to the temple."

"I could carry you," Sasha offered, and even with his mouth obscured, Galen could see his smile.

"Ha!" Galen choked out. "No, Sasha. That won't be necessary. We could just send a runner, probably. I wonder if there's a Kipper around. They always help the temple when they're asked."

Sasha nodded and said, "Jess likes to hang out by your house at night. I've seen them. Probably making sure that I'm not doing something I shouldn't. I'll bet we can get them to act as a runner."

"Yeah, all right," Galen said, nodding and squeezing his eyes shut. "I think I can probably make it home. Do you mind if I lean on you?"

"Not at all, sweetheart," Sasha said, and Galen could hear the grin in his voice. "In fact, I insist on it."

Galen rolled his eyes, but he allowed Sasha put a supportive arm around his torso and start leading him home. He was stumbling, barely able to keep upright. It wasn't just the exhaustion from working all day, or from expending all his magic, which he hadn't done in years. There was an emotional toll that was weighing quite heavily on his heart as well. He had worked so hard to save Old Harry's life despite everything that the man had done to him. And it had all been erased by someone who was trying to destroy Candiru Quarter.

Eventually, when his house was just two streets away, Galen gave up and let Sasha carry him. It would be mortifying when he talked to Jess, but well worth it to not immediately fall asleep as soon as he got to his stoop. Sasha was quiet, just rubbing his hand up and down Galen's side as he stomped through the streets, mask firmly in place. Galen had dropped his somewhere, but it was fine. He had more and could deal with the smell for the time being.

When they were on Galen's street, he heard something that made him push up in Sasha's arms, eyes wide. He gripped Sasha's shoulder tightly and listened carefully. He heard an animal, and it sounded like it was in pain. He remembered the way that Miller had looked at Muffin and his offer to send an exterminator.

"Sasha," Galen said in a harsh whisper.

"What?" Sasha asked, just a few steps from Galen's house.

"Listen," Galen said, looking into the dark night as another cry pierced the air. "That sounds like—"

"Muffin," Sasha finished, his eyes wide and full of concern.

Galen panicked. "Miller said something about an exterminator. He wouldn't have really, would he? Muffin is harmless, he has to be okay, right?"

Sasha set Galen gently down and looked towards the sound as another cry rang out. He was clearly torn about what to do. He looked desperately at Galen and let out a frustrated groan.

"Please, Sasha," Galen said, stumbling a bit. "Please. I'm already home, I'll be fine. But I need to…Muffin needs to be okay."

"Okay," Sasha said, huffing and running a hand through his hair. "Okay, but stay by the house, okay? If you see Jess, call them over. Don't do anything stupid."

"I won't," Galen said, smiling with relief. "Thank you, Sasha."

"I'll be right back, okay?" Sasha said, and in response, Galen rose up on his toes to kiss him. He missed his mouth, instead pressing his lips against Sasha's chin, but Sasha didn't seem to mind.

Sasha turned and ran in the direction of the blink fox's cries. With that, Galen stumbled up to his house, careful not to trample the freshly grown dandelions. He knew if he sat, he'd likely fall asleep, so he propped himself against the wall.

Galen closed his eyes, pressing his head back against the hard surface. He thanked the Lady of Flowers in a whisper, glad that he had been given the power to stop the parasite from hurting him or anyone else. Then, reluctant though he felt after using the gift, he asked for her help again. Of course, no answer came.

"Excuse me, would you happen to be a healer?" A raspy voice broke through his mental fog.

Galen opened his eyes and turned his head. He saw someone with a mask pulled up over the bottom half of their face, long, sandy hair pushed away from their forehead, and a rather nice black cloak pulled around their shoulders. They were fumbling with something in their hands and shrinking away from Galen. Ah, they had a bit of an odd accent; they were likely new in Candiru, or even new to Dragonet City. New citizens were always a bit nervous about asking for help, even if they had been told to look for yellow.

Galen smiled at them as gently as he could, praying that his scars wouldn't scare them off, and said, "Yes, I'm Brother Galen. I'm a devotee of the Lady of Flowers. I can help you; we don't charge. If it's something beyond my abilities, I can always try and get a temple doctor for you."

"Ah, good," the stranger's low, odd voice continued. "Thank you, but that won't be necessary. I just wanted to make sure that I had the right person."

"The right person?" Galen asked, his brow furrowing. "I'm sorry, I don't follow."

Galen glanced in the direction that Sasha had gone, wishing that he would find Muffin alive and well already so he could come back. Something about the stranger was making the hair on the back of his neck stand on end and his hands turn cold.

"You do seem like a nice person," the stranger sighed. "I feel I must apologize. I don't like when the job makes me hurt priests."

Galen's first thought was not helpful at all: *But I'm not a priest.* The second wasn't helpful either: *Oh, fuck.*

Then it didn't matter much what he was thinking.

The stranger with the fine cloak grabbed the back of Galen's head to keep him in place. As Galen opened his mouth to scream for help, their other hand, heavily gloved, shoved something into Galen's mouth. Galen knew what it was instantly from the feel of tentacles writhing against the roof of his mouth and the insides of his cheeks.

Galen tried to scream again, but the parasite used the opening to propel itself down his throat. Gods have mercy, it felt like fire scorching him from the inside. He grabbed his throat and collapsed to his knees.

He looked up and saw the stranger wiping their gloved

hand with a cloth. Galen gasped as fire blazed through his body, an all-too-familiar feeling. He was there again, in the moment when the inferno of his former home collapsed around him, scalding and scarring him. Flames ate away at his flesh then, and they seared within him now.

Painfully, Galen blinked back tears and looked up at his assailant. The stranger, what he could see of them, did look apologetic. They adjusted their mask and cloak, then turned and ran away.

"Galen!" Sasha's scream broke through the pain.

Galen was holding one hand to his throat and the other to his stomach, and he could feel the parasite within him sucking up his strength in giant gulps. His fingers were shaking, and he couldn't tell if it was because of the creature within him or his general exhaustion. Somehow, he was on the ground. Then Sasha's face came into view.

"Fuck! Who was that?" Sasha cried. "Oh, fuck! You're out of magic!"

Galen couldn't respond very well; he just said, "T-temple..."

"Yes, yes of course," Sasha said, and then Galen was up in the air.

"M-Muffin?" Galen asked.

Sasha looked baffled for a moment, then realization dawned. "He's fine. He was in some kind of magic cage, but I broke the lock and he blinked out. He's fine, Galen, I promise."

Suddenly, there was another voice screaming. "Hey! Who the fuck was that? What did they do?"

Jess's face appeared in Galen's line of vision, and they looked furious.

"I don't know!" Sasha cried. "They gave Galen a parasite. I've got to get him to the temple. They're the only ones who can treat it."

"We'll find that bastard!" Jess shouted as they ran away. "Don't you let him fucking die, guard dog!"

"I wasn't planning on it," Sasha said. Then to Galen he said, "Gods above, hold on."

More words were exchanged, but Galen couldn't keep track of them as darkness enveloped him. He was vaguely aware of being carried through the streets of Candiru, and of something writhing within his chest.

CHAPTER 31

A GARDEN STROLL

SASHA

SASHA STAYED AT GALEN'S SIDE. HE HAD KNELT ON the floor for a while, head resting on the bed beside Galen's unconscious form, but eventually the healers convinced him to sit in a chair. He had to admit that it was a lot easier on his knees.

Sasha had burst into the temple, Galen dying in his arms, and screamed for help. He was still covered in the black ichor, some from Old Harry and some from Galen, and was soaked with sweat. He gave the two pledges who were watering flowers near the entrance quite a fright. He couldn't let go at first, but after some coaxing, the healers were able to pry Galen from Sasha's hands and tend to him.

The healers took care of the parasite as quickly as they could, killing it with the now-familiar healing light. They told Sasha that if it had been a bit longer, they didn't know if they would have been able to save Galen. Sasha knew that they meant it as a comfort, to tell him he had done well, but it just terrified him to his core. He had been so close to losing Galen. The line that had formed between Galen's brows eased, and Sasha's heart finally slowed down.

But Galen didn't wake up, not like the others had. A healer explained that it wasn't just the parasite, but also the exhaustion from expending all of his magic. He needed a bit of time to rest and recover.

Rest. Galen never had time to rest, never. The man deserved it, yes, but did he ever get it?

Sasha buried his face in his hands, muttering half-thought-out prayers to Lion in Glory, to the Evening Star, to the Scaled Maiden, to Rising Dawn, to every god he could think of except the god whose temple he currently sat in. He hardly had any right to ask her for anything, and he was sure that the other devotees had her covered.

"Well, this is unfortunate, isn't it?"

Sasha sat up and saw Sister Amber standing next to his chair in full speaker robes. Her hands were folded in front of her, and she was looking down at Sasha with a sympathetic smile. Sasha sniffed and couldn't look her in the eye. The slow rise and fall of Galen's chest was all he could focus on. Sister Amber placed a hand on his shoulder and hummed softly.

"I know," she said comfortingly. "He will be okay; he just needs to rest."

"It's all my fault," Sasha said, his hands gripping his knees. "I should have protected him. It was the one thing I was there to do, and I couldn't even manage it."

There was a drawn-out silence. Then Sister Amber said, "Sasha, I think you need to go take a bath."

Of all the things she could have said, that might have been the one that he least expected. He finally tore his gaze from Galen and stared up at her wide-eyed.

"Look, dear, you are covered in slime and muck and you are exhausted. A nice soak will help with that," Sister Amber said, smiling. "You don't want Galen to wake up to you like that, do you?"

"I suppose not," Sasha said.

"Honestly, you should also eat something, take a walk in the gardens, clear your head," Sister Amber said. "Do you really want Galen to have to tend to you when he first wakes up?"

Sasha stood from the chair, now towering over the priest, and said, "Of course not."

"Good, we're agreed then," Sister Amber said. "I'll stay with Galen, you go clean yourself up and catch your breath. I promise he'll be here when you get back."

She gently shoved Sasha out of the way and then perched on the chair. He stared at her in surprise, but she just shooed him away, giving him directions to the baths. In a daze, Sasha went where he was told.

Sasha haltingly explained his situation to the bath attendant, who took things in stride even though Sasha was heavily armed, extremely filthy, and double their size. He was led into a private bath, where he stripped down without waiting for the devotee to leave, which also didn't fluster them. Sasha slowly sank into the water and watched as the attendant gathered up his filthy clothes.

"I'll bring in guest clothes for you to wear while we clean these up," they said.

"Thank you," Sasha grunted.

"And I am going to lock up your weapons until you leave, sorry," they said, not appearing the least bit sorry.

"Understandable," Sasha said, trying not to grunt again.

"Take all the time you need. The soap's over there, towels are on the bench," they said, then bustled out.

Sasha submerged himself in the bath for as long as he could hold his breath. Because it was a temple to the Lady of Flowers, flower petals floated on the water. As he resurfaced, he had petals in his hair and more stuck to his skin, his chest and arms dotted with soft spots of pink and white and blue. He felt them on his face as well, and he imagined that he looked rather foolish with blossom freckles all over his cheeks and nose. Quickly, he wiped them off with shaky hands.

Sasha spent a long time scrubbing, then soaking in the heated water. He had no idea what the mage runes on the tub said, but the water stayed warm and clear long past the point where it should have been cold and dark with filth. He couldn't imagine the cost of that magic.

When he pulled himself out and started drying off with the fluffy towels, he spotted the fresh clothes. The devotee had probably sneaked them in while Sasha was pretending to drown himself.

They were simple, a linen shirt with a few pink embellishments, including an embroidered pink flower at the collar, dark linen pants to match, and well-worn sandals. Sasha dressed quickly and walked out. The devotee looked up and smiled at him, then continued their work.

"Thank you," Sasha said.

"No worry," the devotee said. "Happy to serve the Lady."

"I, uh, would you happen to know where I could get something to eat?" Sasha asked, and then his question was punctuated by his stomach growling loudly.

The devotee laughed and directed him to the kitchen. Sasha continued his unguided tour of the temple of the Lady of the Flowers, making his way to the next stage in the quest for his own recovery.

The kitchen was much busier than the baths, but a bowl of hearty vegetable stew, a heel of bread, and an apple were shoved into his hands with a warm smile. He followed a line of devotees to an outdoor dining area. There were tables with long benches as well as areas for sitting on the ground surrounded by large trees and gardens of vegetables, herbs, and flowers.

Sasha felt like a young recruit standing and searching for a place to eat on his first day of training, but not for long—a few young devotees noticed him and motioned him over to join them. It was late, but the temple was still busy as ever, and the dining area was still full. The colors of tunics were mixed, healers and growers and speakers all mingling together, laughing and talking. Sprinkled throughout were a few people wearing pure white robes like Galen and Sister Amber had worn and other guests dressed in the same linen clothes as Sasha.

"Hey there! I'm Sister Bailey," a devotee in the dark green of a grower said, beaming. "This is Sister Sam and Brother Pax."

The other two waved, both wearing the deep blue of speakers. They looked friendly enough.

Sasha nodded to each of them as he sat, and said, "Hello, I'm Sasha."

"Nice to meet you," Sister Sam said. "What are you in for?"

"What?" Sasha asked.

"Well, you're a bit old to be a pledge," Sister Sam said. "And visiting devotees always wear their colored branch tunics. Besides, I would have remembered someone as handsome as you."

She propped up her chin and smiled at him until Brother Pax elbowed her in the ribs and said, "Sam! Knock it off!"

"Sorry, I'm...I'm spoken for," Sasha said, hearing the words break as he said them.

Immediately, all three of the devotees sobered up and Sister Sam said, "Oh, by the Lady, I am very sorry. Is your beloved very ill? The healers have them?"

Sasha stared at his stew and said, "Something like that. They said he'll be all right, but I'm still worried."

"Understandable," Brother Pax said. "What happened? If you don't mind us asking."

Sasha took a breath, and then said, "Well, I'm Brother Galen's guard and—"

"Oh," Sister Bailey said, her eyes wide. "Oh, you're him. That explains it. Don't worry, he'll be fine."

"You know who I am?" Sasha asked.

"The guy who walked in soaked with black tar carrying the poor healer from Candiru? Of course, it's all anyone is talking about," Sister Sam said, then winced. "Sorry."

"It's fine," Sasha said. "I wanted to stay with him, but Sister Amber told me I needed a bath, and a meal, and..."

Sasha trailed off, and Brother Pax asked, "And what? Sister Amber's cures are always right, you know. What was the third thing?"

"A walk in the garden," Sasha said, and then was surprised when the three devotees exchanged glances. "What? What's wrong with that?"

"Nothing," Brother Pax said, smiling. "Nothing, it'll be good. Finish your meal, the cooks work so hard. And I think that Sister Bailey grew the carrots in the stew, right?"

"I did," Sister Bailey said happily. "Hope you enjoy it."

Sasha did enjoy it. The food was all good, and it was reminiscent of Galen's cooking, which made sense. He finished off the apple and then looked back at the three devotees, who were once again staring at him. They played it off, directing him to the dishwashing station and then, finally, the gardens.

Saying 'take a walk in the garden' was tantamount to saying 'walk around the entire temple' given that flowers and plants grew from every available surface. It made sense, since this was the Lady of Flowers, but it still made finding a place to walk rather difficult. Finally, a senior grower took pity on him and directed him into the inner garden, which Sister Amber must have meant. It seemed rather abandoned in the night air, but Sasha opened the gate and strode inside, desperate for whatever peace he could find.

As Sasha walked down the path, he couldn't help but notice the little floating orbs of pale yellow light that reminded him of magelights at first. However, this was proven wrong when Sasha moved closer and reached out to touch one. The light wasn't an orb at all, but a small creature. It looked like a cross between a tiny human and a mouse. It was mouse sized and had the rodent's round ears and black eyes, and its features were rather mouselike, including whiskers. But the body was like a chubby human toddler's, dressed in flower petals and leaves. Two large, mothlike wings sprouted from its back, and it landed on Sasha's palm, blinking up at him.

Sasha was fascinated by the little creature; he had never seen anything quite like it. He softly said, "Hello, little one, what are you?"

The answer came from behind him in a voice as sweet as honey and as smooth as silk. "Flower fairies. They're native to the lands outside of Dresia, but every temple has some. They're the Lady's chosen."

Sasha turned to see a stunning woman with deep, rich brown skin. Hair as dark as the sky at midnight flowed down her back. She not only wore a flower crown but also had a rainbow of flowers woven into her hair. Her eyes, the deep, verdant green of fresh, growing things, were surrounded by thick lashes. Her pink dress, decorated with the colors of the different paths, yellow, green, and blue, resembled the bishop's, but it was long and pooled at her feet, the edges stained with grass and dirt. Despite that, it didn't seem messy. Dirty, yes, but the lively, fresh, healthy dirt you would pick up from working in the garden all day.

She held out a hand, and one of the flower fairies flew over and landed in her palm. It gazed up at her in adoration. She smiled at it, and Sasha saw that, just like Galen, she sported a gap between her two front teeth. She looked up at him, and he saw that same gentleness that he had seen so many times in Galen's eyes, and Sister Amber's, mixed with determination. Oh. This had to be another bishop. Maybe she was visiting.

"Hello, uh, they seem to like you," Sasha said, watching as more of the fairies landed on the woman's arms and shoulders.

"They do tend to, yes," the woman said, a small laugh escaping from her lips. "But tell me, Sasha, how are you?"

Ah. Well, of course a woman as beautiful and competent as this would know who he was. The devotees he had eaten with had known, so why wouldn't a high-ranking official of the temple? Sasha smiled sadly at her and shrugged.

"Honestly, not well, ma'am," he said.

"Hmm," the woman said, her eyes softening as she stepped towards him. Amazingly, she was even taller than Sasha. "Would you like to talk about it?"

Sasha took a shuddering sigh. "I know that all of you people have the impulse to just forgive, to say that whatever someone did doesn't matter, because everything is about growth, everything is about how you can move forward and become better, but that just isn't true."

"I assume by 'you people' you mean—"

"Lady of Flowers people," Sasha said, and then, realizing he interrupted her, he winced. "Sorry."

"No worry," she said, smiling at his expression. "Why are you so concerned about forgiveness?"

"I don't deserve to be forgiven," Sasha said. "I never deserved it."

He didn't know why he was suddenly pouring his soul out to this woman whose name he didn't even know, but perhaps it was better this way. He was unlikely to see her again, so he could say everything he wanted to without worrying about future embarrassment.

"Why?" she asked.

"Why what?"

"Why don't you deserve to be forgiven?"

Sasha groaned, and he said, "I keep having this conversation."

"And yet you keep picking at it like an old scab," the woman said, and it was a wonder she was able to read him so quickly. "It will never heal if you keep doing that. It will only fester."

"I'm a bad person."

"That seems rather absolute, especially given that you have been protecting and loving a healer of this very temple," the woman said, smiling at him. "They do tend to be good people."

"Galen is good enough for the two of us. He's the sun that lights up my darkness," Sasha said, feeling immense shame. "I couldn't even protect him. I couldn't even do that, and it's my job. I don't deserve to be forgiven."

"Would Galen forgive you?"

"Yes."

"So, are you saying he has bad judgement?" the woman asked, pulling Sasha's arm and sitting on a stone bench, forcing him down beside her.

"No, of course not," Sasha said, looking down at the flower fairy, which had started hugging his thumb. "I've just deceived him into liking me, like I do with everyone."

"Oh, really? Who else have you deceived?"

"Tracker, my captain," Sasha said. "She still believes in me; she sticks her neck out for me. But I've let her down so many times."

"And yet she continues to care for you?" the woman asked. "Are you saying *she* has poor judgement?"

"No, she's one of the smartest people I know," Sasha said.

"Then why are you unworthy of the forgiveness that she so freely offers you?"

"Because it shouldn't have been me."

"What do you mean, Sasha?"

"It shouldn't have been me," Sasha said, staring at the fairy, fat tears rolling down his face. "I shouldn't have been the one to survive. I don't... Why wouldn't Anya live? Everything would be better if I had died instead of her. She had a purpose, she had a reason for living, and even though I was the one who lived, I never found that reason. I never found any reason until I met Galen, and then I let him get hurt."

The fairy hugged his thumb tighter and nuzzled against it comfortingly. Sasha choked down another sob. He felt a cool, steady hand gently squeezing his shoulder, but the woman waited for him.

"I'll never forgive myself for being the one who lived," Sasha said. "I don't think I can. And I didn't even realize that was my problem until... Well, now, if I'm being honest. I spent so long cursing a god who had nothing to do with it, who only tried to help. How can that ever be forgiven?"

"That has long since been forgiven," the woman said gently.

Sasha turned his head to the woman, who was as peaceful and serene as if she was speaking for the goddess herself. Sasha swallowed, but he felt the truth of it. He had been forgiven.

"Humans are often so silly. Any decent god will forgive a slight such as that," the woman said. "Now, there are jealous, petty gods, don't get me wrong, but..."

"But the Lady of Flowers is not one of those." Sasha stared at her, trying to bite back further tears.

"Exactly," the woman said, grinning at him. "So, Galen forgives you, Tracker forgives you, the Lady of Flowers forgives you, who's left? Oh, right. You need to forgive yourself."

Sasha laughed, but it was a small, broken thing. He lifted a hand to wipe his face, and the little fairy flew up with it and then hugged his cheek. Sasha fell stock-still and was even more shocked when the tiny creature kissed his cheek before fluttering back down.

"She's saying that she'll forgive you if you can't forgive yourself," the woman said.

"You understand them? How? She didn't speak," Sasha said, glancing again at the woman, who had acquired even more fairy attendants.

"You learn to pick up on cues," she said, shrugging. "I've spent a lot of time with them."

Sasha nodded and looked down at the fairy. "Thank you, but I think I do need to learn how to forgive myself. It seems like an important skill."

The little fairy nodded and sat down in his palm. He breathed in deeply. There was no hint here of the summer stink that pervaded Candiru, just the scent of flowers and fresh-tilled earth. Galen had said his eyes were like fresh-tilled earth. Galen. Gods above, he loved Galen so dearly, and he knew that Galen would forgive him. Maybe, if he could do it for Galen, then he could learn how to do it for himself.

"It wasn't my fault," Sasha said quietly. "It wasn't my fault that Anya died."

"No, it wasn't," the woman agreed.

"And I have made mistakes, I have been cruel, but I'm trying," Sasha said, looking up to the sky. "I am trying to be a better person now."

"You are," the woman affirmed.

"And because of that, I deserve forgiveness," Sasha said, blinking back tears, amazed that he had any left. "I deserve forgiveness, and I deserve happiness."

"You do," the woman said, and he could see her gap-toothed grin out of the corner of his eye.

"I deserve it," Sasha said, and he stood, turned around, and gently set the fairy down.

"Yes, Sasha," the woman said, taking his hands in hers. "You are going to grow into such an amazing person. I can already see how you're sprouting now. I cannot wait to see where you end up."

He hadn't noticed it before, but at their feet, dandelions were growing all around the bench. Some of them were the white puffs that would spread their seeds in the wind, but most were the bright yellow flowers that Galen loved so much. Seeing them, Sasha's heart warmed.

"It's because of Galen," Sasha said, and then he smiled. "He follows what the Lady teaches. He tended to me, and I started to grow. I don't... I don't know what power you have here, but please help him. He needs help, more than just healing from this attack."

"I know," the woman said, squeezing his hands. "I have a plan. Trust me."

"I do," Sasha said automatically, easily. "I do trust you. I need to get back to him. Thank you."

"Of course, Sasha," she said, and then stood to kiss each of his cheeks.

Sasha turned to leave but then stopped and turned back around. "I'm so sorry, I was very rude. I didn't ask your name."

"Oh," the woman said, grinning and showing her gap teeth as the flowers in her hair bloomed. "Most people just call me the Lady."

CHAPTER 32

UNRAVELING THE WEB
GALEN

GALEN BLINKED AWAKE AND IMMEDIATELY CLASPED his belly where the parasite had been writhing. It was no longer roiling. He took in a gasp of air and reached for his throat, but there was nothing squirming within him. The parasite was gone. Thank the Lady.

He looked around and immediately recognized where he was. The large glass windows, propped open in the day to let in air, the long rows of beds with crisp white sheets, the garish yellow tiled floor, the scent of yarrow and peppermint in the air; he was in the temple's healing quarter.

Galen's revelation was interrupted by a loud snore from beside him, and he looked over to see Sasha, dressed in visitor's clothes and fast asleep in a chair pulled as close as possible to his bedside. Galen winced; Sasha was going to have an awful crick in his neck with the way his head was thrown back. Warmth bloomed in Galen's chest where the parasite had been. Sasha had stayed with him. Sasha had saved him. Galen reached out and took Sasha's dangling hand.

The guard woke with a start and turned his head immediately to Galen. His face ran through a gamut of emotions; fear, surprise, relief, and then settled on pure and simple love. Sasha squeezed his hand and then fell out of the chair, sending it clattering, to kneel at Galen's bedside.

"Galen," Sasha said, taking his hand and pressing it to his lips. "Galen, you're awake. You're all right. They told me that you would be, but..."

Words seemed to fail Sasha, but Galen was happy to take over. "I'm all right, Sasha. Thank you, thank you for saving me."

He watched as Sasha bit something back, and then he said, "Of course, Galen. Of course. I love you so much, I will always, you understand, I will always..."

Sasha's words fell away as he gazed at Galen, and Galen said, "I'm sorry."

"What for?" Sasha asked, his face twisted in confusion.

Galen smiled at him and said, "I should have listened to you. You were right, but I didn't believe you and—"

"Galen," Sasha said, his face falling into a soft, gentle smile. "Galen, you have nothing to apologize for. I'm just so glad that you're still here. I don't know what I would have done if I had lost you."

Sasha stood then and gathered Galen in his arms, holding him to his chest in pure relief. Galen squeezed him back as best he could, but he was still so very tired. It was several minutes before Sasha released him and lowered him back to the pillows.

"Is there anything I can get you?" Sasha asked, his voice desperate.

"Water? Maybe something to eat?" Galen said, smiling weakly. "How long was I out?"

"Three days," Sasha said, and then started waving down another healer.

"What?" Galen cried, sitting up suddenly.

"Whoa, take it easy," Sasha said, kneeling back down. "Relax, it's okay."

"But Candiru, everyone there..." Galen was breathing hard, thinking of how he had abandoned them all.

"Galen, they sent in a substitute," Sasha said, brushing Galen's hair back from his face. "Well, actually they sent in four altogether because the first one reported back that it was too much work for any one person."

Galen laughed at that, his voice breaking. Gods above, it really was too much. He had secretly suspected for years that he was overwhelmed because of some personal failing, but no. It really was too much. He had the right to be exhausted.

Eventually, a tray arrived with water and porridge. Sasha and the other healer helped Galen sit up and then set the tray over his lap. Galen drank and ate as though he were dying of thirst and hunger, and Sasha watched over him like a hawk the entire time.

"Galen, I have something I need to tell you," Sasha said excitedly as Galen scraped the bottom of the bowl.

"Hmm?" Galen asked, lifting his brows as he looked at Sasha.

Galen's lover seemed oddly at war with himself, a tumult of emotions raging on his face as he worked up to whatever it was he wanted to tell him. Galen nodded, encouraging him, and Sasha took a breath.

"All right, so, Sister Amber made me take a walk in the garden while you were out. She said it would be good for me, and she was right," Sasha said.

"Okay?" Galen said, not wanting to dismiss what Sasha had to say, but also very confused.

"Well, when I was there, it was the inner garden, you see," Sasha said, rubbing the back of his neck. "I met someone. Oh, uh, not like that. But someone very important. I haven't really told anyone else, but I met—"

"Brother Galen!" Bishop Rose said, arriving and cutting Sasha off. "Welcome back to the land of the living. We have much to talk about. Do you feel well enough?"

Galen glanced over to Sasha, who shook his head and said, "I'll tell you later. Are you well?"

Galen didn't really feel well enough; he wanted to sleep for another week at least. However, he also couldn't stand the thought of staying in bed for another minute. He took a breath and then nodded to the bishop.

"Excellent!" Bishop Rose said. "We're going to head to my office; it's a bit more private. Sister Amber will join us. Mister Rider, could you help Brother Galen?"

Galen didn't realize how weak his legs would be. Well, logically, he knew three days of bedrest after a mortal attack would leave anyone weak. But somehow, in his mind, it hadn't applied to him. The moment that he stood, he nearly collapsed. He would have been sprawled on the floor had Sasha not caught him.

The walk from the healers' quarter to the bishop's office seemed to last forever, but he didn't really mind leaning heavily on Sasha, and Sasha certainly didn't seem to mind being leaned on. Compared to the governor's office, the bishop's office was cramped. She had a large window to let in light, and candles strewn about for when the sun was absent or insufficient. Her desk took up a decent amount of space, but every spot was taken up with something necessary and practical.

Besides Sister Amber, they were joined by Sibling Hanan and Brother Chester, the highest-ranking members of the healer and grower branches in Dragonet City respectively, along with a mousy little woman who was not in devotee garb. There was hardly enough room for all seven of them, let alone enough chairs. However, Galen was immediately given one.

He was eternally grateful for that; he already felt ready to collapse.

The others engaged in a polite dance about who would get the two remaining chairs until Sister Amber insisted that Sibling Hanan take one because of their bad hip and the mousy woman take the other since she would need to access a flat surface. Once they were arranged, with the bishop behind the desk combining piles, Sister Amber started.

"Brother Galen, after your attack, we reported to Governor Maple, of course," Sister Amber said. "However, even though the report showed a clear and present danger in Candiru, the governor still refuses to take action. So, we're taking matters into our own hands."

"Oh," Galen said, looking around at them in amazement.

"Yes," Bishop Rose said. "I am so sorry that it took you being hurt to finally get this moving. But we had our hands tied before this, you understand. We will be moving very quickly now."

Galen nodded and said, "Okay, but what does that mean?"

"We're going to catch the governor," Bishop Rose said, folding her hands on her desk and grinning at him. "And you're going to help."

Galen stared in disbelief at all the high-ranking members of the temple for a moment, then shook his head. He didn't know how to explain to them that he wasn't the person to help, that he didn't know how to take down the governor, that he was too small and too tired for that. He was just opening his mouth to say something when the office door flew open with a bang.

"We figured it out!" a very familiar voice shouted, and Galen looked over his shoulder to see a triumphant and disheveled Jess standing there with their hands on their hips. Their hair was escaping from their usual braid, their orange Kipper bandanna was askew, and their dark clothing was covered in a thin layer of filth.

"I am so sorry, bishop," a harried-looking devotee said from behind them. "I tried to stop them, but they wouldn't listen to me."

"That's all right, it seems that they have rather important information," the bishop said, and the devotee dipped her head and shut the door.

"Galen! You're awake," Jess said, stepping over and ruffling his hair. "I'm so glad you're okay, you scared the shit out of me. No more talking to strangers, young man."

"I am older than you," Galen said, batting their hand away but grinning at them.

"What? No, you may have a year on me, but I'm spiritually older than you are," Jess said, leaning up against Sasha, much to the guard's clear annoyance.

"I serve a goddess!" Galen said with a bark of laughter.

"And you have corrected me that you are not a priest," Jess said. Jerking a thumb at Sasha, they added, "Plus, you're sleeping with this guy, so you must not be fully mature yet."

Sasha rolled his eyes and shoved Jess off him as they cackled, then they were interrupted by the bishop clearing her throat. Galen turned and started to apologize, but she waved it off with a good-natured smile.

"Hello again, Jess," Bishop Rose said. "Good of you to pop in. Your timing is impeccable as always."

"Ma'am," Jess said with a grin and a bow. "Happy to be of help."

The mousy little woman had been ignoring the scene around her and carefully setting large bundles of papers on the desk. Finally, it looked like she had finished, and she cleared her throat with a breathy *ahem*. Despite the softness of the sound, it immediately drew the attention of everyone in the room.

"Ah, yes, this is Ellyn Staple. She's a clerk who was once employed by the Palace," Bishop Rose said. "She now works for the temple of Lion in Glory, but they've loaned her out to us."

Galen had trouble imagining the little woman working alongside the tall, burly paladins of Lion in Glory, or even the ever-stoic clergy. Then she gave a toothy grin, and Galen could see the hunger in her eyes behind the fringe of her hair.

"Indeed," Ellyn said, stretching her arms and cracking her fingers. "Lion in Glory is a close friend of the Lady of Flowers; we are always happy to help. Especially if it is exposing a snake hidden in the weeds."

Her voice was soft and airy, but there was a strange strength behind it. It was almost anger, and Galen sat up at alert despite his exhaustion, like there was a predator nearby. Ellyn untied a stack of papers and pulled out several pieces of yellowed parchment covered in neat, exact handwriting.

"So, the downfall of every great villain is due to one thing," Ellyn said, straightening up like a priest about to give a sermon. "Does anyone know what that is?"

"Hubris?" suggested the bishop.

"Overreach," Sister Amber offered

"Greed," Galen said.

"Stupidity!" Jess grinned.

"A sword in the throat," Sasha added.

There were a few more suggestions, but Ellyn shook her head at each one. Finally she said, "All of those can contribute, sure, but in truth, it's paperwork."

"Paperwork?" Sasha asked, clearly not convinced.

"Paperwork." Ellyn nodded, then grinned like a cat who had cornered a mouse. "You see, when civilization became, well, civilized, we started writing everything down. It makes things easier, right? I'm sure your temple has rooms full of paperwork."

"Of course." Bishop Rose nodded.

"And how often is that paperwork audited?" Ellyn asked, pointing a finger at the bishop.

"Admittedly, not often enough," the bishop said. "We get caught up in the day-to-day of the temple and the work we do."

"Ah, see? That's where things fall apart," Ellyn said, beaming. "People think that they can hide things in the paperwork and get away with it, because everyone gets behind on it. But they never expect someone like me! That's the real reason I was fired from the palace."

"You were fired?" Sister Amber asked, glancing at the bishop.

"Because I am a relentless auditor," Ellyn said, her toothy grin looking especially sharp. "And sometimes, that's exactly the opposite of what people in power want. I imagine that's why Governor Maple hired an auditor that she could keep under her thumb. Mister Victor Miller, I believe. Loathsome toad of a man. However, Lion in Glory loves a true auditor, like me. Finding where the snakes are hiding and all that, but none of his usual followers are very inclined to it. They enjoy swinging swords around much more."

Ellyn gave Sasha a knowing, pointed look. Galen felt the guard shift uncomfortably behind him.

"So, how does this help us?" Brother Chester asked.

Ellyn grinned rather like a lion showing its teeth and said, "I've done some digging, and I think you'll appreciate what I've found."

She outlined a series of strange transactions in the palace records, excessive payments to contractors for very vague projects. There were plans that simply didn't make sense: blueprints for buildings that there was no room for, trade routes that couldn't exist, expansions of upper districts that were completely hemmed in. Unless...

"Candiru," Galen said as Ellyn was outlining another strange plan.

He thought he had said it quietly enough to escape notice, but everyone's eyes were on him immediately. Galen shifted uncomfortably at the attention, but Sasha brought a hand down on his shoulder and squeezed it gently.

"I was building to that," Ellyn said, the mountain of evidence teetering beside her. "But yes. It appears that the governor has been making plans for the space that Candiru occupies. As you all know, space in Dragonet City is highly valued. And Candiru takes up a large portion of that space. It is the largest and most densely populated district in the city."

"And I was servicing it by myself," Galen said, mumbling.

"It's incredible that you were," Ellyn said, shaking her head. "It's not called Candiru Quarter without reason. Twenty-three percent of the population lives there."

Galen nearly fell out of the chair. The only reason he didn't topple to the floor was that Sasha and Jess caught him swiftly. He had not been working twice as much as the other healers; it must have been at least ten times as much. He felt sick, he felt betrayed, and he felt so, so tired.

"That cannot be correct," Sibling Hanan said suddenly. "We had thought it was nearly fourteen percent, which is still outrageous, but it cannot be that much. We cannot have abandoned Brother Galen alone down there with that much work. Surely the Temple would have fought that despite the governor's orders."

"It sounds right to me," Sasha growled out. "I've been down there with him every day for months. Do you know what his schedule is like?"

Sibling Hanan seemed to shrink in shame, but Ellyn was undeterred. "I imagine that it was exhausting. But the numbers don't lie, even if the governor's office does."

"We will remedy this, Brother Galen, I swear by the Lady,"

Bishop Rose said, communicating the firmness of her intent through her gaze as she met his eyes before turning back to Ellyn. "What was the plan with Candiru?"

"The plan seems to have been to rid it of the current population, then tear it down and rebuild," Ellyn said.

"But that makes no sense!" Galen cried, finally breaking out of his shock. "The people of Candiru serve so many roles in the city, and they are her citizens. How would she... How could she..."

"Galen is right, it makes no sense," Sister Amber said. "And what about the initiative with the guards?"

Sasha shifted uncomfortably, and Ellyn said, "It was a cover. Apparently, Brother Galen's guard was meant and expected to fail to protect him. Then Governor Maple would refuse to allow the Lady of Flowers to place anyone in Candiru, saying it was far too risky."

"A lot of trouble for all of this," Sasha said, anger barely repressed in his voice.

"Not to mention that tearing down that much infrastructure and losing so much of the workforce. That'd be expensive," Brother Chester said, rubbing his chin.

"Well, it was buried quite effectively, but there have been some potential contracts with a mage school. A magical university here would bring in magecrafted tools that would make things much easier, wouldn't it?" Ellyn said. "Free labor from the students to earn university credits and money into Dragonet City to help with the costs. It would be rather simple."

The room was silent for a moment as everyone took this in. Then Galen said quietly, "But they're her people. We're her people. Does she really hate us that much?"

Jess had been strangely quiet for all of this, until they said, "She doesn't hate us. She just doesn't see us as people. We're pests, vermin. Remember what they call us?"

"Candiru rats," Sasha said, not quite under his breath.

Galen took a breath and said, "It was meant to look like a plague. But they needed to be able to control it better. That's why it was a parasite."

"Admittedly, a brilliantly engineered parasite," Ellyn said, sighing. "They brought in a mage, who apparently wanted to be the one to infect people personally."

"Bastard," Sasha growled.

"They're quite notorious, it seems," Ellyn continued, nodding in agreement. "According to this, they were banished from Cyathus City for similar experiments with these monsters. All they want to do is have them thrive."

"Someone made that on purpose?" Galen asked breathlessly. He thought he knew the depths of human cruelty, but evidently he had only scratched the surface.

"Yes, there's a whole market for it," Ellyn said, lip curling up in disgust. "The new weapons of war, they say. These ones have been named death seekers, created by a mage named Ramil. Luckily, the monsters are being outlawed in most cities because they're heinous."

"Lady of Flowers," Sister Amber muttered.

"And this Ramil, that's who's been infecting people?" Galen asked, picturing the odd look in the stranger's eyes, the fine cloak around their shoulders as they turned away.

Ellyn gave a curt nod. "Part of the reason Cyathus City gave them the boot was because they apparently greatly enjoyed inflicting their creation on the test subjects. I suppose that they're quite pleased to have found a city where the governor is all too happy to let them test their horrifying creation to their heart's content."

Galen's hand lifted to his throat, where he had felt the parasite burrowing its way down into him. For the life of him, he could not imagine someone finding joy in causing that much pain in another person. That horrified him nearly as much as the parasite itself.

"So, what are we going to do to stop her?" Sasha interjected.

"I have a few ideas, but I am not entirely sure what will work best," Bishop Rose admitted.

"Actually," Jess said, clearing their throat and smiling. "That's where I can help."

GALEN HAD NOT EXPECTED HOW MUCH THE UPPER echelon of the temple was going to apologize to him. But they did. Profusely. Apparently, they had known it was bad, but not exactly how bad. Galen tried to wave them off, saying that it wasn't their fault, but none of them would hear it.

With a plan in place, they decided that Galen had served his role in the matter. More than anything, he needed to rest. They dared not put him in danger again after what had happened to him. Instead, they put him up in the guest quarters meant for visiting bishops. Galen was shocked at the luxury, but he could hardly say no.

The set of rooms was nearly as big as his entire house. There were an en suite washroom, a gigantic bed made up with fine linens, and a receiving room with a window that opened out into a courtyard. He was able to spend time in the gardens, to relax and just be. This was something that he had rarely had a chance to do since he started working in Candiru Quarter.

Galen was under strict orders from a temple doctor to get plenty of rest, and that meant a full night's sleep to start with. That first night, however, Sasha finally got him alone and after kissing him until Galen saw spots, Sasha sat him on the bed and grinned at him with a smile that threatened to break his face in two.

"Galen, I know that there's so much going on right now," Sasha said, squeezing his hands tightly.

"That is rather the understatement," Galen said, a small laugh escaping his lips.

"Okay, yes, sorry, but I need to tell you this," Sasha said, and looked at Galen with shining eyes. "I don't know if you'll believe me."

"I'll do my best?" Galen said, and he couldn't help but laugh again.

"I met the Lady of Flowers," Sasha said, smiling, his eyes sparkling.

There was a beat of silence until Galen laughed. "Okay, sure, make fun of me then."

Sasha looked utterly flabbergasted, and he said, "No, I'm not making fun."

"Sasha, really?" Galen said. "Okay, what does she look like?"

Sasha huffed in frustration, and said, "Well, she was really beautiful."

"Uh-huh." Galen rolled eyes and gave Sasha a fond smile.

"No, listen," Sasha said, and he went on to give the most accurate description of the Lady of Flowers that Galen had ever heard. There were depictions of the Lady, but they weren't common public knowledge. Unless Sasha had been spending time deep in the temple's libraries, he was telling the truth.

When Galen had recovered from his shock, he said, "What...what did she say? Sasha, this is incredible! Have you told the bishop?"

"No, I wanted to tell you first, silly," Sasha said, clearly relieved that Galen believed him. "She mostly wanted to help me forgive myself."

"Really?" Galen asked, his eyes surely bulging out of his face, and he turned completely to face Sasha. "Sasha, that's incredible. Gods above, I knew that you were special, but you must be someone incredible for the Lady to give you her personal attention."

Sasha blushed a bit, then he reached forward and cupped Galen's face in his hands. "I think it was also because of you."

Galen's world was spinning, and he asked, "Truly?"

"Galen, I'm not lying to you," Sasha said. "She said she was going to help. I asked her to."

Galen let out a laugh and then felt saltwater rising in his throat. He tried to fight down the tears, but they came anyway. Sasha looked concerned, but Galen shook his head and smiled.

"Sasha, thank you," Galen said. "Gods above, I love you."

Sasha beamed at him, and then asked, "How's your throat?"

"What?" Galen was caught off guard. "Oh, it's fine. They healed me well. I'm mostly just tired now."

"Good," Sasha said, leaning in and kissing his neck. "I'd love to make you just a bit more tired tonight. We actually have a bed that can fit both of us."

Galen burst out laughing and said, "Wow. Very smooth."

"I try to be," Sasha said, hand snaking around Galen's waist.

Galen did not follow the doctor's orders; he hardly slept at all that night.

CHAPTER 33

HORROR IN THE TUNNELS

SASHA

IF SASHA HAD THOUGHT THAT CANDIRU QUARTER smelled bad, it had nothing on the tunnels. The tunnels that he hadn't even known existed. Jess had regaled them all with the tale of how they and three other Kippers tried to chase down the mage who infected Galen. To be honest, Sasha hadn't really believed them until Ellyn confirmed that the tunnels existed.

Apparently, the Kippers had chased the mage through the streets of Candiru. Jess was very fast, but they lost precious time when they stopped with Galen and again when they called the others. They saw them vanish down a hatch Jess hadn't known was there, but by the time Jess dropped into the tunnels after their quarry, they had vanished.

"It was wild," Jess said. "Just poof! Like magic. Like that little stinky fox you got running around, Galen."

Galen had laughed, rolled his eyes, and described Muffin to the rest of the group, who had been rather confused by the mention. Despite Ellyn's deep curiosity about the blink fox and its origin, Bishop Rose kept them on track. Well, until

Galen nearly fell out of his chair a second time. This time, it was from exhaustion, and they decided that he needed to rest.

The next three days were nice, even though Sasha didn't let Galen rest that much on the first night. Galen slept in every day, and Sasha finally got to watch Galen sleep peacefully in the morning light. His face was relaxed, and he slept on his side, the sunlight playing against his skin and his scar.

Sasha had really looked at him then. He hadn't thought about it much in the past months, but Galen did tend to always turn his head to one side to hide the scar as much as he could. Sasha still wanted to throttle whoever had made Galen so self-conscious about something that was hardly his fault, but now... Now it looked like a part of him, a mark of all he had been through and how he had grown from it. Sasha wanted to kiss him there, to show just how much he loved him, all of him.

But after Galen had recovered a bit more, it was time to enact their plan. It was convoluted and precarious, and Sasha was all for it until Galen insisted on accompanying them. Galen had already been hurt, and every other person who was a part of the plan had agreed with Sasha's point of view. Galen did not need to be there; he needed to stay safe. Galen protested this, of course, but was overwhelmed with opposition.

"I've been fighting against this the whole time," Galen said. He was leaning on a chair as he stood, which did not help his case. "Please. I need to be there; I need to see it through."

"What you need, Brother Galen," Sibling Hanan said, taking Galen's arm and trying to get him to sit down, "is rest."

"Please, it's not fair." Galen shook off Sibling Hanan, only to stumble into Sasha's chest. "I want to see it finally fall apart. This whole thing is for Candiru. I am from Candiru. I deserve to be there."

"What's not right is how you were left to die, Brother

Galen," Bishop Rose said, shaking her head. "You were treated as fodder, and I will not risk you again. You are too precious for that."

"I'm not precious or breakable," Galen said desperately, though he was struggling to stay standing and his hands were shaking. "I need to be there. I need to end this."

"Galen, Flower Boy," Jess said, placing a hand gently on his shoulder. "I'll be there for Candiru. I promise, I'll make sure that it gets done right. We'll get justice. I don't want to risk you either. You don't deserve that."

"I don't need to be coddled, Jess," Galen said, his voice breaking as he bit back angry tears, tears that Sasha had seen before. "I don't care what happens to me, I need to be there!"

"And what if you're attacked again, Galen?" Sasha said suddenly, turning Galen to face him. "What then? What if you die trying to avenge Candiru? Do you think that every single person in Candiru wouldn't be heartbroken? That Jess and I wouldn't be devastated?"

Galen stared up at him, mouth opening, then closing, then opening again. Finally, he pursed his lips, looking down and shaking his head as his arms hung limply at his sides.

"Fine," Galen muttered. "Fine. At least let me go home when you start the plan."

Sasha didn't want to let him; he wanted Galen to stay safe at the temple. Candiru itself might be less dangerous than he had thought just a few months ago, but someone was certainly out to get Galen. Sasha looked around at the rest of the people in the room and saw the same hesitation mirrored on their faces. Galen crossed his arms, standing as steadfastly as he could, even though he still swayed. Finally, Bishop Rose sighed.

"All right, we can do that," she said. "We'll need to find someone to guard him, though, since Mister Rider will be coming with us. Perhaps the temple of Lion in Glory could spare a couple more paladins…”

“Oh,” Jess said, smiling and clasping Galen’s shoulder. “That won’t be necessary. The Kipper Gang will take care of him.”

“The Kipper Gang?” Ellyn sat up, suddenly very interested in the conversation.

“Candiru Quarter’s own specialized defense force,” Sasha sighed, eyeing Jess, who was grinning like a cat again. “I think Jess might be their leader or something.”

Jess barked a laugh, and said, “Oh, gods forbid, no. I’m nowhere near that high in the organization. But I’ve got enough influence that I can get Galen a personal guard. Easy enough. Is that all right with you, Flower Boy?”

Galen rubbed his very tired eyes and muttered, “Yes, that’s fine.”

Sasha rubbed Galen’s shoulders. He understood his lover’s anger and frustration, but he also wanted to make sure, more than anything, that Galen was safe. And if that meant locking him up in his little house with the Kippers watching him, so be it.

But now Sasha was creeping through the secret tunnels under Dragonet City with Jess in front of him and a few people from the temple of Lion in Glory, including Ellyn Staple, behind him. She had insisted on coming on the reconnaissance mission for ‘research purposes,’ whatever that meant.

They were moving silently through the muck and darkness. Sasha watched Jess’s careful progress and placed his own feet in precisely the same spots. His eyes had gotten used to the darkness, but his vision was by no means perfect. He just had to trust that the Kipper knew where they were going.

The muck that they were crawling through seemed to be mostly human waste. The refuse of the upper districts had to be transported to the river somehow, and this was how. After a few hours, though, Sasha noticed something different about the sludge running past their boots, and he grabbed Jess's arm.

They spun around, their long braid whipping against his face, and scowled at him until Sasha pointed it out to them: along with the usual waste ran a steady stream of black ichor. At least they knew they were headed in the right direction, Sasha reflected darkly.

Jess bit their lower lip, then nodded at Sasha and continued their trek through the tunnel. About half an hour later, they saw a light up ahead and heard voices. Sasha glanced back and saw that the two paladins from Lion in Glory had their hands hovering over their swords, ready to draw at a moment's notice. Ellyn had a notebook open and an incredibly expensive self-inking quill up and ready to write. He didn't know which weapon would prove more dangerous.

Three voices echoed down the tunnels, and Sasha recognized all of them. There was Miller, clearly frustrated and on the defensive. There was Ramil, the mage who had attacked Galen, their odd, gravelly voice rasping at his soul. And finally, dripping with irritation and disdain, was Governor Maple herself.

Sasha grabbed Jess's arm again, causing them to turn around and glower at him. He motioned *wait, be quiet, listen* with his free hand. Jess's silent eyeroll said eloquently that Sasha was an idiot not to realize they were already planning to do those things. Sasha shrugged and turned to listen.

"This is your fault, Miller," Governor Maple spat. "This was your plan and it's falling apart. I will not be taking the blame for this, do you understand? I will not be held responsible. I've worked too hard and come too far for you to ruin it all."

"Well, my lady," Miller said obsequiously. "In truth, it wasn't really my fault that the devotee survived the attack.

And that's really the crux of the issue. If you have a problem, you should take it up with Ramil. They're the one who infected him."

There was a moment of shuffling before Ramil said, "Oh, it would have worked. The death seeker I infected the devotee with was especially potent. It should have killed him in an hour, maybe two if he had his magic. But unfortunately, you failed to get rid of the guard you yourself installed. Remind me, what was the reasoning behind that, again?"

"Yes, Sir Miller." Governor Maple's sharp voice rang through the tunnels. "Why was that a good idea?"

Flustered, Miller snapped, "Plausible deniability was your goal! That was the reason! By all accounts it should have worked. Sasha Rider was a useless fuckup and he should have failed within the first month. I don't know what happened."

Jess turned to him and silently mouthed 'ouch.' It was Sasha's turn to roll his eyes. He didn't give a shit what Miller thought of him.

Governor Maple groaned, then said, "We're in too deep now. The university wants to start building next year. We've got to clear out the rats now. What is Plan B?"

"We've already gone through Plan B," Miller said with a sigh. "And Plan C. And a half-assed Plan D. I don't know what else to do."

Sasha heard a derisive snort from behind him. He turned to see Ellyn, who smirked in the darkness.

"Very foolish not to have planned all the way through Z," Ellyn whispered. Sasha held a finger to his lips, silently begging her to stay quiet.

"It's funny that you say that," Ramil said, and Sasha could practically hear the grin in their voice. "I actually have had a backup plan for when Sir Miller failed for a while now."

"Oh?" Governor Maple said.

"It's a bit extreme," Ramil said. "But I guarantee that it

will clear out Candiru Quarter. I'll just need a bit of help from you, my lady."

Jess and Ellyn started creeping forward again. Sasha groaned internally but crept along with them. There was a gap in the tunnel wall, and it allowed for a view down into a large, cave-like room that was bright with magelights. Sasha could see all three figures.

Miller cradled a large ledger as though it were a newborn child. Governor Maple was dressed down from her usual expensive look but still was clearly the wealthiest person in the room. Her tunic was plain, but new and untouched by the usual wear and tear of everyday use, and her boots bore only a hint of mud. And then there was Ramil, the mage. They had their fine cloak still around their shoulders. The most haunting thing about them was that they looked so normal. They had a plain, unassuming face, sandy hair hanging down to their shoulders, nothing out of the ordinary apart from the look in their eyes. There was something off there, but Sasha couldn't get a clear read on it from where he hid.

All around the room on long tables there were jars that held small, squirming, pitch-black creatures. Sasha's eyes went wide. These were the death seekers that Ramil had been infecting Candiru quarter with. There had to be at least a hundred jars in the cave. Sasha clamped his lips tightly against a scream. If they released all of those, if they infected everyone in Candiru with those death seekers, the quarter would be wiped out within a week.

"Now," Ramil was saying to the governor, "I must admit. It won't be very good optics. But it will be efficient."

The governor glared at Miller, then looked back to Ramil with a nod. "Let's hear it. I'll have to take what I can at this point."

Ramil nodded and led Governor Maple over to a large sackcloth curtain. "What I'll need you to do is close off

Candiru Quarter for a day. Make sure that not a soul comes in or out. Then we'll release these into the tunnels. They will go directly to the quarter."

Ramil tugged the curtain down, and a screeching sound like the release of a thousand bats tore the air. Everyone in the tunnel covered their ears. Jess squeezed their eyes shut, but Sasha and Ellyn kept looking.

Behind the curtain was a massive glass container, as tall as Sasha and twice as wide, roiling with thousands of death seekers. They were scrambling over each other, pushing against the glass and trying to reach the warm bodies on the other side.

Miller had his ledger up in front of him like a shield, and Governor Maple had retreated in fear. Only Ramil got close enough to the glass to touch it, reaching out as tenderly as to a pet.

"We do that," Ramil said, grinning, "and your Candiru problem will be solved in a day. And I'll get to see just how wonderfully my precious death seekers work."

Miller and Maple exchanged worried glances, but it was the governor who cleared her throat and asked, "And you will be able to stop them? Afterwards."

"Oh, of course," Ramil said, waving a hand dismissively. "It's easy enough. It works on the same principle that allows the magic of the Lady of Flowers to destroy them. They're antithetical to life, so that's what stops them, you see?"

"I see," the governor said, though she clearly did not. "And when do you want to do this? How long will that glass hold?"

Ramil laughed. "The glass will hold until I don't want it to hold. As soon as you're ready, my lady, we can begin."

Sasha's gaze was frozen on the scene in front of him, but Jess grabbed his arm and pulled him back the way they had come. Their party traveled silently, the horror of it all hanging over them like a miasma. Sasha didn't want to believe it, but it had been spelled out plainly before him.

When they finally reemerged, they washed off silently before heading back to Bishop Rose's office. Sasha was grateful that Galen wasn't there to hear what they had seen—more grateful than he had ever been in his life. As Jess and Ellyn recounted the meeting to the horrified upper echelon of the temple, Sasha gazed at the ground with unfocused eyes. He was going to kill that mage. This was all a game for them. They were excited to play with their creations, not thinking at all about the human lives it would cost.

Sasha thought about the people of Candiru, their faces, their voices, their hopes and dreams, and gritted his teeth. Even if he hadn't been overwhelmingly in love with Galen, he would have stood to protect the people of Candiru. They deserved someone willing to fight for them.

"I know exactly which bit of the city that cave is under," Ellyn was saying when Sasha started listening again. "We'll be able to come at them from both above and below."

"Where is it?" Sasha asked, stepping forward and staring at her desperately.

Ellyn smirked. "Directly beneath the palace."

CHAPTER 34

BLOOMING

GALEN

GALEN WALKED BACK HOME SHADOWED BY TWO young Kippers, Danny and Fynn. He knew that there were likely others around, watching him and making sure that no one did anything to him.

He hadn't spoken to Sasha since his return from the tunnels. Something that Sasha had seen there was clearly haunting him, but he refused to say what it was. He just held Galen to his chest, kissing the crown of his head and telling him that he'd be all right. That everything would be all right. Galen was frustrated to say the least.

However, he did understand the concern. He didn't want to be a liability, and surely that's what he would be if he went with them. He knew they planned to head to the palace, both in the tunnels and above ground, early the next day. He'd just have to stay in his little house and pray to the Lady, asking her to help and to watch over his friends and his lover.

As he had left the temple, he had told Sister Amber that that was his plan. She nodded at him firmly and said, "Brother Galen, be sure to listen carefully to how the Lady responds.

Remember, she knows best, despite what our earthly plans might be."

Galen had laughed and said, "Oh, yes. I know. She's telling me that I need to rest, that it's been far too long since I've had a break and that I desperately deserve one. I know, Sister Amber."

Sister Amber smiled at him and cupped his face in her hands. "Look for her signs, Galen. She'll make herself known."

Galen had shaken his head, but thanked her before kissing Sasha goodbye, hugging Jess, and wishing them all luck. And then he went home. It was a long walk, but he was honestly feeling much better after the days of forced rest. For the first time in what seemed like forever, it didn't feel like he was dragging his feet through mud or carrying a pack of heavy stones on his back. He felt a bit lighter, too, knowing that Candiru was still being cared for. He wasn't alone in this.

When he entered Candiru Quarter, a couple of citizens spotted him immediately, even without his yellow healer's tunic. In moments, he was swarmed. They all wanted to make sure that he was okay. He had been gone for over a week, and they were desperate to know where he had been, if everyone had been respectful, and of course who had hurt him so that they could form a mob.

Danny and Fynn had their work cut out for them controlling the crowd so Galen could walk to his house unmolested. He couldn't help laughing at the perturbed looks on their faces. And as person after person rushed him to welcome him back home, it struck him, truly struck him for the first time.

He had never really been alone in Candiru.

As much as he cared for them, they cared for him. By the time he got back to his house, even more dandelions growing in front of it than last time, he was absolutely overwhelmed by the love all around him. Fynn pushed Galen inside, laughing, and Danny slammed the door shut, but not before Muffin came racing inside.

The blink fox was so excited to see him that he blinked up into his arms, chirping happily and rubbing his chilly fur against Galen's scarred cheek. Galen couldn't stop giggling and collapsed on the sofa with Muffin in his arms as the two Kippers stared at him.

"Rising Dawn, Brother Galen," Danny said, blowing out air. "I knew you were popular, but that was something else."

"You've got so many fans," Fynn said, sighing. "But, I mean, I was worried when you disappeared too. You've been seeing me since I was twelve, you know. I remember the time you gave me candy after I broke my nose."

As Muffin licked Galen with his cold tongue, Galen asked, "Wait, how old are you now?"

"Nineteen!" Fynn said, puffing out her chest and placing her hands on her hips. "Plenty old to be taking care of you!"

"Oh, I believe it," Galen said, laughing. "I just feel old now."

Fynn grinned at him, and then there was a knock at his door. The two Kippers turned around, seemingly ready to tell the intruder to leave immediately, but Galen wasn't so eager to be left alone. He gently set Muffin on the sofa and went to the door despite the Kippers' protests. He wasn't about to be a prisoner in his own home.

Galen opened the door and saw Miss Kingley holding a plate full of food. Before he could say anything, she pushed into his kitchen and set it on the table, tutting and cleaning the mess left behind after his attack. Galen couldn't have protested if he wanted to.

Others came also. Adrian brought enough bread to feed an army, which was lucky with the Kippers around. Nina and Mandy brought him a few new pots and then spent time helping Miss Kingley clean. Angelica and Charlie came, little Marigold in tow. They let Galen hold her as they changed his sheets and did his laundry. Galen's heart felt as though it would burst.

After Mister Priestly and his twins came, bringing a feast big enough to feed all his visitors, Galen was exhausted. Fynn and Danny had to chase off the well-meaning citizens of Candiru, each of them giving him well-wishes as they left. Even though it was late, Galen set up his little altar, found his prayer beads, and went through his prayers. He didn't whisper. Somehow, he doubted that his neighbors would mind hearing them.

After praying that the Lady would watch over all those he loved, that she would guide them to do what was best, he felt much better. He drank the nectar, finished the prayers, and rose. Muffin was still in his house, curled up on Danny's lap as he snored lightly on the couch. Fynn sat to his left, trailing her fingers through Muffin's cold fur.

"I'm going to bed now," Galen called to her.

Fynn gave him a sleepy smile and nodded. Galen moved into his bedroom, which was probably the neatest it had been since he moved in seven years previously. As he shucked off his clothes, continuing his bad habit of just tossing them on the ground, his eye caught the white healer's robe from the temple.

Charlie or Angelica must have hung it up, because it swayed slightly from its perch on the rafter. He gazed at it, arms crossed, and thought about the fact that he had earned it. For the first time in his life, he felt as though he had done enough to be recognized the way that Candiru recognized him. And he knew that he wasn't alone.

Being with Sasha had helped with that. He knew that Sasha would always be there for him, and now he knew Candiru would be too. He laughed lightly to himself, shaking his head at his own stupidity. Why had it taken almost being killed by an evil magical parasite to realize what he should have already known? He climbed into bed, blew out the candle, and almost immediately fell asleep.

THAT NIGHT, HE DREAMED THAT HE WAS WALKING through a field of wildflowers. It had to be a dream, because there were no fields in Dragonet City. It was beautiful. The air was clean and clear, and the ground all around him was carpeted with a rainbow of flowers. He breathed in their scent and sighed. He would love to visit a place like this someday. Then he realized he was not alone.

He had seen her in a dream once before, when he was much younger, and one did not easily forget the Lady of Flowers. Immediately, Galen dropped into a deep bow, but of course the Lady laughed and brushed him off. Galen flushed as he stood upright.

"Oh, come now," she said, grinning warmly at him. "None of that, my child."

"Sorry, my lady," Galen said. "Thank you for visiting me."

"You've been neglecting some of your directives, haven't you, Galen?" the Lady asked, taking his hands in hers.

"I'm sorry," Galen breathed out. "There just hasn't been time. There's always so much to do, and for so long I had been doing it alone and I didn't know how to get help and—"

"You're not in trouble," the Lady said gently. "I know. Things have been impossibly hard for you, and that was unfair."

Galen nodded, keeping silent as he gazed upon his goddess.

"And I am so sorry about that," she said, reaching out and stroking his hair. "It's almost over, my dear."

Galen smiled and nodded. "I know. After tomorrow, things should be better. We should be able to end all of this. Then Candiru can truly grow and flourish."

The Lady smiled at him again. "Oh, my little dandelion. It's not just Candiru that will do that. You will too. You've already grown so much. I cannot wait to see how you bloom. Just remember, your voice is important as well, dear. Don't give up."

Galen looked at her, nodded, and said, "I won't."

Then he snapped awake. Morning light was seeping in through the window. The night had seemed to pass very quickly, but Galen had never felt so well rested. The Lady's visit had invigorated him. He felt so very full, not just of energy, but of love and life.

As he sat up, Fynn poked her head into his room. "Uh, good morning, Brother Galen."

"Good morning, Fynn." Galen stretched and stood up.

"Um, Brother Galen?" Fynn said. "You might want to come outside and see this. I promise, we didn't do nothing."

Galen eyed her with suspicion, then pulled on a tunic and headed to his front door. Danny and Fynn stood in the kitchen watching him carefully with Muffin at their feet. He laughed a bit and then opened his door. Oh. Oh, by the Lady.

His entire front stoop and the street in front of his house and beyond were covered in dandelions. Galen stood in shock, looking out at a sea of yellow punctuated by spiky green leaves and the occasional white puffball. He blinked, but they didn't disappear.

Muffin leapt out past his feet and pounced on one of the puffballs, causing the seeds to explode upwards, where they were caught by the wind and flew out over Candiru. As he watched Muffin play in the miniature field, he smiled broadly. He knew what he had to do.

He gathered a bundle of dandelions, then sat at the

kitchen table, weaving them into a crown, the sticky white nectar running down his fingers. He didn't care. The crown finished, he went into the bedroom and changed.

When he emerged, he was wearing trousers and his bright yellow tunic with the white healer's robe over them. He set the crown on his head, slipped on his shoes, and turned to the two young Kippers, who had been watching him uneasily.

"I need to go to the temple," he told them simply. They didn't argue.

The bells of Rising Dawn had long since finished ringing by the time he arrived at the temple of the Lady of Flowers. Just as he suspected she would be, Sister Amber stood waiting for him beside the same carriage they had taken to see Governor Maple a few weeks previously.

"About time!" Sister Amber called, grinning at him. "I was starting to worry that you weren't actually coming."

Galen beamed at her and said, "I wouldn't miss this for the world. I want Governor Maple to know exactly who she messed with."

"Just what I wanted to hear," Sister Amber said, throwing open the carriage door. "I love your crown. Not traditional, but very you."

Galen wouldn't have been able to wipe the smile off his face if he tried. "Thank you. It was a gift."

CHAPTER 35

IT FESTERS

SASHA

SASHA'S HEART WAS BEATING SO HARD THAT HE WAS sure it was echoing down the tunnels, giving away their position and ruining their plan. No one else was reacting, though, so it must have been his imagination. He gripped his sword with a gloved hand and breathed deeply through the mask tied around his nose and mouth. It smelled of rose oil, reminding him of Galen giving him one just like it. His heart continued to pound.

Once again, he was creeping behind Jess, who led him and even more paladins from Lion in Glory than on their previous venture down the tunnels. He could hardly see them, though; much like him, they were completely covered except for their eyes. As far as they knew, a death seeker could somehow infect them through touch, and face masks had somehow protected Sasha and Galen. They weren't going to risk an unprotected inch of skin.

Behind him, there was a soft sneeze, and he whipped around to see a healer pulling down her mask and wiping her nose. The only thing that they knew was completely effective against the death seekers was healers' magic. They had brought along as many volunteers as the temple could spare. Which was only seven, not including Sibling Hanan, and a few of them were newly out of their pledge years. The paladin behind the young healer stared at her, and Sasha shook his head.

"Sorry," she said far too loudly. "I don't like the smell of the rose oil; it keeps tickling my nose and—mmph!"

Jess had appeared and clapped their hand over the healer's mouth. They widened their eyes, cocked their head, and then lifted a finger to their mouth to indicate that she needed to stay silent. The healer nodded, and Jess lowered their hand. She mouthed 'sorry' and pulled the mask back up.

Jess moved back to their position in front, and Sasha continued to follow them, listening to the footsteps of the healer close behind him. He knew that Galen was praying, asking the Lady for help, but he decided that it wouldn't hurt to add his voice to the plea.

With each step that he took, Sasha silently beseeched the Lady of Flowers. The gods only had so much power, but he couldn't imagine that the Lady would just stand by and let something so heinous happen here, especially when her worshippers were at the center of it. He prayed that Bishop Rose, Ellyn Staple, and Captain Tracker would thoroughly distract Miller and Governor Maple and that they would be too preoccupied with the accusations to notice an infiltration. He prayed that Ramil would be nowhere to be found.

When they finally got to the break in the tunnel that led to Ramil's lair, Jess reached a hand back to Sasha. Sasha unhooked the rope from his belt and handed it up to them. Moments later, they had tied and secured it and were dropping silently into the space below. Sasha followed them soon after. Luckily, the room was dark and seemingly empty.

The paladins were fine getting down; it was the healers who struggled. Most of them didn't spend upwards of twelve hours walking around a district treating patients almost every day like Galen did, and they were already exhausted from the long trek through the tunnels.

Sasha had to catch Sibling Hanan when they lost their grip halfway down the rope. They made a soft *oof* sound as he caught them, which made him whip his head around and search for any movement, but it appeared that they were alone. Jess was stalking through the room, looking for any sign of the conspirators, and the paladins from Lion in Glory were clearly on alert.

"We can't see anything," whispered the young healer who had sneezed.

"I think we're alone," Jess called from across the room. "Give me a moment."

Light suddenly filled the room as Jess somehow activated all the magelights. And then the room was filled with gasps and shrieks from the healers and paladins who hadn't seen the death seekers before. Most of them were small, probably the kind that Ramil had been using in Candiru quarter, but some of them were nearly bursting out of their containers.

Sasha met the eyes of a queasy-looking Sibling Hanan and said, "Well?"

Hanan nodded firmly. "Come on, get ready. Brother Galen said that he used a standard healing spell, and it killed them. Don't expend all your magic on the small ones, you must make sure you have enough for the bigger ones. Let's get to work."

The devotees, though clearly worried and unsure, got to it. A devotee would walk up to one of the glass jars, lay their hands on it, and start praying. The familiar pink glow appeared, and then moments later, the squirming death seeker within went motionless, dissolving into dark ash shortly after. Sasha watched them for a bit as the paladins moved around the edges of the room, their hands resting on their swords.

Sasha watched as the healer who had sneezed in the tunnel

lifted a jar from the table and allowed the light of the gift to explode out in a huge, blinding burst. Soon, Sibling Hanan was at her side.

"Sister Petra," Sibling Hanan said, grabbing the young healer's hand, "not so much. You're going to run out of the gift before you finish five at that rate."

"Right, sorry," Sister Petra said, pulling down her mask and wiping her nose.

Sasha sighed and sent another prayer up to the Lady that this would work. His fingers were tapping nervously at his side as he watched the healers move from jar to jar and winced as the younger ones started to look worn out.

"Gods above, I hope this works," Jess said, suddenly beside him.

Sasha, who had learned not to jump when Jess appeared, just nodded. They shuddered as they watched the healers work, expending their gift in a way that Sasha doubted it was truly meant to be used.

"What are we going to do about..." Jess trailed off, but they tilted their head back towards the curtain that hid a tank full of the creatures.

"Ramil said they had a failsafe," Sasha said. "Hopefully, that's what the others are getting right now."

"Well," Jess said, shrugging as bursts of pink light filled the room, "keep praying."

Time passed slowly. Three of the devotees had run out of magic and were sitting on the ground, breathing heavily. Sibling Hanan was still going strong, but Sasha saw a familiar exhaustion in the eyes of the remaining healers. There were at least twenty jars left. Sasha rubbed his eyes and looked over his shoulder at the door that led up to the palace. Nobody had dared to open it, just in case it would summon the governor.

The worst thing about the situation, besides the squirming death seekers that might kill them if someone dropped a jar, was the not knowing. There was no way to know exactly what was happening with the governor and the bishop. There was no way to know if the other half of the plan was succeeding, or if they were wasting time down here. Sasha hated it, and Jess surely hated it just as much.

They always had so much energy, and right now, it was pent up in a small space with nowhere to go. They paced back and forth, breathing heavily with fists clenched at their sides, muttering behind their mask. It was excruciating.

As Sibling Hanan started on the next death seeker, shouts broke out on the other side of the door. Everyone froze and stared, but when the chanting stopped, Sasha whipped around.

"Keep going!" he shouted, and then the door flew open.

On the other side was Ramil, the architect of the death seekers, their eyes wide and horrified. They released a bloodcurdling scream at the sight of the jars full of dead parasites. They collapsed to the floor, muttering and clutching their head, as more people descended into the room.

Bishop Rose was first and threw a hand out towards the scene. "Explain this, then, Governor Maple. Why is your basement full of these creatures?"

Governor Maple, pale and shaken, descended the stairs, followed by Miller, holding the large ledger in his arms. Tracker was behind them, sword drawn and ready, and Ellyn Staple came down last, looking infinitely smug.

Maple looked down at the heap that was Ramil and back up to Bishop Rose. She spread her hands wide and put on a well-practiced smile. Bishop Rose, of course, was not buying any of it.

"Bishop Rose, please," Governor Maple said. "Obviously, I wasn't actually going to go through with that plan. The citizens of Candiru Quarter are, of course, my citizens as well. A different space would have been found for them, perhaps outside the city. This was just meant as...a motivator. A little fear can go a long way."

Miller looked a bit green, but he said, "As you well know, these parasites can be treated easily with healing from your own temple. Brother Gary had been easily treating everyone who got infected. No one was in any true danger."

Bishop Rose's eyebrows nearly disappeared into her hairline as she asked, "Do you, perhaps, mean Brother Galen?"

"Yes, of course," Miller said, shaking his head. "What did I say?"

"Brother Gary," Bishop Rose said, disgust evident in her voice. "Well, what do you think, Mistress Staple?"

Ellyn's grin was wild and wicked as she stepped next to Bishop Rose. "Hello, Governor Maple. Do you remember me?"

It was clear from her expression that she did. "I have no earthly idea who you are."

Ellyn was unperturbed as she said, "Lie as much as you like, Governor Maple. It never helped you in the past." She tapped her pile of papers. "But all right. Let's try this out. The healers haven't finished destroying all the highly illegal death seekers yet. You and Miller. Why don't you allow yourselves to be infected? Prove to us that there is no danger."

Both of them stood stock-still. Sibling Hanan, bless them, stopped chanting over the death seeker in their hands and brought it over to the bishop. The little parasite shrieked and smashed itself against the glass as they held it out towards Governor Maple.

Governor Maple looked at the monster, looked back at

Bishop Rose, and said, "Of course I'm not going to do that. Do you take me for a fool?"

"I thought it was perfectly safe," Ellyn Staple said, her grin very much like a lion's.

Governor Maple was silent; her face grew red as she clenched her teeth. Miller broke and ran back towards the stairs. He didn't get far as Jess appeared from nowhere and stuck out a leg to trip him. He fell with a resounding crack of his chin against the hard stone floor.

As two paladins lifted him up and held him in place, he spat out blood and a tooth onto the cold ground. Jess's eyes, the only part of them that was visible, were full of fire as they growled, "That was for Figlove Lane."

Miller groaned, glaring at the floor, his arms held behind his back. Jess bent down and scooped up the ledger, offering it to Ellyn, who took it with glee. The governor still said nothing.

"I think it's time to admit it, Elizabeth," Ellyn Staple said, tilting her head to the side. "You were caught red-handed. There's no coming back from this."

"I'll testify against her for a lesser sentence," Miller said, locking eyes with Bishop Rose.

"Aw, Miller, I knew I could count on you, you spineless worm," Ellyn said, smirking at him.

Bishop Rose smiled, though, and said, "We'll have to confer with the temple of Lion in Glory, but I think it's time to head to the temple of Rising Dawn. We'll confirm everything with a truth-seeker. First, though, we'll need that fail-safe to finish this off."

Sasha had been so focused on the scene in front of him, feeling triumphant and honestly shocked that the plan had worked so well, that he hadn't been watching the mage. It appeared that no one had. It wasn't until the young Sister Petra shrieked that anyone realized that they had moved off.

"What are they doing?" Sister Petra screamed as Ramil pulled the curtain down and revealed the enormous tank seething with death seekers.

"Ramil!" Governor Maple shouted, finally breaking her silence. "What are you doing?"

Ramil's eyes were furious. The fine black cloak hung precariously off their shoulders and their hands shook. They glared at Governor Maple and the rest of the gathering. Then they lifted their hand and pressed it against the glass.

"You don't appreciate my creations," they growled. "You let them destroy it all. They were my masterpieces, and now they're gone. They're all gone..."

"Somebody stop them!" Bishop Rose cried.

Sasha started running, but he was too slow.

Ramil's face softened into a crooked smile. "I'm sorry. I've said it before. I don't like to hurt priests."

Then the glass cracked.

CHAPTER 36

IT ENDS

GALEN

SISTER AMBER WAS A GENIUS. GALEN KNEW THIS well. But the way that she spread the information about exactly what Governor Maple had done confirmed that for him ten times over. Sister Amber had a reputation for being the best speaker in the temple, and now he thought she might be the best speaker in the world.

Rumors had a magic all their own, especially in the upper districts. Galen hadn't realized just how powerful they could be until he saw them in action. The truth spread like wildfire as Sister Amber had breakfast then morning tea then brunch with one person after another. Along with the evident hubbub at the palace, it was incredibly effective. Galen sat awestruck as he sipped his tea.

"You are terrifying," Galen said as he climbed into the carriage after their fifth stop.

"Oh, thank you," Sister Amber said, beaming at him. "That's high praise from one of the best healers this temple has ever seen."

Galen flushed. "Oh, I don't know about th—" He caught

the look on Sister Amber's face, so he just laughed and said, "Thank you."

"Good!" Sister Amber said, clapping her hands together. "Let's see how things are going at the palace, shall we?"

Galen agreed, and then they were off. Sister Amber had explained the plan to him, something that Sasha had refused to do. Galen would be having words with him about that later. It seemed incredibly risky, but he had no idea what else they could have done. It seemed to be working so far.

It was now in fashion to be appalled at Governor Maple's plan, and everyone that he met declared that they would never want a mage school in place of Candiru Quarter. Just think how many servants and goods came from there, and how expensive everything would become! Compassion for Candiru would have been better, but at least they were opposed.

Galen rested his head against the wall of the carriage as they continued the climb, closing his eyes and sending another prayer to the Lady of Flowers. *Please let this work. Please keep them safe. Please let Sasha be okay.* He breathed in deeply, and Sister Amber chuckled.

"He'll be all right, Galen," she said, smiling as he opened his eyes. "They all will. You'll get to chew him out for not telling you, I promise. Bishop Rose, Mistress Staple, all of them are very smart. They'll be safe."

"I hope you're right," Galen said, smiling. "I'm just a worrier. Let me worry."

Sister Amber laughed and then patted his knee. Galen reached up to fiddle with the dandelion crown. It wasn't as carefully woven as the ones the growers in the temple made, and he'd had to fix it a few times. But he was glad he wore it. The yellow-stained tips of his fingers looked right.

They soon arrived at the palace, and Galen was taken aback by its emptiness. The guards and the staff were gone, and it was more a mausoleum than a grand palace. For the first time, Sister Amber looked a little worried. Her steps were not the slow, carefully measured ones that Galen had grown so used to. Instead, she made a rapid beeline towards the governor's office with Galen at her heels.

They got to the office only to see the giant portrait swung open like a door, revealing steps leading down into the dark. Sister Amber smirked and offered a hand to help Galen up to the entryway, and they started descending.

At first, they moved slowly. It grew colder as they went lower, despite the blistering heat outside. Magelights were enough to see by, but they were far from perfect. Galen tripped and stumbled a few times, catching himself on the wall. Sister Amber didn't stumble, but he could feel her unease.

In a few minutes, they heard voices. At first, it was conversational. People speaking in low tones, an occasional shout or laugh peppered in, but as they approached the bottom, all they could hear was shouting. And then a very familiar shriek, like bats screeching in the night. Galen broke into a run.

He burst in through the door at the bottom just in time to see a huge tank full of death seekers crack open and release its contents into the room like a wave crashing onto a shore. It was utter chaos. The tide of creatures surged over people, trying to dig into their skin when they couldn't reach their mouths. The mage who had created them just held their arms wide and let themself be enveloped.

Paladins from Lion in Glory swung swords, slicing death eaters in half, but it was futile. Galen could see flashes of pink healing, but it was weak, nearly spent. Bishop Rose was crowding towards the door with Ellyn Sharp and Governor Maple in tow, and when she saw him, her face twisted in surprise.

"Galen? What are you doing here?" she cried, trying to push him up the stairs, but he wasn't having it.

"The Lady told me to come," he said, looking the bishop in the eyes. "And here I am. Let me help."

Over her shoulder, he saw Sasha, knee-deep in death seekers and trying to fight them off with a sword. At the sound of Galen's name, Sasha looked up towards the door. Sheer panic in his eyes, he yanked down his mask and screamed, "Galen! R—!"

As soon as his mouth was free, a death seeker leapt up and started to burrow its way into his throat, blocking his shout. Sasha clutched at his face and crashed to the ground, eyes rolling back. Galen screamed and pushed past the bishop, leaping into the room.

Something very odd happened then. The death seekers tried to surge towards him, to attack him like they had every other person in the room, but when they got close to him, they shrank back, hissing and shrieking. Galen blinked at them and touched his chest just below his pendant.

He felt it lifting inside of him: an inexhaustible well of the gift. It was as though the sun itself filled him, begging to burst out. Galen took another step forward, and the death seekers scrambled back, away from him, as if in pain. Galen lifted his hands and started the healing spell.

The pink glow washed out from him like a wave. The light was brighter, more vibrant than it had ever been. It was as though morning was breaking over the room, bathing each inch of it in the Lady's power. Everywhere it touched the death seekers, they shriveled into husks. The dusty ashes of their remains soon covered the floor of the room as Galen walked through, chanting and spreading the light of the Lady.

As the magic rushed out of him, filling the room, the gentle pink glow left behind flower petals. Galen did his best not to crush them; they were pink primrose. Those were the Lady's favorite flowers and another clear sign that she was here, using Galen as a vessel for her will. Galen didn't mind in the slightest.

Soon, he made it to Sasha. His skin was covered in rapidly-spreading black spots and the ichor leaked from his mouth and eyes. Galen dropped to his knees and bent over Sasha, taking his face in his hands and turning it towards him. Sasha coughed, but his eyes were unfocused.

"Please, Sasha," Galen said, and a dandelion from his haphazard crown fell and landed on his guard's cheek.

Would it work? Galen still felt a never-ending river of magic within him, but he had already lost so much, and he could feel the man he loved slipping through his fingers. He started chanting again.

The magic flowed through him like the Haplin River just below them. The pink light enveloped his entire body, filling it with the comforting, warm presence of the Lady of Flowers in all her glory. The warmth of a spring day, the colors of freshly blooming flowers, the joy of having loved ones close, all of it became a part of Galen's magic. And all that love rushed into Sasha.

It took longer than Galen would have liked, but it worked. Sasha coughed and turned his head to hack up sludge onto the floor. Then he sat up and looked around in utter disbelief. He turned to Galen and released a sound somewhere between a laugh and a sob before grabbing Galen's face and kissing him until he saw stars. Sasha tasted of black ichor, but Galen didn't care.

As Sasha broke the kiss, clutching Galen, he said, "Gods above, remind me to never second-guess you again. We really did need you here."

Galen laughed, and they stood together, supporting each other. He pushed his face, wet with tears, against Sasha's chest, holding onto him and breathing in his scent. It was finally, finally over.

They were interrupted, of course, by a shout.

"Hey! Flower Boy!" Jess yelled. "If you're done with him, could you please help over here? You'll have plenty of time for that later, promise."

Galen turned from Sasha with a laugh, but looked back to say, "Duty calls."

As Galen stepped away, Sasha grabbed his hand, pressing a kiss to it and saying, "You look beautiful."

Galen smiled a wide, gap-toothed grin. "Thank you."

GALEN'S INCREDIBLE WELL OF MAGIC LASTED LONG enough for him to destroy all of the death seekers and heal all those infected, including Sir Miller and Governor Maple. Ramil had not survived the initial wave.

As Galen laid his hands on Governor Maple and chanted, the pink glow enveloping her and healing her, she glared at him. He lowered his hands and met her glare with force.

"Why in the gods' names would you heal me?" Governor Maple asked, her brows low.

Galen sighed and said, "No one deserves a death like that. Not even you."

Governor Maple sneered at him. "Do you think you're better than me for showing me such mercy? Are you proud of yourself, little priest?"

Galen smiled, showing his gap teeth, and said, "Not at all. Just, if you were dead, I couldn't tell you how I really feel."

"And how's that?" Governor Maple ground out. "Do you want to tell me how I should care about all the citizens again? All the dirty little rats down in Candiru?"

"No," Galen said, shrugging. "That'd be a waste of my energy. I mostly just wanted to say fuck you."

Governor Maple's face twisted into a mask of impotent fury as the paladins pulled her away. Jess whooped and punched the air. Then Sasha scooped Galen up from behind and spun him around, even though he squawked and demanded to be put down.

After he had healed the last infected person, his borrowed power drained away. The exhaustion hit him like a wall, and he fell to his knees. Sasha was there, because of course he was, and he lifted Galen in his arms and carried him up the stairs.

Maybe being carried like a child should be embarrassing, but Galen felt strangely at peace. He nestled his cheek against Sasha's shoulder as they walked through the palace. As they emerged into a bright summer day, Galen looked back. Emerging from a crack between two perfect, white stones grew a bright yellow dandelion.

EPILOGUE - SIX
MONTHS LATER

GALEN

GALEN WOKE UP AND WAS SURPRISED AT THE LACK of a warm body beside him. Although they had finally gotten a larger bed—which Charlie and Angelica refused to let them pay for, much to Galen's embarrassment—Sasha still nearly smothered Galen during the night because he wanted to be so close. Ever since the confrontation with the governor, Sasha didn't like Galen further than five feet away, let alone out of his sight. So it was surprising that Sasha wasn't there pinning Galen into place.

Galen sat up and rubbed his eyes with a yawn, then sniffed the air. Was that...was that ham? Instead of putting on his own clothes, Galen found one of Sasha's tunics thrown across the back of a chair. On Galen, it would reach his knees. He stretched languidly and then pulled it over his head. It was so nice to have time to stretch.

There were now seven other healers stationed in Candiru. He couldn't believe it. *Seven.* The Lady had tested him, yes, and oh, did she reward him. The bishop had been so appalled that she decided that Galen would have three days off a week, instead of the usual two, for at least as long as he had been alone down here. And on one of those days, no one was allowed to call on him for emergencies. He was to rest. Today was that day. Galen hummed happily to himself.

Normally, on these days, Sasha held Galen captive in bed for hours. They usually wouldn't even do much of anything. Sasha would just hold Galen to his chest and they would talk softly to each other until Galen finally pushed himself off Sasha to use the chamber pot or say his prayers. Sasha was always dramatic about it, but eventually he'd roll out of bed too and follow behind him like an overeager puppy.

It was odd, but very nice, that Sasha had gotten up and made breakfast. Galen walked out into the kitchen. He watched Sasha silently for a few moments, smiling to himself as Sasha whistled away. On the table were apples, eggs, and muffins, along with butter and honey, and mugs already set out with tea steeping. Galen grinned at just how domestic Sasha had gotten since he left the guards.

Galen crossed the distance between them and wrapped his arms around Sasha's waist, leaning into his back and murmuring, "Good morning."

"Ah, damn," Sasha said, turning around and bending to kiss Galen. "I didn't mean to wake you. I wanted to give you breakfast in bed."

Galen grinned, then said, "And how were you planning on doing that? There's a ton of food here. Were you going to carry the whole table into the bedroom?"

Sasha cupped Galen's face gently. "If I had to."

Galen laughed and said, "I'm in love with a ridiculous man."

"I'm very glad you are," Sasha said, stepping back to check the ham, but pausing to scan Galen's form in admiration. "And I am even more glad that you decided to come out wearing that. I'm going to hide all your other clothes so that you can only wear my shirts."

"An extremely ridiculous man!" Galen laughed and sat down, propping his chin on his hand.

Sasha just grinned and took the ham off the heat. Galen had been delighted to find out that Sasha was quite a good cook. When he had met Sasha's parents for the first time, Sasha's mother had been appalled that Galen was doing all the cooking. Not because Galen was a poor cook, no, but because she had taught her son everything she knew in the kitchen and couldn't believe that Sasha was letting it go to waste.

Meeting Sasha's parents had been daunting, but Galen had had no reason to worry. They were kind and grateful that he had helped Sasha find his way. Sasha's mother had squeezed him close, demanding that he call her Katya and apologizing for Sasha's behavior. Sasha's father had an endless curiosity, and he asked Galen innumerable questions about the Lady of Flowers, magic, and the temple. Sasha had to force his father to stop.

Now, seeing Sasha in the kitchen, memories of those visits up to Medaka washed over Galen. It was so nice. He wished that he could have introduced Sasha to his family, but that was simply not fated. He wished he could have met Anya, but he supposed that he could find her when he was taken by the Crow, whenever that would be

Soon, they were eating, looking at each other as they always did when they shared a meal. Things had truly gotten so much better, and it had only taken both of them nearly dying. Finally, as Galen took a long drink of his tea, Sasha cleared his throat.

Galen lifted his eyebrows. "Something you want to say?"

"Yes, well," Sasha said, leaning back in his chair and slipping his hands into his pockets. "There is. Something. I want to ask."

Galen smiled, and said, "Okay, out with it then. You all right, Sasha?"

"Yes, of course," Sasha said, his face turning red. "I'm fine. More than fine. I, uh, you said that you've never left Dragonet City, right?"

"Right?" Galen said, lifting a brow.

"Want to take a vacation together?" Sasha blurted. "Anywhere you want. Anywhere. We could go to Dresia, if you want. See the Grand Temple there, right? Or anything. Wherever you want to go. If you want?"

Galen wasn't sure what to say. He smiled and said, "Um, all right? That would be fun. I'll definitely be a bit lost, though."

"That's all right," Sasha said, a smile breaking out. "I'll make sure nothing will happen to you, I promise. You know I'll always protect you."

Galen laughed, rested his arms on the table, and leaned forward. "I know."

Just then, the door flew open, letting in a blast of cold, snowy air, as well as Jess and Muffin. The snow landed on the floor, melting soon after as Jess stomped their boots and slammed the door closed. Galen shivered violently at the sudden cold and then yelped as Muffin blinked up onto the table, snatched a muffin, and ran off with his prize.

"Gods above, these city council meetings are going to kill me!" Jess said, stalking into the kitchen and grabbing a muffin themself. "I finally understand why Governor Maple fired Ellyn Staple. I felt my eyes glazing over at least ten times during the budget discussions. The meeting lasted all night, Galen! There's an eighth hell, and it's budget meetings."

Jess had earned their place on the city council. Governor Maple and Miller were now rotting in jail, as they deserved for all that they did, but Dragonet City still needed leadership. The previously weak city council had been expanded greatly.

Now, the city was run by representatives from each district, along with leaders from the various temples and guilds. Because of its size, Candiru Quarter had five representatives. Jess had run a very aggressive campaign to be one of them and was easily elected. It would be good to have a Kipper there. However, they loved to show up to Galen's house to complain about the endless meetings.

Galen laughed despite the annoyed look on Sasha's face and said, "That bad, huh?"

"I know I asked for this," Jess said, looking up at the ceiling for divine intervention, "but this is testing me. Congratulations, by the way."

Jess took a bite of their muffin, and Galen furrowed his brow. "On what?"

"On…" Jess's mouth dipped into a frown and then looked over at the extremely red Sasha. "You haven't asked him yet?"

"I was about to before you burst in and stole our muffins!" Sasha said, thrusting a hand at the misappropriated morsel.

"Muffin. Singular. I only stole one," Jess said. "I have no control over the fox."

Sasha groaned in frustration, and Galen asked, "What is going on?"

Jess grinned, catlike, and nudged Sasha with their boot. "Well? Go on then."

"It was meant to be just the two of us," Sasha said, throwing his hands up. "I don't want to embarrass him."

"Oh, you won't embarrass him," Jess said, waving a hand through the air as though dismissing his concern.

"He's right here, and he'd like to know what's going on," Galen said, looking between his best friend and his lover.

Sasha swallowed, and then said, "Sorry, just a moment."

He got up and moved to a cupboard. He moved a few things and finally pulled out a crumpled, crushed bouquet. It was made entirely of roses. Galen's eyes went wide, and he held his breath as Sasha turned around.

Sasha smiled at him and said softly, "I'm guessing you already know what this means."

Galen nodded, still in shock.

"Good, because I'm about to change it, just a bit," Sasha said.

He reached into his pocket and pulled out a handful of dandelions. Galen couldn't help but smile. They were wilted and crushed, but Sasha sat down and started to try and place them among the roses. Galen laughed lightly and knelt in front of Sasha, who went very still, and then Galen started to help thread the dandelions in with the roses.

When they were done, Galen stood, as did Sasha. He held the bouquet, beautiful if messy, much like them, and smiled a very nervous smile. He licked his lips as he looked down into Galen's eyes.

"So, you already know what I want to ask you, right?" Sasha asked.

Galen nodded, smiling wide.

"But you're going to make me say it, aren't you?"

Galen just kept smiling.

"Fine," Sasha said, laughing. "All right. Galen, the man who lit up my life, who finally taught me how to change and grow, who is possibly, no, definitely, the best person that I know, will you please marry me?"

Galen took the flowers from him and held them up to his face, inhaling their scent deeply. He closed his eyes for a moment, savoring the fact that this wasn't a dream, that it really was his life. And then he opened his eyes to look up at Sasha, into those deep, brown eyes as rich as freshly tilled earth.

"Well," Galen said, smiling at the ridiculous man that he loved. "Since you said please."

THE END

ACKNOWLEDGMENTS

The Need for Dandelions wasn't meant to be my second book. Originally, I had planned to take the time to work on an epic fantasy romance series (that I will complete one day) and get that out next. It was that, or another fantasy romance novel that is always about to be trunked because I have fought with it so much. I had just finished that manuscript, and I needed a break before I touched it again. So, on a whim, I decided to write out the opening chapter for a couple of characters that I had been playing around with in daydreams. Those two characters were Galen and Sasha. Then I was sucked immediately into their story.

Much like that other fantasy romance story, I fought with this plot so much. There are two people that I need to thank immensely for their help saving this book from being abandoned. Justin and Keiran, you were both incredible. I would never have been able to write this book without you and your brilliant ideas to help make this story work. Dom, thank you for always answering my questions and giving your opinions. You were the reason I finally settled on a title. And, of course, Alec for all your encouragement. I know I can always count on you to cheer me on.

Additionally, I have to thank Sammy for lending me his expertise. Wishing you the best of luck with your future career as a midwife. Chris Zable, my editor, was absolutely invaluable to making this book the best it could be. Her work is so thoughtful. Alex Dingley, the cover artist, brought Galen and Sasha to life with his stunning illustration. And, of course,

Talli L. Morgan, whose formatting always looks incredible. I also appreciate the indie author community on Bluesky so much. It really feels like a home. Your encouragement and support mean the world.

Finally, thank you for reading this. I hope that you enjoyed reading it as much as I enjoyed writing it.

About the Author

Alex Larkspur is an author of queer fantasy books such as *Sweet & Wild* and *The Need for Dandelions*. They live in San Antonio, Texas with their dogs. There, you can find them reading, writing, and playing TTRPGs.

Their books are available online wherever books are sold.

You can find them online on https://alexlarkspur.weebly.com/ and @applesncinnamon.bsky.social